Dear Reader,

No matter how busy your day, there'll *always* be time for romance. TAKE 5 is a new way to indulge in love, passion and adventure—and still be on time to pick up the kids! Each TAKE 5 volume offers five condensed stories by top Harlequin and Silhouette authors. Now you can have the enjoyment and satisfaction of a full-length novel, but in less time—perfect for those days when it's difficult to squeeze a longer read into your hectic schedule.

This volume of TAKE 5 features five love stories of home and family...five *heartwarming* escapes! In *All in the Family New York Times* bestselling author Heather Graham proves father doesn't always know best! Elda Minger's *Wedding of the Year* and *Seize the Fire* are two tales of love *almost* lost and found. And Dallas Schulze's *Tell Me a Story* and *Saturday's Child* celebrate the courage of love.

Why not indulge in all four volumes of TAKE 5 available now—tender romance, sizzling passion, riveting adventure and heartwarming family love. No matter what mood you're in, you'll have the perfect escape!

Happy reading,

Marsha Zinberg
Senior Editor and Editorial Coordinator, TAKE 5

Heather Graham describes her life as "busy, wild and fun." This master storyteller, with over 10 million copies of her books in print around the world, once dreamed of acting on the Shakespearean stage. But happily for her fans, fate intervened, and now she is a *New York Times* bestselling author. Married to her high school sweetheart, this mother of five spends her days picking up the kids from school, attending Little League games and taking care of two cats. Although Heather and her family enjoy traveling, southern Florida—where she loves the sun and water—is home.

Dallas Schulze has written more than forty romance novels, both contemporary and historical. *Romantic Times* named her Storyteller of the Year, and her titles appear regularly on the *USA Today* bestseller list. She describes herself as a sucker for a happy ending, and hopes that her readers have as much fun with her books as she does. Dallas and her husband live in Southern California.

Elda Minger's passion for writing is in her blood; both her parents and an uncle were authors. Now a bestselling author herself with more than twenty titles to her credit, Elda has been a finalist for the Romance Writers of America coveted RITA Award, and her novel *Night Rhythms* won a *Romantic Times* W.I.S.H. award for its hero. When she isn't writing, Elda enjoys gardening, traveling, going to the movies and subjecting her family to home renovation projects on a house that's been in her family for several generations.

TAKE5

Quick Reads. Great Escapes.

**NEW YORK TIMES
BESTSELLING AUTHOR**

Heather Graham

Dallas Schulze

Elda Minger

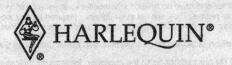

HARLEQUIN®

TORONTO • NEW YORK • LONDON
AMSTERDAM • PARIS • SYDNEY • HAMBURG
STOCKHOLM • ATHENS • TOKYO • MILAN • MADRID
PRAGUE • WARSAW • BUDAPEST • AUCKLAND

ISBN 0-373-83494-2

TAKE 5, VOLUME 3

Copyright © 2001 by Harlequin Books S.A.

The publisher acknowledges the copyright holders
of the individual titles as follows:

ALL IN THE FAMILY
Copyright © 1987 by Heather Graham Pozzessere

TELL ME A STORY
Copyright © 1988 by Dallas Schulze

SATURDAY'S CHILD
Copyright © 1990 by Dallas Schulze

WEDDING OF THE YEAR
Copyright © 1989 by Elda Minger

SEIZE THE FIRE
Copyright © 1985 by Elda Minger

CONTENTS

ALL IN THE FAMILY

Heather Graham

She had been watching him for a long time when she finally came to the fence that day. She'd seen him first in the hallway with his friends, and had noticed his hair. Not just blond, it was nearly white, and one lock slashed across the tan of his forehead like a silk ribbon. And his eyes, blue like the sky, were as startling and arresting as that hair.

He was about six-foot-two and should have been a California beachboy, not a West Virginia mountain man from Bolivar.

Yet it had been his smile that had really drawn her. They had seen each other on her very first day, across the crowded hallway. Their eyes had met, and the world had stopped. Suddenly there was no one else, no one who mattered....

A whistle shrilled, and the boys went running off the field. But he remained. He tossed the football up in the air, caught it, tossed it again, caught it. And then he walked toward her.

He reached the fence, and they stood just inches apart.

She was in love. Head over heels in love, and she would never love again as she did at this moment. They watched each other with all their feelings in their eyes.

"You're Sandy Marquette," he said at last.

"You know my name."

He smiled. "I know everything about you. You've just moved here from D.C., your father is some kind of historian and..."

His voice trailed away. Then that smile touched his face again. "You're the most beautiful girl I've ever seen. You must be here to break the hearts of all us poor mountain boys."

She laughed, a husky sound that caught in her throat. "I'd take a mountain man anytime."

It wasn't meant to be sexy; she was just being honest. She barely knew him—all she knew were those looks that had passed between them.

"This mountain man?" he inquired softly.

"No other. Ever," she whispered.

The spring breeze picked up, touching them both. His fingers curled over hers where they clung to the fencing. Just touching.

"I've got to shower," he finally told her.

"I'll wait."

When he walked back to meet her at the fence, they smiled again. She was sophisticated, he told himself. She was superior to anything that had ever touched his life before.

Hold something back, she warned herself. He was the most popular guy in school, and she was just the new girl. She had to be careful....

That slow smile lighted his face again, and he held out his hand, watching her eyes as their fingers intertwined.

"Want—" He had to clear his throat. "A soda or—"

"I don't care. I don't care what we do."

"We could drive—" he began, then laughed. "Except that I don't have a car. I came with Pete, then I took one look at you and forgot everything."

"I have mine," she said.

She led him to the parking lot and her red sports car.

He groaned inwardly. She was a rich girl, and he...

She handed him the keys. He drove to a quiet place by the river and parked. They talked, and finally darkness fell.

He talked about the river and the cabin up in the mountains by the stream. He told her about the deer that would eat right out of your hand, and about how when a fire crackled in the hearth and night descended, there was no better place to be. She tried to tell him about her life, but couldn't think of much to say, because it felt as if nothing before him mattered.

He began to dream of her, awake and asleep. He was going to marry her. As soon as possible.

He told her so the next day. At first she was stunned, but then she hugged him. Then the bell began to ring for class.

That afternoon, they wandered to the stream by the cabin. They wound up laughing and showering each other with the cold mountain water. He built a fire to warm them up.

By its gentle light they gazed into each other's eyes, and then he touched her, and then...

Love led the way for her, a gentle, tender path to an ecstasy that was both sweet and torrid.

She'd known she belonged to him since their eyes had met across the hall, but now she felt as if he would be a part of her forever. They would marry, yet marriage could be only a legal sanction of what they had already shared.

*

"TAKE THAT, you dastardly, devilish dragon!"

Kelly tried the words aloud, shrugged, grimaced, then added more pencil strokes to her paper.

Umm. Hard to judge. But this installment of the children's comic, Dark of the Moon, was due tomorrow, and she simply had to take care of the Fairy Queen and Daryl the Devilish Dragon by tonight.

The doorbell began ringing. Kelly looked up in disgust. "Jarod!"

Was he even home? Maybe he'd forgotten his key. He was very forgetful lately.

Kelly padded barefoot to the door. She should have looked through the peephole, but she was annoyed at having been interrupted, so she merely threw the door open.

"Where's your father? I want to see him now!"

Kelly felt fury settle over her as she stared up at a total stranger. His hair was dark auburn, and he wasn't just tall; he was solidly built.

He had flashing dark eyes, a straight nose, and a square jaw. And he looked as furious as Kelly felt. He might have been handsome if his features hadn't been so hard and angry.

"Where is your father!" The words thundered out again.

"My father, sir, is in Vancouver—I believe. I don't keep a schedule of his whereabouts."

"Get me your mother then. Now—please."

A sigh of irritation escaped her, and she felt her own temper rise as he brushed past her into the hallway of the old house, critically surveying everything in sight.

Kelly set her jaw grimly. "My mother is deceased. Now, since you've barged into my home—"

"You live here alone?" he demanded.

"Not exactly. I live with my son."

"You're his mother!"

He spoke with such astonishment that Kelly paused. "If being 'his' mother means Jarod McGraw's, then yes. Now—"

"Where's your husband?"

Kelly gritted her teeth, wishing that she had the size and strength to pick the man up by his collar and deliver him outside. She said, "Also deceased, I'm afraid. So, since you've barged so rudely into my house, I suggest you tell me your business. Otherwise I'll feel obliged to call the police."

He didn't scare easily. But then, he didn't smile, either. "I've been considering the possibility of calling in the police myself, Mrs. McGraw. But, please do call them," he drawled. "I really don't know that much about the law. The charge might be statutory rape."

"What—what are you talking about?" Kelly asked.

"Rape, Mrs. McGraw. Statutory. Your son Jarod."

"Jarod? Never! I don't know who or what—"

"Who? My daughter, that's who, Mrs. McGraw. An innocent young girl with a good head on her shoulders until your barbarian of a half-back—"

"Jarod has more manners and style in his little finger than you'll ever have in your entire body, mister! Now if your little tart of a daughter offered herself—"

"Lady, don't you ever—" He reached her in a single stride, and his hands fell on her shoulders. But suddenly he seemed to realize his anger and potential for violence. He drew his hands back and stared at them.

Perhaps we're both barbarians, Kelly thought. Parents defending their offspring.

"Don't you ever come flaming in here like a torch again, attacking Jarod! You have no right. You can't—"

She broke off as the front door flew open.

Jarod was there.

Beautiful, tall, blond Jarod, a frown furrowing his handsome brow. "Mom?" He said the word as a question.

"Jarod?" the stranger asked him.

Jarod nodded. And then Kelly began to feel ill. Something like recognition had entered her son's eyes.

"Sandy?" he gasped. "You're Mr. Marquette, Sandy's father, aren't you?" Jarod asked the stranger. "Nothing's happened, has it? There hasn't been an accident or anything?"

"No," Marquette said with deceptive calm. "Sandy is pregnant."

Jarod hadn't known that, Kelly realized. He stumbled slightly, turning white.

He looked broken. Well, he should, Kelly thought. He wasn't even eighteen. Every promise in the world lay open to him. Destroyed, if this was true.

She reeled under a new onslaught of fury. There was Marquette, so convinced of his little girl's innocence. Well, it couldn't be true! Marquette's precious daughter might have been running around with the entire senior class, and chosen Jarod's name simply because he was every young girl's fantasy!

Kelly said scornfully, "Come on, Mr. Marquette. Perhaps we should call in the police. Or perhaps you should take greater care with your accusations. The father is so often the last to know."

"Just what do you mean, Mrs. McGraw?"

"What I'm saying, Mr. Marquette, is that your daughter might have seduced not only my son, but half of the senior class. What I'm saying is that—"

Kelly wasn't sure quite what happened then. Marquette stiffened, the expression on his face explosive, and took a step forward. Jarod let out a gasp and came charging in. He swung at Marquette who ducked, then straightened.

"I'm sorry, Mrs. McGraw," Marquette said suddenly. Kelly stared at him, a bit incredulous at his change.

But he hadn't really changed, she thought. He was just more polite.

"I shouldn't have come over this way. I'm afraid I reacted out of pure anger. I wanted to be reasonable, and I wasn't."

Kelly lowered her head, wishing that they had remained on the battleground, because now she was forced to admit that she had replied in kind. She had all but called his daughter a little whore, and really, she didn't normally behave that way, either....

"I'll leave you now. I'll call, to see when we can discuss this situation."

To Kelly's amazement, Marquette turned and strode from the room.

Jarod called, "Mr. Marquette! Wait, please!"

The man was already out the front door, but he paused on the walkway. Jarod leaned down and kissed Kelly's forehead, looking at her anxiously. "I'm sorry, Mom. I've never been so sorry about anything in my entire life. Honest to God. But I've got to go. I have to see Sandy. She's—she's pregnant. She's going to have my baby.''

He kissed her forehead again, then started for the door to catch up with Marquette.

''Jarod, wait! This is serious! We have to talk.''

''Mother, please! I just have to see that Sandy is all right! I'll be back, and then we'll talk.''

The door banged. Kelly could see them through the window: her tall, handsome son, and the even taller red-haired man. Leaving together.

''Jarod, I'll...I'll clobber you for this!'' she swore. And then she started to think about Marquette again. ''Damn you, Jarod! If you had to get a girl pregnant, couldn't you have picked one with a different father?''

Then she started to laugh, because the thought was so ridiculous. And then, all alone, she started to cry.

Because it was just like history repeating itself, and she didn't know if she sympathized more with her own son—or with the girl she had never seen.

NOT KNOWING what to do with herself after such a shock, Kelly simply returned to her drawings. She turned Daryl the Devilish Dragon into a new type of monster—one with Marquette's face— and she let Esmeralda, the Fairy Queen, chase him around with a fat wooden spoon, catch him, tie him up and clobber him.

Of course, she had to get some real work done. And letting Esmeralda behave so violently would never do. But it had felt awfully good for the moment.

''Work!'' she murmured aloud disgustedly. Who could work when her teenage son was likely to be slapped with a paternity suit?

She threw down her pencil, but just when she thought she would scream, the front door opened and Jarod came into the house.

He looked dazed. Starry-eyed. He was smiling a dizzy type of smile. He was completely gone over this girl who had just destroyed his life. Kelly wanted to slap him, but before she could even talk, he came and knelt before her, taking her hand in such a way that all her anger escaped.

"Mom, I am sorry, very sorry, for the way I've disappointed you," he said softly.

She jerked her hand away. She couldn't be soft—not now. "Jarod, really, get off the ground, please!" He did, and she found herself growing annoyed all over again. He was sorry, but not for the deed, only because she was upset.

"Jarod—" she began, "don't you see what you've done?"

It took him a long while to answer.

"I love her, Mom," he finally said. She didn't say anything, and he hesitated again.

Then, "Mom, you don't know her," he said. "You have no right to judge her."

"I'm not judging her! If she were a saint, you'd still be in the middle of a disaster!"

"A child isn't a disaster, Mother."

Great. All she needed was Jarod preaching to her—and sounding ridiculously wise.

"Jarod, I know that. But a child is a tremendous responsibility. A baby is constant, Jarod. It won't wait, unattended, while you go to school, to football practice, to a concert with your friends. Then there are the hospital costs, the pediatrician, the diapers—"

"Mom, I know all that!"

"And?" She turned around, one brow arched.

"I'll deal with it."

"You're not even out of high school!"

Kelly didn't want to alienate him—she wanted to help him. But he was being so blasé!

He returned her stare evenly. "When the baby is born, I'll be out of high school."

"College lies ahead of you, Jarod. Four years of it."

He shrugged. "If I have to wait, I will."

"What will you do in the meantime?"

"Get a job."

"Doing what? Doing what?" Her voice was rising. "Oh, Jarod. And what about Sandy? Think about her for a moment, saddled with an infant. What if they won't let her finish high school? What about college for her? What about her dreams?"

"Do you want Sandy to get an abortion?" Jarod broke in coolly.

She winced, closing her eyes. No, she didn't want that. She

couldn't bear the thought. Still, this wasn't her life they were discussing. It was Jarod's life, and Sandy's.

"Mother?" he pressed softly.

"Don't, Jarod. Don't push me. I'm not saying that. Besides, what I want doesn't matter. What's best for the both of you is what matters. We've just got to—well, we've got to really discuss it."

"Mom..."

His voice was very soft, and he was on his knees again, beside her chair, and they were hugging each other. She found that she was crying again, smoothing back his beautiful blond hair. "I just had such dreams for you! And maybe that wasn't fair. I can't dream your dreams for you—that's your own right...."

Jarod looked up at her, taking both of her hands in his. "I love you," he told her. "I didn't want to leave you, but I had to see Sandy. The way her father came in...well, I had to tell her that I really loved her. That I'd never cop out on her."

Kelly nodded feebly.

"It's going to be okay. We're going to talk. All of us, okay?"

"All of us?" Kelly frowned.

"Sandy—oh, wait till you meet her. She's wonderful! Me, you, Mr. Marquette."

"What about Sandy's mother?"

"She doesn't have a mother right now. Just her father. And he's asked us over for dinner tomorrow night. It's the next step. Mr. Marquette said so."

"Mr. Marquette said so," Kelly mimicked. "Well, at least you're not calling that awful man 'Dad'—yet," Kelly murmured.

*

"YOU'RE NOT going to wear that, are you?"

Halfway down the stairs, Kelly paused to face her son.

"What's the matter with it, Jarod?"

"You look like—someone's mother," he said unhappily.

"Jarod, I am someone's mother."

"Grandmother, then. Mom, you look like a nun."

Kelly smiled vaguely and continued on down. She knew she didn't look that prim. Her skirt was long and her blouse had a

Chinese collar, but it was a silky teal blue that was becoming to her eyes and hair.

"Jarod, my outfit is fine," she said. "You're determined to marry Sandra, and I don't want to meet my prospective daughter-in-law looking like Bubbles La Tour. Now, get the car, dear."

He gave her one last exasperated glance, then went outside. Kelly turned to the hall mirror to give herself a quick once-over.

Was she dressed too old? Maybe, but her height was such a drawback when she was trying to stand her ground, and she must—maturely—tonight.

She had her hair piled on top of her head. Her heels were three inches high, but she still felt short. "That's your fault, Jarod!" she said heatedly. It was impossible to feel tall around him.

He beeped the horn, and she gave herself a little shake. Face it, she told herself wryly, Marquette had mistaken her for a child at their first meeting, and she was determined to prove to that obnoxious individual that she was not—in the least—a child.

Kelly gasped at her first sight of the Marquette house. It seemed to rise naturally from the mountain, all granite and redwood and glass, immense and beautiful. From the driveway she could see the living room, with its walls of glass, and through that glass the stone fireplace, the warm earth tones of the Indian rugs and casual furniture.

"It's nice, isn't it?" Jarod demanded a little smugly.

Kelly turned on him. "I thought Marquette was some kind of historian. You didn't tell me that he was well-off. And don't you dare sound so smug. This doesn't change anything."

"Mom, you're just so worried about money! We won't starve. Don't you see—"

"If you take a penny of his money, Jarod, I will be so disappointed in you that I'll—I'll scream."

The front door opened before they could reach it. Marquette was standing there. Kelly hesitated, but Jarod's touch got her moving again.

Marquette looked...good.

Really good. He had on a light, casual jacket, a shirt open at the neck, and nicely tailored trousers. He smiled when she came nearer, a deep, inviting smile, and she realized that he was handsome, very handsome. With those dark eyes of his and the white

slash of his smile against his bronzed, rugged features, he was
alluring...and exciting!

"Jarod, Mrs. McGraw, come in."

Marquette took her hand in one of his, and his scent, from some
kind of clean, woodsy soap, seemed to wash over her. She wanted
to shriek, let go of my hand! And even in heels she had to tilt
her head back to meet his sardonic smile.

"Mom," Jarod prodded her. "This is Sandy."

Kelly didn't know what she had been expecting, but Sandy
was, quite simply, beautiful. She was dark, like her father, with
big dark eyes, and long hair that was one of the richest shades of
auburn Kelly had ever seen. She was tall, too. About five-foot-
nine—how irritating!

The whole world suddenly seemed tall! Kelly felt a bit like
Alice in Wonderland. Here she was, so tiny, with a bunch of
normal-size people, as if she had eaten something strange.

"Sandy, how do you do?"

She offered the words softly, and gave the girl her hand with
a nice smile. How could you be so perfect? she thought in despair.
You've ruined his life!

"Can I get you a drink?" Marquette said.

"Ah, yes, thank you," Kelly murmured.

Unlike her, Dan Marquette was perfectly at ease. "Come into
the kitchen with me, Mrs. McGraw."

Sandy and Jarod were staring at each other, oblivious to anyone
else. Kelly glanced at them uneasily, then followed Dan Marquette.

The kitchen, too, was beautifully contemporary. Light oak cab-
inets, a big butcher-block island, restaurant range, rows of gleaming copper pots, and a booth against another glass wall.

Kelly wandered over to the window as Dan got ice from the
freezer. She could feel him watching her all the while.

"What will you have?"

"Wine. A spritzer or a cooler, something like that."

He poured wine and soda over ice and offered her the glass,
his own amusement so evident that Kelly snapped at him. "What
do you find so funny?"

"You, Mrs. McGraw. You are appalled that we've left the
children together. Alone."

"Yes, I guess I am," Kelly replied coolly.

"Aren't you trying to close the barn door after the horse?"

"Are you trying to encourage outrageous behavior?"

"Not so outrageous. Natural, I believe. Just how old are you, Mrs. McGraw?"

"What?" Kelly gasped. "It's none of your business!"

"Oh, but I think it is. You're condemning those kids, when you were apparently running around yourself at a very young age—"

"It's none of your business!" Kelly repeated in fury. She slammed her glass down so hard that it shattered, but she barely noticed. She stared at Marquette.

"You're just a kid yourself, aren't you?" he asked softly. "That makes this whole thing very hard."

"Mr. Marquette, I'm not a kid. I'm unhappy about this entire situation because it's going to be very, very hard on those two children!"

He listened to her, then turned quickly away, moving into the pantry to get a broom, and clean up the glass she had shattered. She moved to help him, and as she did so, she slipped on the wet floor and fell to her knees. She winced sharply; some glass had cut into her knee.

Marquette, instantly concerned, put his hand on her shoulder.

"Just let me go. The glass—"

But he stood, and she found herself swept up into his strong arms. Instinctively she wound her own arms around his neck for balance.

"It's nothing."

"It's deep."

He set her down at the table and quickly reached into a cabinet for antiseptic and a bandage.

"It's nothing, really."

"The stocking has to go," he murmured, his hand on her leg. Kelly leaped up, found her garter, and released the offending garment. Marquette removed her shoe and was sliding the stocking down her leg as Jarod and Sandy made their appearance in the kitchen.

"Mother!" Jarod said.

"Dad...?" Sandy queried.

Kelly felt color flooding her entire body. She was sitting, Dan Marquette at her feet.

"Your mom's glass broke," he said smoothly, picking up the antiseptic. "She cut her knee."

Kelly was sure that she could have heard a pin drop, but Dan just daubed the antiseptic on her knee attentively.

"Is it okay, Mom?" Jarod asked anxiously.

"Oh, yes, really. I, uh, I—"

"Sandy, do me a favor, please?" Marquette asked her. "Finish picking up that glass. Jarod, why don't you make your mom another spritzer?"

Sandy began to clean up, while Jarod made Kelly a drink and brought it over. She sipped it quickly, and her vision swam for a moment. All she saw was that dark masculine head bent over her knee, and her impulse was to run her fingers through that thick hair. They actually itched to touch him.

"There, that should do it." Marquette looked up at her. He was smiling. A devilish, fascinating smile. Then he rose.

"Jarod, the salad is in the refrigerator. Sandy, you check on the roast and the potatoes."

Sandy laughed. "Hey, Dad! What's your job here?"

"I'm going to help Mrs. McGraw hobble out to the table. That other shoe needs to go, too." He was already slipping it off.

"How do you ever walk in these things, anyway?"

"I manage fine," Kelly retorted.

He grinned, offering her his hand.

"Her name is Kelly," Jarod offered.

"Kelly," Dan Marquette murmured. "Nice. Irish...green."

"Short," Jarod teased.

"Jarod!" Kelly gave him a sharp warning. But Marquette's hand was out, and she had little choice but to accept it. He led her out—barefoot—to the dining room, a beautiful room simply decorated in an Oriental style.

When everyone was seated, Jarod glanced at Dan Marquette and his mother, then mouthed out a quick grace. Then he commented on how delicious the food was and Kelly found herself echoing the sentiment. She asked Dan whether he or Sandy had done the cooking.

"Neither," he responded. "Reeves is the cook."

"Reeves has been with us all my life," Sandy explained. "What is he, Dad? Sort of a gentleman's gentleman, I suppose.

After all these years he's still very proper and very British. He's great."

Reeves apparently had his own room at the back of the house. "He needs a certain independence," Sandy explained.

"I think we're all done with our salad," Dan murmured. Sandy and Jarod collected the plates and disappeared into the kitchen. Kelly felt Dan Marquette staring at her.

"What's wrong?" he asked.

"Wrong?" She sipped her spritzer. "What could be wrong? Those two are children, with no apparent sense of responsibility, and they're going to have a child. Unless—"

"Unless?" Marquette was smiling, but his dark eyes were narrowed as he leaned closer. "What are you suggesting, Mrs. McGraw? That Sandra have an abortion?"

His blunt suggestion made her color again. "I'm thinking of your daughter more than of my son," she said flatly. "Both their lives will have to change, but it's the woman who bears the brunt of whatever comes."

He leaned back again, watching her. "I think you're missing the main point here, Kelly. These two know what they're going to do. We can be their friends or their enemies, but we can't change their minds."

Sandy came back in with a smile that quickly faded when she saw the way the adults were looking at each other.

Jarod sailed back in with a huge platter of parsleyed potatoes and broccoli in cheese sauce. His smile faded, too.

Kelly looked down at her plate as Dan carved the roast. She was vaguely aware that he had started using her first name when he asked for her plate and piled it high with food.

They all sat down to eat in silence.

"Mrs. McGraw, your glass is empty," Sandy said softly. "Can I fix you another drink?"

Kelly smiled. "Are you trying to ply me with liquor? Ask Jarod—my tongue just gets sharper."

Sandy flushed and laughed, and Jarod assured her that they were going to hear from his mother one way or another that evening, anyway. Dan Marquette disappeared with both glasses, returning with them refilled, and Kelly suddenly felt more comfortable.

"Sandy, I'll start off with the tough stuff," Kelly began. "I

admit that I'm deeply disappointed in both of you. You seem like
a lovely young lady, but what you did was—''

"Mother," Jarod interrupted. "Come on! We're seniors.
Everyone—''

"Everyone?" Kelly murmured. "'Everyone' isn't expecting a
child, and 'everyone'—''

"Well, Mom, we weren't planning what happened the first
time!"

"You were careless and irresponsible!" Kelly retorted. "And
now you act like you're being Mr. Magnanimous, Jarod! Sandy
is going to do most of the paying—have you thought about that?
Sandy, have you thought about it? I can't change your minds and
I'll be honest, I don't know what the 'right' thing really is. But,
Sandy, you have options. You don't have to have this baby—and
none of us has the right to make you!"

Sandy had gone ashen. Marquette looked as if he were about
to explode and Jarod seemed ready to strangle his mother, but
Kelly kept going. This was for Sandy, between the two of them
as women.

"Or you could give the baby up for adoption."

"Oh, my God!" Sandy whispered, close to tears.

Kelly leaned closer to the girl. "I wouldn't want that, Sandy.
That baby is my grandchild. To be honest, what I want is for you
and Jarod to marry each other. It's just that it's going to be mis-
erably hard. I want you to see that. I want you both to see your
options, and then, once you two make your decision, I swear that
I'll back you and help you in any way that I can. If I've hurt
you, I'm sorry."

There was silence, complete silence. Then Sandy burst into
tears and raced from the room, Jarod behind her.

From somewhere Kelly heard a clock chime. Dan Marquette
was still, but Kelly couldn't look at him.

She heard him rise, then walk over to the window. Felt him
when he turned to watch her.

"Are you going to rip into me for hurting your daughter? Go
ahead. But everything I said was important and—''

"Yes, it was." He was smiling at her. "It is going to be hard,
and it is important that they think about what they're doing."

He came back to the table and sat down next to her. Kelly felt as if the temperature in the room had risen by ten degrees. She could feel his smile, feel those dark eyes.

"You don't want to talk to me, Kelly McGraw, but I know you were ridiculously young when you had Jarod. How old are you now? Thirty-five?"

"Forty-five!" Kelly lied quickly.

He only laughed again. "Things went badly for you—I'm sorry. But you should know that things that start off well can go badly, too. Sandy was planned, Kelly. Her mother and I met in college. We got married right after graduation. Sandy was born a year after our wedding day. But her mother left when Sandy was five days old. So much for planning. I think Jarod loves Sandy—and I know she loves him. Yes, it's going to be hard. Let's help them make it, shall we?"

She turned slowly to stare at him. At the dark eyes gazing so intently into her own. At that smile. His hand was stretched toward her. He wanted her to take it.

Kelly stared from his hand to his eyes. "We still haven't gotten anywhere here," she murmured. "They have to finish their senior year. We have to decide how to—handle this!"

Kelly looked at him, suddenly wide-eyed with confusion. There really was so much to do!

"It will go much better," Marquette murmured, "if you and I are friends. Don't you think?"

His hand closed over hers, and Kelly stared at it.

No, she thought. No, no, no...

She realized that she was afraid to be his friend. He would demand a great deal of a...friend.

KELLY LET herself into the house smiling. She felt so much better about things.

"Jarod!"

He came running down the stairs, a pencil stuck behind his ear. That made her feel better, too. He hadn't forgotten about his schoolwork.

She could even admit that since everything had come out in the open, especially since they'd gone to the Marquettes' for dinner, Jarod had been doing better. Straight A's in school, and a note from the coach stating that by the time the season was over, he would be able to attend the college of his choice on an athletic scholarship alone.

"Well?" he asked her anxiously.

She smiled. Well, why not? Sandy Marquette was going to be Sandra McGraw soon enough. It would be foolish, Kelly had decided, not to enjoy her only son's wedding.

Kelly smiled, threw her arms open to Jarod. "The priest says that the first Saturday in June will be fine."

"Super!"

He accepted her embrace, then whirled her around the hallway.

"Well, what did he say? Did you tell him that Sandy...I mean, did you explain—"

"I didn't lie, Jarod." But Kelly couldn't help grinning. "The man is a Roman Catholic priest, so he was glad that you two are going to get married."

"By June..."

"By June Sandy will be about four and a half months along. Not necessarily noticeable at all." Kelly shrugged. "If people know, they know. If they don't—well, we won't announce it. This is a once in a lifetime affair. Sandy should have a beautiful white dress and a mile-long train, the whole nine yards."

Jarod looked at her anxiously. "You really think so?"

"Definitely."

He hugged her again. "Sandy will be thrilled."

"Why don't you call her and tell her?"

"She's on her way over now."

"Now? Why?"

"Oh—I forgot. They're both coming. We're all going out," Jarod said happily.

Kelly shook her head. "Uh-uh! You all can go out, but—"

"Mom, I said you'd go. I told Dan that you loved tubing, that you loved anything to do with the water."

"Jarod, you can't run around telling—"

"Mom, please, for my sake, for Sandy's sake. Come on, they've just moved here. From D.C. Going tubing is new and exciting for them."

The doorbell chose that moment to ring. Kelly stared at Jarod; he stared at her. Kelly went to answer it.

Sandy, her beautiful dark eyes bright with pleasure, greeted her.

She was in a bathing suit, and she looked so young and lovely that Kelly had to smile.

"Oh! You're not ready!" Sandy said.

Kelly smiled. "I'm not coming, Sandy. I've really got an awful lot to do."

"Oh, come on! Please. Dad just got the tubes. And he already dropped off the meat for the barbecue at the cottage. Please? He won't come if you don't."

"What's wrong?" It was the man himself, in a pair of cutoffs that left very little to the imagination.

How old are you? she wondered, unaware that she was staring at his bare chest. Thickly covered with hair and hard with muscle.

He should have been skinny! Weren't scholars supposed to be pale and scrawny, with horn-rims and...

"Is something the matter?" he asked.

"No, I'm just a little busy today, that's all."

He shrugged. "What a shame. The kids had said that you could go. I guess I'll stay home, too. Third wheel, you know."

"That's foolish," Kelly protested. "Sandy said you'd set up for a barbecue at some cottage."

"I bought a little house along the Shenandoah. I'm just fascinated by the river."

Kelly kept smiling. "All the more reason why you should go."

Jarod came up behind Kelly and whispered in her ear. "See, Mom, if you don't go, he won't go. And Sandy and I will be all alone."

She spun around. "Not amusing, Jarod. You're in no position to be giving me that kind of grief, young man."

He grinned and grabbed Sandy's arm.

"We'll be in the car, Dad!" Sandy called.

"Are you coming or not?" Marquette asked Kelly very softly.

Damn him! He knew darn well that he made her uneasy. That she was much more aware of him as a man than she wanted to be.

"Can't handle the big time, huh?" he dared her.

She certainly couldn't let herself retreat after that. "Step inside, Mr. Marquette," she said smoothly. "I'll just be a moment."

A FEW minutes after leaving, they were in the river. Jarod and Sandy were drifting along behind them—their hands entwined.

Dan Marquette was quite relaxed, as if he'd been tubing all his life. His head was back, his feet dangling in the water, and an extra tube containing an ice chest was tied to his. Kelly shrugged and leaned back.

Dan took a look at the kids, then smiled at Kelly. He pulled his second tube closer and dug into the ice.

"Beer, Mrs. McGraw?"

"Thank you, Mr. Marquette."

She smiled as she sipped it, then leaned back and rested her head against her tube. The river was easy here; the current was slow, but she grinned to herself. Washington city dweller. Wait until they hit the rapids! The water was a little bit low, and maneuvering over the rocks might turn out to be tricky.

She opened her eyes. "Just what do you do for a living, Mr. Marquette?"

He shrugged. "I write—historical pieces, nonfiction."

Kelly lifted an eyebrow. "You seem to do rather well at it."

He laughed. "I've never had anything on the *New York Times'* bestseller list. But what I write doesn't change. Universities order so many a year." He sipped his beer and went on to tell her that he had been doing a book on early American life in Washington. He liked this area because it offered easy access to so many of his research sources.

Kelly found herself warming to the subject, telling him how things had changed since she'd been little, how the National Park Service had really saved the area after numerous floods. She told him that he would have to go on the "ghost tour," and started to list some of the books the local small press had published.

"You know quite a bit about the region, don't you?" he asked her.

"West Virginia, born and bred." She laughed.

Laughter from behind distracted her, and she turned to see a group of people on a raft passing by. They were all throwing water at each other. Someone missed and hit Sandy, who shrieked with laughter; Jarod responded by dousing the group on the raft.

Watching it all, Kelly smiled, then rested her head against the tube again. It really was fun. Had it been almost eighteen years since she had felt like laughing this way? Eighteen years since she and David had been like Jarod and Sandy—so young, and so much in love with love! But they hadn't gotten much help. Her mother had been dead, and David's parents had been furious. She and David had started out with nothing, and she'd spent almost five years rushing from work to pick up Jarod and back to work.

Not too much time for love, either. They had both been too tired. David from his schoolwork and his part-time job; she from her nine-to-five job and trying to be a loving parent in the hours that were left. And then David had gotten out of school, and it had been her turn to start studying art.

Hard...everything had been so hard. And then, ironically, as soon as she had finished school—another five-year span—David had gotten into that stupid hang-gliding club and...died.

Almost seven years ago. Years in which everything had gone on being hard. Raising Jarod alone, worrying about the bills, wishing she had majored in something more practical than art....

"A penny for them. Hell, I'd even give you a dollar." Dan Marquette was staring at her intently.

"They wouldn't be worth it," she told him. And then grinned. "Rapid coming up," she said lightly.

He nodded.

Kelly smiled serenely as her tube began to pick up speed. She maneuvered skillfully past the rocks, loving the cool spray against her face. She heard a shriek behind her and saw that Jarod had just saved Sandy from capsizing.

Dan Marquette was still there, serenely sipping his beer, undaunted by the rapids.

He laughed. "What's the matter, Mrs. McGraw? Was I supposed to have been dashed to bits?"

"Of course not!" she retorted. She lay back again and let the water carry her along. It felt so good!

Suddenly her tube got snagged on a submerged branch, and she was plunged face downward into the river, with her tube flying off into the distance.

Coughing and sputtering, she came to the surface. The water was no more than four feet deep, and she ended up sprawling across a rock.

And he was leaning over her. His hands were resting on either side of her face, and she could feel the heat of his body.

He leaned closer. "You missed that branch, Mrs. McGraw."

There really was no other choice. She made a frenzied swish

with her hand and sent a wall of water flying up into his handsome face.

He coughed; he sputtered. And then she was lifted off the rock and dragged beneath the water. In defense she grabbed at his legs.

"Oh!"

She came up for air, only to find herself dragged below again, then back up, gasping. Finally she was dragged to shore and laid out flat, with the sun shining through the tree branches and Dan Marquette stretched above her.

She was smiling, she realized. Smiling and laughing and staring into his dark eyes.

She was dying to touch him. She inhaled sharply, and held her breath, then realized that he was staring down at her, his breath held too. The dark flame in his eyes was the flame of desire, and the heat that emanated from his body was something like...need.

"Kelly..."

He reached out and touched her, running his thumb over her lower lip, brushing his knuckles over her throat. And she couldn't protest. Didn't want to.

Not at all. Something was growing in her. A sweet throbbing, an excitement. His breath caressed her cheek. She wanted to wrap her arms around him. She wanted to press her body against him. She wanted...

"Mom! Dan! You two okay? Where are you?"

Jarod's voice broke the spell. Dan Marquette sprang to his feet and reached a hand down to Kelly. She took it, and he pulled her to her feet. Kelly felt herself flush.

"We're fine," Dan called out, exhaling raggedly. "We're fine. We're right here."

He looked at Kelly, caught her chin and spoke huskily. "Don't you dare try to deny it! I simply won't let you."

And Kelly knew that her world would never, ever be the same again.

*

"THERE'S NO GAME tonight?" Kelly called over her shoulder to Jarod. She was perched on her stool, staring blankly at an equally blank piece of paper. Thank God she didn't have an imminent deadline.

Jarod came up behind her and kissed the top of her head. "Mom, I told you, the game is tomorrow night. I'm going over to Sandy's to watch television."

"Is her dad going to be there?"

"I don't know, Mom," Jarod said. "But Reeves will be."

The doorbell started to ring just as Kelly brought her pencil down to the paper. "Jarod! Get that, will you?"

But Jarod must have gone down to the basement. She slid off her stool and went to the door. Dan Marquette stepped in.

"Hi. What are you doing?"

"Working." Kelly held up her pencil.

He took it out of her fingers. "I need some help. Want to go to dinner with me?"

Kelly swallowed. She did want to go to dinner. She was dying to leave the house, because she wasn't in any mood for work. And the way he looked, she would love to go anywhere with him.

"Hi, Dan!" Jarod had appeared in the hallway.

"Hi, Jarod."

"You're not at home," Jarod blurted.

Dan grinned. "No, I'm not. But Reeves is."

Jarod looked at the floor, blushing. "I know."

"I came to see if your mom wanted to go up to the Hilltop House for dinner."

Jarod looked at his mother, who refused to meet his eyes.

"I'd have to shower and change," she murmured.

Dan shrugged. "Whenever you're ready."

Kelly nodded vaguely and started up the stairs. Jarod watched her and stared at Dan.

"Yeah. Well, I'm, uh, on my way, I guess. Can I get you something while you're waiting? A beer? Scotch?"

"A beer would be nice."

When Jarod returned with it, Dan was still in the hallway. "Uh, why don't you have a seat in the parlor?" he suggested. "Mom won't be long. She's real quick. She's not a primper."

"Jarod..."

"Well, I guess I'll be going. Sandy is expecting me. Have a good time, huh?"

Dan nodded. "Thanks, I'm sure we will. You, too." He picked up a magazine and walked into the parlor with it.

But at that very moment there was a piercing scream—Kelly's—from upstairs.

Dan dropped both the magazine and his beer and bolted up the stairs.

KELLY HAD BEEN quick. She'd chosen a light blue silk dress—a halter-type garment, strapless, with a full skirt—and laid it out on the bed. She'd pulled back the shower curtain to start the water and frowned, thinking that she must remember to open the bathroom window afterward. The tile was molding because she never remembered.

Kelly hesitated, then went ahead and opened it. Who could possibly look through her bathroom window? Her neighbors were hundreds of yards away through the trees.

She opened the window and started to hum. She was trying to forget about everything, in fact. Such as falling for the man who was going to be Jarod's father-in-law. The complications were endless.

No, she told herself. She wasn't falling for him....

Kelly sudsed herself and set her face beneath the spray. Don't think! she reminded herself. I wanted to kiss him, she admitted silently. I wanted to run my fingers through his hair, and...

She turned around, letting the water sluice through her hair, and as she opened her eyes, she screamed.

Someone was staring at her. Someone two flights up from street level, just beyond the bathroom window.

"Kelly!"

She couldn't breathe or gasp out a reply. She could only stand with the water sluicing over her. She wasn't a coward, she told herself. She was just short.

"Kelly!"

She dimly heard the bathroom door crash open; then the curtain was ripped back. And she was standing there in her birthday suit.

Dan Marquette was standing there, too. Tense, anxious, concerned, ready to do battle.

And the eyes were still there. Kelly pointed.

Marquette looked, just as Kelly threw herself against him. All of her. Dripping wet.

"Didn't you see them! Oh, my God, Dan! The eyes! Staring in!"

He was holding her. All of her. And she was perfect! Smooth, sleek, and quivering in his arms. Her flesh was softer than silk....

"Dan, there were eyes! Staring at me!"

"What? Eyes? Oh, yes. I—oh!"

He handed her a towel. "I'll go check."

"Dan, be careful! There's someone out there!"

She thought that he might be in danger. The danger was when he returned!

Kelly managed to wrap the towel around herself, but that was as far as she got. She stood there shivering, then steeled herself to go to the window, to look out. Someone was standing by the big oak.

"Dan?"

He looked up. "Kelly, I can't find anything. Whoever or whatever was here is gone now."

She nodded, and a moment later he was back in the steaming bathroom. She was still standing in the tub with nothing but a towel between them.

Kelly McGraw, you don't know this man very well, she warned herself. It's wrong.

"You—you couldn't find anything?" she managed.

He cleared his throat. "There are some broken branches. Someone or something did go up the tree."

His eyes never left her face, but his gaze was like a caress. He stood so still, so tall, filling the room. "Should I get you anything?" he asked. "A drink? Some brandy?" Me? he added silently. All of me. You'll never be afraid again. I won't let you— I swear it.

He should leave, of course. The danger was gone. Gone—or just beginning?

Water clung to her in delightful droplets. Her hair was drying in soft golden wisps. The towel wasn't really around her—just kind of against her breasts. She looked so tiny, delicate, exquisite....

He took a step toward her, and she didn't move, so he took another, then lifted her over the bathtub rim and against him. He felt the tremendous shivering that seized her body. She didn't look away from him. She tilted her head back, and her eyes met his. He could have sworn that his heart stopped.

"I promised your son we'd go to dinner," he said.

"We will," she told him.

He bent down and kissed her with all the yearning in his heart and soul. His tongue slid over her lips, grazing against her teeth, plunging and delving into her sweet hot depths.

The towel slid from between them. She was kissing him back now. Her tongue, a sweet torment, was deep in his mouth; her fingers were entwined in the hair at his nape. They merged together in that kiss, and the night stopped. Time ceased to be. When they finally pulled apart, neither of them could breathe, and neither of them cared. He saw only her beautiful eyes, blue and open and honest, searing into his own.

"Oh, Kelly," he whispered, and then he kissed her again. When he drew away this time, there was nothing that needed to be said. What was happening between them was so right that it couldn't be denied.

"Oh, Kelly," he whispered again, and he swept her naked body into his arms.

He barely knew the way, yet his footsteps led him surely to her bed. He laid her on it, but when he tried to draw away to undress, she parted her lips and smiled, and pulled him into a kiss again.

He kicked his shoes off, and when the kiss ended, he was above her. Their eyes remained locked as he removed his tie, as she eased away his jacket, and they fumbled with the buttons on his shirt and vest together.

Things went in every direction. His vest to the left, his shirt to the right, his belt to the foot of the bed.

Only then did her fingers falter. He stood and shed his trousers and briefs, then fell down beside her again. For a long moment they remained that way, feeling the marvel of their bodies meeting.

She made a little sound and moved against him, and suddenly the world was filled with brilliant color. He burned with desire. It raged within him as he swept his arms around her and felt the liquid motion of her body beneath his. Too fast, he warned himself. They had just met, and he couldn't let passion take control.

But it had.

A hoarse, guttural cry escaped him, and he shifted his weight over hers. He let his trembling hand roam free over her breast, then touched that seductive flesh with his kiss, with his tongue, holding her nipple within his mouth, warning himself to slow down, ignoring that warning as her body arched against him.

Kelly decided that she had gone mad. But she deserved to be mad, she told herself. She was an adult.... And this was paradise! Once she had thought herself a decent lover. She had loved her husband, and life had been good.

But this was new. This was so intense it was painful. So delicious that denial would be akin to death. This was something that she had never known.

She whispered his name out loud, harshly, hoarsely. His teeth were grazing her nipple while his fingers stroked the soft inner flesh of her upper thigh, and she seemed to become liquid, hot and molten. She emitted a small sound, and then a louder one, and then a searing cry as his touch probed deep within her. The sensation electrified her, and she shuddered because it felt so good, so intense.

He told her to open her eyes, and she did. She stared at him with wonder, enchanted with the passion she could read on his face. He shifted again, smiling, entering her, and she cried out boldly. For a moment she was horrified at the sound, but he laughed with such triumph and pleasure that she buried her face against his shoulder and wrapped her arms around his back.

She savored each second, each movement, each slow, subtle thrust that brought him deeper and deeper into her, made him more and more a part of her.

Her blood seemed to sing in her ears, her entire body moved to the music, his touch. She flew, and she soared, and she sobbed, because she had to reach the pinnacle, yet he held her back again and again, so that she was forced to fly and soar again.

Finally she reached it: a moment so high, so wonderful, so good, that light had never been so explosive, color had never been so brilliant. She felt as if the stars were colliding inside her, yet she knew that she was completely of the earth. As she drifted downward she smiled, because once again she could hear her breath and his, hear her heartbeat and his. Feel her flesh, damp and slick, against his.

She smoothed the hair back from his forehead, ran her fingers over his cheek. He kissed her fingers.

"I think I'm in love," Kelly murmured.

Then she suffered a pang of remorse. What an asinine thing to say! Anyone with any sense knew that love and lovemaking weren't the same, that a man might run if such words were spoken too early.

But he didn't run. He grinned. And kissed her forehead.

"Kelly, do you have any idea how sweet, how fresh, how wonderful you are?"

She colored and curled against his chest, fingering the damp curls of dark hair there.

"Really?" she whispered.

He slipped his arms around her and held her close. "What do you think the kids are going to say?"

Kelly frowned, then sat up, laughed and straddled him. It was a wonderful feeling, natural and easy. "Actually," she told him, "I had no intention of telling them."

He nodded. "Well, they are going to realize that we're getting along much better."

"Are we?"

"I thought we got along just splendidly," he said, his dark eyes alive with sensual fire. "If you've forgotten already, I can refresh your memory."

"Mr. Marquette," she murmured primly, "when I woke up this morning, I most certainly did not intend to spend the evening in bed with you. But once we made the...connection...oh, that doesn't sound right, does it?"

Grinning, Dan said, "It sounds divine, Mrs. McGraw. Divine." He leaned down to kiss her.

"Dinner," she murmured. "You're forgetting, dinner comes early around here! If we don't eat soon..."

Dan glanced at her clock and shrugged. "We can always drive over to Charleston. It's not that late." He smiled, lowering himself against her. "We've got plenty of time," he told her.

And she didn't protest.

TWENTY MINUTES later they were in the shower—with the window closed. But when Dan made an openly amorous move with the soap, she hopped out of his way, pointing at her watch.

"We really will miss dinner!" she told him. "I keep telling you, this isn't New York or D.C.!"

He laughed, remembering that he had wanted to go to the Hilltop House because they could walk after dinner and take in the beautiful view.

They managed to get into the dining room just in time, and get seats right next to the window, too. Friday night dinner was a buffet, and their waitress warned them to get their food quickly, before the chef began to put things away.

They didn't speak much until they had eaten, and then they both laughed again, because they had been so hungry. Kelly ordered a coffee liqueur and Dan a black Irish coffee when they had finished the meal. Only then did his fingers fall over hers, and she smiled a little awkwardly in return.

"You know," Dan said lightly, "Sandy is crazy about you. I'll never be able to thank you enough for that."

Kelly felt her cheeks flush, and wondered how on earth she could still blush so easily around him. "She's a beautiful girl, and you know it."

Dan agreed, then he frowned. "You know, they have to decide on a college they can both go to."

Kelly shrugged. "Jarod wanted Georgetown. He wants to be a politician eventually."

"Sandy wanted the University of Miami. Premed."

"Well, they're going to have to compromise. And they probably should—" Kelly began, but they were interrupted by a sweet, feminine voice.

"Kelly McGraw! How good to see you, darling!"

Kelly swung around, feeling only the slightest dismay. The woman coming toward them was a very pretty natural redhead. Kelly had known her—though not always liked her—since high school. She was also sophisticated and elegant—and tall.

Dan was already politely on his feet. Kelly said, "Dan Marquette, June DeMarco. June, Dan Marq—"

"Marquette, yes, I know," June said serenely, pulling up a chair to join them, even before Dan could help her.

June grinned at Kelly. "Mr. Marquette is the talk of the town, Kelly. And you know each other?"

"Our children are engaged," Dan supplied.

June's eyebrows shot up. "Kelly! You didn't tell me!"

"June, honestly, I haven't had a chance," Kelly said, but June had already linked a long arm through Dan's and was telling him that she ran a simply wonderful antique shop down in the historic section. "You really must come by!"

"I'm sure I will," Dan said noncommittally.

Kelly laughed. "Down, June! Dan, forgive her. She's only been divorced for two years, and we're still trying to teach her proper behavior."

"Oh, nuts to you, Kelly McGraw!" June teased. "We've been trying to teach Kelly that widowhood does not mean instant membership in the nunnery!"

Dan choked on his coffee. Kelly reddened and quickly asked June about her daughter.

They talked for a while about casual things; then June suddenly frowned and asked Dan, "Your daughter isn't home alone, is she?"

Dan shook his head. "No. Jarod is over there, for one. And Reeves—sort of a butler, sort of an old friend—who lives with us. Why?"

June stared at Kelly uneasily. "Haven't you heard? The police, the sheriff's office and even the FBI are after an escaped Tennessee convict. He's called the Peeper. He was convicted of thirteen assaults!"

Kelly gasped. "The Peeper!" she nearly shrieked.

"Calm down, Kelly, you don't know for sure. Kelly thought someone was watching her tonight," Dan said carefully.

"Thought!" Kelly exclaimed. "I saw those eyes!"

"Thank goodness Dan was with you," June purred.

"Yes, thank goodness," Dan murmured.

June said that Kelly should call the police anyway, and she did, from the inn. Dan spoke to them, too, and then they walked out to look at the view.

"You're not staying home alone," Dan said bluntly.

"But I won't be alone! I have a son, remember?"

"Kelly, the police made it sound as if this man is really dangerous. It might have been him, right outside. You are going to stay at my house."

"I can't! What—"

"You'll stay, and Jarod will stay."

"Oh, great! The kids will adore that!"

"Kelly! You can have your own room, and so can Jarod. My house is enormous. We'll tell the kids what happened—"

"We will not!" Kelly yelped.

"Not that!" Dan retorted. "We'll tell them about the Peeper, and the eyes staring in at you. That's all."

"I don't know, Dan," Kelly began.

"I do," he said, and she was still tempted to argue.

But she was a little bit frightened, too, so she didn't.

*

KELLY GNAWED lightly on her lower lip. Dan and Jarod and Reeves had been insistent that she not go home alone, not with the Peeper still on the loose. She and Jarod had been staying at the Marquette house for a few days now, but she had work to finish. She could do preliminary drawings at Dan's, but she needed her board and her T-square and her pastels to do the final work.

Her work was a monthly project; Dark of the Moon was a comic book that came out twelve times a year, and she had just handed an issue in. But she was wasting an incredible amount of time. Dan didn't waste time. He had needed to research something on the flintlock pistol, so he had apologized profusely and taken off for Washington.

"I can't stay away from my house forever!" Kelly said out loud. She paused in front of the house. Jarod would be at school for at least another hour.

She hesitated, then decided not to park in the driveway. She went around to the empty Ipsom house behind hers and parked underneath the oak.

Kelly was a little nervous when she let herself in: she hadn't been alone in the house since she had heard about the Peeper. But she reminded herself that, after all, she hadn't been hurt, just frightened. The Peeper—if that's who the eyes had belonged to—hadn't been inside.

She would be fine. She'd just work for a few hours, lock up, then go back to Dan's.

Images seemed to fly onto the paper. But it was her hand that flew. There was just nothing like love.

"And I am in love!" she whispered.

Only then did her hand pause. Was she really in love? Could love come that quickly? She wouldn't dare to tell Dan that she loved him. It was one thing to murmur in the afterglow of passion—yet suddenly she knew that she was willing to take chances. Even if it meant getting hurt. This would be an adult relationship. There wouldn't be any "have to's" this time. She wouldn't have to marry him. If and when things went further, she would know that it was what they both wanted. Kelly smiled. And then she froze.

Someone was at her front door.

She slid off her stool, determined to walk out and look through the peephole. But her front door was already opening.

Glancing quickly around the room, Kelly saw a heavy vase. She grabbed it, then looked for someplace to hide.

The footsteps were coming closer. Any minute now the intruder would be in the room with her.

Kelly made a mad dive for the doorway, then stood there.

The footsteps hesitated just outside the doorway, as if the intruder knew she was just feet away.

Another step.

He was there; one more step and she would have to strike.

A floorboard gave; the step was taken.

Kelly let out a loud cry, then rushed from behind the door with the vase raised. The intruder's head was way above her. The room was dim and shadowy—crash!

And—slam!

She was gripped violently by the shoulders, then slammed back hard against the wall.

"Kelly!"

"Oh!" she cried. Her panic faded as she stared with dismay at Dan holding his head between his palms and staring back.

"Dan! What are you doing here?"

"What the hell are you doing here?" he demanded.

"I live here!"

"But you're not supposed to be here!"

"Neither are you!"

"Ooh...damn!" he groaned, and felt his head gingerly. He headed for the kitchen and nervously, Kelly followed him. He was digging into the freezer for ice. She got a towel to hold it for him. Still staring at her furiously, he slid into a chair at the kitchen table.

"What are you doing here?" she asked. "You're not supposed to be in town. How did you get in?"

"I have Jarod's key. They're coming to put in a security system, and I had to be here. And I didn't tell you because I was pretty sure you wouldn't have let me do it.''

"I wouldn't have...I won't," she protested, as his mouth came down on top of hers. Possessed it, owned it, ravaged it—and it was wonderful.

They broke apart, and she slipped her arms around his neck, then pressed her face to his shoulder. His hand went to her throat and then her breast, and she thought of all the times when she had wanted so desperately to be with him, when they hadn't touched each other, hadn't dared, because Sandy and Jarod were with them.

"Dan," Kelly said at last. "Dan, I can't let you do this. I don't know what a good security system costs, but I can't afford it right now, and I can't let you—"

She broke off, because his expression was dark and furious. "Dan?"

He stood up slowly. "Kelly, I can't take it anymore. Can you? Hell, I didn't have to leave town! I just couldn't bear you being in a bed in my house without me in that bed, too!"

"But...but..."

"Kelly, you can let me put this system in so that you and Jarod can come home, or we can say, 'the hell with whatever the kids think,' and you can move into my bedroom. I can't stand this any longer. We're adults, but we're trying to act chaste because that's the way we want our kids to behave. But it's too late. And I'm not going to do it any longer!"

Kelly inhaled slowly and shakily. He was making her furious, and she didn't like his set of choices!

"You'll be able to come home Friday or Saturday," Dan said harshly.

She felt all the tension—sexual, wonderful, frightening—in the man before her. She wanted to give herself to him completely. But not quite yet.

ON SATURDAY afternoon they all went to Jarod's game; it was an all-star game, with the income from ticket sales going to a local charity.

Jarod, Kelly noted, shone. He outdid even himself that day. He couldn't miss. If he passed, the ball was caught. If he ran, he gained yard after yard.

"He could probably go pro," Dan said.

I don't want him to go pro, Kelly thought, but she didn't say it; it wasn't her decision. Jarod wanted to go into law and politics, and Kelly personally thought that such a life had to be better than one spent having knees put back together.

She shrugged. "He'll have to decide when the time is right."

Dan laughed softly. "So if luck goes your way, he won't play pro ball, huh?"

"Dan, that's not—"

His laughter, warm and husky, caught her up.

"Oh, go buy some peanuts, will you!" she snapped.

"Peanuts aren't going to solve our problems, Kelly."

"Dan, I can't talk about this in the middle of the game!"

"You have to. Because later the kids will be back, and I know you—you won't want to talk in front of them."

"Dan!" she whispered suddenly, vehemently. "You know I want to be with you!"

"You will be." He paused, then went to buy a sack of the hot roasted nuts.

Someone hailed him when he started back up the stadium steps. It was Sandy, Kelly saw. She looked a little tense. She was smiling, but she was tense.

Because a lot of girls were watching Jarod, watching him like tigresses on the hunt.

He won't hurt you, Sandy! Kelly wanted to promise her. He'll smile, because he's Jarod. He'll be flattered, and he'll be polite. But he really loves you, and he would never hurt you. I hope you know that!

The clock ticked down, and the game was over. The rest of the players on the winning team lifted Jarod up like a god, while the crowd screamed and people began to rise from the stands.

Kelly stood hastily, feeling uneasy, although she wasn't sure why. Then Sandy was with them, asking if she and Jarod could do something that night, all in one breath.

"Hold it! Hold it!" Dan commanded.

"Everyone is going, Dad! I mean everyone—" she insisted.

"Jarod isn't," Kelly interrupted. "Because he hasn't said a word to me yet."

"Oh!" Sandy spun around. "Oh, Kelly, he will! He just has a hard time getting away from the other kids." She paused. Her words had held a touch of bitterness. But her enthusiasm washed it away. "Dad, Kelly, really, it's totally innocent, and it sounds wonderful!"

"Totally innocent," Dan repeated, grinning. "What are you talking about, Sandra?"

"Well, Coach Harrison said he wants to take the team up to Skyline Drive for the night. There's a special nature hike first thing in the morning. Coach said that he'd take the first string and—"

"Since when are you first string?" Dan demanded.

Sandy blushed. "Da-aad!" she wailed. "It's not just Coach Harrison going! It's his wife, and two other teachers and their wives, and six other girls. Separate cabins—and Mrs. Harrison will be in with us."

Dan glanced over at Kelly. She smiled, knowing that he was trusting to her greater knowledge of the situation. "I think it'll be okay," she said slowly.

Sandy threw her arms around her and nearly suffocated her with gratitude. "Oh, Kelly! Thank you! I'll go tell Jarod."

She went rushing away. Kelly and Dan stared at each other, laughed, then shrugged.

"Hmm. I say dinner on the highway," said Dan. "That new place that just opened. I hear it's wonderfully romantic. Italian food, great wine, and a strolling violin player. Then we can catch the last ghost tour, and then..." He winked.

Kelly moved closer to him, taking both his hands, holding them between hers.

"Dan, I own a cabin up in the mountains. It's the most beautiful place in the world. There's a stream and a fireplace, and deer that eat right out of your hand. It's so peaceful. The tour ends at ten—"

"You've got a date, Mrs. McGraw. Shall we collect our offspring and hurry them on their way?"

"Sounds good to me!"

WHEN THEY reached the driveway Jarod reached into the trunk to bring out his gear, then stopped cold to look at Kelly.

"Mom, they haven't caught this Peeper guy, have they?"

"Not that I know of."

His shoulders seemed to sag. "I can't—I mean, this overnight thing isn't that big a deal."

Kelly inhaled sharply. "What are you talking about?"

"You! Oh, Mom! I can't leave you here alone!"

"There's a brand-new security system in this house!"

"But you would still be alone! Mother," Jarod went on primly, "you must know that for a parent you are...very nice-looking." He grinned. "I've actually gotten into a few fights 'cause of you. That sickie would think he'd died and gone to heaven if he found you alone."

Kelly blinked, and nodded slowly. "Thank you for the compliment—I think. But, Jarod, I'm going to the new Italian restaurant with Dan and—"

"Oh! You can go back over there for tonight! And I won't have to worry, because Reeves will be there!"

"I could, uh, stay with Dan, yes."

He smiled, relieved, then started for the house.

Kelly waited behind him guiltily for a moment. Then she shrugged and followed him. She hadn't lied to him; he had simply made some assumptions. Why should she correct him?

By the time she reached the front door, he was upstairs in the shower. By the time she had her sneakers untied, he was out, clad in his briefs, drying his hair. "I'm going to get dressed. When is Dan supposed to be here?" he asked.

"Soon, I guess."

"I'll stay until he gets here. Go on, take your shower. I'll be downstairs. And if you see anything, scream your head off. I may not be old, but I'm tough."

Kelly laughed, brushing his cheek with her knuckles. "I know you're tough, hotshot. And, hey, I was proud of you today," she added softly.

He grinned. "I know, Mom. Thanks." He gave her a quick hug, then turned back to his own room.

A little nervously, Kelly threw off her dirty clothes and stepped beneath the shower. She was glad that Jarod had decided to wait with her. She started smiling, thinking of Dan. They would have all night together. Up at her cabin...

She paused, remembering Jarod's admission that Sandy had gotten pregnant at the cabin. And, of course, Jarod had come into existence there.

But it still meant everything good to her. The cabin had been David's, and it represented everything good about him, too.

"I loved you," she whispered aloud. "I really loved you, David McGraw."

But he was gone, and he'd been gone a long time. They had lived together long enough to know that love was not a fantasy, that it was real. Could be real again.

And then she realized that she was standing in the shower, not moving. She turned off the faucet. David wouldn't begrudge any of them the cabin. He would secretly have laughed if he'd known about Jarod and Sandy....

Just as he had always smiled when the cabin and Jarod's name were mentioned together.

He would smile now. He could be jealous, he could be possessive—but he would like Dan Marquette. Kelly felt it with certainty, and that made her feel very, very good about herself. And about the evening ahead.

JAROD LET Dan in when he came to the front door. They talked about the game for a moment, then, to Dan's surprise, Jarod let out a great sigh of relief. "I'm so glad my mother is spending the night with you!"

"Ah—what?" Dan asked.

"With this Peeper guy running around."

"Oh, yes."

Jarod grinned. "Old Reeves can hear a pin drop, you know. I leaned over to give Sandy a kiss on the cheek when we were watching TV, and the next thing I knew, he was standing between us."

Dan nodded, grateful when Jarod kept talking.

"Thanks for letting us go on this trip. And you have a good time. Well, don't have too good a time."

"Goodbye, Jarod. And be careful." Dan heard him run up the stairs to say goodbye to his mother, then rush back down and out the front door.

Kelly came downstairs a few minutes later. She looked beautiful in an emerald-green knit dress with a mandarin collar and long sleeves. He didn't realize he was staring until she smiled a bit nervously and hurried over, rising on tiptoe to kiss him.

"Well?"

He laughed ruefully. "Lust is roaring through me," he told her. More than lust, Kelly, he added silently. Drawing a ragged breath, he set his hands on her shoulders and smiled ruefully.

"We'd better get going. I made reservations."

She nodded, then said, "Oh! Wait!" and fetched a massive suitcase.

"For one night?"

"Ah, but you don't know what's in it."

He took the suitcase from her and marveled at its weight. "Hot bricks?" he asked.

"Never you mind, Mr. Marquette."

When they reached the restaurant he ordered champagne and made a toast to her beautiful blue eyes. She laughed, but then he made another toast, taking her hand across the table. "Kelly, thank you. Thank you for inviting me someplace that is really special to you."

She moved her fingers idly over his hand, and when she looked back up at him, he knew he was staring at her too intently. But he loved her so much that he wanted to learn everything there was to know about her.

"Hey!" she protested. "People are looking at us." She smiled playfully trying to break the mood.

"I think it's because you're beautiful."

She grinned again. "I think it's because we're beautiful—together. Dan, thank you. I feel young and beautiful with you."

He sipped his champagne. "You are young."

"Not that young. Just short."

"You're not that short. But come on, Kelly, tell me. How young?"

"Well, I'm not underage."

"Thirty-four to thirty-six?"

"Thirty-six in October."

He whistled softly. "Aha!"

"Aha, what?" She stared at him, then flushed. "Well, it was never any massive secret. I made it through my senior year on a real wing and a prayer. David and I were married in June, and Jarod was born in August." She stared at him suddenly, defiantly. "Just like Sandy and Jarod. And that's why I know how hard it's going to be for them."

Dan leaned toward her. He took both her hands in his. "Kelly, you stayed married, didn't you?"

"Yes, but—"

"Kelly, people should never get married because of a child. There are options. More today than you had. If Sandy had become pregnant by the man in the moon and wanted to keep the baby, I would have stood beside her all the way, whether the boy did or not. But Jarod loves her. And she loves him. It's going to be tough, but love will keep them together. Your life might have been hard, but, Kelly, you two beat the odds. I think Sandy and Jarod will make it, too."

She smiled wistfully at him. "Think so?"

He kissed both palms of her hands. "I know so. And guess what? I think their parents are going to make it, too."

*

THERE WERE at least fifty people on the ghost tour that night. It was something Kelly had done a dozen times, but she loved it. It was really called "Harpers Ferry Myths and Legends," and the proprietress was a marvelous storyteller who didn't swear that ghosts existed, merely pointed out certain unusual occurrences in the city.

When the tour was over and people began to disperse, they stood holding hands, gazing at each other.

"You liked it?"

"It was wonderful. I love this place. It's nice at night. It's as if the entire world belongs to us, and only us, right now."

When they came to Dan's car, Kelly gave him directions through the park to the highway and over the border. They actually drove through three states, but it took barely fifteen minutes, and in another five they were halfway up the mountain, parking beside the stream.

Kelly scampered out of the car, up the walk and into the cabin, hoping Jarod had kept the place clean.

He had.

It was just a rough-hewn, one-room cabin, the only addition being the bathroom. The fireplace took up almost an entire wall, and Jarod had stacked plenty of wood. The spring night was just cool enough for a fire.

Dan came in with Kelly's suitcase. He gazed around at the comfortable sofa and chairs, the Indian rug in front of the fireplace, the warm orange and brown curtains.

"It's wonderful," he told her, touching her mouth with his. "It's the warmest place I've ever been."

She smiled and stepped past him quickly to heave the suitcase up on the counter. It contained a stick of pepperoni, several cheeses, crackers and a vintage red wine.

"Dynamite." Dan laughed. "I'll make the fire if you'll cut the pepperoni and pour the wine."

She nodded, but then he pulled her against him, and all she could see was the dark fire in his eyes. She gazed at him with something like wonder. This was real life turning into magic. His touch could make her tremble, melt, yearn to join him in love.

She stared at him, touched his cheek softly.

"I won't be able to make the fire."

"I think you've already made it," she murmured.

He didn't reply. She saw a shadow fall over his face, something that sent a thrill racing up her spine. She felt his hands on the zipper of her dress, felt the fabric slide down against her flesh. When the dress had fallen to the floor, she carelessly kicked it away.

She wondered at his intentions for a moment when he lowered himself to his knees, and then realized he had knelt to remove her shoes. She braced herself against his shoulders; then her fingers tightened, as his hands slid along her thighs to the top of her stockings. She caught her breath and cast her head back, dazed by the rising sensations inside her.

He remained kneeling before her, and she realized that she had never known what it was to feel so adored. At first she felt strong and pleased at her power over his desires, then incredibly weak, then he touched her so deeply with his caress.

He stroked her with a heat and tenderness that filled her until she had no will of her own. He swept her again and again to the brink, eased her down, swept her up and up and...over.

Panting, gasping, she stared down in amazement, slightly embarrassed. He had been so...intimate, and she was already quivering, drenched....

"You—you shouldn't—" she gasped.

"Why not?"

"Well, I—I—"

He stood and swept her into his arms, then carried her to one of the chairs and set her there. Again she felt tremors, ripples, a quivering inside. She heard the rasp of a zipper and, oh, what a sound could do....

She felt it all over again. The warmth, the soaring, the rhythm that went on and on, the throbbing need for him.

She rested her cheek against his shoulder, damp, gasping, savoring his body against her, inside her. He filled her with a staggering pleasure, hot and alive and full. She kneaded his shoulders and back, and felt the fabric of his shirt. Deliriously, she wanted to rip it to shreds. Instead she unbuttoned it slowly, shuddered and touched the bare flesh of his chest, then gripped his shoulders and stared into his eyes.

They were dark with hunger, his features taut, straining, almost grim. His eyes closed, and he moved within her, one final thrust, exquisite in the volatile pleasure it gave them both....

They clung together for a moment, panting. Then he raised his head, his eyes alight with amusement, and she flushed.

"I thought you said you shouldn't?" he teased her.

"Well, I didn't think...." she began primly, but lowered her lashes at the sound of his laughter.

"Don't worry, okay?" he murmured, then picked her up again and collapsed into the chair with her on his lap. He kissed her lightly and she began to feel a different warmth, the kind she had felt in town, when the tour had ended and the darkness closed around them like a blessing. I love you, she thought again with awe. It wasn't the lovemaking—although that was so wonderful she still couldn't believe it. It was the warmth, the pleasure she felt just in holding his hand, in listening to him talk, in watching the stars reflected in his eyes.

"I—I have to get dressed," she murmured. "I'm supposed to be cutting pepperoni."

"The pepperoni will taste a million times better if you cut it...undressed."

Kelly laughed. "You're terrible! And you're still dressed. Well, sort of..."

"I'll strip," he swore solemnly. "Right now." He slid his loafers off while she was still on his lap. Then, holding her tightly, he shed his shirt with a speed that left her gasping.

Then he stood abruptly, deposited her on her feet and bent over to shimmy out of his jeans.

She turned and raced for the shower, shivered beneath the cold water, and hopped out quickly. Then she grabbed a towel and wrapped herself up in it.

When she walked back out Dan was naked, comfortably hunched down while he set the logs and started the fire. He sat back, whistling a tune, smiling complacently, and merely arching a brow while she strutted by defiantly in her towel.

"No fair," he charged. But then he shrugged and sat on the rug, edging back to lean against the sofa. Kelly poured out two glasses of wine. She dug around under the sink for a cutting board and started on the cheese, then the pepperoni.

Dan went to the closet and procured an armful of pillows and her feather comforter to create a marvelous little nest in front of the fire.

Kelly ate some pepperoni, then sipped her wine. As she leaned over to set the glass down, she studied Dan. She loved him so much. Everything about him. His dark hair, the slant of his nose, the little lines beside his eyes, the deep tan that bronzed his whole body—except for the whiteness of his rump!

Other women had probably loved him just as much before her, she reflected.

"Out with it," he said.

She shrugged. "I was just thinking about you. According to the kids, I should be wary."

"Why?"

"Well, they say you've 'loved 'em and left 'em.'"

"Oh? And how well do they know me?"

"I should think Sandy knows you quite well."

"Great. The little minx has been gossiping."

"Well..." Kelly lightly tapped his chest. "I did hear that you...had been around. And now, seeing you in action, well, you are something of an expert."

"I try."

Kelly flushed. "That's not what I meant." She picked up her wine. Suddenly she didn't like the way he was watching her; it made her uncomfortable about the way she was feeling. She was falling in love with him, but he... Who knew what—if anything— he felt for her.

"Kelly," he said softly, "I think Sandy would have liked me to have been serious a few times. She's been good to almost everyone I've ever dated. I just never fell in love before. Sandy thinks I'm hung up because of her mother. I'm not. I even understand—a little bit. It never bothered me that she left me—it killed me that she left Sandy. But she wanted something else out of life. I was drafted, and she was alone."

Love... I just never fell in love before....

That was what he'd said.

They were the most beautiful words she had ever heard, and they made her laugh with delight. Laugh and laugh until he took the glass from her, stretched her out, and she felt his kisses, burning, sweet and hot, against her shoulder, her mouth, her collarbone. Her breasts and her ribs and her waist and...

They made love.

Again and again... Before the fire, the blaze casting gilded patterns against their skin. It was a night of discovery. As long as she lived, Kelly would remember kneeling while he knelt, touching his shoulders, drawing her fingers across his skin, then leaning over and pressing her lips along the same path.

In the end Kelly had no desire to make up the bed. She was too comfortable there before the fire and she began to doze after the perfection of their lovemaking.

Dan nudged her.

"I can't," she groaned. "I really can't."

He laughed. "I was going to ask if you have another blanket. Then you can keep your cute little tush on the comforter and I can put something else over us."

"There's a whole pile of blankets in the closet."

She was so tired she could barely speak, but she felt him stand, heard him pad over to the closet.

She must have dozed then, if only for a few seconds. She came awake and realized that he was standing there, silent, still, his expression like a thundercloud. He was holding something. "Dan?"

Then he was shaking something white and lacy in front of her.

Sandy's bra, Kelly realized. Damn them! They hadn't only got Sandy pregnant—they'd left half their clothing behind.

"Do you know what this is?" Dan demanded.

"A bra," she said dully.

"No, not a bra!" he stormed at her. "Sandy's bra! This whole thing was your fault!"

"My fault!" Kelly shrieked. "What do you think—that I dragged Sandy up here? That I sent her an invitation?"

She found her panties and stumbled into them, then her slip.

"Jarod sure as hell invited her up!"

"She could have said no!"

Fumbling, Kelly managed to shimmy into the rest of her clothing. Dan must really have been floored by his discovery of the "scene of the crime." Apparently he hadn't even noticed that she was dressing.

"What the hell do you think you're doing?"

"Leaving!" Kelly retorted.

"In the middle of the night?"

"You guessed it, Sherlock."

"Oh, no, you're not!"

"Oh, yes, I am!"

She had slammed her way out the front door before he could stop her. Kelly smiled grimly, wishing she'd taken his keys—but willing to walk down the mountain. She knew it like the back of her hand, and she had a good head start. He couldn't come rushing out stark naked.

But as soon as she was on the path to the stream and the trail that went on down to the highway, an uneasy sensation stirred at the base of her spine. She heard a rustling in the bushes.

It's a deer, she told herself.

But it wasn't an animal. Not the four-footed variety, anyway. She knew it. There was someone evil behind her. Someone who meant to slink through the darkness and assault her.

She inhaled, desperate to scream. But who would hear her? Would Dan? How far had she come?

She turned; she could keep her back to the danger no longer. And she saw them. Those eyes. Those same horrible eyes that had stared at her before. Eyes filled with pure menace...

There was enough light for her to see that they belonged to a man. Reaching for her in the darkness.

She screamed at last, loud and long. Then, when he was just about to touch her, he fell instead.

Something was on top of him. Something bronze, except for a little patch of white. On the rump.

Dan.

Of all the deplorable—absolutely fantastic!—gall.

He hadn't bothered with his jeans, or even his briefs! Now he was embroiled in a horrible fight.

She screamed again. "Oh, God!"

"Kelly!"

"Dan! That must be him! The Peeper! And, Dan! It was him! The other night, staring at me..."

He was there, her naked savior, taking her into his arms. Trembling, shaking, she fell into them.

"Shh, Kelly, it's all right. He's unconscious. We've got to call the police."

She nodded, trembling, and they went back to the cabin together, Dan dragging their captive along.

*

THE GOOD NEWS was that they had caught the Peeper.

The bad news was that the story was plastered over the front pages of newspapers as far away as D.C. and Knoxville.

Thank God Dan had gotten into his jeans before the police had come!

Still, the papers reported that she and Dan had been in the cabin on the mountain. The police had been called at 3:48 a.m. and had arrived to find the Peeper still unconscious.

It would have been impossible to tell Jarod that they had driven to the cabin to feed the deer.

He and Sandy came back around eleven to find Kelly, Dan and Reeves sipping coffee in Dan's living room. Jarod had burst in like a small tornado, with Sandy in his wake, waving a newspaper.

"Mom!"

He raced over to give her one of his massive hugs, the kind that she was afraid would break her one day.

Sandy gave her a much gentler hug. "I would have been just terrified. Thank God they caught that awful man and locked him up again. I'm so glad you and Dad were together...." Then she kissed and hugged her father, telling him he was a hero.

Jarod had moved to the window, hands clasped behind him. He turned to Kelly with a curious smile. "What were you doing out on that path at three in the morning, Mom?"

Kelly hardened her features and her heart and stared at him coolly. "Walking, Jarod."

"So you two were up at the cabin together, huh?"

"Yes, Jarod—" Kelly began, but Dan was on his feet.

"And do you really want to know what your mother was doing on that path, Jarod?" he said easily.

"Yes, I do!" he announced defiantly.

"Jarod!" Sandy said in alarm, trying to calm him down.

Even Dan said, "Stay out of this, Sandy."

"Now, wait a minute—" Kelly began.

"You, too, Mom!" Jarod snapped.

"I'll tell you what she was doing on the path!" Dan seemed to roar. "She was walking out on me. We were arguing, Jarod. It's funny. The truth had just slapped me in the face. There I was, picking up pieces of my daughter's underwear, and something just made me snap. I knew what you two had done, but I hadn't known where you had done it, and suddenly I was forced to stare it all in the face. So I blamed your mother, Jarod. It wasn't fair, but I wasn't being rational. And she was furious, so she walked out on me. I tried to catch her, to apologize. That's the full explanation, Jarod. But do you know what, son? I think that if you have any sense at all, you won't mention that cabin to me again. Or ask either one of us what we were doing in it.''

Jarod stared at him for a long time, fists clenching and unclenching. Suddenly he turned to Kelly. "Mother, I'm leaving. Are you coming?"

"Jarod, I think—"

"I think you're acting like a spoiled brat and that you'd better watch your step with me, young man," Dan warned.

"Watch my step!" Jarod growled. "We've been through this before. I love Sandy. There's a big difference."

"Jarod, really!" Kelly snapped. "I'm your mother! I've raised you, and I have the right—"

"It has nothing to do with rights, Mother. It has to do with him. Don't you see? It's humiliating. He only wants—it's just like being his whore."

There was a deathly silence. Kelly was too amazed to talk; Sandy—and Dan—seemed to be in shock.

Jarod turned and stormed out of the house, slamming the door in his wake.

"I'm going to kill him!" Dan swore suddenly. "Take him apart limb by obnoxious limb—"

"Dad, no!" Sandy cried. "Dad, he really doesn't mean anything." She ran to him, clutching his arm. "Dad, please! Let me talk to him. He's upset. He'll apologize!"

She tried to smile at them both, her face ashen. "Please!" she whispered.

Kelly still couldn't move. She felt frozen. She could only watch as Sandy went racing out after Jarod.

Through the huge window, Kelly and Dan could see them clearly; Sandy trying to soothe him; Jarod shaking off her desperate grip on his shoulder.

Then Dan was suddenly in motion. He started toward the door, but Kelly raced after him.

"Dan!"

"I won't have her out there like that! Whining and pleading with that obnoxious, overgrown brat!"

"Dan, damn you, she's going to marry him! She's carrying his child, and he's my son! My son!"

"And you didn't do a damn thing to shut him up!"

Kelly jerked away from him as if he had burned her. "That's right, Marquette, I didn't. Like I said, he's my son. Even if he is an obnoxious brat, he's being protective. And if you so much as go near him, I'll never speak to you again.''

''Kelly? You're defending his behavior!''

''Damn right,'' she said, picked up her purse and marched toward the door.

Outside, she went sailing by Jarod and Sandy, but a second later he had caught up with her. He opened the passenger door for her, then moved to the driver's seat.

They drove home in an awful and absolute silence.

''Mom...'' Jarod began once he had parked the car.

But Kelly had nothing to say to him. She slammed the car door and started for the house.

He followed. ''Mother! Don't you see?''

Still silent, Kelly unlocked the front door and stepped inside.

Jarod was right on her tail. ''The cabin, Mom!'' he exclaimed in sudden fury. ''How could you? How could you go up there with that man and sell out?''

Kelly slapped him. Hard. And then, even as he clutched his cheek in astonishment, she backed him up against the staircase. ''I own that cabin, Jarod—you don't! And without my knowing a damn thing about it, you brought that man's daughter up there. And she's pregnant. And we went out of our way to try to smooth the way for you. We're both trying to see things rationally, and we're both willing to help—and you repay me like this? Jarod...''

There were tears in his eyes. Real tears. ''It was my father's cabin!'' he shouted back. ''It was all right for me to be there! It wasn't all right for you! You betrayed him. I was conceived there! It was my father's place!''

Kelly stopped short. ''Jarod, I haven't betrayed your father! Your father is dead.''

Jarod suddenly sank down on the bottom step. ''It was Dad's cabin,'' he repeated softly.

Kelly sank down beside him, slipping an arm around his broad shoulders. ''Jarod, I loved your father. A lot of things were very hard, and we made it anyway. But, Jarod, he's gone. I miss him, you miss him, but I've been alone a long, long time! Now, I don't have anything else to say on the matter, and quite frankly, Jarod, I really don't want to talk to you right now! Excuse me, please!''

She went up to her room, closed the door, then locked it.

She sat down on her bed and lifted her hands helplessly, then started to cry. She hated them. Both of them! How dare Jarod call her names? How dare he think that he could dictate to her?

And Dan! What was the matter with him? Couldn't he understand that Jarod would be upset? Couldn't he have a little patience, a little empathy? Sandy didn't remember her mother. Jarod did remember his father. And he was a sensitive young man; maybe something about the cabin really was sacred to him.

She stopped crying and lay back on her bed, staring up at the ceiling. Damn Dan! Except that she loved Dan, too. Jarod didn't know that, and she was afraid to tell him. She had been coming to trust Dan, to believe in him, to believe that he loved her, too.

And now...

Maybe he would call her. Maybe he would apologize. He couldn't disappear. They would have to see each other again, because of the kids. Jarod and Sandy were still going to get married.

Kelly sighed. She was exhausted. She'd barely had an hour's sleep, and her crying jag had exhausted her further. She sighed again and fell asleep.

DAN WALKED out into the backyard, where the air was cool and the trees offered some shade, a place where he could try to curb the awful heat of his temper. He walked, because walking would burn steam.

I love you, Kelly McGraw, he thought, chewing a piece of grass. I love you, and I want you, and I'm...

"I'm sorry!" he swore aloud. But as much as he wanted her, he'd be damned if he was going to call her and apologize and tell her, sure, let her son run around acting as if their being together was something dirty and illicit. If Jarod had been anyone else and he had called Kelly a whore, Dan would have decked him.

But he was her son....

I miss you! he thought again.

She'll call me! he promised himself. She would call, because she was wrong. She had to call.

BUT KELLY didn't call. She didn't call on Sunday, and she didn't call on Monday. Or Tuesday.

On Wednesday Dan discovered that Sandy had taken his side. She hadn't said a word to Jarod since he had walked away on Sunday.

She wouldn't really talk to Dan about it, but when he asked

her if she had seen Kelly, she said no, certainly not, that she hadn't even spoken to Jarod.

"Sandy," he had reminded her softly, "you and Jarod have to straighten this out. Not talking doesn't seem to be the answer. Maybe I should—"

"No!" Sandy interjected fiercely. "No, Dad! Jarod has to grow up! I will not let our situation influence yours again!"

She was gone before Dan could say more.

He spent Thursday and Friday working, then discovered on Saturday that he hadn't really accomplished anything.

The weekend passed. Sandy moped around the house, and so did he. Reeves kept walking around pretending that nothing was wrong, but Dan could tell that even he was upset.

Dan talked to Sandy again. He reminded her that she and Jarod were planning a future—the rest of their lives—together. That whether he and Jarod were best friends or not really didn't matter, but that whether the two of them got along did.

Dan decided—in silence—that if Jarod didn't come around to see him by the next weekend, he would go find the boy. But on Wednesday night, everything changed.

Sandy came home nearly hysterical. In the end Dan discovered that it was all because Jarod had been talking to a redheaded cheerleader. To his credit, Dan stayed fairly calm. He was convinced that Jarod had tried to make Sandy jealous because she had been giving him the silent treatment.

He calmed her down, then decided that this was the time to find Jarod himself. But when he picked up the phone to call the McGraw house, he stopped. Sandy was already on the line—to Jarod. She could clearly handle this one herself.

A few minutes later he heard her hang up. A second after that, the phone rang. Dan picked it up.

"Dan, Mr. Marquette! You can't let her do it! Please, sir, you can't."

"Who is this?" Dan asked, smiling.

"Me. Jarod. Sandy is mad at me over some little thing—"

"Jarod, this is not 'some little thing.' Son—"

"I'm sorry!" Jarod exclaimed. "Oh, God, I'm sorry! Sir, I know I offended you, but you've proved my point. You really don't care anything about my mother—"

"We're getting off the real subject here, Jarod, but a son who lives with his mother does not refer to her as a whore. And that goes for whether you want to consider me Mr. Right or not—"

"Please, I'm sorry! Please—"

"I think you owe your mother the apology."

There was silence for a minute.

"Yes, sir," he said very softly. "I know I owe you both an apology. But, Dan—Mr. Marquette—sir! Sandy is thinking of giving up the baby. She can't do that! That baby is mine, too. She has no right—"

"Maybe she doesn't. Decisions regarding the baby should be made by the two of you." He hesitated. "On this, Jarod, I do agree with you."

"Mr. Marquette, she says she's going to go take care of the paperwork right now. Please, don't let her leave the house. Not until I get there."

"I'll try."

Dan hung up the phone, smiling. Sandy came out of her room and smiled back at him.

"Dad?"

"Yeah?"

"He's on his way over here, isn't he?"

"Yes."

She threw her arms around him. "I love you, Dad!"

"And you love Jarod, too, huh, baby?"

She nodded, beautiful eyes wide.

"As mad as I've been at Jarod, Sandy, I believe with all my heart that he loves you."

She nodded. Then she smiled. "And you love her, don't you? Kelly. You love Kelly."

"Yeah. I think I do, babe. I think I do."

*

A few months later...

KELLY HAD BEEN standing by the fence watching Dan for a long time. Watching everything about him. His hands on the ball. His smile. His hair, catching in the breeze. His eyes, when he glanced her way.

Kelly had come to watch him quite specifically. Of course, she couldn't have missed him. He was six-foot-three—a standout in any crowd. Striking, handsome—young, she thought. He was absolutely beautiful.

Yet none of those superficial things was what had drawn her. Not from the beginning, and not now. It had been his smile, and his passion, and all the things inside him. Oh, he was far from perfect. He was temperamental, with his ego and his stubborn streak and his impatience. But he was always able to see his mistakes, and he was always quick to apologize. She knew that always, through thick and thin, they could talk, and he would always be there for her.

It had begun the first time she saw him: love at first sight. And that love had deepened and grown with every step they took together.

Now he looked her way, and she smiled.

He stood still, tossing the football up in the air, then catching it. At last he came toward her.

He stood by the fence, and they were just inches apart. She was in love. Head over heels in love. She felt as if she would never love again as she did now.

"Hi," she said. "Want to go for a ride?"

"Yeah."

"I love you."

"I love you...." His voice trailed away, his heart catching at the sight of her smile. "You're the most beautiful creature ever to walk this earth."

She laughed, a husky sound that caught in her throat. Warmth raced through her.

"You're a liar. I look like a blimp! But I...oh, I love you. I love you, and I need you, and I want you...."

It wasn't meant to seduce; it wasn't even meant to be sexy. They were honest words, meant for a lifetime.

The breeze picked up, and he walked through the gate to stand in front of her. A slow smile lit his face, and he raised his hand, palm flat, toward her. She put her own hand against his, and their fingers entwined.

"Do you have your car?" he asked her.

"Yes. Where do you want to go?"

"I know this wonderful place. It's a cabin, up in the hills."

She laughed, and they walked toward the car. In no time at all, it seemed, they were at the cabin.

While it was still light they wandered down to the stream, where they wound up laughing and showering each other with the cold mountain water. Naturally he built a fire as soon as they went back inside.

As they sat beside it, he touched her cheek, and in the gentle firelight they gazed into each other's eyes. Finally their clothes were shed.

He'd never seen anyone more beautiful. She had wonderful hair, and it seemed to be a part of the fire, cascading over her breasts, glowing against the ivory of her flesh. Her breasts were beautiful and perfect and full, and when he looked at her, he could barely speak. Yet when she was in his arms he did, telling her how much he loved her. Each time he touched her body he murmured of her beauty, and she laughed, but he told her it was true: she was more beautiful than ever.

Finally their laughter faded. Love led the way for her, a gentle, tender path to ecstasy, sweet and torrid.

She belonged to him, with all her heart.

No one had ever loved so well. And no one had ever made love as they did. So deeply, so completely. Heart and body and soul...

She lay with her cheek against his chest, his fingers wound into her hair, and together they watched the flames playing softly in the hearth.

"Sometimes I still can't believe it," she murmured.

"Believe what?"

"How happy we are. From such a beginning! All of us, really."

He held her face tenderly between his hands and looked at her with a rueful grin. "Sometimes, just sometimes, life can be a little like a fantasy. We've found that magic. At least, I have. It's in your eyes."

"Oh, that's so nice."

He grinned again. "Yes, I thought so. Rather good for a grim old historian, don't you think?"

"Humph!" She would have said more, but the phone started ringing. They looked at each other with surprise, because no one should have known where they were.

Jarod. Of course! Jarod had seen them leave, and he must have guessed where they were going. Except that he wouldn't have interrupted them—unless...

"Sandy!" they exclaimed simultaneously.

Dan won the race to the phone, but he held the receiver away from his ear so they both could hear.

"Jarod?"

"It's a boy!"

"A boy! It's a boy!" Dan repeated for Kelly.

"Eight pounds, two ounces."

"Congratulations! We'll be right there."

"Good." Jarod hesitated just a second. "Put your clothes on first, will you, please?"

Kelly grabbed the phone. "I heard that, young man!"

"Sorry! Get here quickly. Mom, he's beautiful!"

"Of course he's beautiful. He's my grandchild!"

She dropped the receiver and stared at her husband. "Oh, Dan! It's true! We're grandparents."

He kissed her lips quickly. "Yes, it's true." He drew her against him. "And," he whispered very softly to her, "thank God for those darling little procreationists! We might never have met without them."

"Never loved."

"Never married."

She smiled up at him. "Let's go see the baby."

"Only if you calm down. Ours isn't due for another two months, and I'd like it to wait until then."

She made a face at him. "I am calm. Oh! My God! We're grandparents!"

"I'll go see that baby without you, Kelly."

"You will not!"

She smiled sweetly, showing him how calm she was, while he helped her back into her clothes.

"Actually," he told her, "you do look like a blimp."

"You wouldn't dare say that if I weren't a grandparent!" she said reproachfully.

He laughed and told her that she was the most beautiful grandmother he had ever seen, and the sexiest. "Definitely the most beautiful pregnant grandmother, ever," he assured her.

And so, naturally, being sophisticated and mature this time around, she stuck out her tongue at him and preceded him out the door.

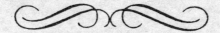

TELL ME A STORY
Dallas Schulze

Flynn was positive that newspapers did not move on their own. This piece of brilliant reasoning burst into his alcohol-soaked mind with the force of a lightning bolt.

He slumped against the wall. If the papers were not moving themselves, he should know why they were moving. After all, this was his alley. Since his family owned the building, they owned the alley, too.

The papers shifted more violently and Flynn's frown deepened into a scowl. That was an arm. Thin and pale and amazingly fragile. He couldn't just walk off and leave it in the possession of these animated and possibly dangerous papers. What if this was the first wave of an invading force from another planet? This could be an alien pod looking for some innocent human to take over their body.

It didn't occur to Flynn that the alley behind a luxury apartment building in Los Angeles seemed an odd starting point for an interplanetary invasion. At five o'clock in the morning, after drinking all night, anything seemed possible.

Filled with pixilated patriotism, Flynn managed to cross the space between himself and the suspicious papers. The lump jerked alarmingly and the papers cascaded in all directions.

"Hey! Get off my foot, you big ox."

Flynn slumped down and found himself gazing into a small heart-shaped face with fine sandy brows drawn together in a fierce scowl. He smiled at the face in a friendly way. "Sorry. Are you a pod?"

The scowl on the little face returned in triplicate. "I'm not a pod. I'm a girl."

Flynn was vaguely disappointed. He'd been looking forward to telling his father that aliens had landed and they'd chosen McCallister property as their landing site. The old man would have had an apoplectic fit at their effrontery.

He sighed. "What are you doing under that pile of papers?"

"I was trying to sleep," she told him with heavy sarcasm.

His brows rose. "Wouldn't a bed be more comfortable?"

"I don't have a bed." The statement was flat, leavened with a touch of scorn.

Flynn's brows shot up until they almost met the heavy fall of black hair that drifted onto his forehead. "No bed? It doesn't seem fair. I have more beds than I know what to do with. We'll go to my 'partment and find you a bed. Bound to be a spare or two lying around the place."

He struggled to his feet, leaning one hand on his companion's shoulder once he achieved his goal. He frowned down at her. "You're not very big, are you?"

She drew herself up straighter, almost unbalancing him as she guided his erratic footsteps across the alley.

The door to the apartment building closed behind them with an expansive whoosh of air. Flynn blinked rapidly in the sudden glare of light. A bank of four elevators lined one wall. With a great deal of concentration, he managed to punch out a short combination of numbers that opened the doors on the elevator. Once on board, Flynn grabbed for the nearest wall as the floor surged upward, leaving his stomach somewhere beneath him.

"Are you okay, mister?"

He closed his eyes in exquisite agony as the elevator stopped and the doors slid open, revealing a wide foyer and two beautifully carved wooden doors on either side.

Using her shoulder as a brace, he steered her out of the elevator.

"Which door, mister?"

Flynn turned slowly and then pointed to the door on the left with a gesture worthy of Lady Macbeth. "Don't go near that door. A dragon lives there. She has red hair and cold green eyes and she can freeze your bones with one look."

His new acquaintance shook her head, her small face twisted in an expression of adult exasperation.

"You're drunker'n a skunk."

Flynn frowned. He followed her lead to the other door and reached out to push the door open. They stepped onto thick, soft carpeting and the door clicked quietly shut behind them. He spun on one heel with more enthusiasm than sense and stumbled. He gave her a smile that had been known to make little old ladies swoon with pleasure.

She was not impressed. Her small mouth was pursed in stern disapproval.

He stumbled down the two steps that led into the living room and almost sprawled onto the carpet. Some rapid and surprisingly graceful footwork kept him upright, and he turned to grin at her triumphantly.

"Fred Astaire, eat your heart out," he exclaimed expansively.

She caught the twinkle in his eye and giggled. "You're very silly."

"Thank you. I do my best." He swayed for a moment before regaining his balance. His lips twisted in a rueful smile. "I'm afraid my night of wicked carousing is catching up with me." He blinked to clear his foggy vision. "We'd better get you settled before I collapse."

He set his feet down with neat precision, each step carefully planned and executed as he led the way through one of the doors that faced onto the hallway. The bedroom was beautifully done in shades of brown and slate blue. Plush blue carpeting and drapes formed a background for the rich mahogany furniture.

Slowly, the little girl moved into the room, staring around her with wide gray eyes. In her childish eyes, the room was reflected as a palace and, for an instant, he saw her vision, pushing aside the hurtful memories that tainted it.

She tiptoed across the thick carpet and reached out to touch the heavy bedspread, drawing back before her hand made contact.

He crossed the room in a few quick strides and grabbed hold of the bedspread, jerking it off the bed and tossing it carelessly on the floor.

"It's so beautiful." She bent to touch the discarded bedspread reverently.

"It's beautiful, but it's only a thing." He looked down at his diminutive companion. "Make yourself at home. This is a good room. It used to belong to my brother," he said.

She watched him silently, only speaking when he would have pulled the door shut behind him. "Hey, mister, could you leave the door open?"

He stuck his head around the door and grinned at her. "You bet, and I'll leave the hall light on, too. My bedroom is two doors down on the right. If you need anything, just come in and poke me. Good night, urchin."

Flynn walked the few feet to his bedroom, deliberately encouraging the alcoholic fumes to cushion his mind. Once in the room, he collapsed on the wide bed. He groaned softly. God, he was drunk. He hadn't been this smashed in years. Not since he and Mark... No. He didn't want to remember. Not now. Not when his defenses were at an all-time low.

The memories faded and were replaced by tiny features capped with a mop of raggedly cut sandy hair. His mouth tilted up. Cute little thing. Who was she? Good Lord, he didn't even know her name! Oh, well, in the morning he could find out her name and who her parents were, and he'd get her back where she belonged.

The mists of drink and exhaustion gradually thickened, creating swirling pockets of peace in his tired thoughts. The faint lines beside his mouth smoothed out as his breathing deepened and slowed.

FLYNN'S NOSE twitched and his eyelids flickered. His head hurt with a relentless, pounding throb that moved from the top of his skull all the way down his body. His nose twitched again. What was that smell? Acrid and smoky.

"Are you awake, mister?" He rolled onto his side. The little girl from the night before was perched on the edge of the bed. "I made you some coffee."

"Bless you." He dragged himself into a sitting position. He lifted the cup to his mouth and took a sip. Flynn's eyes sprang from half-mast to wide open. He was about to spit the foul liquid back into the cup when his eyes fell on his small houseguest. Wide gray eyes peered from beneath ragged, sandy bangs. Without another thought, he swallowed, praying that his stomach lining was tougher than it felt.

"It's wonderful."

His companion smiled. "Mom says you can't start a day without coffee."

"I...ah...feel the same way." Flynn tried to look casual as he held the cup as far from his nose as possible. "I don't think we were properly introduced last night. I'm Flynn McCallister."

"I'm Rebecca Antoinette Sinclair. You can call me Becky. Do you want some more coffee?"

"No! I mean, one cup is my limit." He looked at Becky. "It's been a while since I was your age, but I'm sure I'd remember if sleeping in alleys was normal. Where's your mom and dad?''

"I don't have a daddy." Her chin thrust out. "He left when I was real little."

"Okay. What about your mom? Where is she?"

The tough little chin quivered. "I don't know. She was s'posed to come home a couple weeks ago. She went away with one of her boyfriends. She was supposed to come back on Monday. Only she didn't. Mrs. Castle said she was going to report me to the welfare people. Mama told me all about them." Becky's brows came together. "I couldn't let the welfare people take me away. They'd never let me see her again."

Flynn closed his eyes, half hoping Becky would turn out to be a figment of an alcohol-soaked imagination. But when he opened them again, she was still sitting there, her eyes fixed on him.

"You won't call the welfare people, will you?"

He looked at her, wondering what imp of fate had chosen to drop her into his lap.

"No, I won't call the welfare people." Flynn thrust his fingers through his hair and stood. "The first thing I'm going to do is to pick up the paper and the mail and then I'm going to take a hot shower. Then we'll sit down and talk about what we're going to do with you."

Flynn went to the front door. He stepped into the hall just as the elevator came to a halt. His smile took on a wicked edge.

Ann Perry had lived in the apartment across from him for two years. She was young, attractive, single, and she sternly disapproved of him. He could never quite resist the urge to reinforce her image of him as a worthless, womanizing playboy.

He leaned against the doorjamb. He knew exactly the picture he presented. It was four o'clock in the afternoon. He was unshaven. His hair was tousled. His feet were bare. His shirt was unbuttoned to the waist and his belt was unbuckled. He looked the very picture of worthless masculinity. It was perfect.

The elevator doors slid open and Flynn felt a twinge of guilt. In the instant before she saw him, she looked tired. There was a vulnerable droop to her shoulders. But the moment her eyes fell on him, her shoulders stiffened.

Flynn slumped against the wall, letting his eyes trail insolently over her.

"Ms. Perry. Home from a day of saving lives?"

She tilted her head. "Mr. McCallister. Home from a night of drinking?"

She stalked to her door, stopping to pick up her mail and the newspaper.

Ann was aware of Flynn McCallister's eyes following her every move. She fumbled with the key before stepping into the haven of her home. She resisted the urge to slam the door. She wouldn't give him the satisfaction of knowing he disturbed her.

Three feet away, her housemate launched himself into her arms. It was Oscar's preferred method of greeting. She carried the huge tomcat into the kitchen and set him on the floor.

"I saw McCallister in the hall. He looked like he'd been up all night. Again."

Oscar murmured sympathetically. He was familiar with the problem of McCallister.

It annoyed Ann that McCallister could read her so easily, and it annoyed her even more that she couldn't control her reaction to him. She was a doctor. People's lives rested in her hands every day. Control was essential in her work, and it carried over into her private life. With nothing but a look and a quirk of an eyebrow, Flynn McCallister managed to weaken that control, and she resented it.

The phone rang, startling her out of her thoughts, and she jumped. It would be her father. He would want a progress report. How did she tell him that a medical career wasn't like being a corporate executive where every day she could report some deal closed, some new advance toward a vice presidency? The triumphs of helping a patient didn't interest him in the least. He wanted to know where her career was going. He thought she was progressing too slowly.

Twenty minutes later she put down the phone, feeling more drained than when she'd left the hospital.

She'd planned to go out and do some shopping, but maybe it would be a good idea to take a long hot bath and unwind. She had the next two days off, and a relaxing evening at home would be a nice way to start her little vacation.

She left the kitchen and headed toward her bedroom, but she was sidetracked by Oscar, who was sprawled flat on his back in the middle of the living-room floor. She stopped to scratch his ample tummy, and he took it as an invitation to play.

The sudden pounding on the door interrupted the wrestling match. Oscar rolled to his feet and streaked for the bedroom.

She grasped the doorknob, ready to give whoever it was her iciest look.

The last thing she'd expected to find on her doorstep was Flynn McCallister, clad in nothing but a towel and a panicked expression.

She dragged her eyes from his chest and looked at his face. Something was wrong. What was he saying?

"...in the shower and she fell. There's blood all over."

The doctor in her took over. "I'll be right there."

FLYNN WAS kneeling on the floor next to one of the sofas, his naked back blocking Ann's view.

"She's a doctor and she'll know just what to do." His voice was soothing and full of confidence.

"But you said that a dragon lived next door." The voice was definitely feminine and just as definitely under ten years of age.

Ann filed the words away to examine at some other time. Right now, what mattered was her patient.

Stepping around Flynn, she knelt by the sofa. Other than being female, the child bore no resemblance to her hasty image of a woman who'd been cavorting in Flynn's shower. She was small-boned and fragile, with a mop of badly cut sandy hair. Her gray eyes were swimming with tears.

"I was in the shower and I heard her fall. I don't know what happened. Becky was looking at magazines when I went into the bathroom." Flynn's voice was tight with concern.

"I was just trying to get a closer look at that picture on the wall, Mr. Flynn. I stood up on the sofa, but I slipped on a book and hit my head on the table." Ann glanced over her shoulder at the coffee table. It was a massive affair of glass and wood. Becky was lucky the damage was as minor as it was.

Becky's eyes met hers solemnly, more than a trace of uncertainty in their depths. Ann smiled and the look faded a bit, but it wasn't replaced by trust. Ann had a feeling that this was not a child who trusted easily.

"It REALLY wasn't a very big cut, just a nasty one. In a few days you'll hardly be able to tell that you were ever hurt."

She lifted her head and was surprised to find that Becky was holding out her hand, her small face very solemn. "Thank you, Miss..." Her face scrunched up in thought and then she shook her head. "I can't remember your name."

"Ann. Ann Perry." Since it seemed to be expected of her, Ann took Becky's hand and shook it. "You're very welcome. I'm glad I was here."

Flynn stood at the top of the steps, having returned from getting dressed. His expression was anxious. He looked like a tousled satyr.

"Well, urchin, you certainly look a lot less gruesome than you did."

"Ann says that in a few days I'll be good as new."

Becky lifted a worn shopping bag and carefully took out a stuffed giraffe. Next came a well-thumbed book. Ann picked up the giraffe.

"That's Frankie," Becky said. "I've had him since I was a baby."

"Did your mother give him to you?"

Becky hesitated a minute and then shook her head. "I think Daddy gave him to me."

Ann fingered the distinctive button in the toy's ear and picked up the book. It was *A Child's Garden of Verses*, a beautiful leather-bound edition, old and much worn, showing the love of more than one generation.

"Was this your daddy's when he was a little boy?"

"I don't know. Mama doesn't much like to talk about him." She took the book from Ann and set it next to the giraffe, clearly saying that the subject was closed. Ann accepted her lead, knowing that you didn't win a child's confidence by pushing.

"Becky, why don't you go out and take a look at the plants on the balcony. I want to talk to Flynn."

Flynn looked at Ann, one dark brow arching in question. Becky looked from one to the other and her pale brows puckered.

"Are you going to fight?" Becky looked at Flynn, clearly more willing to trust his judgment than Ann's.

"Go on out, urchin. There's some hand tools in the box next

to the door. Why don't you dig in one of the empty planters. I promise we're not going to come to blows."

Ann hired professional gardeners to care for her garden. It was lovely, not a leaf out of place, and she seldom paid any attention to it. Flynn's garden was considerably less neat. Some of the planters were empty, while others held such a wealth of vegetation, it was hard to distinguish one plant from another. It was the perfect place for a child to play. She watched Becky disappear into the jungle of growth, trowel in hand.

The smile that softened her mouth disappeared when she turned to look at Flynn. She settled onto an off-white overstuffed chair and then realized it was a tactical error. The huge puffy cushions practically swallowed her. She shot Flynn an annoyed look.

"She said that you found her in the alley last night and offered her a bed. Is that true?"

"Pretty much."

Ann ground her teeth together. "Flynn. Didn't it occur to you that her mother would be worried about her? I've always known that you were irresponsible but I wouldn't have believed that even you would do something like this. That poor woman must be out of her mind with worry."

"You've always known that I was irresponsible? On what do you base this sweeping judgment?"

Ann opened her mouth but he cut her off with a sharp gesture. "I don't really want to hear it. Becky's mother disappeared two weeks ago. The landlady was about to turn Becky over to Social Services. Becky is terrified of them so she ran away. She's been living on the streets for the past few days. No matter how irresponsible I am, I think I'm a better bet than the streets."

"That's not the issue. She says you were intoxicated last night."

"Smashed to the gills."

"You can't possibly think that's a good influence for a child."

"It was my brother's birthday."

"And that's supposed to make it all right? The two of you go out and—"

"Not the two of us. I was alone. Mark died three years ago."

Ann wondered if it were possible to coax the huge chair into swallowing her completely. "I'm sorry."

There was a moment of silence and then Flynn ran his fingers through his hair. The crooked smile he gave her was half apology and wholly charming.

"I'm the one who should be sorry. I know you're concerned about Becky and I shouldn't be giving you such a hard time."

"She can't just continue to stay here. What are you going to do?"

He rubbed his forehead. "Either I'm getting too old to drink like that or hangovers are getting worse. I thought I'd take her out to my parents' home tomorrow. They may have some ideas. You're welcome to come along just to make sure that I don't sell her to the white slavers." He grinned to show her that there was no rancor behind the words.

"If you wouldn't mind, I'd feel better seeing this a little farther. I don't know why. I hardly know Becky."

"There's something about her that sort of gets under your skin."

Ann nodded, suppressing the thought that Becky might not be the only one.

LYING IN the huge bed that night, the covers tucked under her chin, Becky's youth and fragility were more apparent than ever.

Flynn sat on the edge of the bed and brushed the hair back from her forehead. He smiled at her. Ann was stunned to feel a twinge of envy.

"Could you tell me a story, Mr. Flynn? Mama always tells me a story 'fore bedtime."

Ann barely listened as he began to spin a story full of dragons and princesses and handsome princes. She didn't want to hear the soft rise and fall of his voice. She didn't want to see the way his eyes softened when he looked at Becky. She didn't want to like him. It wasn't safe.

She was so absorbed in her thoughts that she jumped when he touched her arm. Becky was fast asleep, her lashes lying in soft crescents against her cheeks. She didn't stir as the two adults eased themselves off the bed and tiptoed out of the room.

Flynn followed her to the door and Ann was vividly aware of him every step of the way. She stepped into the hall, feeling as if she were escaping some fatal temptation. "I'll see you tomorrow, then."

He nodded, stifling a yawn. "I'll come knock on your door around ten."

When she opened her own door, she turned, lifting her hand in what she hoped was a casual gesture.

As she shut the door, Oscar looked up, his yellow eyes full of polite inquiry.

"Oh, Oscar. What have I gotten myself into?"

*

THE MCCALLISTER home in Santa Barbara smelled of old money—lots of it. Some of the antiques were one of a kind pieces—all of them were exquisite.

Ann hadn't given much conscious thought to what Flynn's father would be like, but she'd had a vague image of an older version of Flynn—tall, lean, with elegantly masculine grace.

She hadn't expected a stocky man a few inches short of six feet. His features were blunt, his eyes a clear, sharp gray rather than electric blue. The only resemblance she could see was the thick black hair, now heavily streaked with gray.

His handshake was firm, his look direct, lacking the lazy charm that made his son so fascinating—and so exasperating.

David McCallister nodded to his son, his eyes cool. "Flynn. I thought you might call this week."

"So Mom told me. You know how I always hate to do the expected. Besides, we would have quarreled and that seems like a hell of a way to honor Mark's birthday." His tone closed the subject and there was an uncomfortable silence in the study.

Ann looked around the room, admiring the walls of books, most of them leather bound. One shelf held trophies, another family photographs. The silence lengthened. She moved over to the photos, studying them with interest. It wasn't hard to identify the family members. There was a stocky young man who showed up in most of the photos. That must've been Mark. Flynn was in some of the pictures, sometimes in the background, sometimes with his arm over his older brother's shoulder. But there were no photos of Flynn alone. Ann turned away from the pictures, not wanting to think about the implications of what she was seeing. She cleared her throat.

"You have a lovely home, Mr. McCallister. Flynn tells me he grew up here."

His eyes snapped to her, dark and fierce. "Did he mention his brother?"

Ann glanced at Flynn, but he didn't shift his eyes from his shoes. She was on her own. "Flynn told me that his brother died three years ago. That must have been a terrible time for all of you."

"My son Mark was a wonderful boy. He was a police officer. Died in the line of duty."

"You must have been very proud of him."

"I was." Father and son stared at each other across an abyss that had obviously been there for a very long time. Flynn smiled, the insolent smile that Ann had seen so often the past two years.

"Hey, Dad, don't feel bad. One out of two ain't bad."

The older man's face darkened, and Ann braced herself for the explosion that was sure to follow. She'd seen that look in her own father's eyes too often to mistake it. Why had Flynn provoked him?

The explosion didn't come.

Louise McCallister stepped into the room. The older woman's eyes took in the situation immediately, and Ann caught a glimpse of her distress before she set about smoothing the waters.

"Becky is settled in the kitchen and Maggie is teaching her how to bake cookies. What a charming child. I'm so glad you brought her to see us, Flynn."

The next few hours passed on a calmer note, though Ann had the feeling that the hostilities lay just beneath the surface. By the time Becky's immediate future was hammered out, Ann felt as if she'd witnessed a battle between the superpowers.

It was agreed that Becky's terror of the welfare department eliminated the possibility of calling the authorities. On the other hand, something had to be done about finding her mother. It was Flynn's suggestion that they call a private detective and, very reluctantly, his father agreed that it seemed like a reasonable alternative.

"MARK AND I used to play on those swings. I bet they haven't been used since we were kids." Flynn waved at Becky, who was happily absorbed in pumping herself as high as possible on the swings in the backyard.

"You and your father don't get along very well, do you?" Ann hadn't planned on asking the question.

"A masterpiece of understatement if I've ever heard one." Flynn's voice was heavy with sarcasm. "As far as he's concerned, I haven't done anything right since I was born."

Ann stared at Becky without seeing her. Flynn's words brought back her own childhood too vividly for comfort. "It must have been hard to please him."

Flynn shrugged. "I quit trying long ago."

"How can you not try to please your father?" The concept was foreign to her.

"I suppose I might have been more inclined to try if it hadn't been for my older brother. You see, Mark was perfect." His smile twisted with memories. "Captain of his football team, captain of the debating team. He was intelligent, polite, handsome and had a great sense of humor. It was all absolutely sincere. He was truly the greatest older brother any kid could want."

"But you couldn't compete." Ann's voice was soft. She knew just how he felt, though her competition had been the ideal of a son who'd never existed outside her father's dreams.

"I couldn't compete. I sometimes think I became a rebel just to give myself an identity. At least Dad noticed me as something other than Mark's shadow. I can't say I don't enjoy doing exactly what I'm doing. The fact that it irritates Dad is just a side effect."

"Just what do you do?" He slanted her an amused look and Ann flushed, realizing how critical the question sounded. "I mean, you don't seem to go to work or anything...."

The smile he turned on her was brilliant. "I'm a professional playboy. The truly useless man-about-town." He bowed low before her.

She shook her head, unable to imagine a life without the limits of work or school to frame the days. "I can't imagine not having a job."

"That's the trouble with the world today. Nobody can imagine life without jobs."

Silence fell between them. There was something about him that disturbed her in ways she didn't understand. He was so... different. She'd never known anyone like him.

"Hold still." His voice was hushed and Ann froze as he reached toward her. She felt his hand in her hair and when he pulled away, there was a ladybug resting on the tip of his finger. He held his hand up and blew gently. The tiny insect hesitated a moment and then flew away.

"You know, for a dragon, you're pretty nice." Flynn's hand came up to tug at a lock of red hair that had escaped from her braid. His head was lowering toward hers, that brilliant blue gaze fixed on her mouth.

His mouth touched hers and her eyelids fell shut as if attached to weights. She could smell the faint tang of after-shave. Her mouth opened the smallest amount and the kiss deepened. Their breath mingled until it was impossible to tell where one began and the other ended.

She could feel something waiting just out of reach. Something exciting and dangerous and full of promise. Something she wasn't sure she was ready to reach for.

"Mr. Flynn."

The voice seemed to come from a long way away. At first Ann couldn't even make sense of what it was saying.

"Mr. Flyyynnn."

Her eyes opened slowly as Flynn's mouth left hers. In his eyes she could see some of the same surprise she was feeling.

"Becky wants you. I....ah...I think I'll go see if I can help your mother with dinner." She walked away before he could say anything.

IF ANN HAD seriously believed that her involvement with Becky and Flynn was going to end after the visit to his parents, she was doomed to disappointment. Over the next few days, the focus of her life seemed to shift. Whether she wished it or not, she was caught up in Becky's life. And through her, Ann was caught up in Flynn McCallister's life. There just didn't seem to be anything else to do.

"LOOK AT IT GO, Mr. Flynn. I bet it could go clear to the moon."

Flynn reached out to steady Becky's small hands on the spool of kite string and then leaned back on his elbows, staring up at the bright scarlet kite that floated high above them. Not since Mark's death had he felt so relaxed. He shifted one hand, touching

Becky's slim back affectionately. It felt so right to be here with her. He'd never thought of himself as a family man, but Becky was making him reconsider. And Ann. Ann was making him reconsider a lot of things. Like Becky, she'd become an integral part of his life.

Dangerous thinking, McCallister. Next thing you know, you'll be thinking about rings and babies.

And why not?

He sat up, oblivious to Becky's startled look. He'd begun to think of himself as a confirmed bachelor. He hadn't thought about marriage and children in years. Now, suddenly, the idea didn't seem quite so alien. Almost appealing.

"Something wrong, Mr. Flynn?"

ANN TRIED not to think of how impossible the day had seemed. Her heart hadn't been in the job, and that was a dangerous thing for a doctor. She'd gone through all the motions and done all the right things but, in the back of her mind, she'd wondered what Becky and Flynn were doing. She'd wished she were doing it with them.

"So what did you two do today?" she asked during dinner.

"Mr. Flynn got a big kite and we flew it for a long time, only then he got it caught in a tree."

"I prefer to think of it as the tree got in my way."

Ann answered his grin with a smile, surprised to realize how right it felt to be sitting across the table from him.

After dinner, Ann loaded the dishwasher with only a few token protests from Flynn. She insisted that it was the least she could do, and he didn't argue long.

She wandered out into the living room to find Flynn and Becky sitting on the sofa. A box was on the table in front of them. Ann crossed the soft carpet and sank onto the sofa on Becky's other side.

"What have you got?"

"Pictures." The succinct answer came from Becky. Flynn appeared to be half dozing.

Ann reached for a handful of the photographs that were scattered across the table. She expected to find family pictures. But the first was a picture of the park across the street. A little boy was wearing a bright red raincoat and hat, with incongruously bare feet. The camera had caught him in the act of jumping into a shallow puddle, his face ecstatic. Leaning drunkenly against a bench nearby was a pair of red rain boots.

The next photo was of an old woman. Her face was weathered with decades of hard living, but there was pride in the set of her chin, in the clarity of her eyes. Pride that wasn't dimmed by the shopping cart of belongings that sat next to her.

Ann blinked back tears. "Did you take these?"

"It's a hobby."

"They're beautiful."

"Thanks. I've got a small darkroom and I enjoy playing with it."

"You've done a lot more than play with these. You could get them published."

He took the pictures she still held and put them in the box with the others. "I probably could. But I don't want to."

"Why not?"

"Ann, if I sold some photos, it would cease to be a hobby and become a career. I couldn't play with it anymore. People would expect me to take wonderful photos according to their schedules. It wouldn't be fun anymore."

"But you can't just take pictures like that and not do something with them."

"Why not?"

The simple question seemed to stymie her. She stared at him blankly for a moment. "You just can't."

Flynn stood up, abandoning the subject. "Time for bed, urchin." He ignored the inevitable protests and herded her toward the bedroom. Ann followed. Becky was soon tucked into bed with Frankie the giraffe snuggled beside her.

"Tell me a story, Mr. Flynn." Flynn told her a story about a frog who became a prince and the princess who loved him even when he was a frog.

He finished the story and reached up to tuck the covers under her chin. "Good night, Becky."

"Mr. Flynn? Do you think I'll ever see my mama again?"

Flynn was aware of Ann coming to stand behind him. What was he supposed to say? Life didn't offer any guarantees. Not even to children.

"We've got a man looking for her, honey. He's very good at

finding people. All we can do is cross our fingers that he'll find her soon.''

*

ANN LOOKED at the clock in her apartment and frowned. Flynn had only been gone a little over an hour. As soon as he'd talked to the private detective and found out if there were any leads to Becky's mother, he'd come home. There was no sense in watching the clock.

When the doorbell rang fifteen minutes later, Ann practically flew to the door, Becky hard on her heels.

''Flynn—''

''Mr. Flynn—''

Both sentences came to an abrupt halt. The man standing outside the door was short, stocky and balding, and the expression on his face bore no resemblance to Flynn's lazy charm.

''Dad.'' Ann knew her tone fell short of enthusiasm.

''Ann.'' He nodded. ''Obviously, you were expecting someone else.''

She stepped back, aware of Becky retreating to stand next to Oscar. ''Dad, this is Rebecca Sinclair. She's staying across the hall and I'm taking care of her for a little while. Becky, this is my father, Mr. Perry.''

He acknowledged the introduction with a short nod.

''Staying with the McCallister fellow, is she? I thought you were steering clear of him.''

Robert Perry believed that children should be treated as if they were part of the furniture, which included not only silence, but deafness.

Luckily, the doorbell rang again before Ann had to find an answer for her father's comment.

''Flynn.'' They had only an instant in the semi-privacy of the hall. There was no time for Ann to ask any questions about his visit with the private detective. Her eyes met his and he shook his head slightly before Becky clutched him around the knees.

''Hi, urchin.'' He bent and swooped her up. Her giggles drew a smile from Ann, a smile that died when she looked at her father.

''Flynn, this is my father, Robert Perry.''

Robert Perry's face expressed his disapproval of both Flynn

and Becky. "I understand Ann has been baby-sitting for you. My daughter is a very busy woman. I hope you don't plan to intrude on her time like this again."

"Dad!" Ann could feel the color coming up in her cheeks. She looked at Flynn, half expecting him to stalk out in a rage. But, of course, Flynn McCallister never did the expected.

His mouth twisted in a half smile that brought an angry flush to Robert Perry's face.

"I think Ann can take care of herself. She's never hesitated to speak her mind in the past. Of course, you have to be willing to listen to hear what she's saying." His words fell into a little pool of silence.

He shifted Becky from one arm to the other, tugging the door shut behind him, cutting off the sound of Becky's giggling pleas to be put down. Ann stared at the door for a long moment, surprised by the strength of the urge to follow him.

THAT NIGHT after they put Becky to bed, Ann slid farther back on Flynn's sofa and leaned her head against its back. How had it happened that, in the space of a few short days, Flynn McCallister had gone from being a thorn in her side to being an oasis of calm?

Flynn swirled the wine in his glass.

"How did the visit with your father go?"

In her current relaxed state, not even the mention of her father could seriously dim the warm glow Ann felt.

"The same as usual. I should be further along in my career. I don't attend the right gatherings. He doesn't like my cat, my apartment, my lifestyle."

"And Becky and me."

"It's nothing personal. He just worries that I'll let things get in the way of my career."

"Things like personal relationships?" He leaned forward and picked up the wine bottle, filling Ann's glass. "You know, I've found that you can't always fulfill your parents' dreams for you."

Ann frowned into her glass. "Did you know that I wanted to be a veterinarian when I was a kid?"

"Why didn't you?"

She swallowed the wine. "My father thought it was dumb. Doctoring people is more important than animals." She yawned.

"I'm sorry. I should have warned you that wine makes me sleepy."

"That's okay. Do you ever regret it?"

"That wine makes me sleepy? It doesn't cause me much trouble." She blinked at him owlishly. Her eyelids felt so heavy. "I really should be going home."

Flynn watched as her head slipped slowly to the side, her eyes shut, her mouth the slightest bit open as she slid into sleep. There was a funny ache in his chest. She looked so vulnerable. He looked at her a moment longer and then left the room.

When he returned, he was carrying a pillow and a blanket. Ann didn't twitch when he tucked the pillow under her head. He covered her with the blanket, and she cuddled under its light warmth.

Thirty-three was a hell of a time to fall in love for the first time. He'd almost begun to think it would never happen. He tucked the blanket more firmly around her shoulder and moved away, scooping up the glasses and the half-empty wine bottle on his way to the kitchen.

THE JANGLE of the phone was an unexpected intrusion and Ann jumped. What if it was Flynn? In the two days since she'd awakened on his sofa, she'd managed to avoid much contact with him. There was something about him that made it all too easy to reveal things she didn't want revealed, say things she didn't even want to think.

The phone rang again, and she took a deep breath and reached for it.

"Ann?"

"Oh, hello, Dad." The relief was only temporary.

"I wanted to let you know that I've taken matters into my own hands."

"What matters?"

"When we talked about that child that McCallister is keeping, I told you that the only thing to do was call the Social Services. After giving it careful thought, I felt it would be best for all concerned if someone did the right thing, so I called Social Services this morning."

"You did what?" Ann hadn't thought it was possible to be so angry so quickly. "How dare you interfere like this? You had no right!" She slammed the receiver down.

She had to warn Flynn. Barefoot, she flew out of the apartment and across the hall. It seemed like hours before the door opened.

"Flynn, I'm so sorry. My father called—"

"Come in and meet Ms. Davis, Ann. She's here about Becky."

Ann looked past his shoulder to the woman who sat in the living room. She stretched her stiff facial muscles into a smile and hoped she didn't look as sick as she felt.

"Is SHE gone?" The adults turned to find Becky peering into the living room, her eyes wide and uncertain.

"She's gone."

"She's not going to make me go away with her?"

"Nobody is going to make you go anywhere." Flynn bent to catch the little girl as she flew across the room to him. He swept her up easily, accepting her arms around his neck and returning the hug. Ann swallowed a lump in her throat.

"She wanted to take me away, didn't she?" Becky's voice was muffled by Flynn's shoulder.

"She wanted to make sure that you were all right."

"Is she going to let me stay with you?"

Flynn stroked the back of her head, offering her physical reassurance as well as verbal. "She's going to let you stay with me. She was just worried about you and she wanted to make sure Ann and I were taking good care of you."

Becky snuggled her head deeper into his neck.

Apparently that was all the reassurance Becky required. If Mr. Flynn said it was going to be fine, she'd believe him. Her arms loosened around his neck, her world set right again.

Flynn set Becky down and she skipped off, confident that all was right with her world as long as Flynn was in it.

Ann shifted toward the door, her eyes settling on a point somewhere beyond Flynn's shoulder. "I...I'm sorry about what my father did."

"Where are you going?"

Her eyes flickered to his face and then away. "I didn't think I'd be welcome."

Flynn caught her arm. "Ann, you can't possibly think I blame you for what your father did? It had nothing to do with you. I know that."

His voice was so gentle that Ann had to blink back tears. It had been a long time since anyone had used that tone with her. It made her want to lean her head on his chest and let him take care of her.

His head lowered, and Ann closed her eyes as he kissed the tear from her cheek.

Her hands slid around his neck, pulling him closer. She felt as if all her life she'd been only half-alive.

She couldn't pretend anymore that life was going to go back to the way it had been before she'd opened her door to Flynn's towel-clad, panic-stricken presence.

*

"TELL ME a story, Mr. Flynn." This had become a nightly ritual. Ann moved quietly around the room putting away the day's accumulation of clothes and toys, while Flynn's voice spun a quiet story about elves and princesses.

The story was only half over when Flynn's voice stopped, and Ann turned to see that Becky had fallen asleep, her lashes making dark crescents against her flushed cheeks. Flynn eased himself off the bed and dropped a kiss on Becky's forehead. They tiptoed from the room, leaving the door open just a crack.

In the living room, the atmosphere was suddenly awkward. The two of them were seated on the thick carpeting in front of the fireplace. Huge pillows bolstered their backs. It was a warm, intimate setting and part of Ann couldn't believe that she was here, courting disaster like this.

She stared into the fireplace, afraid to look at Flynn, afraid to look too closely at what she was doing. Afraid to stay and even more afraid to go.

He didn't move, didn't speak until, at last, she could bear the tension no more. She turned her head. The flames cast shadows over his features, making it difficult to read his expression.

"You are so beautiful." His voice was husky, soft. His thumb brushed her earlobe and she shivered. Her lips parted, anticipating, needing, wanting.

And then he was there.

His mouth claimed hers hungrily. Ann moaned low in her throat as her lips opened, welcoming the invasion of his tongue.

He tasted of wine. He tasted of madness. He tasted of all the things she'd denied herself for so many years.

She was barely aware of his hands shifting to her shoulders, lowering her to the thick carpeting. Flynn's mouth slid down her throat, his tongue tasting the pulse that beat frantically at its base.

He was warm, so warm. She slid her hands up his chest, feeling the shudder that ran through him. For the first time, she realized the power of her femininity. It was a heady feeling. But she didn't have long to savor the feeling, because Flynn soon showed her that it worked both ways.

She opened dazed eyes as he stood up, bending to lift her in his arms. The fire continued to burn in the hearth, the flames lower now. Her eyes met Flynn's, reading the hunger that still burned in him.

He carried her easily, kicking the door of his bedroom shut behind them, reminding Ann that they were not alone in the apartment.

She stared at his chest as he shrugged out of the loosened shirt and let it fall to the floor. His fingers went to his belt buckle, and her eyelids fluttered.

He bent forward to kiss her and her mouth softened instantly. Need burned in him. When she at last lay naked beneath him, he thought he would surely explode with hunger. Her hair spread like fiery silk across his pillow. And her eyes. Her eyes seemed to burn into his very soul.

His hands stroked her body, stroking the slumbering fires to new life. She arched beneath him, tangling her fingers in his hair.

The pleading tug of her hands stripped away the last of Flynn's fragile control. He slid his body over hers, feeling her stiffen and then melt as she felt the heat that burned in him.

He began to move, slowly, savoring the feel of her tight warmth. Ann matched his movements, gradually picking up the rhythm. The hunger had been building for so long that the fulfillment could not last long. Flynn felt the delicate contractions grip her body and he moaned a protest. He wanted it to last forever. Then his own climax took him, sending him spinning after her into a place where the only reality was each other.

The return to earth was slow. Flynn lifted his head, feeling as if the entire world had been rearranged in the last few minutes.

Ann lay still beneath him, her body lax, her face utterly peaceful. He kissed her, tasting her satisfaction in the softness of her mouth.

He was pleased with the slightly glazed look in her eyes. She looked like a woman who'd been well and thoroughly loved.

He slid his arm beneath her shoulders, pulling her to his side. Ann's head snuggled into his shoulder, feeling so right that he wondered how he'd ever slept without her small body tucked against his.

SHE STOLE quick glances at Flynn, terrified that he would wake up before she could slip away. She couldn't face him right now. It was foolish, childish even, but she just needed to get away.

Once dressed, she hesitated for a moment. Part of her wanted to climb back into bed and wake him. She wanted to find out if it was possible to know the kind of pleasure she remembered from the night just past. Surely, she must have dreamed the total satisfaction she'd felt. She backed away, physically resisting temptation. She hurried from the room, carefully shutting the door behind her.

WHEN THE knock on the door came, Ann jumped, spilling milk on the counter. She'd known that she wouldn't be able to avoid Flynn forever. But she hadn't expected him to come knocking on her door when she'd been home from work less than twenty minutes.

He was going to want to talk about last night and she wasn't ready to talk about it. She wasn't sure she'd ever be ready. This was one problem she hadn't been able to put aside by going to work. It had nagged at the back of her mind all day, like an aching tooth that couldn't be ignored.

She pulled open the door to find Flynn's hand raised to knock a second time. All her carefully selected phrases flew out of her head when she saw his face.

He looked old and tired. Deep lines bracketed his mouth, and there was a dull hurt in his eyes. He was far removed from the man she'd left sleeping only twelve hours ago.

"My God, Flynn. What's wrong?"

"They found Becky's mother. She's dead."

*

FLYNN HAD no idea what time it was when he came out of a light sleep, aware that something was wrong. He was surprised that he'd fallen asleep at all. After tucking Becky in once they'd told her about her mother, he and Ann had shared a glass of wine and then she'd gone back to her apartment, leaving instructions to call her if he needed her.

Looking in on Becky, he'd experienced a feeling of total unreality. She slept so peacefully, as if this night were no different than any other. Was death really such an abstract concept to a child that she didn't realize what it was going to mean in her life?

The sound that had awakened him came again and he slid out of bed and padded down the dim hallway. Pushing open Becky's door, the sound was clearer, easily identifiable. She was crying.

He crossed the room, easing himself onto the edge of her bed and gathering her shaking body into his arms. Her arms came up to circle his neck and she buried her face in the thin silk over his shoulder.

"Mama. I want Mama." The words were muffled by sobs but Flynn felt them like tiny knives in his heart. "Mama."

"I know you do, sweetheart. I know you do."

He had no idea how long she cried. He held her, rocking her, brushing the tangled hair back from her face, murmuring soothingly and wishing that there was something he could do to take her hurt away.

It had been one hell of a day.

"DR. PERRY to emergency please. Dr. Perry to emergency." The tinny voice echoed over the PA. The elevator was empty for once, and Ann allowed herself the luxury of leaning against one wall and closing her eyes. Her heart wasn't really in it these days. A part of her wondered if it ever had been. She was so tired. Tired of thinking, tired of trying to decide what was right, tired of worrying about what her father wanted. She wanted to get up and walk out of the hospital and never come back. She wanted to go home to Flynn and Becky and shut the door and not come out for a month.

What were they doing right now? Had they gone to the park? The new school year had started two weeks ago, but Ms. Davis had agreed that it might be best for Becky to stay home. It was a difficult time for her. Unspoken was the thought that, when they placed her in a foster home, she probably wouldn't be in the same school district that she was now, anyway. Flynn refused to talk about foster homes.

Flynn. Another subject she'd been avoiding examining. There were a lot of things she needed to think about. Like the direction her life was going; did she want to spend the rest of her life in medicine; and what would it be like to fall in love with Flynn McCallister?

The next afternoon, she was no closer to answering any of her own questions, but the questions themselves had been pushed aside by more pressing matters. Sitting on Flynn's sofa, she watched him pace back and forth across the living room, his strides full of coiled energy.

"Maybe Ms. Davis just wants to check and make sure Becky is all right."

Flynn shook his head. "She was here three days ago."

"Did she say anything then that might give you a clue?"

Before he could answer there was a knock on the door. Their eyes met, each wanting some reassurance that neither of them could give.

None of his feelings showed in his face as he opened the door. "Come in, Ms. Davis."

Flynn followed her into the living room, wishing that he could read something from her face. "Was there a problem with your visit Monday?"

"No problem at all, Mr. McCallister. I'm afraid I have some good and some bad news."

Flynn smiled slightly. "I've always had a healthy distrust of conversations that start out on that note."

"I'm afraid it won't be possible for you to adopt Becky, Mr. McCallister."

Flynn was aware of Ann's head jerking toward him. He should have told her what he had in mind. "I can't believe that my reputation is so bad that it would earn me an immediate rejection."

"It really has nothing to do with your reputation, Mr. McCallister."

He leaned forward, his eyes pinning her to her chair with their intensity. ''What if I were to get married?''

His eyes shifted to Ann. She stared at him, feeling her own eyes widen with shock. He was suggesting that they marry for Becky's sake. It was amazing that he could even consider such a thing. She wanted him to want her for herself.

The thought was so stunning that Ann jerked her eyes away from his.

''Your bachelorhood really doesn't make any difference, Mr. McCallister. Becky's father has been located and he wants his child.''

The words fell into a pool of silence, as if each were a small stone, sending out ripples as they hit the water.

''Her father?'' Flynn's voice was dazed. ''You're just going to hand her over to some flake who couldn't be bothered with her for the last three years?''

Ann wondered how Ms. Davis could be so calm. Flynn was a more than slightly intimidating figure.

''I understand your disappointment, and I would have given you my recommendation if Mr. Traherne hadn't turned up.''

''Who's Mr. Traherne?''

''Becky's father.''

''Traherne? Becky's last name is Sinclair. If this Traherne couldn't even be bothered to marry Becky's mother, how can he lay any legal claim to Becky?''

''They were married, Mr. McCallister. You see, three years ago Becky's mother left and took their child with her. Mr. Traherne has been looking for both of them ever since. He's a doctor. The Traherne family has been in Denver for over seventy-five years and they are all respected members of the community. We feel that it's in the best interests of the child if she can be with her natural father.''

Ms. Davis reached for her briefcase. ''He should be here day after tomorrow.''

Flynn's smile was strained as he stood up to show her to the door. He was losing Becky. The thought brought a hollow ache to his gut. And with Becky gone, what was going to happen to his relationship with Ann? Would Ann still want to be with him or was he going to lose her, too?

FLYNN AND Ann decided not to tell Becky about her father. If there was some mistake, there was no sense in getting her hopes up only to have them dashed. There'd been enough disappointments in her young life.

The day Becky's father was supposed to arrive, Ann stayed home from the hospital. Becky was playing on the balcony when Joe buzzed up from the lobby to say that Mr. Traherne was here. Flynn felt as if the world had come to a halt.

At six feet tall, Rafferty Traherne was built like a bulldozer. There was nothing here that reminded Ann of Becky's delicate bone structure. Nothing to show that he was related at all, until she looked into his eyes. They were the same clear gray as his daughter's. And they gave her that same feeling that they could look right into her soul.

She watched him sink into one of the living-room chairs. Like Flynn, he dominated the overstuffed piece of furniture without effort.

"What I'd really like to know is why your wife ran away. I've had Becky in my care for over a month now, and if you hadn't turned up, I was going to adopt her. The government may be satisfied with the fact that your name is on her birth certificate but, until *I'm* satisfied, Becky is staying right where she is."

Flynn was deliberately trying to antagonize the man. The two men stared at each other, weighing and measuring in some way that Ann couldn't follow. Whatever he saw apparently decided Rafferty in Flynn's favor. He nodded slowly.

"Maryanne was a very high-strung, very sweet girl. And I use the word 'girl' deliberately. She just didn't seem to know how to grow up. I thought maybe she'd grow up when Becky was born but she didn't. I'm not sure she ever really figured out that Becky wasn't a doll to play with." He was silent for a moment, lost in memories. He shrugged. "I wanted her to grow up and she wanted me to be a father figure. There was no middle ground.

"Maryanne...did something that she thought was going to make me very angry. She thought... Hell, I don't know what she thought. When I got home from work, she was gone and she'd taken Becky with her. I hired investigators but no one could turn up a trace of Maryanne or Becky. For all I knew, they were both dead, until I got the phone call from Ms. Davis."

Rafferty had told the story without fanfare or dramatics. But

Ann had watched the way his fingers knotted over one another and she knew just how much it had cost him to dredge up the old memories. She looked at Flynn and could see that he was impressed despite himself.

"It's going to be awfully hard on Becky to just pack up and move. To her, you're a total stranger."

Rafferty nodded. "I know. She's just lost her mother. You two are the only security she knows right now." He thrust his fingers through his hair, tousling it into waves of gray. "I want to get to know my daughter again. You two know her a lot better than I do. What do you think would be the best way to tell her who I am?"

It was clearly not easy for him to ask for help. Flynn answered the pained question. "Becky's been through a lot lately. If we just drop it on her that her father has arrived, it's going to be pretty hard on her. You can stay here. It will give her a chance to get to know you without any pressure. We can tell her that you're a friend of mine." Flynn's offer was made without expression, and Rafferty studied him for a long moment before nodding slowly.

Ann allowed herself to relax for the first time since hearing of Rafferty's existence.

*

IN THE last two weeks, Becky had come to adore Rafferty. Which was just as it should be. Flynn was doing what he could to loosen the ties between himself and Becky. It hurt but it had to be done. She needed to transfer her dependence to her father. He was glad that she was doing so.

His eyes caught Ann's. They'd barely spoken since the night they made love. It seemed as if something was always taking priority. First there'd been the death of Becky's mother, then finding out about Rafferty and then Rafferty himself showing up. Their relationship had taken a giant step and had then been frozen in time.

Becky and Rafferty had gone to the movies, leaving Ann and Flynn in the quiet apartment. He didn't want to talk about Rafferty or Becky or the fact that soon they'd be going away. He wanted to pull Ann into his arms and feel her soften against him.

"Do you realize this is the first time we've been alone in three weeks?"

Awareness flickered through her eyes for a moment. He was so close that his breath stirred the hair that curled against her temples. Slowly her eyes came up to meet his.

"Flynn..." He stilled her whispered protest with a quick kiss, stealing away her voice.

"Stay with me tonight."

"I can't. I..." He kissed her again and she forgot what she'd planned to say.

"Stay with me. I just want to hold you."

She started to shake her head but his mouth stopped the movement. The kiss was longer this time. His mouth molded hers, stealing not only her breath, but the ability to think.

She wasn't quite sure how they'd gotten to the bedroom. Sometime during that drugging kiss, he must have eased her in here. She didn't remember walking but he certainly hadn't carried her. He reached around her to turn down the covers on the bed.

She hesitated, aware that this was a crossroads in some way that she couldn't quite define.

Flynn waited. He could feel Ann's hesitation and he held his breath. He wouldn't pressure her but, if she walked away now, he felt as if something inside him would die. She looked up at him, her eyes bright green with questions he couldn't read, and then she turned and slid onto the bed.

He released his breath in a rush. He reached out, pulling her close, feeling complete for the first time in a very long time.

FLYNN CAME awake slowly, aware of feeling completely rested. He didn't have to open his eyes to know the source of his contentment. He kissed his way down her face, planting soft kisses at the corners of her eyes, on the tip of her nose, on the delicate skin just under her jaw. Her lips parted, inviting him.

Ann moaned against his mouth as his hand cupped her breast. The sleepy passion took on an edge of urgency, and Ann met him with demands of her own. All that mattered was touch.

Her legs parted, cradling him. His mouth caught hers, his tongue plunged inside at the same moment that he sheathed his aching hardness in the damp warmth of her body. He moved, feeling her body shift to accommodate his.

Ann shivered beneath him, her body contracting around him, and Flynn groaned, following her to the culmination of their passionate love.

Not a word had been spoken, but they communicated as fully as was humanly possible.

RAFFERTY woke suddenly, aware that he was no longer alone. He was lying on his stomach, his face near the edge of the bed. He opened his eyes to find Becky seated on the floor next to the bed. Clutched in her arms was the tattered brown giraffe he'd given her for her second birthday. Her eyes were wide and solemn on his face.

"Are you my daddy?" The question was so totally unexpected that Rafferty wondered if he was dreaming.

"Would you like it if I was your daddy?"

She shrugged. Her fingers twisted an ear on the battered stuffed toy. "How come you left me and Mama? How come you left us?"

He chose his words carefully, knowing that what he said now could affect their relationship for a very long time to come. "Your mother took you and she left. I looked for the two of you but I couldn't find you. I never stopped looking, Becky." He closed his eyes. "We used to have a lot of fun together when you were little. You probably don't remember much of that."

Her eyes flickered up at him. "You used to throw me up in the air. And sometimes you'd tell me a bedtime story. Only you'd read it out of a book. Your hair was all streaky. Not one color like it is now."

Rafferty ran his fingers through his iron gray hair. "When your mother left, my hair hadn't gone completely gray yet. It runs in my family, you know. Your grandfather's hair was gray by the time he was thirty."

"Grandfather? Do I have a grandfather?"

"Sure. And a grandmother, too. And you've got two aunts and three cousins."

Her eyes widened at this bounty of relatives. "All those?"

Rafferty's arms closed around her and he buried his face in her sandy hair. She smelled of soap and baby powder. His chest ached as her arms went around his neck. He'd lost so much time with her. Three years gone never to be regained. He'd never lose sight of how lucky he was to have her back with him.

*

No matter how quickly said, the goodbyes were still painful. Becky had been part of Flynn's life a relatively short time, but she'd wound herself deep into his emotions. It wasn't easy to say goodbye.

"Don't cry, Ann. You and Mr. Flynn will come see us soon, won't you?"

"You bet we will, urchin." Flynn crouched next to the little girl, his eyes going over her face. He ruffled her hair, keeping his smile tacked in place. He stood up and held out his hand to Rafferty. "Take care of her."

Ann's smile was shaky as she bent to hug Becky. "See you later, Becky."

Flynn's chest ached as the elevator door slid open. Rafferty stepped in but Becky tugged her hand loose from her father's and ran back.

Flynn dropped to one knee, catching her as she flew toward him, burying his face in her hair, breathing in all the sweet little girl smells that he'd grown to love.

"I love you, Mr. Flynn."

"I love you too, Becky." His voice broke on the words and he held her tighter. "I'll come and visit you soon. I promise."

He turned her around and gave her a gentle push toward Rafferty. She took two steps and then hesitated, looking back at him. He smiled, hoping she wouldn't notice the unnatural brightness of his eyes. She looked at him a moment longer, her gray eyes full of uncertainty and then turned and ran to her father. Rafferty caught her hand in his and stepped into the elevator. Flynn stood up, watching as the elevator doors slid shut, blinking rapidly against the burning in his eyes. Behind him, Ann sobbed quietly.

"I'm going to miss her so much." The words came out on a hiccoughed sob and Flynn's heart twisted.

"I know, love." He pulled her head to his shoulder and Ann collapsed against him, one hand curling around the edge of his shirt.

She cried for a long time, crying out her grief over losing

Becky, but also crying out the confusion that seemed to have taken over her life. Nothing fit into the neat patterns she'd devised for herself. Most of all, Flynn McCallister didn't fit into any pattern.

When she lay still against him, he brushed the tangled hair back from her face. He dropped a kiss on her flushed forehead, tilting her face back to place another kiss on her still-trembling mouth.

"I must look awful." It was a measure of her exhaustion that she didn't try to hide her tear-streaked face. "I guess I'll go home. Oscar probably thinks I've died."

Flynn felt a surge of panic. He had the feeling that, if she went home now, they might never find each other again.

"Dinner."

Ann looked up at him, startled by the way the word came at her so forcefully. "Dinner?"

"Dinner." He smiled crookedly. "I know a great restaurant where the lobster is slathered in butter. I'll call and see if I can get reservations."

THE EVENING seemed to have a fairy-tale quality to it. The table was tucked in a dimly lit corner. And Flynn's eyes couldn't seem to get enough of her.

"You should have ordered the lobster."

Ann cut into her beef, finding it meltingly tender. "It's impossible to eat lobster neatly and I don't want to end the evening with butter on my chest." She took a bite of beef and then looked up to find Flynn's eyes on the décolletage of her dress.

"I'm sure I could think of some way to get it off." His eyes swept up to hers, and Ann forgot how to chew.

Flynn dipped a bite of his entrée in butter and held it across the table to her. "You can't possibly get butter on your dress this way."

Her teeth sank into the succulent white meat and she closed her eyes in ecstasy, savoring the buttery richness of it. When she opened her eyes, she found Flynn staring at her. The need she saw there made her feel like a siren.

"Once I get you home, I'm going to strip that sexy dress off of you a little at a time and I'm going to taste every single inch until you beg me to make love to you."

Though she knew the food was exquisite, Ann couldn't really

say that she tasted much of it. All her attention was for the man across from her. They said very little during the meal, but she could feel the tension building to a boiling point.

They both refused dessert and Flynn paid the bill. He put his hand against the small of her back as they walked from the restaurant, and Ann wondered if the sparks that seemed to shoot from that light touch were visible to the other patrons.

Neither of them said a word on the drive home. The tension inside the low-slung sports car was so thick, it seemed to be almost breathable.

He carried her through the silent rooms to his bedroom, laying her on the bed and following her down, pinning her with the sensual weight of his body.

She couldn't have said if it were hours or days later when they at last fell asleep. She was conscious of nothing beyond the warmth of Flynn lying next to her, his ragged breathing slowly steadying. He'd kept every promise he'd made her in the restaurant.

THE NEXT morning, she opened her eyes and sat up, feeling more alive than she had ever felt before. She cocked her head, listening, but the apartment was quiet. Her clothes were neatly folded and stacked on a chair and she flushed, remembering how quickly they'd been discarded the night before. Lying on top of her silk slip was a folded piece of paper. She picked it up, feeling as quivery as a schoolgirl.

Ann,
    Sorry I'm not here to kiss you awake but I'd probably end up making you late for work. I had to go out to my parents'. Some papers Dad needs me to sign. Let's have dinner again tonight. I'll pick you up at eight. Wear the green dress again. I had such fun peeling it off of you.

                                                        Love, Flynn

Ann hugged the note to her chest, her cheeks pink with the memory of their lovemaking the night before.

But, as the day wore on, some of the glow faded, to be replaced by a host of uncertainties. What was she getting into? Never in her wildest dreams could she have imagined that she would be attracted to a man like Flynn McCallister. He'd been wonderful with Becky, but there was more to life than being kind to small children and animals. There was dedication and ambition and...Well, weren't dedication and ambition important enough? And he didn't have a trace of either one.

Ann Perry was a very practical woman who knew better than to think that love alone could support a marriage.

*

HE TOOK her to another quiet restaurant. Flynn tasted the wine and nodded to the waiter before turning his full attention to Ann. "How was your day at work?"

"It was okay." She shrugged, feeling tension creeping into her shoulders.

He leaned back as the waiter set spinach salads down in front of them. "Do you ever think about what your life might have been like if you'd become a veterinarian?"

"No!" His eyes jerked to her face and Ann flushed, realizing how abrupt the word had sounded. "I mean, why would I? Being a doctor is important work." Ann picked at her salad. Why did the words ring so hollow? "How was your visit to your parents?"

"Pretty much the same as always. Dad wants me to take an active role in the corporation." He half laughed and, at another time, Ann might have heard the pain in the sound. "I don't know why he can't get it through his head that I'm not like Mark."

"I thought he was a police officer."

"He was, but Dad always figured Mark would quit the force and join the company after a few years, and he's probably right. But I've got a lousy head for business."

"Maybe it disappoints him that you don't have more ambition." Ann pretended not to notice the way Flynn's eyes widened at her tone.

"We can't all be ambitious. I'm content."

"Are you?" She was suddenly brimming with anger and frustration.

Flynn half laughed. "Why do I have the feeling that I've done something to upset you? Is it my tie?"

"You can joke all you want, but you're wasting your life and you're wasting your talents."

His mouth tightened. "Where the hell is this coming from? You be ambitious and I won't be and we'll do just fine."

"It just seems to me that you're a little old to still be defying 'Daddy.'"

"I beg your pardon." The tone was icy.

She gestured angrily. "Isn't it time to grow up?"

Flynn's knuckles whitened around the delicate stem of the wineglass. "At least I haven't let my entire life be run by my father like you have. Sleeping with me is probably the first thing you've ever done that you didn't ask Daddy's permission for. Or did you call and check it out with him first?"

The crack of her hand against his cheek echoed in the quiet room. Ann drew her hand back, pressing it against her mouth, her horrified eyes on the red imprint of her palm. "Oh, my God."

There was a sharp ping and she looked down to see that the stem of his wineglass had snapped in his fingers.

Flynn raised his hand to the waiter, who was staring at them in stunned silence.

"The lady and I will not be dining tonight after all. Please tell Mike to put the meal on my tab."

Seconds later, he was sitting beside Ann and the car's engine growled as he pulled away from the curb.

"Flynn—"

"Don't. Just forget it."

There was such command in the simple words that Ann subsided into her seat.

The car came to a halt outside their building. She glanced at Flynn but his eyes were focused on the windshield. "If you didn't bring your key, Joe can let you in."

He didn't look at her. It was as if, in his mind, she'd already ceased to exist.

THE NEXT few days were an exercise in torture. Ann could not stop going over the disastrous evening in her mind. The events replayed themselves like a broken record: each word, each gesture, had to be taken out and examined again and again.

She'd deliberately set out to pick a fight with Flynn. There was no other possible explanation. She'd been looking for a reason to break off their relationship, looking for some terrible flaw in him. She'd found a flaw, but it was in herself, not in Flynn.

She saw him twice in passing over the next three days. Each time she ached with the need to say something—anything—to break through the terrible wall that lay between them. But she said nothing, did nothing. Just looking at him seemed to paralyze her vocal cords.

A week after the disastrous dinner date, her father came to see her.

"I understand that little girl McCallister was keeping is gone now." Robert Perry leaned back in his chair and sipped at the coffee his daughter had just handed him. "Best for all concerned. Gets McCallister out of your life, lets you concentrate on your career."

Ann sipped her coffee, trying not to be irritated by the cavalier way he dismissed Becky. She set her cup down with careful deliberation. "Actually, I've been thinking about giving up my practice and going back to school to be a veterinarian." The words could not have had stronger results if she'd just announced that she was going to become a terrorist.

"Veterinarian!" He made the word sound like an obscenity. "Don't be ridiculous!"

"Dad, I'm not happy with my work." Her tone pleaded with him to understand.

"I forbid it! Do you think I spent all that money for your schooling just to watch you throw it all away on a whim?"

"This isn't a whim. I think this will make me happy."

"Happy? Life is about getting somewhere, accomplishing things, making something of yourself. It's McCallister, isn't it? He's filled your head with a lot of twaddle. What's he accomplished in his life? Look at him. Nobody respects him."

"*I* respect him."

"I should never have let you move in here."

Ann stared at him. "Dad, can't you hear what I'm saying? This has nothing to do with Flynn, though he's the one who made me see how foolish it is to waste my life. *I'm not happy.*"

"I can't be proud of someone who's wasting their time on a bunch of filthy animals."

He glared at her, and Ann looked at him over an abyss so vast that there was no crossing it.

"You don't care about me at all, do you?"

"Don't be melodramatic." He stood up. "When you've calmed down, you'll see that I'm right about this."

"I don't think so."

She listened to the door close behind him and waited for all the pain to come crashing down on her. But the only feeling that emerged was a tremendous relief. The turmoil of the past few weeks was suddenly gone. She knew exactly what she wanted out of life.

And the first step was to find Flynn. Nothing else in her life could be right until he was back in it. Flynn was the key to everything. Why hadn't she seen that from the start?

She knocked on Flynn's door and waited impatiently for him to answer. He would understand. He had to understand.

She knocked again, waiting for a long time before finally admitting that he wasn't home. She leaned her forehead against his door.

"I've got it all straightened out now, Flynn. Where are you?" The whisper went unanswered.

THE RAIN poured down with steady persistence. It was after one o'clock in the morning. She'd been knocking on Flynn's door every half hour since eight.

She'd built a fire earlier but it was down to embers now. Ann leaned her head back, closing her eyes. She had to talk to Flynn. It couldn't be too late for them. It just couldn't.

She had no idea how much later it was when she was startled upright. Ann stumbled to her feet, groggy and disoriented. She pulled the door open and all her thoughts shifted into instant focus.

Flynn stood outside. A Flynn she'd never seen before. The brilliant blue of his eyes was dulled to steely gray. His skin looked pale and his face seemed much older than his years. He looked like a man who'd seen the death of all his dreams and had nothing left inside. He looked absolutely shattered.

His mouth quirked in a frail ghost of a smile. "I...didn't know where else to go." His voice was hollow, lost. Ann felt as if her heart were breaking.

ANN HAD made coffee and sandwiches and thrown enough logs on the fire to create a roaring blaze. There was still that rather frightening emptiness at the back of his eyes but his skin was not quite so gaunt.

"What happened?"

Flynn had been staring into the flames and it was a moment before he dragged his gaze to her.

"My father and I had a fight."

Ann waited, but he settled back against the cushions and stared into the fire.

"I suppose we quarreled about you, indirectly." He spoke so abruptly that Ann jumped.

"Me? What about me?"

"He thinks you were smart to get rid of me. He agrees with your opinions. He thinks I'm worthless."

"Flynn, I didn't mean those things I said." Her fingers knotted around her cup.

He glanced at her. His smile sweet. "I knew you didn't mean it. Not like he meant it."

"Flynn, what did your father say to you?"

"It wasn't what he said to me. It's what I said to him." His mouth twisted bitterly, his eyes on the fire. "I broke a promise. I did it because I was hurt. Not a very good reason. He started telling me how, if Mark had lived, Mark would have given him a grandson by now." He stood up, staring down into the flames. "I told him that wasn't likely. It's the truth but, God help me, I had no right to say it."

He turned his head to look at her and she almost cried out at the self-loathing in his eyes. "Mark was gay. Tonight, I blurted his secret out like a child. Just because I was hurt. My father called me a bastard. I can't even blame him." He put his head down, resting his forehead on his arm, his shoulders slumped in absolute defeat.

Ann got up and went to him. All the hurt that lay between them was forgotten. This was the man she loved and he was in pain.

"I'm sure Mark would understand. And your father will come around. Just give him some time. He was hurt and shocked, but he'll come around."

He turned suddenly, his arms going around her, clutching her.

Ann felt the dampness of his tears on her neck and her arms tightened. She didn't know how long it was before he moved. He backed away. His eyes looked anywhere but at her.

"It's late. I should go home."

It was Ann's turn to look away. "You could stay."

The silence seemed to stretch out endlessly.

"I'd like that."

Ann let out her breath in a rush, only then aware that she'd been holding it.

She knew what she had to offer him. An unconditional love. Someone who accepted him with all his faults and all his good points. Someone who'd never compare him to another and find him wanting.

Someone who'd love him just as he was.

HE WAS standing in the kitchen doorway the next morning and she couldn't imagine how it was possible for a man to look so gorgeous.

"I love you."

Her head jerked up, her eyes meeting his. "Oh God." She slumped back against the counter, her knees shaking.

His brows shot up. "Oh God?" He was across the kitchen in an instant, his arms going around her, holding her close.

"Do you love me or do I go jump off the balcony?"

"I love you." His arms tightened, drawing a squeak of protest from her.

"I still don't have any ambition."

"That's okay. I've got enough for both of us."

His hand slid into her hair, tilting her head back. She smiled at him, her eyes sparkling through a film of tears as his mouth came down on hers.

*

FLYNN PICKED his way through the turmoil of packing boxes until he reached her side. He crouched in front of her, reaching up to tuck a stray lock of hair beneath the scarf she was wearing.

"Rafferty called," she told him. "He says he's got all the real estate ads marked for us. Becky's looking forward to helping us pick out a house."

"Are you sure this is what you want to do? We're making a lot of changes all at once. You quitting your job, moving to a new state, trying to get into school and having a baby. It's a lot to take on."

She smiled at him, feeling contentment fill her. A year of marriage hadn't softened the intensity of their love. He'd supported her through the difficult decision to leave her job and apply to a school of veterinary medicine. He'd stood by her when her father all but said she was no daughter of his. When Flynn found out that the school she wanted to go to was in Colorado, he'd suggested that they move there, confident that she would be accepted. He believed in her more than she believed in herself.

"I love you, Flynn McCallister."

"I love you, too."

She watched him move over to the box she'd been packing and start wrapping the china in tissue.

A knock came at the door. She started to get to her feet but Flynn waved her back.

A minute later her eyes widened as Flynn stepped into the living room with his parents. Not just his mother, who had visited them on a number of occasions, but his father, too.

Ann came forward, holding out her hands. "Louise. David. How nice to see you." She looked at her husband, but Flynn was looking at one of the packing boxes. She could see the muscle that ticked in the side of his jaw.

The two women sat on the sofa and the men remained standing. David cleared his throat awkwardly.

"Your mother tells me that you and Flynn are going to be having a child."

"Yes, we are."

"That's wonderful. Wonderful." David took his hands out of his pockets and stared at them for a moment. "You're... ah...moving to Colorado, I understand."

"That's right." Flynn would have left it at that but he caught Ann's eyes, reading the plea in them. "Ann's going to be going to school there."

"Good. Good." The silence stretched again. "We...ah...that is, your mother and I thought we'd like to maybe help out with the...house. We...that is...I didn't get you a wedding present and it would mean a lot to us if you were to consider the house a wedding gift."

Ann held her breath, waiting for Flynn's answer. He had to see how difficult this was for his father. Surely, he wouldn't turn him away. Flynn glanced at her and then looked at his father.

"Thank you. Ann and I would be happy to accept your gift."

Ann let her breath out in a rush, feeling Louise do the same next to her. "Thank you, David. The house will mean even more to us, knowing that it comes from the two of you." David McCallister shifted uneasily beneath the warmth of her words.

"You know, Flynn, you've got a real treasure here."

Flynn's face relaxed in a half smile. "I know."

"Your mother tells me that you're quite a photographer. I never knew that. She says you've even submitted some things to a few magazines."

"That was Ann's doing. She can be pretty stubborn." His smile was so loving that Ann had to swallow the lump in her throat.

"Well, good luck with them. I'm...I'm proud of you, son."

Flynn's eyes widened as he stared at his father. "Thank you..." The two men stared at each other across the years, across a lot of hurts. "It means a lot to me to hear you say that."

Ann sniffed, unashamed of the tears that filled her eyes.

Ann didn't urge them to stay. At the door, she hugged Louise tightly and then hesitated a moment before putting her arms around her father-in-law's stocky figure.

Flynn hugged his mother and then faced his father. After a moment, David held out his hand and Flynn took it. More was said in the fervency of their grips than could have been said with words.

"Keep in touch, Flynn. Losing one son in a lifetime is enough for any man." He was gone before Flynn could reply.

Flynn stared at the door for a moment and then turned to see Ann watching him, tears running down her face. He held out his arms and she stepped into them.

"I love you so much." His voice broke on the words and he buried his face in her hair.

Her arms tightened around his waist. As long as she had him to hold on to, everything in her life was right.

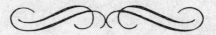

SATURDAY'S CHILD

Dallas Schulze

Lying in bed, Katie McBride stared up at the dark ceiling, waiting. She'd been waiting for over an hour now, and the church bells had long since tolled midnight. In respectable neighborhoods, people were abed, sleeping peacefully. But respectable was not a word for San Francisco's Barbary Coast.

Here, the hours of darkness brought peak business for the areas' gambling halls, saloons and bordellos. The Barbary Coast never slept. An hour's sleep would cost an hour's profit.

Profit was not on Katie's mind. For her, money was survival—and maybe, someday, a way out of this shabby room in its tumbledown neighborhood.

Katie had spent all her nineteen years moving from place to place. Her parents, Sean and Maggie McBride, had come from Ireland, determined to make a better life.

The theater was in their blood. They'd brought their infant son with them, and a few years later, Katie had been born during a brief stop in Cleveland.

The McBrides had dreamed of founding a new theatrical dynasty, and Katie had been on the stage before she could walk. Later, she'd danced and sung in theaters from Boston to Los Angeles. Once she'd even had a role in a Broadway play with Ethel Barrymore.

Her older brother, Colin, had left the family act almost three years ago, tired of the endless wandering. Liking San Francisco, he'd settled there.

Katie had stayed with her parents until their deaths eight months earlier in New York City. They'd been crossing the street in front of their hotel when an automobile careened around the corner at high speed—nearly thirty miles an hour, one witness had guessed.

The impact had killed them both and orphaned Katie. But Colin had sent for her and she'd come across the country to join him.

On the journey, she'd tried not to hope for too much. Colin had said little of his life in his few letters. Still, Katie had allowed herself to dream—just a little.

A small house maybe—nothing fancy—just a cottage where she could grow a rose or two. They'd rented a house one summer in Connecticut and she'd never forgotten the scent of the roses that grew over the porch.

But there was no cottage. There was just this one room, with a bathroom down the hall and one window that looked out on a shabby street.

When Katie arrived, Colin had taken a job as a dealer in a saloon on the Barbary Coast. It was no job for a man of his talents, but it put food on the table. It hadn't taken Katie long to see the necessity of finding work herself. But her future didn't lie in the theater. She was tired of the tawdry trappings and the only certainty in life being uncertainty. She wanted a home and a family, a place to put down roots.

She turned over and stared at the ceiling again. Nearly 3:00 a.m. and Colin still wasn't home. Not that he hadn't worked this late before, but it never failed to worry her.

But what if something had happened to him?

Her eyes flew open and she stared at the ceiling, waiting, listening.

KATIE STARTED UP in bed at the sound of footsteps in the hallway.

"Katie?" Her brother's soft voice followed on the sound of a key in the lock and then the creak of the door. "Katie, I've brought a man who's hurt."

Katie swung her legs off the narrow bed, reaching for her light flannel wrapper and buttoning the collar high on her throat.

She brushed aside the curtain that separated her bed from the rest of the room, blinking in the sudden light as Colin lit the lamp, then staring at the stranger who stood near the door.

He was taller than Colin. His shoulders were broad, filling out his formal black jacket. His hair was golden brown, his features perhaps too strong to be considered handsome, but compelling all the same.

But it was his eyes that threatened to steal her breath away. They were deep blue in color, not like a summer sky but more like a sapphire she'd seen once.

Katie flushed as those eyes swept over her thinly clad figure, a spark in them that told her he liked what he'd seen.

"I'm sorry to intrude on you in this boorish manner, ma'am.

I'm afraid your brother overestimates the extent of my injury."
He swept a battered silk hat from his head and bowed.

Katie's eyes found the dark stain on his sleeve and she hurried forward.

"Help the gentleman to a seat, Colin, and let me take a look at that arm."

Colin eased the stranger to a chair, then stepped back and watched as Katie knelt in front of him.

"Colin, get me some water in a bowl and bring my sewing basket." With a quick movement, she split the coat sleeve up the side, exposing the white silk of his shirt. Gently she eased the fabric away from the deep slash in his upper arm.

Studying the wound, Katie tried not to notice the muscles that rippled under the golden skin she'd bared, more muscles than seemed right for a man who wore silk hats and expensively tailored evening clothes.

"It should have a stitch or two to make sure that it heals properly. If you'll trust me, I'll see to it."

She was sponging the blood from around the wound as she spoke. When the stranger didn't say anything, she reluctantly shifted her eyes to his face. He was looking at her hair, which spilled in fiery disarray across her shoulders.

"Your hair is the most beautiful color I've ever seen, though I'm sure you think it forward of me to mention it."

Katie's cheeks flushed. "I do," she said bluntly. "Will you be wanting me to tend to your arm or not?"

He shifted his gaze from her hair to her face. "Yes, please." He said it softly, sweetly, like a child requesting a treat. Hastily, Katie bent her head over her sewing box.

"You must hold still. 'Tis likely to hurt a bit," she warned him as she motioned Colin to shift the light closer. Lifting the chimney off, she held the needle over the flame.

"I shall be steady as a rock. I do believe I have imbibed enough liquor this past night to prevent any but the greatest of pains from bothering me. Please, do not concern yourself."

True to his word, the stranger didn't flinch, and no one said a word until she'd set the last stitch and clipped the thread. She sat back on her heels.

"With a little care, you should do. 'Twould be best if you tried not to do any heavy lifting with that arm for a week or two."

The man turned to look at the neat row of stitches slashing across his tanned skin.

"You've done a fine job. And I thank you for it."

"It would be better thanks if you'd stay out of dark alleys where trouble is likely to seek a man out."

"You're quite right. If it hadn't been for your brother, I've no doubt that I'd have been beyond patching. But I don't even know who I'm thanking."

Katie rose, stepping back as he stood up. Odd how he seemed to dominate the room.

"I'm Colin McBride and this is my sister, Katie," Colin said.

"Quentin Sterling at your service." The stranger bowed low. Katie dipped a small curtsy.

"It's a pleasure to make your acquaintance," she said politely.

He reached to pick up his hat, bowing again to Katie. "I thank you, ma'am, for your kindness and your skill with a needle."

Colin opened the door, leaving no time for Katie's response, if she'd had one. Quentin Sterling's eyes met hers for one long moment before he turned to step outside with her brother.

Katie stood staring at the blank panel, feeling slightly breathless. Then she turned back to the cubbyhole that sheltered her bed. She knew as well as Colin that she'd never see Mr. Quentin Sterling again, but would it hurt to dream a little of what it might be like to have a man like that fall in love with her?

*

KATIE HURRIED across the street. It had to be nearly seven o'clock, and Mrs. Ferriweather believed in punctuality the way others believed in the power of prayer.

Mrs. Ferriweather's establishment was much too elegant to be called a dress shop. She catered only to the finest clientele, turning lengths of silk and soft woolens into sophisticated gowns in the latest fashions.

For the past six months Katie had spent ten hours a day, six days a week plying her needle. The pay was nearly thirty-five dollars per month, and if she could take over Miss Lewis's position in the summer when she married... Well, maybe she and Colin could afford to rent a little house somewhere. A real home.

By noon, Katie's back ached. On one side of the room several sewing machines hummed as the girls worked the treadles. Sometimes Katie worked there, but her talent for fine embroidery meant that she mostly worked by hand.

Today she was applying an elaborate design of soutache braid to a pale green jacket.

"Ladies, I have some wonderful news." Katie looked up as Mrs. Ferriweather stepped into the room, waiting until all eyes were on her.

"We have been asked to provide a seamstress to assist in preparation for one of the season's biggest weddings. Miss Ann Sterling is to wed Mr. Jonathon Drake in less than three weeks. It seems that the seamstress the Sterlings had hired has fallen and broken her wrist. Such a pity," she added dutifully.

Katie heard little beyond the name. Sterling. Was it possible that they were any relation to *her* Quentin Sterling? Not that he was really hers, but she couldn't help feeling a bit possessive.

"Since we have provided several gowns to Mrs. Sterling and she has expressed her satisfaction with our work, she has made this request. Our work must be of the very highest quality, since providing even a part of the trousseau for Miss Sterling will be a feather in our cap."

She paused, beaming at her workers fondly. Katie hardly dared to breathe.

"It will certainly be a great deal of work, ladies. And long hours. Though much of the work will be done here in the shop, Mrs. Sterling wishes to have a seamstress in residence at her home. She's offered to provide a room."

Was it Katie's imagination or was Mrs. Ferriweather's eye lingering on her?

"Miss McBride?" Katie jumped at the sound of her name.

"Yes, ma'am?"

"I believe you live with your brother, don't you?"

"Yes, ma'am, I do."

"Would he object to you taking such a position temporarily? It would mean a few additional dollars, of course, to compensate for the extra hours."

"No, ma'am." Despite the breathless feeling that threatened to overcome her, Katie's voice was steady.

It couldn't possibly be the same family. But if it was?

"MAYBE I SHOULDN'T have come home."

Tobias MacNamara looked up from the chessboard, focusing faded but still shrewd eyes on his grandson. Quentin was staring out the window at another foggy winter day.

"Why *did* you come home, boy?"

Quentin stirred restlessly. Why *had* he come home?

"I don't know." He moved a bishop.

"Must've had a reason, boy. You didn't come home for this shindig of your mother's." Tobias's contempt for the wedding preparations was clear.

"I thought the least I could do was return for my sister's wedding," Quentin said. "Besides, winter in Wyoming can be a bit harrowing. I decided I could use a break."

"A break, is it? Or did you want a taste of your old life again? Your sniveling wimp of a cousin couldn't wait to tell your mother all about your return to your wicked ways."

Quentin's smile held an edge. "It was quite a surprise to find Joseph across the table from me at the saloon."

"Do you still blame him for young Alice's death?" Tobias asked gruffly.

Quentin shot the old man a look. "I do not wish to discuss Alice."

"I know you don't. You haven't discussed her in eight years, not since she died. Well, time is supposed to heal all wounds and though I think Joseph Landers is a liar and a cheat and probably not above murder, the girl's death wasn't his doing."

"Why are you defending Landers? As I recall, you've threatened more than once to forbid him ever to set foot in this house again."

"That I have. And if it hadn't been for your mother's weeping and carrying on, I'd have stuck by it. But that should be enough to convince you Alice's death wasn't his fault. You know how your mother felt about Alice and your engagement. The fact is, boy, there was nothing anyone could have done but what Landers did."

"He left her there alone," Quentin said.

"He went for help," Tobias corrected. "When she fell through the ice, he couldn't pull her up himself. That damned gown must have weighed fifty pounds and the ice was rotten. *You* couldn't have done anything but what he did."

Quentin stood up, the memories roiling inside him. He couldn't argue with his grandfather's words—or bring himself to agree with them. For so many years he'd focused his anger on Joseph Landers, who deserved it on a hundred other counts. He'd simply never let himself accept that, in this one instance, he might be innocent.

Because if Joseph wasn't to blame, he'd have to accept some of the responsibility for Alice's death himself. If he hadn't gone away... If they'd married as everyone had expected...

Quentin stared out at the wispy fog that draped Nob Hill. He'd been in the Yukon when word of his fiancée's death had reached him. By the time he received the letter, she'd been dead and buried nearly a month.

Quentin had known Alice Mason since they were children. And he'd known they were going to marry since he was fifteen and she was twelve. They might have wed already but for the restlessness that stirred in him, the urge to see more of the world.

He turned from the window abruptly. "Maybe Alice's death wasn't Joseph's fault, but it must be the first time he's been blamed for something he *wasn't* guilty of."

"I'll not argue with that." Tobias leaned back in his chair. "You still haven't told me why you came home."

Quentin looked up from the fist-sized piece of gold ore he'd been studying. The first chunk of ore his grandfather had ever mined, taken from the Sutter's Mill strike back in '49 that had founded the family fortune.

"I've decided to marry."

Tobias said nothing for a moment, then responded, "Well, you're of an age for it. A man should have a wife and children. It steadies him, gives him a purpose in life. Who's the girl?"

"I don't know yet. I've come home to find a wife."

"Have you mentioned this to your mother?"

"No. I thought I'd wait until after Ann's wedding. Then maybe she'd like to throw a few parties, introduce me to some eligible females. I've met few enough of those in my wanderings," he said.

Tobias fixed his gaze on Quentin. "Don't do it, boy. Don't say a word to your mother about this. You're not going to find a wife in this house."

Startled, Quentin crossed the room to lean his arms on the back

of the richly upholstered wing chair. The chessboard lay forgotten
between them.

"Why not? You mean Mother doesn't know any eligible females?"

"She knows plenty, depending on what you want them to be
eligible for. The girls she'd introduce you to would know all
about going to parties and running a big house with plenty of
servants. Are you planning on that sort of life?"

"No, I'm going back to the ranch as soon as I've found a wife.
I need a girl who can run a home five miles from the nearest
neighbor."

"Well, you're not going to find a girl like that at any party
your mother gives," Tobias told him bluntly.

Quentin sat down, hearing the truth of his grandfather's words.
It had all seemed so simple back in Wyoming. Now he stared at
Tobias in silence, seeing all his plans crumbling.

A soft tap on the door interrupted his thoughts. Tobias frowned.

"Nearly four o'clock and I always have my tea at three," he
muttered. "I swear this household is falling to pieces. Come in,"
he barked.

A maid entered bearing a heavy tray. "Your tea, sir."

"Where have you been, girl, dallying with one of the stable
boys?" Tobias asked.

The tray hit the table with a little more force than was necessary. "I'm sorry if your tea is late."

"What happened to the girl who usually brings it?"

"Edith is polishing the silver, I believe."

Something about the sound of her voice tugged at Quentin's
memory, but he could see little beyond a neat back wearing one
of the gray gowns all the maids wore. Her hair was gathered in
a heavy knot at the back of her head, though a few strands of
dark auburn had slipped from beneath the plain cap she wore.

"You're new here, aren't you?" Tobias asked.

"Yes, sir. I'm the new seamstress, helping with the wedding."

"And a very fine seamstress, I'd say," Quentin said, suddenly
placing the voice. He touched his shoulder.

Katie jumped. Hidden in the wing chair as he was, she hadn't
even realized he was there.

She turned, feeling the color leave her face when Quentin stood up, a smile lighting his eyes. He was just as handsome as she remembered.

"I didn't think I'd see you again. What a coincidence."

"Yes, sir." She got the words out with difficulty as the color rushed back into her face.

"I was going to come back and thank you properly, you know," Quentin said. "But I couldn't find you once I'd sobered up." His smile was self-deprecating. "That will teach me to drink more than I should. I'd thought of going back to see your brother too, but I got the distinct impression he didn't approve of me."

"I'm sure that's not true," Katie mumbled, focusing on his neat cravat. In the two weeks since she'd been here, she'd heard mention of Mr. Quentin, but since their paths hadn't crossed, she'd begun to forget the reason she'd been so anxious to come here. Now she was tongue-tied.

"I must go," she muttered, and, bobbing a curtsy, she fled.

"What was that about?" Tobias demanded.

"Excuse me, Grandfather. I'll be right back." His departure was abrupt.

Katie was halfway down the hall when she heard him behind her.

"Miss McBride. Katie." She slowed, her eyes on the narrow flight of stairs that led to the upper floor and sanctuary.

She turned reluctantly.

"What can I do for you, Mr. Sterling?" She fixed her gaze on the top button of his coat.

"I thought you might like to know how your patient progressed," he said lightly.

"How is your arm?"

"Almost healed, thank you. But tell me, what are you doing here?"

"As I told Mr. MacNamara, your mother wished to have a seamstress here full-time. She approached my employer, Mrs. Ferriweather, who sent me."

"Remind me to thank Mrs. Ferriweather."

Katie flushed, glancing over her shoulder as she heard the jangle of keys that announced the housekeeper's approach. Mrs. Dixon was not one to tolerate any conversation between servants and the family.

"I have to go."

She turned to hurry up the stairs. Quentin didn't try to call her back, aware of Mrs. Dixon's chilly gaze taking in the meeting from down the hall.

He turned away from the stairs. Odd that he should run into that girl here in his own home. She was just as pretty as he remembered, her hair just as rich a color. He wondered if it could possibly be as soft as it looked.

IT WAS ALMOST a relief when the last few days before the wedding swept the household up in a frenzy of activity. The huge house bustled with guests and servants, all intent on preparations.

At the last minute Mrs. Sterling decided that her daughter's wedding dress required more alterations. Whatever the reason, Katie was called on to do the work. Carrying the heavy gown upstairs, she muttered to herself, "It already looks like a Christmas tree. Maybe I should just put some candleholders on the shoulders so that Miss Sterling can go to her groom all lit up like a holiday."

The image made her smile and she took the last few steps more quickly, coming to an abrupt halt as she stepped onto the landing and found herself face-to-face with Joseph Landers. Her smile faded, her hands tightening on the heavy gown.

He looked at her for a long, silent moment and then his tongue came out, flicking over his lips. "Well, it looks as if you've quite a lot to do," he said, his eyes lingering on her bosom.

"I've enough to keep me busy." Her tone was polite.

"You don't like me, do you, little Katie?"

"It isn't my place to have an opinion, Mr. Landers."

Disappointment flickered in his eyes and she knew that he'd have preferred a more fiery answer. The man actually found the idea that she detested him exciting.

"You like my dear cousin Quentin, don't you? You think he's a gentleman. Well, perhaps I'll have the chance to show you how much more interesting a real man can be."

Anger flared deep inside her, chasing caution away. She'd been working long hours with too little sleep.

"And where do you propose to find a real man to show me?" she spat.

It took a moment for the question to sink in. Joseph's face paled, then flushed red. He controlled himself with an effort.

"You'll regret that, my girl. I'll show you exactly what a real man does with impertinent servants. Soon, my girl."

She met his eyes bravely, and he brushed by her. She hurried into the sewing room, shutting the door and wishing that there was a key in the lock.

"You've made a mistake, Katie McBride," she whispered. "You've only sparked his interest."

*

By THE DAY before the wedding, there was nothing to be done but row upon row of beading on the bodice of the gown. Katie applied herself to the task, hardly lifting her head.

The monotony of the stitching left too much time for thinking and she found her thoughts turning, as they did far too often, to Quentin Sterling.

"Yes, you *are* a fool, Katie McBride. Even setting aside that he's a Sterling—and wealthy in his own right, too—what would he see in you?"

The thought was surprisingly depressing, all the more so for having been said out loud. Maybe that was why she felt slightly light-headed. Or perhaps it was that she hadn't eaten. She'd gone down to the kitchen for a cup of tea and a slice of bread and butter that morning.

Edith, with whom she'd become friendly, had promised to bring her noon meal as soon as she could, but she was likely as busy as Katie. Not that she was hungry. But this odd, hollow feeling in her head might have something to do with a lack of nourishment.

She heard the door open and, looking up, blinked to focus on her visitor, expecting Edith. But the figure in the doorway was much too large.

"Mr. Sterling." Her voice was hoarse.

"Hello, Katie. No, don't get up." She obeyed his command, uncertain that her legs would hold her.

"What are you doing here?" She realized how blunt the question sounded. "I mean, what can I do for you?"

"Nothing." He stepped into the room, leaving the door open for propriety. "The whole house seems to have gone mad with wedding preparations. I'm seeking a small sanctuary. Do you mind?''

''Not at all. But there aren't many places to sit.''

''Don't worry about it. I've sat more these past few weeks than I have in years. I'm not accustomed to spending so much time in a sitting position, unless I'm on a horse. Do you ride, Katie?''

She thought of the one time she'd awkwardly ridden a horse about Central Park.

''I've ridden,'' she said cautiously.

''In Wyoming I spend most days in the saddle.''

''You sound as if you miss it.''

''I do. More than I'd thought possible.'' He crossed the small room to look out the window.

''Are you thinking of your ranch?'' Katie's quiet question made him realize he'd been standing there wrapped in thought.

He turned. ''I do believe I've spent too much time alone. I've forgotten my manners. Yes, I was thinking of my ranch.''

''Is Wyoming pretty?''

''No, I wouldn't call it that. Wild, exciting, stunning, perhaps, but not pretty. It's too big, too raw.''

''And you love it for its wildness.''

''Yes. I suppose I do. There's something exciting about a land that won't ever be tamed. It's a challenge.''

''It seems to me that land is the one constant thing. The one thing you can depend on to always be there. A place you can sink roots and grow.'' She leaned her head back, her eyes dreamy. For the first time Quentin noticed her pallor, the dark circles under her eyes.

''You look as if you've not slept.''

Katie shrugged. ''I'll sleep tomorrow. There's still much to be done.''

''And I'm keeping you from it.''

''That's not what I meant.''

''But it's the truth. I'll find somewhere else to hide from the turmoil. I thank you for the moment's respite.''

Walking down the narrow flight of stairs, Quentin wondered just what had possessed him to seek out Katie McBride. If any of his family should discover it, they'd think he'd gone quite mad. Stepping into the second-floor hall, he nearly bumped into Edith.

''Mr. Sterling, sir.'' Edith bobbed a curtsy.

"Edith. Just the person I was looking for. I'd like you to have cook make up a tray—just some soup and bread. Oh, and one of the cherry tarts we had at lunch."

"Yes, sir. Do you want it brought to your room?"

"Take it up to Katie. I don't think she's bothered to eat today."

"No, she hasn't. I was going to take her something just as soon as I could."

"Well, do it now and tell anyone who argues that it's on my orders."

Quentin watched her hurry off before starting toward his grandfather's room.

"You're wise to keep the girl's strength up, cousin."

Quentin turned to look at Joseph, who slithered out of the reading alcove that had concealed him.

"I suggest you not say another word, lest I be forced to knock your teeth through the back of your head." Quentin's tone was quietly icy.

"There's no need to be so touchy, cousin," Joseph protested. "I'm not the sort to tell Aunt Sylvie what's going on under her nose. We men have to stick together. I only thought that you might consider sharing the bounty, keeping it in the family, as it were."

Quentin grabbed a fistful of his cousin's shirt, startling a cry from Joseph.

"You are to stay away from that girl. In fact, you are to stay away from every female in this household. If I find that you have laid so much as a finger on anyone under this roof, I shall take great pleasure in tearing your sniveling head from your body."

WHEN THE WEDDING at last occurred, it seemed almost an anticlimax to all the preparations.

Katie heard the whole story from those servants who'd been allowed to stand in the back of the church. Miss Ann had been pretty as a picture and the clothes worn by the guests had proven the city's claim to being the Paris of the Pacific. All in all, it had been a dazzling spectacle.

Katie's fingers throbbed and her shoulders ached, but the job was done, and well done. Mrs. Ferriweather should be pleased.

She stretched, aware of a hollow emptiness in her stomach. Food suddenly seemed very appealing, but even more, she wanted to be out of this stuffy little room. If she hurried, she might make it home in time to see Colin before he left for the night.

Sliding off the bed, she shook out her dark skirts and put on her shoes. Shrugging, Katie lifted her coat from the chair. She could hear the sounds of laughter drifting up from the first floor.

Katie had no intention of lingering. All she wanted was home and food, in that order. She yawned again. And sleep. She felt as if she could sleep for a week, but Mrs. Ferriweather would be expecting her at the shop promptly at seven.

She started toward the door, only to fall back, startled, when it was pushed open.

"What a pleasant greeting, my dear. I wasn't expecting such a welcome." Joseph Landers stepped into the room, turning on the gas lamp she'd just shut off. Katie backed away, uneasy but not yet frightened.

"If you'll excuse me. I was just on my way out."

"But I won't excuse you." He said it pleasantly enough. "You and I have a bit of unfinished business, my dear. Now seems as good a time as any to finish it, don't you think?"

"I don't know what you're talking about." She edged to one side, her eyes flickering to the door as Joseph pushed it closed.

"Just to insure that you don't make too hasty a departure. I want to be sure we have plenty of time."

"I think perhaps you've had too much to drink. If you'll just let me past, I'll say nothing of this." She was stalling for time.

"It doesn't matter. Who would believe you—a seamstress, a servant? And even if they believed you, who would care? Are you going to fight me?"

Katie felt her stomach roll. He'd enjoy subduing her. Perhaps if she didn't struggle, he'd lose interest.

Yet, when he lunged suddenly, gripping her arm, her response was instinctive: her other hand slapped his face. He bit off a curse but only dragged her closer despite her struggles.

Three floors below, laughter and music floated upward, at odds with the nearly silent struggle going on in the small room. Even if she'd had the breath to scream, Katie knew it would not be heard.

She dragged her nails down the side of his face, feeling a savage satisfaction at his howl of pain. But a moment later, he swung her around, catching her with an openhanded slap that made the world go gray.

Before she'd regained her spinning senses, he'd thrown her across the bed, pinning her down with the weight of his body, catching both her hands in one of his, stretching her arms over her head. Katie arched frantically, but couldn't throw him off.

"Now let's see how high and mighty you are."

Katie thought she'd never seen anything more evil than the set of his face. He hooked one hand in the high neckline of her dress, bruising her throat as he wrenched at the fabric until the buttons popped loose.

She lay beneath him, bare but for the fragile protection of her chemise. In an instant, that was gone too and he stared down at her naked breasts.

"Lovely," he murmured. "So pure." He lifted his head to meet her terrified eyes, closing his free hand over one delicate mound. "Am I the first? Of course I am," he answered, his eyes glittering with unholy lust. "I'll make sure that your first experience is a memorable one, little Katie."

The cruel sound of his laughter broke the frozen moment and Katie bucked frantically upward, crazed with the need to have him off her. She knew that her struggles only excited him more but she couldn't stop.

Her frantic struggles seemed to amuse him for he laughed again, the sound drowning out the quiet click of the door opening and then closing, as footsteps hurried down the stairs.

"WELL, ANNIE HAD her big send-off and Sylvie got to put on her show. Now, maybe we can have a little peace in this house." Tobias lifted a forbidden glass of brandy, sipping it slowly.

Quentin lifted his own glass, settling back deeper into his chair. Two floors below, the guests were still celebrating.

Suddenly the door was thrust open and Edith tumbled in, her cap tilted over one eye.

"What the devil?" Quentin rose. "What is it?"

"It's Katie, sir." She paused, trying to catch her breath. "It's that Mr. Landers. They were struggling. I came as quick as I could. I didn't know where else to go. Hurry, sir. Please hurry." But she was speaking to empty air.

Quentin took the narrow stairs three at a time. By the time he reached the door to the sewing room, he felt rage explode in his chest. His cousin's back was to him and for a moment, he thought he was too late, that Joseph had accomplished his foul aim. He lunged forward, grasping the other man's shoulder, tumbling him off the bed. Relief surged through him. Though Katie's dress was torn, Joseph was still fully dressed.

He had only a glimpse of Katie, pulling together the front of her bodice, her face white. Then Joseph came up off the floor, aiming his fist at Quentin's jaw.

The fight moved onto the landing and Katie heard the harsh sound of a fist striking flesh, a solid thud and then silence. Looking at the doorway, she felt numb.

When Quentin stepped into the room, Edith behind him, she stared at them solemnly without saying a word.

"Are you hurt, Katie?"

"No, I don't think so. My dress is ruined, though, and I don't think I'll be able to mend these stockings." She turned her head.

Quentin reached out, snagging her cloak from where it had landed when Joseph ripped it from her. Edith took it from him, her eyes meeting his. She handed the wrap to Katie.

"Are you sure he didn't hurt you, Katie?" That was Edith, her voice gentle.

"Didn't I tell you I was fine?" Katie asked. "My garments have taken more damage than my person. Now I want to go home."

"Perhaps you should see a doctor," Edith said.

"I don't need a doctor. I just want to go home." Katie's voice rose.

"All right. We'll take you home," Quentin told her. "Edith, go and tell Graves to bring the carriage around to the side entrance. Say nothing to anyone about this."

Edith nodded and hurried from the room.

"Are you ready to go now?" Quentin asked.

"I've told you I'm fit," Katie said, but her legs didn't seem to have gotten the message. When she slid off the bed, her knees threatened to buckle. Her startled gasp brought Quentin to her side, offering support.

With Quentin's arms about her, now carrying her away from the scene of her terror, Katie felt almost safe. But deep inside she thought she'd never feel truly safe again.

With a soft sigh, she turned her face against the fine wool of Quentin's dinner jacket, shivers racking her body as reaction set in at last.

The carriage was waiting at the side door. Quentin set Katie down. Her skin still carried the pallor of shock and there was a hollow look about her eyes, but she seemed more in control.

"I would appreciate the use of the carriage, but there's no need for you to come with me," Katie said.

"Edith and I are both coming with you," Quentin said firmly. "I'll get my coat and hat and tell my grandfather what's happened. I was with him when Edith came to get me," he said. "He'll want to know that you're safe."

When they arrived at the scarred door of her room, Katie's hand was shaking too much to fit the key into the lock. Quentin took it and unlocked the door.

"Katie!" Colin was home, still in his shirtsleeves. He started toward her, his smile of welcome fading when he saw that she wasn't alone. "What's wrong?"

"Nothing, really," Katie said quickly. "Just a small incident. Mr. Sterling was kind enough to insist on seeing me home."

But then her voice wavered, and she pressed her free hand against her mouth as Colin's figure blurred before her.

"Katie!" Colin reached out, drawing her close as a sob broke from her. He couldn't remember the last time he'd seen Katie cry.

Feeling his strong arms around her, Katie's control dissolved and she sobbed into his shoulder, crying out all of the fear, the deep exhaustion of the past weeks. Then she drew back, wiping at her eyes.

"I'm sorry. I don't know what came over me."

Edith bustled forward. "You need some rest, that's all. Let me help you."

Colin waited until the two women had disappeared behind the curtain that set Katie's bed off from the rest of the room before asking Quentin, "What happened?"

Quentin told him in as few words as possible.

"She wasn't hurt?"

"I believe her hurt was more emotional than physical," Quentin said.

"I should never have let her go out to work," Colin said angrily.

"And watch the two of you starve?" Edith stepped through the curtain, her eyes flicking over Colin contemptuously.

"I beg your pardon?" Colin seemed confused.

"Well, it's plain to see that you don't hold with working. Just getting out of bed at this hour."

"As a matter of fact, I *have* just gotten out of bed." Colin's temper flared. "But, contrary to your opinion, Miss—"

Quentin broke in then. "I would guess that Miss McBride would sleep easier if it were a trifle quieter."

They glared at each other a moment longer before Edith gathered her wrap and swept by Colin. She paused at the door. "Sleep is the best thing for her now. Tell her I'll be by to see her tomorrow after I've left work."

QUENTIN WAS fastening his cuffs when someone knocked on the door of his room. Glancing up, he bade the person enter.

"I've just come to tidy your room, sir. If you'd prefer, I can come back later."

"No, this is fine. I was just leaving." It wasn't until he turned that he realized it was Edith. "Did you see Katie yesterday evening? Is she well?"

"Yes, sir. I saw her." Edith's eyes were lowered.

"And how is she? Is she rested?"

"A permanent rest is what she'll be getting," Edith said. "She was given her walking papers yesterday from her position at the shop."

"Where did you hear this?"

"From Katie herself. Mrs. Ferriweather has let her go. Seemed she regretted it, but after Katie had made improper advances to one of the wedding guests, she had no choice in the matter. So there's poor Katie, booted out of her job and no one to care about it."

"I care," Quentin said quietly. "Thank you for telling me this, Edith."

"Well, Katie wouldn't thank me for it."

"*I* thank you for it." Picking up his walking stick and hat, Quentin left the room.

"EXCUSE ME, Mother, but I fail to understand why you complained to Miss McBride's employer about her. Are you aware that she has been fired?"

"Really, Quentin, what her employer sees fit to do is none of my concern. I simply told her what had occurred."

Quentin sighed. Staring at his mother's vacant but still pretty face, he reminded himself that she was not an unkind woman. She just didn't believe in thinking—had, in fact, avoided it all her life.

"Mother, Joseph attacked Miss McBride. He could have done her great harm if I hadn't interfered."

"Joseph told me all about it. Naturally, I had to tell Mrs. Ferriweather. After all, I can't have that kind of thing going on in my house. All our girls are virtuous," she added firmly.

"Katie *is* virtuous," Quentin grated. "Did you forbid Joseph to return to this house?"

"Certainly not. The poor boy admitted that perhaps he'd been a trifle naughty but the girl enticed him, Quentin."

"Hellfire and damnation!" Quentin shot from his chair. "Katie would no more have tried to entice Joseph or any other man than...than you would," he said, striding to the door. "I'm sorry I didn't wring his worthless neck."

"Quentin." Sylvie Sterling's voice rang with alarm. "Quentin, where are you going?"

He turned, fixing her with cool blue eyes. "Did I tell you that I'd come to San Francisco looking for a wife?"

"A wife?" She stared at him. It was too incredible to imagine, but there was that look in his eyes. "A wife? Quentin. You're certainly not— You wouldn't?"

"Yes, Mother, I rather think I would." He grinned wolfishly as she fell back, one hand pressed to her bosom. He set his hat at a jaunty angle. "I think Katie McBride might be just the girl I'm looking for."

HE'D ONLY MEANT the words to startle his mother out of her smug complacency, but as he strode down the street, the idea seemed to grow in his mind.

Quentin didn't know a great deal about Katie McBride, but she seemed to be a girl of sound good sense. She understood the value of hard work, and, heaven knew, ranch life provided plenty of that.

She was attractive and seemed intelligent. Knowing how isolated the ranch was, Quentin understood the importance of a woman he could talk to. His grandfather had been right in saying that he'd not find a suitable wife among the women of his own class. But Katie McBride was not ill-bred. In fact, she seemed more refined than some of his sister's flighty friends.

By the time he stopped outside the scarred door of the room Katie shared with her brother, he'd wavered from one side of the fence to the other. As he lifted his hand to knock, his nose wrinkled at the scent of onions that drifted down the hall.

He forgot about the onions when the door opened. Katie stood in front of him, her eyes widening with surprise when she saw him.

"Hello." He removed his hat, trying a smile on her.

"Hello, Mr. Sterling." Her eyes seemed to soften a bit, but she didn't move back from the door.

"How are you feeling?"

"I took no permanent harm. Thanks to you."

"May I come in?"

She hesitated a moment. "Colin isn't here."

"I promise to behave with the utmost propriety."

"I know you will. May I take your things?"

His hat and cane disposed of, Quentin was suddenly at a loss. Looking at Katie, all his indecision faded. She'd make a fine wife, strong, hardworking, the sort of a woman to stand beside a man. It wouldn't be a love match, but then, since Alice there could be no question of that.

Katie wondered what had made him look so fierce all of a sudden. It had been quite a surprise to find him standing in the hallway. She'd not expected to see him again. Not after Mrs. Ferriweather had dismissed her because of his mother.

Oh, Mrs. Ferriweather had been apologetic. And Katie understood, but it didn't make her any less angry. It wasn't fair. But if she'd learned one thing in her twenty years, it was that life was seldom fair.

"May I offer you some tea?" she suggested at last.

"No, thank you," Quentin refused, guessing rightly that tea was a luxury here.

"Would you like to sit?" It was a relief when he nodded.

Looking at Katie, he was struck again by the restful air that seemed to drift about her. She sat, politely waiting for him to speak, her hands together in her lap. Her gown was not in the latest fashion, but it was of good quality. The pale green fabric set off the color of her hair so that it seemed to glow.

"Katie, would you like to see Wyoming?" He heard the question as if it were being asked by someone else.

"I beg your pardon?" She blinked.

"I've a ranch there," he told her. "There's a house. Small, rather untidy, but there's a pump in the kitchen. Another room could be added.

"The house needs work—curtains, rugs, that sort of thing. I've lived alone too long. A woman's touch would add warmth.

"The land is hard but beautiful. There's snow in winter, but in the summer the grass stretches for miles. There's a small garden that could be made bigger. The facilities are primitive but I could install a water closet this summer."

He stopped, wondering what else he should say.

She stared at him uncertainly.

"Are you looking to hire a housekeeper, Mr. Sterling? For I'd have to say I think you could do better."

Quentin opened his mouth, shut it again and stared at her. "Actually, I was asking you to be my wife."

IN THE SILENCE that followed his words, Quentin could hear each separate beat of his heart. From the look on Katie's face, he could tell she was as stunned as if he'd suddenly sprouted horns.

"Did you say—" She was unable to finish the sentence.

"I want you to marry me."

"Why?" She looked at him, her eyes wide. "Why would you want to marry me?"

Quentin leaned forward.

"When I came home, it was not only for my sister's wedding. I'm nearly four-and-thirty, and I had it in mind to find a wife."

"Why me? Surely there are many more suitable choices."

"I think you are suitable."

"Your family is not likely to agree," she commented dryly.

"It's not my family who'd be marrying you. Katie, I need a woman who isn't afraid of hard work. The life I'm offering is not easy, but it can be rewarding."

Katie smoothed her skirt. She'd thought that the events of the past few days had left her numb, but just the sight of Quentin had made her pulse beat more quickly.

He'd haunted her thoughts, and if she was honest with herself, he already held a piece of her heart. If she married him, she didn't doubt that he'd soon hold it all. But to love someone who didn't love her...

"You don't speak of love," she said quietly.

"No, I don't." Quentin met her eyes squarely. "I'll not lie to you. I know women set great store by marrying for love. But it's my feeling that a marriage can be just as solid if it's based on mutual respect and friendship. And I think we've a bit of both, haven't we?"

Katie nodded. She wouldn't have called her feelings for him friendship but it was all she was likely to have. Could she marry him, knowing that?

"I still don't understand why you're marrying at all," she murmured.

"I need a wife. I've had the ranch nearly three years. I've built a strong foundation—cattle, horses and most of the feed to support them. But it's a lonely life. A man begins to crave someone to talk to, someone to share the successes and the failures. I'm building something worth handing on to a son."

"Then it's a real marriage you have in mind," she said, the color rising in her cheeks.

"Yes. But I wouldn't rush you, Katie. I have to go back soon. There's no time for courting before I leave. But if you married me now, we could do the courting after the marriage. I'd give you time to get to know me, Katie. I'm a patient man."

She lifted her head, meeting his eyes directly. "What of your family?"

"They'll come around."

"You've more optimism than sense, if you don't mind my saying so," she commented.

"Perhaps. Is their reaction so important to you?"

"Not to me. But I know how it feels to lose a family. I'd not like to cause you to lose yours."

"You won't. It will be their choice if they can't accept our marriage."

"That's easy to say now."

"Let me worry about my family." Quentin reached out, catching her hands in his. "Katie, we could have a good life together. It's not an easy land, but it is beautiful. I'm offering you a home of your own, a place to put down roots."

She caught her breath. How had he known? How had he sensed her deepest need and spoken of it? A home. A place to call her own, a place to build something permanent and lasting.

She stared at their linked hands. He didn't love her...might never love her. But he'd be a good husband, kind and true. And if she bore him strong sons— Well, wasn't there a kind of love in that?

And if she didn't take this chance, what did she have? She had no job, no reference for another employer.

"Yes." The word was hardly a whisper, but she felt Quentin's hands tighten. "Yes, I'll marry you."

*

Dear Katie,

I hope you are happy in your new home. San Francisco does not seem the same without you.

I was honored that you asked me to be at your wedding. Your brother, Colin, offered to walk me home afterward, and I was glad, for it gave me the opportunity to apologize for my earlier rudeness to him.

That awful night when Mr. Sterling and I brought you home, I made the assumption that your brother was unemployed and you the sole support.

Fortunately, Mr. McBride was quite gracious in forgiving me. I should have realized that your brother could not be other than as honest and hardworking as you are. Though my family would not approve of his current employment.

Please write and tell me how you are going on. Wyoming seems so very far away. Do you miss our fair city?

Now that time has passed, I thought it might interest you to know that the Sterling household was in quite an uproar over your wedding to Mr. Sterling. Perhaps he's already told you about it.

His mother fainted dead away when he told her that he

was planning to marry you, and his father turned quite purple. I happened to be nearby and heard the shouting match that ensued. But your Quentin stayed very cool and told his parents that their opinion held small interest for him. He said that he was marrying a fine woman and was proud that you'd consented to be his wife.

I see I've rattled on far too long, as usual. Please write soon and know that I miss you.

Your true friend,
Edith

Katie refolded the letter and slipped it back in the envelope. So Quentin's parents had been furious. She wasn't surprised, though he'd never breathed a word to her. But when they didn't attend the wedding of their only son, it was not hard to guess.

Quentin had defended her. It was a pleasant thought, for lately his temper had been uncertain at best. She had a pretty good idea of what might be making him so testy but she didn't know what to do about it.

The memories of Joseph's attack had faded and Quentin now filled her thoughts. But how could she tell him? It would seem as if she were asking him to consummate their marriage, a bold move she couldn't bring herself to make.

She sighed, tucking the letter into a drawer, looking out the window. The last of the snow had melted, turning the yard into a sea of mud, but all she saw were rows of young plants, vegetables burgeoning with fruits and flowers turning bright faces to the sun.

It would take time to make the dream a reality but she'd made a start. Joe, the hired hand, had helped her to prepare the vegetable garden, and beside the front door she'd had him dig two holes for the American Beauty rosebushes, ordered from a catalog.

When Quentin had seen them, he'd shaken his head. "They're not likely to survive the first winter, Katie."

She had put up her chin. Roses by the door were a part of her dream. "Then I'll plant them again."

"It's your time," he'd said, shrugging. "We can give them *some* protection in the fall."

So she had her roses, her house and her garden. If she didn't have her husband, surely that would come in time.

Shaking her head, she knelt to open the bottom drawer of the dresser, hoping to find room for a few small mementos, but it jammed on something inside. Katie worked her hand into the narrow opening and pressed down on the offending object, while she pulled the drawer open with the other hand.

The item that had caused the problem was a picture frame. Curious, she picked it up and turned it over.

A lovely young woman looked up at her. She had soft skin and wide-set eyes with a sweet expression. An inner beauty seemed to shine out of her.

Across the bottom of the picture was written "So you'll never forget. With love, your fiancée, Alice."

Katie sat on the floor staring at the picture. So Quentin had been engaged to this beautiful young woman. And he'd loved her. The thought made her heart ache.

"Katie?" Quentin's voice called. She scrambled to her feet, the picture still clutched in her hands.

"Katie?" Quentin stepped into the bedroom—the room he so rarely entered when she was present. "Could you—" He broke off when he saw her with the picture.

"What are you doing?"

"I was just looking for a place to put some things of mine." She heard the guilty note in her voice and stopped. "I didn't mean to pry."

"I know." He crossed the room and took the picture from her, staring down at it without speaking.

"Who was she?"

"Alice," he answered, his tone absent. "Our families were close. We'd known each other since childhood. We were engaged."

"Did you love her very much?" She had to ask.

Quentin nodded slowly. "Yes, I did."

"What happened?" she asked, needing to know.

"She died," he said simply, "and I wished I had died, too."

Perhaps Katie's indrawn breath reminded him who he was talking to. He shook his head suddenly, glancing up at her.

"It's all a long time ago. I'd forgotten where this picture was." His tone made it clear that the subject was closed. Still carrying the picture, he turned and left. Katie moved to the bed to sit down. Vaguely, she wondered what he'd come in for, why he'd called her name.

Alice. Even her name was lovely. A woman from his own world. A woman his family would have welcomed.

Katie wrapped her arms around her stomach as if that could cushion the pain. It didn't matter how often she reminded herself that love had never been part of this marriage bargain, there was still the small foolish part of her that kept dreaming.

The photograph had left those dreams in tatters.

THE CLOUDS that had looked so innocent the day before had built and darkened until they filled the sky to the north. Katie watched them with a mixture of anticipation and concern. If only the rain wasn't too heavy.

Turning away from the window, she moved to the kitchen table and poked an experimental finger into the bread she'd set to rise. The loaves were ready and she transferred them to the oven, once she'd tested the heat by thrusting her forearm inside. It had taken more singed arms than she cared to remember before she learned to judge the temperature. She'd buried any number of ruined loaves behind the woodshed.

But she'd learned. Her bread was as good as any she'd tasted. She wondered if Alice had ever baked a loaf of bread. Katie pushed the oven door shut, exasperated by the way her thoughts kept turning to the other woman. Alice was dead. Quentin was married to *her* now.

But he'd thought he was taking a wife with some expertise in all the myriad tasks that went with running a home, she reminded herself.

"Well, I've learned, haven't I?" she asked aloud.

Luckily, she'd found a garden manual on Quentin's bookshelf, followed it faithfully and now had a healthy patch of young plants. It was the one place where she felt she'd been a complete success.

Her cooking was only adequate. The milk cow seemed to despise her. The chickens showed an amount of tolerance, but that was because she hadn't yet tried to take any of them to the chopping block.

Quentin left early and worked late. They rarely talked, and they still didn't share a bed, so she could hardly say that her marriage was a total success. She couldn't say that she and Quentin knew each other much better now than they had when they married.

Katie sighed, picking up a linen towel to dry the bowl she'd just washed. Quentin was probably sorry he'd married her, and who could blame him?

Just then, thunder cracked, loud enough to rattle the windows. Katie jumped, running to the window as the skies opened.

In all her life she'd never seen such a storm. Rain fell in sheets, a nearly solid wall of water.

She ran to the back door, throwing it open to step out on the little porch. Would the dry ground be able to absorb the rain or were her small plants going to be washed away? Perhaps if she covered them with some of the bushel baskets she'd seen in the shed...

She dropped her shoes onto the porch and stripped off her socks, lifting her skirts as she ran into the storm. Drenched by the time she reached the shed, she found the baskets, lifted a stack of them and hurried out.

She'd taken only a few steps when she realized that the rain had changed to hail. It speeded her footsteps, for the hail surely spelled her garden's doom.

The size of the stones had increased to that of small rocks, striking with force enough to raise welts. But Katie hardly noticed as she set baskets over small plants already showing damage. In her mind, it wasn't just a few plants she was trying to save, it was her marriage, maybe her whole life.

The hail pelted her unprotected head, but she didn't pause.

"What do you think you're doing?" Quentin's bellow startled her. "Dammit, woman, you'll be hurt. Let the plants be and come inside."

"Not until I've covered as much as I can," she said stubbornly.

"Now." She tried to pull back as he took her arm and drew her to her feet. "Let the damn plants take care of themselves," he all but shouted.

"I won't."

A bolt of lightning speared down, striking the earth so near them that the air seemed electrified.

"You will," Quentin said calmly. He stepped forward, scooped her against his chest and strode toward the house. Katie made one convulsive attempt to escape and then held still.

The kitchen was warm, filled with the rich scent of baking bread. He set her on her feet in the middle of the floor. Her hair hung down her back in a thick, wet braid. Her dress was soaking wet.

"Are you crazy?" Quentin demanded, glaring at her. "We can get hailstones the size of a man's fist in one of these storms."

"I had to cover the plants," she said stubbornly.

"Look at your arm," he said angrily, showing her the reddened skin. "And you're soaking wet. You could catch pneumonia. And the nearest doctor is nearly a day's ride away."

"Don't worry. If I catch pneumonia, I'll try to die peacefully without asking you to send for the doctor." She hardly knew what she was saying. Tears blurred his tall figure. "It was the one thing I'd done right," she lashed out, wiping angrily at her tears. "The cow hates me and I can't kill a chicken, but those plants were growing."

"Katie." Quentin's voice softened when he saw her distress. He reached for her but she twitched away.

"I don't need your pity," she snapped, her chin coming up. "You married me out of pity. I knew that. You went to San Francisco to look for a wife and you felt sorry for me. Well, I don't need your pity."

"Katie." He reached out. "I didn't marry you out of pity." His hand slipped under her chin, tilting her face up. "I thought we could make a good marriage together. Only a fool would marry for pity."

She could see nothing but honesty in his eyes. "Then why haven't you—"

She broke off, feeling her cheeks flush as she looked away. But Quentin understood.

"I said I'd give you time." He let his hand slip from her chin to rest along the side of her neck. "I didn't want to rush you, Katie."

"You're not rushing me," she said, cheeks burning at her own boldness.

He pulled her a step closer. "Look at me, Katie." Her lashes lifted slowly. She could only guess at what he saw in her eyes, but the look in his sent a shiver down her spine. "Are you afraid of me, Katie?"

She shook her head slowly. "I know you'd not willingly hurt me," she said.

"Willingly?" He questioned the word. "Katie Aileen Sterling, I promise I'll never knowingly cause you pain. Do you believe that?"

"Yes."

"We've a marriage that isn't. It seems to me time we did something about it. Do you trust me?"

The hands she set against his chest trembled, but her eyes were steady on his as she answered.

"With my life."

This kiss was different. It held more demand, more hunger, more need. It was the need she responded to, opening her lips to him, her tongue entwining with his as she sank against his chest.

After a moment Quentin lifted his head. He looked down into her eyes, feeling his stomach tighten at the innocent sensuality of her gaze. He wanted her. He couldn't remember the last time he'd wanted something so badly. It wasn't just a sexual need, it was a deep visceral hunger that only she could satisfy.

She gasped as he bent, scooping her up in his arms.

"I'm wet."

"I'll help you get dry," he said huskily, his mouth coming down on hers as he carried her into the bedroom.

Outside, the hail had turned to rain. The worst of the storm had passed, but the clouds blocked out the sunlight, leaving the bedroom dim.

Quentin set Katie down next to the bed. He undressed her slowly, his eyes never leaving hers.

When she stood before him at last, clad in nothing but thin cotton knickers and a lace-trimmed chemise, there was no disappointment in Quentin's eyes. He tugged loose the ribbon bow at the top of her chemise, then the tiny pearl buttons fell open beneath his touch. Katie gasped as his hand slid inside to cup her breast. She'd never dreamed a simple touch could start such a fire raging inside her.

She felt a deep sense of loss when his hand left her, but it was only so he could strip off his coat. His shirt followed and her vision was filled with the width of his chest. A thick mat of golden-brown hair covered the taut muscles, tapering to a thin line that disappeared into the waistband of his jeans.

She jerked her eyes up, her cheeks flushing at the glimpse she'd had of his arousal. The flush deepened when Quentin's hands went to the buttons of his pants, but he didn't take them off immediately. Instead, he reached for her hands, holding them against his chest until he felt her relax. Slowly she moved her fingers, feeling the springy mat of hair curl against her hands. Quentin held his breath at her innocent exploration that was somehow very erotic.

Burying his fingers in her hair, he tilted her head back, catching her mouth with his. Katie felt her head spin as he pulled her close, slipping the chemise from her shoulders so that her breasts pressed boldly against the warm skin of his chest.

Nothing could have prepared her for the feelings that flowed through her. In a matter of minutes she could think of nothing but the warm pleasure washing over her.

When Quentin lifted her onto the bed and kicked off his jeans before following her down onto the feather mattress, Katie opened her arms to him. This was her husband—the man she loved with all her heart.

KATIE came awake slowly. Her sleep had been light but restful. She stirred in the big bed, aware of a feeling of fulfillment she'd never had before. Without opening her eyes, she shifted one foot, cautiously seeking. She wasn't sure whether she felt relief or disappointment when she found she was alone.

She was really and truly a married woman now. Odd how something she'd regarded with a mixture of fear and fascination should turn out to feel so natural. Wonderful actually, she admitted to herself, feeling the color flood her face as she remembered the response she'd given so readily.

There was a muffled thud from the direction of the kitchen and Katie swung her legs off the bed. She dressed hastily, muttering over uncooperative buttons, terrified that Quentin would walk in. They might have made their marriage real at last but it was going to take her a while to get used to the idea of sharing his room.

Another thud made her decide against trying to pin her hair up. She tied the unruly mass back with a wide ribbon.

Katie approached the kitchen warily. There was an odd, harsh smell in the air.

"My bread!" She entered the kitchen in a rush as Quentin turned from the stove, the last pan in his hand.

"I smelled them burning," he said. "It's too bad I didn't smell them a bit sooner."

"I followed the steps so carefully this time," she said sadly.

"It was my fault for distracting you."

At that, she glanced at him, the ruined bread forgotten. Her cheeks flushed.

"Don't worry about the bread," he told her, and poured himself a cup of coffee from the pot always left warming on the stove.

She turned from him, finding it easier to sustain her casual air if she wasn't looking directly at him.

"Are you all right?" She jumped when his voice came from directly behind her.

"I'm fine."

"Then why won't you look at me?" His hands settled on her shoulders, turning her to face him.

"I've looked at you," she mumbled to his chest.

"Do you truly think I married you out of pity?"

The question brought her eyes to his face.

"I...I don't know," she admitted at last.

Quentin released her, turning away to pick up his cup. "We haven't talked much, have we?" he said. "I married you for just the reasons I gave you in San Francisco. I felt we could build something together.

"I've lived here alone for several years and I could feel civilization slipping away from me. A true home needs a woman, children," he added softly.

Katie felt a warm glow inside at the thought of children. Even now, she could be carrying his child. It was an incredible thought.

"I needed someone to help me build this ranch," he went on. "Someone strong. A woman who didn't expect to be waited on hand and foot. A woman who could take care of herself."

"You needed a woman who knows about cooking and cleaning and caring for animals," she said. "I should have told you at the start that I'd no experience with such things. We never settled in one place long enough for me to learn."

"Your family moved often?" he questioned, realizing that he'd given little thought to her background.

"We were a theater family," she said.

"Theater?" Odd, he'd never have imagined Katie coming from that background. "*You* were on stage?"

"Yes."

She waited for his reaction. Though times were changing, many still felt that being in the theater put one on the lowest possible social rung.

"Why didn't you tell me this before?" He didn't seem upset or angry, only curious.

"You didn't ask, and I thought I could learn the things I needed to know." She poked one of the blackened loaves. "I wanted you to feel you'd made the right choice in marrying me."

He set his cup down and took her by the shoulders again. "I *did* make the right choice, Katie. I'm glad I married you. You've brought warmth and light into this place. You've turned it into a home, just as I knew you would."

Katie heard little beyond his first words. He was glad. The only thing that would have made her happier was if he'd told her that he loved her.

*

KATIE TOOK UP her pen and wrote.

May 1905
Dear Edith,
It's been too long since I last wrote, I know. I can only tell you that my life has been so full, I seldom have time to write a letter.

I am glad to hear that you and Colin have made peace and that you are seeing him occasionally. I know it's foolish, but I do worry about him. He's a grown man, I know, but it makes me feel better to know that he has friends like you.

We had a terrible hailstorm nearly two months ago and I thought the garden entirely lost. Fortunately, I've found that plants, no matter how fragile they seem, are quite sturdy. Most of them survived, and they are now thriving.

Life in Wyoming is so different from that in the city. The first and most obvious difference is the lack of people. Though we have neighbors, I've yet to meet them, for they live several miles away.

I've seen no one but Quentin and the hands since coming here. I must admit that the solitude can be wearing. I miss having a chance to chat with another woman. It's a lonely life but a very good one, I think.

Please let me know how Colin goes on. I've had only one card from him since leaving the city. Write soon.

Your fond friend,
Katie

The most important news was something Katie wasn't quite ready to share with anyone. She set her hand over her stomach, hardly daring to hope that her suspicion was correct. Carrying Quentin's child would make her life complete, or nearly so.

"You're a fool, Katie, to be always wanting more than you have," she whispered to herself.

She and Quentin had developed a certain closeness over the past two months. It might not be a grand, passionate love, but it was enough for now, or so she'd made herself believe. Love could grow. *That* she did believe.

June 1905
Dear Katie,
I should have written before now, for I have important news for you. But first, I want to tell you how much I enjoyed your letter.

The Sterlings, by the way, had a terrible fight with old Mr. MacNamara. It seems that Mr. Sterling had suggested that he might forbid your Quentin to enter the house again.

Mr. MacNamara, on hearing this, hit the dinner table with his fist and said that, as long as his money was supporting the household, he would be the one to decide who would be welcome.

I had this information from Mary, who was serving dinner that night, for I had already left their employ.

Anyway, Mr. MacNamara said that he felt Quentin had made a fine choice in marrying you and that you were both welcome in *his* house any time you cared to visit.

With that out of the way, perhaps I should tell you my news.

Colin and I are wed. Only a week past, we went to Oakland, which some are saying is the Gretna Green of California, and were married. My parents had forbid the match, because of Colin's employment at the Rearing Stallion. But once the deed was done and they saw how happy I am, they forgave us and welcomed him into the family.

The next day Colin found employment at the Grand Opera House. He said that he would not be dictated to but nor did he wish to cause his new in-laws any concern. I believe it amused my father greatly.

I am very happy to be your sister in marriage, Katie dear. And I hope you will forgive us our unseemly haste. I'm sure you know that, once your brother's mind is decided, he sees no reason to hesitate before taking action.

He asks me to send you his affection and best wishes and the hope that we will all be together again soon.

> Yours,
> Edith

Katie was hardly surprised by Edith's news. She'd almost expected it. Colin married. She was happy for him. And for Edith, but the news made her feel slightly melancholy, too. They'd married for love. How she envied them that.

She sighed. It wasn't that she regretted her marriage to Quentin. He was all that was good and kind. But she sometimes felt as if there were a wall built around him.

"Maybe when he lost his Alice, he truly lost his heart. Maybe he'll never love again," she said aloud.

Could she bear it if Quentin was never more than the slightly affectionate companion he was now? The only place she felt as if he truly belonged to her was in the privacy of their bed. There, she felt no ghosts, no walls. But there had to be more to a marriage than that.

Quentin had said he wanted to build something good and fine. Well, she wanted that, too. But part of what she wanted to build was a strong bond between them, and she couldn't do that alone. Her palm flattened against her stomach.

Would the child she was now sure she carried help her forge that bond? Surely he couldn't keep her at a distance while she was carrying his child, perhaps a son to carry on his dream.

March 1906
Dear Katie,
Colin and I were so relieved to hear that you and baby Geoffrey are both well. You said it was a difficult birth, so I hope you have fully recovered by now.

You will be pleased to hear that we have purchased a house. My father provided us with a reference and much of the initial monies. Though Colin did not care for the idea of accepting help, I persuaded him that it was for the best. After all, my father considers it a good investment, as the value of real estate is sure to go up.

It is a tiny house, sold as an artist's cottage. It is south of Market Street, so we are not on Nob Hill yet. Just five rooms and a bath, but the basement is finished. It cost three thousand dollars and I know you gasp at such a price, dear Katie, but it really is quite a bargain.

Colin is enjoying his work at the Grand Opera House.

Which brings me to my real purpose in writing this letter. Katie, dear, do come and see us. We long to meet our new nephew. Our home is small, but still enough to supply you with all the comforts you need.

You have told me that spring is a busy time on a ranch, so I know better than to suggest that Mr. Sterling join you. But surely he could spare you for a few weeks.

Just send us a wire and let us know when to pick you up at the station.

I'll say farewell for now, but I hope that soon I will be saying hello.

Your fond sister,
Edith

Katie let the letter fall to her lap. Outside, the sun shone with unreasonable brightness. The snow lingered in the shadowed places but most of the yard was a sea of mud.

From the talk around the supper table she knew that more snow was likely. With spring calving just around the corner, a heavy snowfall could be disastrous.

She could see that Quentin was concerned, though he didn't say anything. But then, lately, he didn't say much to her beyond what was necessary.

She sighed, leaning back against the rocker, looking down at Geoff, who was lying on a thick quilt at her feet, gurgling contentedly.

Quentin's withdrawal could be dated to Geoff's birth, but she'd been unable to find a cause for it. She was getting more than a little exasperated. He was a good father, spending more time with the baby than most men would. But to his son's mother, he seemed to have nothing to say.

She'd even asked him if he was upset with her for some reason. He'd seemed genuinely surprised and assured her that nothing was wrong.

"But there is something wrong," she told the baby. "We had drawn closer. And suddenly he changed." She lifted her hands, letting them fall to her lap. "Is it possible he was just being kind to me because I was carrying you?"

Geoff gurgled, waving at a dust mote that floated on a sunbeam above him.

"But that doesn't seem right. He's so reserved. It's as if he doesn't even like me." She picked up Edith's letter. "Maybe some time apart will be the best thing."

Maybe he'll ask me to stay.

BUT HE DIDN'T. She brought the subject up after she'd put Geoff down for the night. Quentin was seated at his desk, making entries in the ranch books.

"I received a letter from Edith today," she told him.

"That's nice. How are she and Colin doing?" Quentin didn't lift his head.

"They've bought themselves a small house. Edith has invited me and Geoff to come and stay with them."

Quentin's pen hesitated a moment.

"Do you want to go?" he asked without inflection.

"Well, Geoff should meet his family. And he will be needing clothes before too long and I could purchase fabric. It's so much better than ordering by mail."

"Certainly, if you wish to go, I don't see any reason why you shouldn't."

It wasn't until she heard him say it that Katie realized how much she'd been hoping he'd say he didn't want her to go—that the idea of her leaving might make him realize how much he'd miss her.

"It would not be worth making the trip for less than several weeks' stay," she said.

"Of course not." He set down the pen, turning to give her an avuncular smile. "I think it will be a very good thing for you. I know you've missed Colin. Besides, you've been looking a little peaked since Geoff's birth. Some time in the city is probably just what you need."

Katie kept her eyes on her knitting so that he wouldn't see the tears that threatened. He sounded as if it didn't matter at all to him that she and the baby would be gone.

"Yes, maybe it will be good for me," she said dully. She stood. "I think I'll go to bed now."

"Fine. I've a few more things to do. When would you like to leave? If the weather holds, the roads should be passable by the day after tomorrow. If we start early, we should reach Laramie by nightfall."

She started toward the bedroom, wanting only to bury her face in her pillow and have a good cry.

"Katie." Quentin's voice stopped her in the doorway and she turned.

"Don't worry about packing a great deal. I'll give you a letter of credit and you can draw on my account. Outfit yourself as well as Geoff."

She nodded, not trusting herself to speak. The door closed behind her with deceptive quietness. Once in the bedroom, she stood, fists clenched, slowly reciting the soliloquy from *Hamlet* to herself. Her father had always sworn that it was the best thing he knew for calming nerves.

That done, she undressed for bed, slipping her nightgown over her head before moving over to the cradle to check on Geoff. The baby slept soundly.

Quentin was sleeping in the room he'd built as a nursery last summer. When she'd asked why he hadn't returned to their bedroom, his eyes had shifted away and he'd mumbled something about Geoff waking in the night. It hadn't made much sense, but she'd felt shy about questioning him further.

Crawling between the cold linens, Katie felt as if they were no colder than her heart tonight. She didn't know why, but she had to face the fact that whatever affection Quentin might have begun to feel for her had died.

Now what she had to decide was whether or not she could continue in such a sterile marriage.

*

"KATIE!" Edith's cry turned several heads as, hitching Geoff farther up on her hip, Katie turned toward the sound. She saw Colin first and felt tears start to her eyes. How could she have forgotten how handsome he was, how tall and strong?

"Katie?" Edith darted around a stout woman who was arguing with the porter. "You look wonderful! And this must be Geoff. Oh, what a big boy he is. May I hold him?"

Geoff, who generally objected to strangers, stared in fascination at Edith. Katie decided it must have been her enormous hat, complete with a stuffed bird that bobbed up and down as she nodded.

"Katie. How are you, lass?" Katie all but fell into Colin's arms, feeling her tears spill over.

"Here, here," he protested, half laughing. "You're supposed to be glad to see me, not turn into a watering pot." He tilted her chin up.

"I am glad to see you." She sniffed, giving him a wide smile to prove it. "Once I've had some tea and a chance to rest, I'll be my old self."

In a short while, she was comfortably ensconced in a wing chair in what Edith proudly called the parlor. A cup of tea steamed by her elbow and Edith had provided a plate of small homemade biscuits.

Colin solemnly warned Katie to have care, as her teeth might suffer if she attempted his wife's cooking. Edith hit his shoulder, blushing and calling him a traitor. He caught her hand and kissed it, promising to break all his teeth on her biscuits, if only he could be forgiven.

Watching their silly play, Katie felt a wave of melancholy. This was what a marriage could be like. Husband and wife as friends and companions. If she couldn't have that, did she want anything less?

IF COLIN and Edith suspected there was more to Katie's visit than the desire to see San Francisco again, neither of them said anything. They gave her just what she'd wanted, time to think.

When thinking grew too much to bear, she shopped, outfitting Geoff with a wardrobe that would last him for the next year or two. And for herself she purchased fabric such as she'd only dreamed of in the past. It was always a surprise to find that the Sterling name brought her a certain deference even in the finest stores.

She indulged in only two ready-made gowns, the first a lovely evening gown of pale green satin with a décolletage that made her blush.

The second was a soft day dress in palest apricot, with rows of lace around the hem and hundreds of tiny tucks over the bodice. She closed her eyes to the cost, telling herself that she was a Sterling now.

But the dress was also for a special occasion. Though Quentin had told her not to visit his parents, Katie couldn't pretend they didn't exist.

So she donned the apricot gown, dressed Geoff in a fine little suit of navy and white and had a carriage take her to the Sterling mansion.

With a sleeping Geoff in her arms, she turned to look down the street, delaying the moment when she'd have to face her in-laws. In the distance she could see the blue of the bay. It looked so calm and peaceful.

Lifting her chin, she turned and walked up the brick path, raising her skirt slightly as she climbed the four stairs to the door. She could hear the bell ring somewhere in the house and felt almost light-headed with nervousness. Maybe Quentin had been right.

But before she could change her mind, the huge door swung open. The maid was no one she recognized.

"Yes, ma'am?" The deferential tone gave Katie courage.

"Mrs. Quentin Sterling to see Mrs. Sterling, please."

The girl's eyes widened. She might have come to work here

in the past year, but she was obviously well caught up on her gossip.

"Oh, my." Without another word, she pushed the door shut, leaving Katie standing on the porch. When the door opened again, it was Mrs. Dixon who stood on the other side.

The housekeeper looked down her thin nose at the woman and child outside.

"Mrs. Sterling is not at home to you," she said coldly, but Katie was prepared for this and had her reply ready.

"Then I'd like to see Mr. MacNamara, please. I'm sure he'll want to meet his great-grandson."

Mrs. Dixon hesitated. Katie knew she longed to shut the door in the intruder's face, but if she did so and Mr. MacNamara found out...

"Come in, please. I'll inform Mr. MacNamara of your arrival."

Katie stepped into the huge marble foyer, her chin held high. She had as much right to be here as anyone, if not for her own sake, then for Geoff's. He was a Sterling and she'd not see him shut away from his family.

Mrs. Dixon came back down the wide staircase. "Mr. Mac-Namara will see you now. If you'll come this way."

If the rest of the Sterling family wanted nothing to do with her or her son, Tobias MacNamara didn't share their feelings. In fact, he positively delighted in their presence in his suite of rooms.

Geoff seemed entertained by his great-grandfather and Tobias got to see him at his sunny best.

It was only when the baby began to tire that the old man turned his attention to Katie.

"So, how's that grandson of mine? Why isn't he here with you?"

"Spring is a very busy time at the ranch," Katie said.

"Pshaw. The boy could get away if he'd a mind to. Not having problems, are you?" He didn't wait for her to answer, which was just as well, because she couldn't think of a thing to say. "He's a good lad, but prone to being moody. He thinks too much. That's been his problem all along.

"Take this girl Alice." He nodded when he saw Katie start at the name. "I thought that might be part of the problem. I'd have warned you at the start, but we hardly knew each other. Not that we know each other all that well now, but this little boy here, he kind of speeds things up.''

"I do feel as if I've known you longer than I have," Katie said shyly.

"I do, too. I was pleased enough when Quentin told me you two were getting married. Hadn't seen a lot of you, but it doesn't take long to see character. And I saw it in you. Strength, too. He made a good choice.''

"I'm not sure he'd agree," Katie said in a whisper.

"Well, if it's Alice you're worried about, don't be. Oh, she was a sweet child. Pretty as a picture, but she and Quentin would never have suited. She was too soft and gentle. Quentin would have found that out sooner or later.''

Katie longed to believe him. But the fact was that Quentin had said he'd wanted to die, too, when he lost Alice.

Setting aside the tragic Alice, there was still no reason to think he cared for her. Before Geoff was born, she'd begun to think it possible, but he'd grown so cool and distant.

Still, the visit with Tobias made her feel better. Maybe she shouldn't give up so soon.

THESE WERE the thoughts that were running through her head the next night as she lay in bed, staring up at the ceiling.

Sighing, she turned her face into the pillow, determined to get at least an hour's sleep before Geoff woke her at six with a demand to be fed.

The mantel clock in the parlor was chiming three as sheer willpower got her to sleep, but it seemed as if she'd barely closed her eyes when she woke to a deep rumbling sound, like the growl of a great animal.

Katie sat up with a start, noting that the furniture was moving as if in some bizarre dance. The rumbling became a roar as the little house shook. Her first thought was for the baby in his crib near the wall. She jumped out of bed, only to be knocked to the floor as it undulated beneath her.

Lying there, she knew the meaning of absolute terror. It was as if the city had been caught up by a giant terrier and was being shaken like a rat.

The shaking stopped and she lunged toward the cradle to snatch Geoff up. She had time for only that before the shaking started again, more fierce this time. Staggering, she grabbed for the bed-post, clutching the baby to her with her free hand.

She watched in horror as the whole side of the house began to shudder, and then suddenly the wall broke loose, falling outward with a sound that only echoed the sounds of shattered masonry and falling brick all around.

Above it all, incongruous as a dream, she could hear the bells of Old St. Mary's Church, north of Market, frantically ringing as if to announce the end of the world.

The shaking stopped and, aside from the bell, it was suddenly silent, the quiet of the tomb. She could only stand there, trembling, holding Geoff close.

From the corner of her eye she caught a movement. A calendar fluttered on the wall, the lovely girl pictured on it a contrast to the destruction she so obliviously presided over.

Katie focused her mind on the date, as if it were of vital importance.

April 18, 1906.

QUENTIN RODE hunch-shouldered and ill-tempered. Why was it that life never worked out as planned? He'd planned to marry Alice and spend his life with her. Then she'd died and he'd sworn never to love again, never to let anyone close enough that her loss could leave him broken and bleeding inside.

And then he'd met Katie.

He'd admired her spirit. He'd found a certain peace when she was near. And he'd told himself that it would be a good thing to marry her. A man shouldn't go through life alone—he should have heirs to inherit what he'd built.

He'd thought Katie would make a good wife and she'd not expect him to love her. It had been a good plan, he told himself irritably. Only that plan hadn't worked, either. He'd made the singular mistake of falling in love with his wife. He loved the way her nose wrinkled when she laughed, the way she frowned while she was cooking. He loved the way her hair always managed to escape its pins. The way she blushed when he unbuttoned her nightgown. And then how passionately she responded to his touch.

When she'd nearly died having his son, he had no longer been able to pretend that all he felt was fondness. Faced with losing her, he'd had to face his feelings. But he'd fought them tooth and nail.

He didn't *want* to love anyone that much again. He didn't want to be so vulnerable. He didn't want all his happiness tied up in another person. He'd arranged his life so well. How dare she destroy his neat pattern?

He'd treated his love for her like an illness that would go away if given a chance to run its course. He'd been a fool, he admitted to himself.

It wasn't until she was gone that he'd learned the true meaning of loneliness. His temper had gone from bad to worse after her departure. She hadn't even been gone a week when one of the hands threatened to quit. Quentin had reined in his ill temper after that, but Tate, his foreman, had finally taken him aside and, with the familiarity of an old man talking to a young fool, suggested that he go to San Francisco and bring his wife home.

Quentin had railed all night against the idea. He wouldn't love her. And then he'd gone into the room they'd shared and stared at the bed where they'd made love, the bed where their son had been born. He'd pushed his boot against the cradle, listening to the quiet rhythm of the rockers against the wood floor.

The house seemed to echo with emptiness. All the heart was gone from it. "I love you, Katie Aileen Sterling." He spoke the words out loud and wondered if it was his imagination that made the room seem suddenly brighter, warmer.

Now here he was, almost to Laramie and frozen half to death. He had fresh clothes strapped to the back of the saddle. He was going to catch the first train to San Francisco, find his wife and tell her just what a fool he'd been. And he wasn't leaving the city without her.

He'd started well before dawn, but it was after dark when he rode into town and made his way to the livery stable. He left his horse to be cared for, and walked directly to the railway station, though his stomach suggested that stopping to eat might be a good idea. He'd eat on the train, if he was lucky enough to catch one tonight.

"Hello, Bill. You're working late." The stationmaster turned as Quentin leaned in the ticket window.

"Hello, Quentin. Goin' somewhere?"

"San Francisco, if there's a train."

"There's one should be comin' through in about three hours. Bringin' relief from Chicago."

"Relief?" Quentin felt a frisson of alarm.

"That's right. There was a big earthquake just this morning. Newspapers are sayin' the city's leveled. No tellin' how many are dead."

"My God." Quentin straightened. Katie and Geoff were there. And the rest of his family.

"You still want to go?" Bill questioned.

"Yes. My family is there."

"Oh, say." Bill's face wrinkled with concern. "I'm sorry about that. I'd forgot you were from the coast." He shifted uncomfortably. "Well, you know how the newspapers exaggerate. Probably wasn't near as bad as they say. Your wife there?"

"Yes. And our son."

"Say, that's too bad, but I bet you'll find them snug as anything. Sure, they'll be fine."

Quentin turned away without answering. Moving to the edge of the platform, he stared toward the west. Katie was there. And Geoff. Everything he loved most in the world. If he hadn't been such a fool... If only he'd told her how he felt, she wouldn't have gone.

THE HOURS immediately following the quake were like a scene from Dante's *Inferno*. Within fifteen minutes, columns of smoke could be seen rising from various parts of the city, many of the blazes in the area south of Market where Colin and Edith lived.

The firemen were well trained and efficient, but they were hampered at first by the scattered positions of the fires, and then a far more serious problem became evident. The water from the hoses slowed to a trickle and stopped. The shifting earth had snapped the water mains, leaving the firemen virtually helpless against the advancing blaze.

All of this Katie learned later. In those first few minutes she could only stand in the ruins of her little bedroom, clutching her son and offering up a prayer of thanks that they had been spared.

"Katie? Katie, are you all right?" Colin's voice was harsh with fear.

"I'm fine. And the baby's fine." He thrust open her door, his face white. "Is Edith safe?"

"Yes." He seemed unaware of the cut on his forehead, probably from falling plaster. "You'd better put on some clothes. I'll gather what food we have. There's no telling what this day will bring."

By noon, one square mile of the city lay in ashes and the fires were still raging. Colin had shepherded his small family out into the street, their food tied in a hobo-style knapsack. In a matter of hours it was clear that their little house, like the whole area south of Market, was doomed.

Without water, Fire Chief Sullivan's brave men could do little to fight the flames. And they later learned that Dennis Sullivan himself had been fatally injured, trying to rescue his wife.

The fire burned for three and a half days. The great Palace Hotel, which had boasted huge water tanks on its roof to provide its own protection from fires, burned before dusk, its water tanks empty.

As Katie and her family hurried through the streets, they saw signs of high comedy and high tragedy. There were men in nightshirts and frock coats, carrying silk top hats and flower vases, whatever had been near to hand when they'd fled their homes.

Several times they stopped to aid in the rescue of some poor soul trapped in the rubble of a fallen building. Twice the aid had come too late and Colin had turned away, his face grim, his hands bleeding.

They spent the night crouched in a small park, wrapped in blankets Edith and Katie had carried from their home. Dinner was beans eaten from a tin can, and they felt fortunate to have that much.

Katie cradled Geoff to her bosom, wrapping the blanket modestly about her as she nursed, grateful that she didn't have to worry about food for him.

The sky was bright with the reflected flames from the blazing city below. It seemed to Katie as if the whole world was burning. Holding Geoff close, she drew what comfort she could from his sturdy little body. She'd seen enough women sobbing in the street, begging for some word of their missing children, to know how lucky she was.

Exhaustion finally overcame numbed shock and she lay back, drawing the blanket about her and the baby, praying that the sun would rise on a better day.

BUT ON THURSDAY morning the fire still blazed. The City Hall, newspaper row and the Grand Opera House were all gone. The fire was nearing the crest of Nob Hill. Katie hoped the Sterlings had gotten to safety. And old Mr. MacNamara.

Colin moved his small family to the Presidio. Tents and shacks were set up among the rows of military buildings, giving shelter to hundreds of refugees. Military rations were passed out to those in need.

Katie managed to rig a sort of pack that held Geoff to her bosom but left her hands free, and she helped out wherever she could, distributing food, bandaging small wounds. She and Edith worked from dawn to dusk, while Colin had gone back into the city to do what he could. All day they could hear the sound of blasting as the fire fighters struggled to stop the flames from consuming the entire city.

But it wasn't until midafternoon on Saturday, three and a half days after the earthquake, that the last of the fires were doused. When the news reached Katie, she sat down on the ground and started to cry. For the first time since the earthquake she allowed herself to believe that they were going to be safe. They'd be able to go home.

She'd hardly let herself think of home these past terrible days. But it had always been there, in the back of her mind. Home and Quentin.

Quentin. Was he worried about her? Isolated as the ranch was, it was possible he didn't even know about the earthquake and fire. Had he missed her at all?

She held Geoff close, laying her cheek against the downy softness of his hair. The smell of smoke was so prevalent she hardly noticed it anymore.

"Colin!" Edith's voice broke on the cry and Katie looked up in time to see her brother throw his arms about his wife. He was filthy with soot and grime, but unharmed. Katie stood up and Colin lifted one arm from Edith's shoulders to draw her close. After a moment she stepped back, reaching up to wipe at the tears that had left tracks on her dirty cheeks. Colin, his arms still around Edith, grinned at his sister.

"I have brought you a present. Someone I happened to run into."

At his gesture Katie turned. Her heart seemed to stop. "Quentin.'' His name was hardly a breath. He stood right in front of her when she'd thought him a thousand miles away. She blinked, trying to clear the tears from her eyes, sure that she was hallucinating.

"Katie." His voice was low and husky. He was as filthy as everyone else, his work shirt torn, his jeans streaked with soot and dirt. It seemed strange to see him here in clothes he'd only worn on the ranch.

She stared at him, searching for something to say. All she wanted was to have him put his arms around her and hold her close, to hear him tell her that he loved her, that he wanted to take her home.

"What are you doing here?" The question was all she could manage.

"I was worried about you and Geoff."

She looked down, stroking her son's hand. Of course he had been worried about Geoff. She'd never had reason to doubt that he loved his child. She blinked back foolish tears.

"Geoff is fine. He's too young to know what's happened."

"That's good." Quentin pushed his hands into his pockets and then pulled them out again, staring at them. Around him were sounds of celebration that the fire was at last out.

"Have you been here long?" Katie asked at last.

"Yesterday. I got here yesterday. It wasn't easy. The rails are damaged, you know." He squinted toward the city. "I couldn't find you. Nearly everything south of Market has burned. It was sheer luck that I saw Colin. I'd still be looking for you otherwise."

"Yes, that was lucky." She stared at his boots, fighting back tears.

"I even went to my family's home."

She glanced up. "Are they all right? We heard most of Nob Hill had burned. I prayed they got out in time."

"The house is gone. Everyone got out safely. My grandfather commandeered an automobile and packed the whole family across the bay Wednesday night. One of the servants told me they were safe. She also told me you'd been to visit them."

She lifted her chin. "I thought they might want to see their grandson. Your grandfather was most kind."

"But my parents refused to see you." He shook his head, narrowing his eyes against the sun. "My mother was so proud of that big house on the hill, and now she's left with little more than her own servants."

There didn't seem to be anything to add to that. Katie brushed her tangled hair back from her face and, glancing up, caught Quentin's eyes on her, a look in them she couldn't quite interpret. He looked almost hungry.

"I was coming to see you before I knew about the earthquake, Katie," he said abruptly. "I was coming to take you home, where you belong."

"Quentin?" She felt her heart slow until she could count each beat. For so long she had dreamed of seeing that look in his eyes.

"Will you forgive me, Katie, and come home? It's empty without you. *I'm* empty without you."

There was a frozen moment where she couldn't seem to move and then she was in his arms, feeling them close, strong and warm, about her.

"Oh, God, I was such a fool." His voice was muffled in her hair, but she heard the words clearly. "I love you, Katie. I love you. I thought I'd lost you forever. I couldn't live without you."

She closed her eyes. If this was a dream, then she didn't want to wake up.

Geoff dispelled the dreamlike atmosphere by letting out a loud cry, indignant at the way his parents were squashing him between them. Quentin's arms loosened enough to allow the baby some room. One hand cupped Katie's cheek, his eyes looking deeply into hers. Katie felt fresh tears spring to her eyes at the expression she saw in his.

All her dreams were coming true. San Francisco would be rebuilt, bigger and better than ever. But she wouldn't be there to see it.

She was going to be in a place where you could look for miles without seeing another person, a place where she'd put down roots, strong and sturdy.

Leaning her head against Quentin's shoulder, their son held close, she knew she'd found the home she'd always dreamed of, right here in Quentin's arms.

WEDDING OF THE YEAR

Elda Minger

The wedding of the year.

Alexandra Michaels stared out her office window. The Los Angeles sky was overcast, and a steady rain had been falling for the past hour. Yet nothing could dampen her elation.

Her intercom buzzed. "Alex? Your mother's on the line."

Almost nothing.

"I'll take it." There was a note of resignation in her voice.

"Alex? Darling, are you there?"

"I'm here." She was nervous already, hating the way her mother sometimes brought out the worst in her. The short, clipped voice. The defensive attitude.

"Alex, we just got back from London, and I wanted to let you know. How are you, darling?"

But Alex knew what that question really meant.

Is there an eligible man in your life?

"Fine, Mother. Just fine."

I'm not admitting to anything.

"Oh. Well, what have you been up to?"

"Work, work and more work. But I do have some good news. I've got the Bradford wedding. They took my bid. I have three months to pull it all together, but this is definitely the wedding of the year."

"Alex, that's marvelous!"

Oh, I get it. There might be a nice, eligible, rich young man at the wedding ceremony—

"Darling, I— That is something to be proud of."

But I'm well on my way to being terminally single.

"I know, Mother. How was London?"

Her mother chatted about her trip, Alex made soothing responses. Both agreed to call later in the week.

Then Alexandra Michaels, director of catering at the Los Angeles Biltmore Hotel, career woman extraordinaire, thirty-seven years old and celibate for the last fourteen months, hung up the phone and walked quietly into her private powder room.

Where she locked the door.

And burst into tears.

ONCE SHE arrived home, Alex got her evening off to a grand start by talking to the cat.

"So I never meet a man, spend the rest of my life catering other people's good times and live here with you, Roscoe. Is that so bad a life?"

Roscoe, a hefty tabby tom, barely looked up from the can of salmon Fancy Feast he was devouring.

"Just like my ex-husband. He only came home to eat and clean up before he was out chasing anything but me."

Alex didn't have to look up to know her housemate, Karin, was standing in the doorway. They had bought the stucco duplex together and got along famously.

But at least Karin had something that passed for a social life.

Karin was daring. Karin had Jesse, of the taut-muscled stomach and incredible shoulders. Of the dark, thick hair, Latin-lover eyes and full, sensual mouth.

Alex was not that daring. Alex had Roscoe, and though he had blazing yellow-green eyes and thick, tabby hair, he had a tendency to bring home fleas.

After dinner, the two women sat in the living room, glasses of wine in hand.

"So you've made it to the top, Alex. And so you're reassessing your goals. There's nothing unusual about that. I do it all the time with my painting."

"I guess I just feel like I've missed out on so much of life. It's like a horse wearing blinders, you know?"

"I do. I felt that way after my divorce. Jim always made fun of my painting, so I put it aside for a long time. When I finally got it back out, I felt all rusty and out of practice. It's the same thing with dating."

"Ugh. What a horrible word."

"I know. It's the pits. But I'm just about due for another party. Give me a weekend you'll be free, and I'll make everyone I invite bring an eligible guy. There's bound to be someone you hit it off with, even if you just go out for a while. You know, like training wheels on a bicycle."

"Yeah. You're right. I just get scared."

"Take it a step at a time."

Alex took another sip of her wine, then turned at the sound of a car coming down the street.

"I think Jesse's home."

"Hmm. I'm gonna run."

After her friend left, Alex sat quietly on the couch in the darkness, enjoying the view that encompassed the Hollywood sign, Griffith Park Observatory and then swept all the way downtown to the Wilshire district. At night, bright lights sparkling, she saw Los Angeles at her sultry, colorful best.

She didn't have time to enjoy it. She was rarely home. And when she was, she was usually asleep.

Enough. She leaned back into the comfort of the sofa and took another sip of white wine. After the wedding, it's time for you to start living your life, she mentally ordered herself.

"YES, MRS. Bradford, I understand you want a Renaissance theme." Alex had dealt with the Constance Bradfords of the world before. The women who sought her professional advice as a caterer smelled of money. Yet this had never intimidated Alex. She had grown up with money, then decided she wanted to make it on her own terms. An only child, she had always been independent.

"I want everything to be as authentic as possible." Constance's china blue eyes were regal and cool. "Now, did you check into getting the pheasants?"

"Yes. That's all taken care of. And I checked about costuming the waiters. The ice sculptures have been ordered. Now, about the flowers—"

"All white. And nothing ordinary. I don't want roses or carnations or—"

"I know just the man. He did the Jamison wedding last year, and everyone talked about those flowers for months—"

"Yes." Constance's eyes were admiring as she studied Alex. "That will do nicely. Only I want more flowers than that, masses of flowers—"

"David's your man."

As Constance checked over other details, Alex glanced covertly at the bride-to-be. Elizabeth "Muffy" Bradford, youngest child and only daughter of the Bradford dynasty. She was a pale little thing and looked nervous.

Who wouldn't be, with that mother of hers?

Bloodless. That was the word.

SEAN LAWTON gazed around the Bradfords' formal dining room with carefully concealed distaste. He had grown up with money and had made even more. He knew the sort of power it gave a person.

He felt Muffy looking at him before he turned and saw her frightened gaze. They were sitting next to each other, across from another couple Constance had invited to dinner. Sean kept his eyes on Muffy's wan face as he took her hand in his. Her fingers were cold.

Bloodless, he thought suddenly. Then, realizing it wasn't Muffy he was thinking of, he turned his attention to the woman at the end of the table.

Constance Bradford. Impeccably dressed in something blue and silk and simple. She was watching them, a slight smile on her perfectly glossed lips.

He smiled back, holding her eyes with his until it became a silent challenge. Phillip, I feel sorry for you. You're going to have your hands full with that one.

He hadn't really understood his best friend's decision, at first. When Phillip asked Sean to meet for a drink after work only a few weeks ago, he'd had no idea what his friend was up to.

"I love Muffy, and I don't know what to do about that mother of hers," Phillip confessed.

"Run off with Muffy," Sean had advised.

Phillip told him, "You don't understand. Muffy—God, Sean, I love her, but she doesn't seem capable of standing up to her mother. And Constance has made it quite clear that I'm not to come around again."

"The only reason that you're not seen as good enough for her precious Muffy," Sean said carefully, "is that you've declined going into the family business. Believe me, if that woman knew you'd inherit all your father's money, she'd find a way to get rid of her own husband."

Phillip gazed morosely at his empty glass, then at Sean's, half full. Reaching for the bottle of Scotch, he tipped it toward Sean's glass, but was forestalled by his hand.

"I've had enough. I'll have to call Brian as it is and ask him to pick me up."

Phillip smiled, then refilled his own glass. "We've had some good times, haven't we, Sean?"

"That we have."

"Remember the time we were in that bar in— What was the name of that country?"

Sean smiled. "When that man threw his chair at me?"

Phillip laughed. "And all over that girl selling shells on the beach."

Sean nodded. "Couldn't have gotten out of that one if you hadn't thought as quickly as you did."

"Well, there's no way that sod would have attacked a priest."

"Father Lawton." Sean started to laugh.

"You've always been there for me, Sean." There was a peculiar intensity in Phillip's voice.

"As you've been for me."

Phillip swallowed a last mouthful of Scotch, then set down the empty glass. "I wonder if you could help me out one last time."

Sean eyed his friend. "Sounds serious."

"It is." Quickly Phillip outlined his plan. "All you have to do is stand in for me. Convince Constance that you want to marry Muffy and let her wallow round in all the wedding preparations. She likes you, Sean. I have no doubt she'd try to marry you herself if she thought the old man would stand for it."

"Not me." Sean grinned. "The money. She'd like to roll around in my money. God knows we've both seen enough of that type."

Phillip went on. "Then, at the last minute, when the minister is reading the final vows, I'll jump in from the side and, before the old witch knows what hit her, Muffy and I will be man and wife."

The idea had its own peculiar type of charm. Sean pictured her serene highness, the venerable Mrs. Constance Bradford, apoplectic with rage. He grinned.

"I'll do it. One last thing, though. Why me?"

Phillip leaned forward, a lock of tousled blond hair spilling over his high forehead. "I trust you. I love Muffy with my life, Sean. If this goes wrong, her mother will keep us apart for the rest of our lives. I think, even now, she may suspect something.

"I've watched her for years, seen what she's done—I know what she could do to Muffy. I love Muffy, and I want to spend the rest of my life making her happy."

Sean finished his drink. "You're a lucky man."

Phillip eyed his friend, then he grinned. "I'll be damned. And to think I bought that bull about living a life on the edge, never settling down."

"You keep my secret, I'll keep yours."

"You're a bigger romantic than I am! Good God, Sean, what's holding up your getting married?"

"If," Sean said slowly, "I could find a woman who wasn't so damned intent on my money and had some feeling strictly for me—"

"You'd marry her in a second!"

Sean nodded. "But, as I don't see that happening, I'll simply continue on my merry way."

"It happens, Sean. When you least expect it."

Muffy's fingers gently squeezing his brought Sean out of his thoughts.

"Mother wants to know about your latest deal."

Her voice was soft, almost childlike. Dressed in a strapless evening gown far too old for her, Muffy smiled up at him. And Sean had to admire her courage. Sheltered and bullied all her young life, this scheme required all the courage the fragile girl had.

Phillip was a lucky man.

The room seemed uncomfortably warm. Sean would stay just as long as he had to, then make a graceful exit. And on to the Biltmore.

Alexandra Michaels. The woman who was in charge of this "Wedding of the Year," as the press had dubbed it. He had to check her out, see if there were going to be any complications on that end.

And, of course, he'd have to keep Constance in a state of happy anticipation over the thought of getting her hands on his money.

They're all the same in the end. Every last one of them.

He could believe in luck for his friend. But not for himself. If there was a woman out there who wanted him and not his money, he had yet to find her.

"I'M LEAVING, Alex. See you tomorrow."

Alex glanced up at Marcy, her personal assistant. Sometimes she secretly envied the woman. Marcy, a petite redhead with amazing curly hair and a dancer's figure, had one of the most interesting lives in the office. Her job was nine-to-five, but her real life began when she left the office, always in a variety of stunning, stylish outfits. The last thing Alex had heard was that she had been at a friend's party and taken up with a Russian dancer who was in town on an extended tour.

Marcy always looked happy. Radiant. Fulfilled.

Everyone has someone but you.

Alex felt as vulnerable as a grade-school girl without a single valentine. The job, the house, the money and status—it wasn't enough. She stood and walked over to the window.

Arms crossed, Alex rubbed her palms up and down her upper arms. The office seemed cold. Probably the rain. The only light came from the lamp on her desk.

I wish... Oh, I wish...

"Miss Michaels?"

The deep, masculine voice caused a delicious little tremor. Alex turned and saw a tall silhouette in her doorway.

"Alexandra Michaels?" That voice again.

"Yes? Can I help you with anything?"

She wasn't afraid. There were still plenty of people on the floor, and this man didn't inspire fear, but something much more elusive. Alex swallowed, then walked slowly toward her desk and the light.

He advanced at the same time, and it seemed to Alex, as the light caught his face, that he was the most handsome man she had seen in years. Thick, dark hair shot with the slightest silver strands. Blue-gray, penetrating eyes. Strong jaw, broad shoulders, a solid body. She'd bet there wasn't any fat beneath that Armani suit.

He was simply devastating.

"I wanted—" He stopped speaking and simply looked at her. Alex couldn't seem to glance away. Her heart was starting to race, but blood seemed to be thrumming throughout her body. Alex quickly sat down at her desk. She felt the need to put something, anything, between her and this man. She motioned him to a chair.

He sat down, then leaned forward. Alex looked up and found

he was studying her again. Her mind was going into overdrive. Could one's libido hyperventilate?

Enjoy this, a lively little voice in the back of her mind was whispering. There's something delicious going on here.

"So, what is it exactly that you want?" She knew her cheeks were slightly flushed, her eyes dancing. He was fabulous.

He hesitated for just an instant, then said quietly, "I wanted to discuss the Bradford wedding."

She picked up a change in the air, but didn't look away.

"What exactly did you want to discuss?"

He seemed angry suddenly, but not with her. There was a sense of pent-up frustration, of something beyond his control.

"Is everything going smoothly?" Now his voice was soft, his gaze back on her.

Alex met his gaze head on. "Yes, it is. Everything's right on schedule."

"Is Constance giving you a hard time?"

Alex felt her eyes narrow, then made her expression smooth and unreadable. Was this one of Constance's little henchmen trying to catch her unaware? She rejected the thought immediately. This man danced to no one's tune but his own.

"No. She knows what she wants, and it's my business to give it to her."

"And Muffy? How is she holding up?"

"I have to believe she's getting what she wants, as well."

His eyes were full of admiration, and Alex had the strangest feeling that what they were saying had not the slightest relation to what was going on.

Her mind started to wander, with visions of the two of them alone, the door locked, the backs of her thighs pressed up against the hard wood of her desk as he slid his hands up beneath her skirt, bent her back and—

She snapped her mind back to the present.

"Was there anything else—" She stopped and cleared her throat. It was tight, all of a sudden. "Mr.—"

Was it her imagination, or were his eyes regretful?

"Sean. Sean Lawton."

"Mr. Lawton. Was there anything—"

She stopped. Frozen. Staring at him.

Fate was playing one of her nastier practical jokes.

"Alexandra—"

"Don't." Her instincts were screaming at her.

"We have to talk—"

"No, we don't." Her voice was resolutely bright.

"And if I say you're wrong—"

"No!" Alex stood up. She grabbed for her suit jacket, shrugged it on, then snatched up her purse. Backing away from her desk, she walked swiftly to the door.

"Alexandra—" He was on his feet now.

The way he said her name made it sound like a caress.

She didn't turn around until the elevator door closed.

Sean Lawton had walked into her office and exploded all of her preconceptions about love—lust, she corrected herself—at first sight.

And she was arranging his wedding.

*

"ALEX? I need your signature on these."

Alex glanced at the memos, scanned them quickly, then picked up a pen and began to sign them.

"Have you seen him yet?" Marcy was always on top of the hottest office gossip.

"Who?"

"Who else? Sean Lawton. I think he looks like that guy who played James Bond in—"

"Timothy Dalton."

"Yeah. With a little bit of Sean Connery thrown in."

"It's the dark hair and light eyes. It's a striking combination, but it doesn't do much for me—"

"Ms. Michaels?"

That voice. She was doomed.

Alex glanced up, praying that Sean Lawton hadn't heard what she'd said. She and Marcy stared as he walked in and sat down in one of the leather chairs by her desk. His dark suit fit him perfectly. He leaned forward, that same intent look she'd remembered last night in his eyes.

Marcy snapped out of her trance. "Would you like some, ah,

coffee? We have tea, too. Or juice? I could get some fresh Dan-ish—''

"Coffee would be fine." Sean smiled at Marcy, and she scooted out. Alex sighed, then turned to face him. The day she'd been assigned the Bradford wedding, she'd gone over the cast of characters. Constance the bulldozer. Muffy the mouse. John Brad-ford, brilliant businessman.

And Sean. In his early forties, he had more money than he'd ever spend. Slowly, he was redesigning the Los Angeles skyline. Lawton Towers. Lawton Place. Every time you picked up the paper, he was in either the society pages or the business section. He had a lineup of beautiful female escorts, but Alex had never seen a picture of him with Muffy.

Maybe it had been a quick romance. Passionate.

Muffy, passionate?

Now he was simply staring at Alex. Sizing her up. Making her nervous.

"Mr. Lawton, unless you have something you'd like to say, I suggest—''

She never finished her sentence, for Pierre came charging in, a tray in his hands.

"Alex, my darling, you have to taste this! It's my idea for the cake. Most wedding cake is—dry. Tasteless. This, this little cake will become the talk of the catering world."

Alex had to smile. She loved passion in her co-workers, and Pierre was passionate about his cooking. A tall, rangy man with sandy blond curls and twinkling blue eyes, he was the consum-mate temperamental Frenchman. But everyone adored him.

Pierre set the tray down. There was a large slice of chocolate cake on a delicate china plate, and a silver fork.

"Tell me the truth," he said quietly. Then, as if noticing Sean for the first time, "Alex, she always tells me the truth. There are not many people with that quality, don't you agree?"

Sean nodded as Alex tried the cake.

It melted in her mouth. Rich, dark chocolate. Raspberries. And something else. That was what set Pierre's cooking apart.

"It's wonderful."

Pierre smiled, then kissed his fingers. "For you, Alex." He turned to Sean. "She's the best. Always working. I asked her to come to Palm Springs with me this weekend. Even the hardest workers need a vacation now and then, don't you agree, Mr.—''

"Lawton. But call me Sean."

Pierre's eyes widened.

"Why don't you try the cake, Mr. Lawton? After all, it is your wedding." Alex was pleased with herself, her tone purely professional.

"Cut me a piece," he replied.

Pierre seemed fascinated as Alex took the same fork she'd used and sliced through the delicate cake. She leaned forward, starting as Sean grasped her wrist and guided the fork to his mouth.

His touch was warm. Firm. Assured.

"Wonderful, Pierre. I think it will be a wedding the guests will never forget." He was still holding her wrist, and Alex gently but firmly pulled her hand away. Pierre regarded them with an amused expression.

"So, *ma coeur*, I will add that cake to the menu."

"Yes. As long as Mr. Lawton has approved it, I doubt if Mrs. Bradford will challenge the decision."

Taking one last look at the two of them, Pierre left the office.

"Now, Mr. Lawton—"

"I've got the coffee." Marcy appeared in the doorway, balancing a huge tray, complete with a bowl of fresh fruit and assorted baked treats.

Alex picked up the silver coffeepot and poured Sean a cup, then passed it to him.

"Danish?" she asked.

"Maybe the blueberry one."

She handed it to him with a napkin, then poured herself a cup of coffee.

Now, perhaps he would tell her why he was here.

But he simply sat there, quietly eating his Danish and drinking his coffee.

What is this, some kind of game to annoy me?

"What is it that you want to talk about, Mr. Lawton?"

"Sean. Please."

"Sean." She took another sip of her coffee.

"I did some checking on you last night," he began.

She could feel herself starting to bristle.

"I was curious, Alexandra—"

"Alex. Call me Alex."

"Alex it is. Don't be offended at what I did."

"I'm just curious as to why."

"I have my reasons. There are a few things I'd like you to do for me."

Alex took another sip of coffee. "What did you have in mind?"

"I'd like you to help me give three parties before the wedding. I have a great many people to entertain. I'd thought of catering the parties out of my home, but it would be so much more convenient to have them here."

She thought about what would happen if she accepted. More contact with Sean. Seeing him with Muffy. Having to fight this ridiculous attraction.

She glanced at the clock on her desk. "My next appointment is in twenty minutes. Why don't you give me a brief outline of what you'd like?"

Fifteen minutes later, Sean stood. Alex followed his lead and tried not to let him see how his handshake affected her. He was almost out the door when an oversight occurred to her.

"Sean! How do I reach you if I need to talk to you?"

His smile was slow. "I've made it easy for you, Alex. You just have to buzz me. I'll be staying in the Presidential Suite until the day of the wedding."

The Presidential Suite. The top two floors of this hotel. He's going to be around constantly.

And, having dropped that little bomb, Sean Lawton slowly sauntered out the door.

"ALEX? ARE you all right?"

Marcy's concerned voice made Alex glance away from the window. Marcy, purse in hand, was ready to leave for the day.

"I'm fine. So where are you going tonight?"

"Where else? The ballet." She fiddled with the strap on her purse, then said, "Look, Alex, that guy—I mean, Peter doesn't even affect me that way! And everyone in the office was swooning. And then, when we heard that he's going to be living here—"

"I'm sure it's just so that he can be right on top of things."

Literally. "If we can pull off this Renaissance extravaganza, we'll be way ahead of the other hotels."

Marcy stared at her, then said, "Louise was right."

Alex was all attention now. Louise Hartson was one of the caterers who worked under her direction. And she wasn't one of Alex's favorite people. There was a streak of maliciousness in her when she wasn't looking for attention or basking in reflected glory. Alex was constantly picking up the pieces of her catering projects, and just last week had seriously considered firing the woman.

Louise was the consummate California beach girl, getting a little older but still holding up well. Her tan was perfect, her streaked hair artful.

And if Louise thought there was anything going on between Alex and Sean Lawton, it would be a total, unmitigated disaster.

"Right about what?"

Marcy looked miserable. "Oh, Alex, I don't want you to think that all I do out there is sit and gossip—"

"I know that's not true. Now tell me what she said."

"She said—she said it was true what everyone had suspected all along, that you had ice water for blood if Sean Lawton couldn't get a rise out of you."

Alex smiled. If she had Louise fooled, she had the entire office fooled. Now for Mr. Lawton himself.

"I'm sorry, Alex."

"Don't be. You can't control what comes out of that woman's mouth. If I let Louise upset me, I'd be a candidate for early retirement. The woman's a pest, nothing more or less."

"She's not doing well with the Farrell wedding."

"Tell me something I don't know."

Marcy smiled. "Thanks, Alex. See you tomorrow."

Once she was alone, Alex sat back in her chair and closed her eyes. Ice water for blood. Louise had never made this personal an attack. And saying it in front of Marcy when she knew it would get back to Alex...Louise had to know how close she'd come to getting fired, and resented it.

But if Alex had fired her last week, it would have meant taking on three more weddings and a bat mitzvah on top of the Bradford Renaissance Faire. It would have been impossible.

If Louise can only hang in for a couple of months— Sensing

someone watching her, she glanced toward the door. Sean stood there, looking concerned. He wore faded jeans and a black pullover.

"I'm fine." She reached for her purse, averting her eyes.

"You look tired."

"It's been a long day. You know all about those."

"Have dinner with me."

She had to admire him; he was direct. "I'm having dinner with some friends."

"Tomorrow night."

If he wanted a challenge, he'd get one. "Sean, correct me if I'm wrong, but you're engaged to be married, and I just happen to be putting together that wedding. I know men generally get nervous before the big day and perhaps contemplate having a few flings. But I'm nobody's fling. Got it?"

She could be as direct as he could. Now she was surprised to see him smile.

"Was what I said so amusing?"

"No. No, Alex, your feelings are dead on."

She was astonished. "So, I've made myself perfectly clear?"

He nodded slowly, his eyes never leaving her face. Alex felt as if she had issued him a challenge and he had taken it.

"I'm nobody's fool—and nobody's conquest."

He shut the door and walked slowly into her office.

"So, what do you suggest we do?" he said softly.

She stared up at him. "About what?"

"About this. Between us."

"This...feeling?" She felt horribly self-conscious.

"Yes."

Suddenly she felt unbearably tired. A part of her ached at the thought of giving up. She longed to throw caution to the wind and not think of Muffy or the wedding or her mother or her job or anything that got in the way of her primitive reaction to this man.

So easy. No one would ever have to know. A few hours, the privacy of a suite, the key turned securely in the lock. A chance to find out what would happen with this man who seemed to ignite her deepest sensuality. This type of feeling came along...what, once in a lifetime?

Lust. Pure and simple. Alex wasn't proud of her thoughts, but they were her true thoughts, and she wouldn't push them out of the way.

"It's nothing that can last," she began carefully. "I mean, you must love Muffy. What's happening between us—I'd label it lust. It's not designed to hold two people together, you know that."

"I disagree," he said quietly. "I think lust has been the driving force that's kept us from total extinction. I think that when a man wants a woman the way I want you, he goes a little crazy and doesn't think about the repercussions. And that feeling, more than anything, has kept mankind alive. I think it's what keeps people together today even when life throws them a curve. And I think feelings that strong don't happen every day, and when they do, they shouldn't be ignored."

He thought like no other man she ever knew, and his logic was giving her a headache. Her fingers clenched into frustrated fists. "What do you want me to do? Surrender to something that can only last a few months, when you'll go off and start building a life for yourself with another woman? No thanks. I'd rather be alone. In fact, it's the reason I have been alone for over a ye—"

She stopped, then locked gazes with Sean once again.

"Don't do this to me. I'm not some deal. I'm not a building you can buy and renovate and then cast aside."

"What if I said we could have more than that?"

She could feel the anger starting to bubble inside. "More than what? You mean I could be your little something on the side? I don't think so, Mr. Lawton."

"Sean. Have you thought, Alex, what we'd be like together? Alone? Have you?"

"I won't deny it. But what you think and what you do—"

"I've always believed in following my instincts."

"Bully for you."

"I'll never hurt you, Alex."

"There's nothing but hurt for me in this."

"Trust me."

"Trust you! I don't even trust the way I feel about you. And it's lust."

He hadn't touched her, but his eyes were so alive, Alex couldn't tear her gaze away from him.

"You make it sound like something distasteful."

"It frightens me. I don't want to feel this way, Sean."

"Do you think I do? If I could have met you at another time, another place—"

"But you didn't."

"Alex." He grasped one of her wrists and pulled her closer. "Alex, don't run away from me. If I told you there was a way we could work things out—"

"There isn't. Let me go."

"I can't."

And she knew it was true. She was up against him now, and her other hand shot out, fingers splayed against his chest. His heartbeat was rapid. She could feel it through the fine wool of his sweater.

His arm was around her waist, pulling her up against him. And all she could think of was getting closer to this man, touching him, feeling the warmth of his body. A rush of pure, primal feeling overwhelmed her, and she closed her eyes.

She felt his hands in her hair, then he was caressing her head, tilting her face up—

She was lost. Now she could feel the solid wood of her desk against the back of her thighs, and he was pressed against her, close enough to make her realize he was as excited as she was.

"Sean?" She didn't recognize her own voice.

A heartbeat later, his mouth covered hers.

He was kissing her as if he were a starving man and she was responding, her hands sliding up into his hair, pulling his face down to hers, arching up against him. And it was more than fourteen months of being alone, more than the desire to be close to someone. It felt right. His hands felt as if they had been made to shape her body, his mouth felt right against hers.

She didn't even protest as his hand slid swiftly up to cup her breast. His mouth caught her sharp whimper, then she bit his lip as a pleasure so brilliant it was painful shot through her body.

Just touching her breast wasn't enough. She felt his impatience as he flicked the buttons of her silk blouse open, then slipped his hand inside. His fingers were warm as they slid over her lacy bra, then moved to the front clasp and did away with the last barrier. When his hand caressed her bare breast, Alex moaned and knew she was lost.

He was kissing her neck now, moving down her throat, and she sensed a raw, wonderfully male impatience. Had she known this was going to happen, was it why she'd fantasized it? Her head went back, her fingers dug into his shoulders for support as he gently bit the taut skin of her neck.

Don't stop, don't stop—

"Alex?"

She recognized the voice and pulled herself back to reality with a jolt. Alex barely had time to notice Sean blocking her view of the door. All she could see was Louise's face over his shoulder as she stood in the doorway.

But that was enough. Her blue eyes were incredulous, then a slow, feline smile spread over her face.

"I'm sorry. I didn't know you were—occupied with a client. I'll talk with you in the morning."

She closed the door softly, but Alex kept staring at it. Her body felt numb. Finally, not trusting herself to look at Sean, she fastened her bra and began on the buttons of her blouse.

"Alex."

She was startled to find he looked as shaken as she felt.

"Alex, I'm sorry."

"It's not your fault. What happened was just as much my—responsibility," she finished tiredly.

What a bland word to describe what had flashed between them.

"Alex, I didn't come here with the intention of—"

"I know that. It's all right." She was reaching for her suit jacket, then her purse.

"Alex, we have to—"

"Talk. I know. But I can't—" Her voice wavered. "I can't tonight. I need to get away from you. Just for a little bit. Just so I can—figure out what I'm going to do."

"I'll talk to you tomorrow, then?"

She nodded, too tired to resist.

He stepped closer and gently kissed her forehead.

That kiss was her total undoing. When the door shut behind him, she burst into tears.

*

SEAN LAWTON stood in one corner of the Biltmore's luxurious Presidential Suite and stared out at the downtown L.A. skyline. The sun was just beginning to come up. Another day. And sev-

enty-eight days until the wedding, when he could come clean with
Alex, explain the entire mess and find out if there could be anything more between them than this incredible attraction.

He'd thought of calling Phillip. Sean was positive he could trust
Alex with the truth—that he was merely acting as a stand-in. But
he couldn't reach Phillip.

The trouble with this entire scheme was that he hadn't antici-
pated meeting Alexandra Michaels.

He wanted to believe she was different, and her background
seemed to prove she was. He'd had her checked out, and what
he'd learned had pleased him immensely.

The only child of James Edward Michaels, Alex had turned
her back on her family fortune after graduating from a Swiss
boarding school. She'd taken some college classes, and had
worked part-time at the Marriott down by LAX. While employed
there as a cocktail waitress and later a bartender, she'd fallen into
the world of hotel management.

She'd eventually finished her degree—in psychology, with a
business minor—then slowly worked her way up the corporate
ladder. Now she was well on her way to making a name for
herself in L.A. And Alex was not a woman to whom money was
a false god.

He watched the sun climb higher and thought about ordering
up a pot of coffee.

Find Phillip. Far easier said than done. Phillip had worked in
computers for many years. The money was excellent, and it had
given him financial independence from his little tyrant of a father.
He had chosen to work one more job before the wedding, but
there were strings attached.

The company that he worked for, Stealthco, was putting in a
bid to design the software for the Stealth bomber. Phillip had
flown to Virginia days after their talk. Now he was holed up at
one of the company's private homes. No one would be let out
until the bidding commenced. That way, it was impossible for
information to be leaked.

Phillip had told Sean that bidding commenced three days before
the wedding. In the meantime, he would be in a forced seclusion.
The job had seemed a good thing at first. Even if Phillip had been
tempted to see Muffy, he wouldn't have been able to.

Tell Muffy. Sean rejected that idea. The girl was as nervous as an overbred poodle. Constance had done a neat piece of psychological work on her daughter, turning her into a pale shadow of what she might have been. He couldn't do it to her.

Phillip and Muffy were counting on him. Their happiness was in his hands. He couldn't put that in jeopardy.

Alexandra. She was beautiful, but it wasn't only her beauty that had attracted him. Though that had hit him at first, she had seemed so vulnerable when he first saw her in the office that day. She chose her words carefully, with a self-protective hesitancy that had gone straight to his heart.

Her eyes. Intelligent and dark, hiding secrets. Hiding passion. She'd come alive in his arms, then frosted over into the coolly efficient Ms. Michaels, director of catering. An enigma.

Suddenly restless and eager for the day to begin, he punched out the phone number for room service. Then he started for the shower.

A plan was already beginning to form in his mind.

"HAVE DINNER with me tonight, Alex," Sean had said.

"No, I don't think so," she had replied uncertainly.

She waited for Sean to come to her office the entire day, but at six-fifteen when he didn't show, Alex finally had to admit to herself she just might have blown it.

"Anything else, Alex?" Marcy said over the intercom.

"Just bring me in the menu for the Bradford wedding. I want to look it over one more time."

A few minutes after Marcy left, Alex sighed and sat back in her chair. Then, knowing she was alone on the floor, she gave in to the impulse, unpinned her hair, kicked off her heels and swung her aching feet up on her desk.

Sean walked silently down the corridor, his footsteps muffled by the thick carpet. He carried a large shopping bag, and he started to grin as he rounded the corner and saw the light from Alex's door. It was partially open, and he peeked inside.

His heart melted.

Alex was sitting in her chair, her feet up, fast asleep.

He studied her face for several minutes, then remembering he had hot food in the bag, he set to work creating dinner for her.

Not wanting to wake her, Sean looked around her office. There was a small table just outside the door that would be perfect....

SHE WAS dreaming that she had died and gone to heaven. It was like one long, continuous party, only all the food was good. The smells were...

In that strange state between sleeping and waking, Alex slowly opened one eye.

Sean was lighting two candles on a small, round table covered with a peach-colored cloth that looked suspiciously like one from Pierre's restaurant.

She moved in the chair, and it creaked. Sean looked back over his shoulder, and their eyes met.

What was he doing here? Alex slowly lowered her legs off the desk.

"You wouldn't go out to dinner with me, so I decided to bring dinner to you."

Something about his persistence was immensely gratifying. She got up and walked toward the small, intimate setting.

He smiled, then pulled her chair out for her. She sat down. Her nap had refreshed her, and she felt competent to deal with whatever he threw her way.

She just wanted to spend a little more time with him. See what was beneath that beautiful masculine exterior. Talk to him.

"That's not food I'm familiar with," she said softly. "Do you cook?"

"I didn't cook this," he said. "It's from the Seventh Street Bistro."

"Oh." He was clever, and she was impressed. She knew the restaurant; Pierre knew the chef. She had eaten there once and remembered the food as exquisite. The Bistro had a reputation for the classiest takeout in town.

"I wasn't sure what you liked, so I ordered a little of everything. Potato pancakes with Sevruga caviar and lemon cream, salmon tartar with ginger and green peppercorns—"

"I like all that so far—"

"Cold poached salmon with herb dressing and goat cheese, mahimahi with spices, broccoli ravioli in a butter-lobster sauce—"

"Oh, my God—"

"And last but not least, venison with a peach-and-apple chutney in a black peppercorn sauce. Is there anything you don't like?"

She started to laugh. "No. I can be a real pig."

There was silence as they both did justice to the food. Sean had brought china plates, silverware, linen napkins, two tall white candles in silver candlesticks and a centerpiece of tiger lilies.

Alex couldn't remember enjoying a dinner more.

"Why a catering career?" he asked.

"Why not?" She laughed, then reached for her wineglass. "I was working at a bookstore for minimum wage. A friend of mine was making terrific money as a cocktail waitress down at the Marriott. She told me there was an opening, so I took it. Then I figured out that the bartender made even more money, and when she gave two weeks' notice, I asked her to give me some on-the-job training.

"After I convinced my boss that I could bartend, I did so for a year and a half, then moved on to another hotel. By the time I took a job here, I was one step away from the director of catering. Five years later, I had the job."

She took another sip of wine, then said, "So now you have to tell me. Why construction? What is it that caught you?"

"I like making deals." He leaned back in his chair, studying her. "Sometimes it isn't even the building. It's the challenge of getting something of quality and turning it into something even better."

"Pretty ruthless."

"I can be—when I want something badly enough."

"This ravioli is incredible."

"You're very good at changing the subject, Alex. But I want you to know that making you uncomfortable was never my intention. I just want to get to know you. I wish we could have met at a different time. But I'm not going to hurt you. I give you my word."

"I wish we'd met at a different time, too," she whispered. "You're not like any man I've ever met."

That seemed to please him.

"What does marriage mean to you, Sean?" she asked quietly.

"Forever. Loyalty and courage. Standing by that person's side and facing life together. Wanting to be with that person more than anyone in the world."

"Muffy's a lucky girl."

"Yes, she is," he said quietly. Then, he seemed to check himself, as if he didn't want to say any more.

They ate in silence for a while, then, "Do you think," Alex began carefully, "that a man and a woman can be good friends?"

"No."

"That's kind of sexist."

"It's the truth."

"Could we be—"

"The way I feel about you, no."

"Then why are we having dinner together? Is this a game?" She could feel herself getting upset.

He glanced away from her, frustration evident in every muscle of his face.

"God, Alex, if I told you the truth, I wouldn't even believe it."

"Are you in love with her?" The words were out before she had time to check them, but she had to know.

His tone was subdued when he answered, "No."

"Yet you're going to marry her. Does Muffy know?"

"No—and you're not to tell her anything. It would only upset her."

"Don't you think it will upset her to find out you don't love her?"

"I do love her. As a friend. But not the way—a man loves the woman he commits himself to."

"Do you love anyone but yourself?"

"You wouldn't believe me if I told you."

The meaning of his words took a minute to sink in, and then she was staring at him. "Me?"

He nodded.

"You love me?"

"It's different for a man."

"I guess so!"

"I can't explain it. I just looked at you and I knew. And I don't believe in wasting time."

Dessert consisted of two pieces of Pierre's incredible chocolate torte. Alex recognized one of his waiters after he thoughtfully knocked and walked in, then cleared away their dishes and served dessert.

After he had left them alone, Alex leaned back in her chair and picked up her wineglass.

"The tablecloth, the flowers—it's from Pierre, isn't it?"

"A very accommodating man, your Pierre. He understands that sometimes our hearts take us places and we have no choice but to follow."

She set her glass down. "I'm really trying to understand this, Sean. What do you want from me?"

"Just this." And he leaned forward, all power and intensity.

He's making another deal. Only it's not a building, it's me.

"All I want," he said slowly, "is a promise to see me until the wedding and not go out with any other man."

Dead silence reigned until Alex said, "What's in it for me?"

"The beginning of the best time both of us will ever have."

She smiled. "Can I give you some conditions?"

"We'll see."

"No sex. I'm deadly serious about that one, Sean."

"I agree. Anything else?"

"I don't want to hurt Muffy."

"I'm in total agreement with you there."

"So," she said, "you've been honest with me, so I'll be honest with you."

"I'd appreciate it."

"I am totally out of my depth with you."

"Will you trust me on this one, Alex? It would mean... everything to me."

You, Alex, are certifiably insane to agree to this little arrangement, she thought. But agree she did.

And she couldn't even blame the wine.

You, Sean, are certifiably insane to agree to this little arrangement. No sex? What are you, crazy?

Now that he had agreed to keep their relationship platonic, Sean found he could think of nothing else. Yet he knew he couldn't take advantage of Alex that way, not when she thought he was going to marry Muffy.

And Phillip was still in seclusion. Why couldn't his friend have taken on a less complicated job, like doubling for Arnold Schwarzenegger? Why did Phillip have to be in hiding somewhere on the East Coast, unable to come to the phone?

Now Sean Lawton, media darling, was consigned to a hell of his own making. He'd faced some of the most powerful men in the city over the bargaining tables, and he had almost always won.

But one woman was going to bring him to his knees.

*

"SEAN, THIS arrangement could be professional suicide for me." Alex kept her voice low as she spoke on the phone. She'd thought a great deal about what he had proposed. She also knew Pierre wouldn't have sent up just anyone to clear that table and deliver dessert. She could trust Pierre to be discreet.

"I'm not asking you to do anything that will compromise you in anyone's eyes. I'm simply asking you to spend some extra time with me before the wedding."

"But...Sean, that first night, when Louise walked into my office. I'm worried about what she might do."

"Has she done anything to you before?"

"No. But I've called her on neglecting some of the finer points of two weddings and an anniversary party. She was pretty nasty about it. To be honest, I've been thinking about firing her."

He said, "I blocked her view, so I don't think she saw anything. But if you'd like, I'll think of a way to fix it."

"I'd appreciate it."

"Point her out to me when I'm in your office this afternoon. Sometimes a second opinion helps."

As it turned out, Louise came into Alex's office while Sean was there.

They were going over the fine points of Sean's first party, a bachelor affair, when she came in.

"Well, well, Alex, working late again?" Her tone was suggestive.

She obviously hadn't seen Sean whose back was to her, hidden in the depths of a large, buttery-soft chair in front of Alex's desk.

"Who are you?" he asked quietly, turning to fix his gaze on Louise, who was clearly startled.

"This is Louise Hartson. She's one of the assistant catering managers."

"Why were you surprised to see Ms. Michaels working late?"

Sean said. "Surely you don't think she became head of the catering department without a lot of long nights."

Louise looked befuddled, but there was a belligerent gleam in her eyes.

"Oh, come off it! You know who her father is. She could buy this hotel if she wanted to."

Alex felt herself start to freeze up inside.

"I'd watch myself if I were you," Sean warned. "You might find yourself looking for another job."

"Not with what I saw the other night. I could call either the *Times* or the *Herald*. I'm sure they'd pounce on that juicy little item for their gossip column."

Alex felt sick, but kept her face impassive and said nothing. She had a feeling Louise didn't stand a chance.

"What are you talking about?"

"When I walked in that night, she was in your arms."

"Yes, she was. What of it?"

Alex had no idea where this conversation was going.

"You'd been kissing her."

"Had I?"

"Well, she was in your arms—"

"Ms. Michaels has been known to go a long time between meals, has she not?"

Louise was looking down at the floor. "Yes."

Alex knew it was common knowledge that she sometimes worked straight through lunch and even dinner.

"We'd finished our meeting, and she had agreed to see to the first of three private parties for me. What you saw, Ms. Hartson, was what happened after Ms. Michaels walked around her desk to see me to her door. She started to feel faint, so I steadied her. Afterward, she was feeling so poorly that she spent the night in a room in this hotel and ordered up dinner. You can check that with the kitchen records. Now, if this ridiculous accusation is quite finished, I'd like to get back to work. Is that all right with you, Ms. Michaels?"

"Yes." Alex turned to Louise and said, "I'd like to see you in my office tomorrow at ten."

"So you can fire me?" Her belligerence was back.

"No. I've arranged meetings with all the catering assistants, so don't feel that I'm singling you out."

After Louise left the room, Sean said quietly, "You're going to have trouble with that one. I'd fire her and cut your losses."

"I can't. There's no way we can cover for her. We've all got our hands full. But after the new year, I'll let her go."

He wasn't pleased by this, she could tell. And it suddenly touched her that he was concerned for her, wanted to protect her. It had been a long time since she had had someone to watch over her. She found she liked the feeling. Very much.

WHERE WAS my great protector now, wondered Alex the following evening?

"Like I said, Alex, we're in trouble. Tony's in the hospital. They think it's diverticulitis."

"Oh, no. Is he all right?"

"Meg said they caught it in time. He's at Cedars right now."

"This is not happening to me," Alex said. "Marcy, what's the name of that school for bartenders?"

"American Bartending School."

"What's the name of that guy who runs it?"

"Jerry. He's great."

"Call him up. We need a bartender."

Moments later Marcy buzzed her back.

"They're closed. His office closed at five. Maybe Pierre knows someone, one of the bartenders from the restaurant."

"But Tony's special. He's really, really good. He does all those little things that make a difference."

There was a pause, then Marcy came back with, "Why don't you do it, Alex?"

"I—no. I couldn't."

"Why not? You bartended for a long time. And I bet you were really good."

"Well—" Alex could feel herself starting to relent. "I don't even think I have a tuxedo shirt left."

"Hang on, I'll be right in."

Marcy came into her office toting a large canvas bag.

"I was going out with Peter to this club in Hollywood tonight, and I had this look all planned, but I can wear something else. We're close enough in size—you'll look just great!"

"What are you talking about?" Alex was beginning to panic.

"A dandy. Remember Julie Andrews in *Victor/Victoria*? It was a great look. Now, here's the shirt...."

EVEN ALEX had to admit she looked great.

The black dinner jacket, trimmed in rhinestones, fit with shoulders pads added. The icy white, ruffled tuxedo shirt was a bit tight, tucked into a pair of black trousers with a satin ribbon down each outside leg. But the ultimate touch was the large, plushy fur coat—fake, Marcy assured her.

"I don't like the shirt. It pulls across your boobs."

Alex glanced down. Marcy was right.

"Don't wear the shirt."

"Marcy, I don't know—"

"Trust me, Alex, I know clothes. Just button the jacket and you won't even need it."

When Marcy was done with her, Alex studied herself in the mirror. She looked incredible. Like no bartender she'd ever seen. What made the outfit incredibly sexy was the subtraction of the shirt.

But it worked. And with the party starting at eight, and no other bartender in sight, what was she supposed to do? She was certain Sean wasn't going to be happy about this, but if she had learned one lesson in her years of catering, it was that the show must go on.

Marcy, insisting Alex needed something around her neck, had fastened a black velvet ribbon with a sparkling rhinestone pin, then a stickpin on the lapel of the jacket. "Insurance, in case someone gets drunk and tries to get a little fresh, you know?"

Marcy then braided Alex's hair back with the silver ribbon she'd planned to wear as a headband.

"Now, go do your makeup. Light face, dark eyes and lips." As Alex did her face, Marcy drilled her on the drinks.

"What's in a Tequila Sunrise?"

"Tequila, orange juice, grenadine. And a cherry."

"A Sunset?"

"Blackberry brandy instead of the grenadine."

"I'm impressed. What about a California Driver?"

"Vodka, orange juice and grapefruit juice."

Marcy was still whispering drinks to her as Sean walked in the large double doors of the Emerald Room.

"A Russian Quaalude."

"Stoli's, Kahlua, Bailey's and Frangelico."

"You got it, Alex. Good luck."

And with that, Marcy smiled and stepped back slightly.

"You look great. Kill 'em."

Marcy was out the door, and Sean was walking straight toward Alex. She could tell that he was not at all pleased to see that she was going to be attending his bachelor bash.

"What are you doing behind the bar?"

"Tony—the bartender I had hired for tonight—is in the hospital. Diverticulitis. I couldn't get anyone else on such short notice, so I decided I'd do it."

"There isn't anyone else in this entire hotel who could bartend tonight?"

"There's no one else who's as good as Tony." Or me, she added silently, her chin lifting just a fraction. "After all, you didn't request a giant cake, so I know there won't be any naked girls running around. And studies show that men just love a female bartender."

He sighed deeply, fingers raking his thick, dark hair. "I know. Alex, I just don't think you should do this."

Realization came so suddenly that she was surprised she hadn't sensed what was really going on. He's jealous. He asked me not to see any other men, and now, if I tend bar, I'll be in the middle of a ballroom full of them. How wonderful.

Jealousy, like lust, was something that had been in short supply in her life. Until Sean. It struck her that she was intensely, fiercely glad that he wasn't a man to do anything halfway.

And there was no way he could deflect the number of men he had invited. The possibilities were endless.

"Will you do something for me?"

"Sure."

"Let Pierre send someone up."

"All right, I'll just go powder my nose."

There was a phone in the bathroom, and Alex dialed Pierre's extension.

"Pierre? Send Carl."

"Chérie, you are a cruel woman."

"He's jealous."

WEDDING OF THE YEAR

"Of what? You, in your little tuxedo without a blouse, among all those men? How silly of him."

"Is Marcy there with you?"

"She's eating one of my truffles right now."

"Tell her thanks."

"With pleasure, *ma coeur*. Carl is on the way."

Carl was a blue-eyed blonde, his surfer good looks barely restrained in a tuxedo. Alex guessed that Pierre must have given him particular instructions as to this job.

"Hey, dude, let's party."

Alex saw the tiniest bit of worry in Sean's eyes and had to bite her inner lip hard to keep from laughing.

"Are you familiar with most standard drinks?"

"Sure. Whiskey and water, Scotch and soda—"

Carl, Alex decided, was priceless.

Sean said quietly, "Make me a Melon Ball."

Carl went straight for the rum.

"Vodka, Carl," Alex whispered, just loud enough for Sean to hear.

"Oh, yeah. My mind just blanked out, you know what I mean? Okay, vodka, and then orange juice, right?"

Alex nodded her head, looking pleased.

Carl set the highball glass up on the spill rail.

"Where's the Midori?" Sean asked quietly.

"Right here." Carl hefted the liqueur bottle, tossed it, caught it, and quickly poured a scant half ounce in the glass. Just enough to fill it to the brim.

He caught Sean's disapproval.

"Oh. Sorry. Here, I'll just dump some of it out—"

"Not on the fresh ice, Carl! Here, over on the side."

"Whoa, what was I thinking? Call me another one, man."

"Let's see you do a gin and tonic."

"Nice—well you got here, dude. I'm impressed."

"Where's the lime?"

"Oh, yeah! A garnish, of course."

"Make me a Ramos Fizz," Sean said. His jaw was beginning to tighten. Alex glanced at her watch. Thirteen minutes till showtime.

Carl, bless his heart, looked at Sean blankly. "You're kidding me, man. That's a drink?"

"A Ramos Fizz," Sean said slowly.

Carl turned to Alex. "Help me out on this one?"

She stepped behind the bar and placed a wineglass with some ice cubes in it on the speed rail. Then she threw ice, gin, cream, sweet-and-sour mix and a few dashes of orange-flower water into the blender.

She separated an egg and threw the white into the blending cup. Then, while the drink was blending, she dumped the ice out of the wineglass, strained the contents into it and topped it off with some soda.

The silence was deafening.

"Well," said Alex, after a short pause, "I'm sure there's some paperwork waiting for me somewhere." As she started to leave the room, she heard Carl telling Sean about the last party he had bartended.

"Alex, wait."

"Yes?"

He strode quickly up beside her. "Carl's not going to work. Is there anyone else?"

As if on cue, a tall, blond man entered the room.

"Sean Lawton! You sure sprung a quick one on all of us! I didn't even know you were seeing Muffy!"

Alex walked over to the bar and smiled at Carl.

"You're wasting your time at the Biltmore, Carl. Have you ever considered going into acting?"

He grinned. "I'm taking acting classes on the side. And my agent is trying to get me a part on a soap."

Only in L.A. "Well, you did a great job here. Now get going before he changes his mind."

"I'm history, Alex."

Within seconds, Sean was back at the bar. Three other men had walked in, and a group of them were talking and laughing by the door.

"Where did Carl go?"

"Sean, he couldn't handle a party like this. Do you think I want that kind of news to get back to my boss?"

He frowned. "All right. You can tend bar, until Pierre sends up someone to replace you. And—damn it, Alex, what happened to your shirt?"

"What shirt?"

The muscles in his jaw tensed again. "What exactly do you have on underneath that jacket?"

"Besides a black lace camisole? Nothing."

The look in his blue-gray eyes was everything she had hoped for—and more.

"Alex, we have to—"

"Hey, pretty lady. How about a rum and Coke?"

"Hey, Sean, only the best for your buddies, right?"

The look in his eyes...

She'd forgotten just how entertaining bartending could be.

"Darling, make me a Tanqueray and tonic."

"A vodka martini, and could I have two olives, sweetheart?"

"Honey, I'd like a Climax."

The look in Sean's eyes was murderous.

"Would you like me to make that a Screaming Climax?"

"Alex, could I speak to you for a minute?" There was a dangerous glint in his eyes.

"Wait a minute, Sean." The man was from Texas, judging from his accent and the languorous way he moved. "She really is a bartender! Now, honey, what was that last one? It sounded mighty interesting."

"A Screaming Climax. You just add vodka."

"Alex—"

The Texan threw back his head and laughed uproariously, then said, "Toss that vodka right in. You make me feel reckless, little lady."

Sean was about to say something when another wave of guests descended on the bar. Alex knew, with a feeling of certainty, that she would pay for this mischief sooner or later.

The party was still going full tilt two hours later. Sean had never strayed far from the bar, keeping Alex within glancing distance for what seemed the entire evening. When all party-goers had cleared the bar area, he walked over to Alex.

"Sean, you can't just spend all your time here at the bar. Parties are for mingling, and you're the host."

"They all end up coming to the bar sooner or later. I can talk to them here as well as I can out there."

She hid her smile as she reached for a lime. She cut more garnishes in silence, then said softly, "I think the party's going really well, Sean. What do you think?"

"I think you're quite a bartender." His tone wasn't grudging.
There was respect in his voice.

"Thank you. I try my best."

"Alex, I—"

"Sean, there you are! Get over here. Carter and I haven't seen
you all evening. Though I can see why you'd want to hang out
at the bar." The man looked like a Ralph Lauren model.

This time, Sean couldn't avoid his guest. With some reluctance,
he left the bar. He didn't like her being here, the lone woman in
a group of handsome, successful men. Now, as she thought of his
wedding—of having to watch Muffy Bradford walk up the aisle—
Alex began to reconsider the allowances she'd been making for
Sean.

Who did he think he was, telling her not to pay attention to
other men? And when would she have a chance like this again?

I'm not a building, Sean Lawton. You can't make one of your
deals with me.

"Hi, babe." The man standing at the bar looked like a young
Nick Nolte, all blond hair and muscles, with the bluest eyes. Very
attractive.

"Hi, yourself. What can I get you?"

"Behind that bar, you mean?"

"Mmm...yeah." She could see Sean out of the corner of her
eye, and she could feel his presence.

It was volatile.

"How about a shot of tequila?" said Nick, as she thought of
him.

"Good choice. I like a man who likes tequila." A corny line,
but it always worked.

"You do?"

He was cute. He didn't stir her up the way Sean did, but maybe
this was what she needed. Someone to show Sean that she wasn't
just waiting for him to walk in so that she could jump up, roll
over, play dead.

Be daring, a sneaky little voice whispered in her ear.

He's going to be furious, the voice of reason shot back. You
may get more than you bargained for....

"So, you doing anything after the party?"

An electric silence. She could feel Sean, sense that he was
within earshot, that he would hear her reply.

"How about a quiet dinner at Bernard's? I'd like to get to know you...someplace we could really talk."

"I'd really like that."

"I'll go make reservations. Think you'll be off in about an hour and a half?"

"I know I will."

"All right." He was giving her an assessing look.

She met his gaze, then smiled slowly. "You have excellent taste—"

"Steven. But everyone calls me Steve."

"Steve. I'm Alex. Bernard's is a very romantic place."

"I hope so." There was a devilish glint in his blue eyes as he turned and walked toward the main door.

She reached for another lime, as she wanted something, anything, to do with her hands so she wouldn't have to meet Sean's eyes.

There was a palpable chill in the air.

"You're not going out with him."

"I beg your pardon?"

"We made a deal. Don't do this, Alex."

"Tell me why you think you have any rights at all when it comes to what I will and will not do."

"I won't let you do this."

"What are you planning on doing, dragging me out of this room forcibly? Locking me up?" She met his gaze, and it was frigid. "This is the twentieth century, Sean, not the fourteenth. Women aren't possessions anymore, even when they do choose to get married. Are you planning on treating Muffy this way? Does she know what you have in store for her?"

There was a perverse little demon riding her. She'd believed she could handle this whole thing, but the thought of Sean with another woman was more than she could bear.

But just then, three men descended on the bar.

"Darling, how about a refill—"

"A Tequila Sunrise—"

"Just Perrier, with a twist—"

Alex immersed herself in the drinks, chatting, laughing, smiling. Sean, looking like he wanted to upend the entire bar, stalked away.

"WONDERFUL PARTY, wasn't it?" Alex said brightly as she sur-
veyed the empty Emerald Room. She and Sean were the only
people left, and she had five minutes to make it to Bernard's.
She'd unbraided her hair, and it cascaded down her back in shining waves. With the thick, plushy fur coat around her, she was
dressy enough for the four-star restaurant.

Sean simply looked at her. "Don't do this, Alex."

"I'll see you in the morning."

"Well," he said, "at least let me help you with your coat."

The tiny, secret part of her woman's heart was upset that he
wasn't going to put up more of a struggle.

"All right."

He walked behind her, holding the coat, and at the same time
she moved her arms behind her.

Too late, she realized he'd trapped her.

The coat, voluminous and fluffy, came down over her head in
a smooth swish, as she felt strong arms lift her up, then thump
her over hard shoulder bone.

The breath left her body in a painful rush.

"Put me down, you rat! Right now! Down!"

In answer, she felt a large hand come stinging down on her
buttocks, and she was shocked speechless.

He was walking swiftly now, and she began to struggle. Her
heart was pounding, but her mouth was dry, and she couldn't
form the words to tell the world that she was in the hands of a
madman.

By the time she did, it was too late.

They were in the elevator now, and frustrated tears filled Alex's
eyes as she realized it was the private elevator that went directly
to the Presidential Suite.

Temporary lair of one Sean Lawton.

*

HE SET HER down on the bed with a resounding thump.

Alex had heard the key scrape in the lock, and as she struggled
up out of the fluffy black fur, she saw Sean slip the key into his
pocket.

"You," she said slowly, with as much dignity as she could
muster, "are a pig."

He said nothing, simply looked at her.

"I'm getting out of here and going downstairs to Bernard's."

"Just try it."

Furious, Alex jumped to her feet. "Give me that key."

"Are you going to go out with Steve?"

"That...is...none...of...your...business!!"

"No." His jaw was set, the blue eyes cold now.

"This is not the fourteenth century—"

"You were the one who gave me the idea."

She could remember her taunting words.

"What are you planing on doing, locking me up?"

Me and my big mouth, she silently mused.

"I really, really hate you."

"I really don't care. Take off your jacket."

"What!"

"Just a little insurance. There's no way you'll call anyone for help if you're up here in your underwear. Now take off your jacket. Or I'll do it for you."

"Sean, you can't be—"

"I want to see that black camisole. I've been thinking about it all night."

"What if I said," she began nervously, "that I would forget this entire incident and go straight home?"

"Too late. Off. Now."

She stared at him.

He leaned back against the wall by the bed, hands in his pockets, a slow, arrogant smile on his face.

She unbuttoned the first button of Marcy's black jacket.

"Sean, I really think we need to—"

"Come on."

The second button was unfastened, and her mouth went dry at the thought of Sean seeing her in her underwear. It was extremely nice—a black silk, lace-trimmed camisole and tap pants—but it was still underwear. And he was still the most devastating man she'd ever met.

Now the jacket was completely unbuttoned.

"Sean, I cannot believe that a civilized man—"

"I'm tired of being civilized. Take it off."

Their eyes locked and held, the only sound the ticking of a clock somewhere in the penthouse. Finally, after what seemed endless minutes, she looked away.

Somewhere, somehow, her fury was turning to the strongest feeling of arousal she'd ever experienced.

Hadn't she thought about this? Fantasized about being alone with him?

So easy. No one would ever have to know. A few hours, the privacy of a suite, the key turned securely in the lock....

"Off, Alex. Now."

She released her jacket, shrugged out of it and let it slip off her shoulders to fall at her feet.

"Now the slacks."

They joined the jacket on the floor and, suddenly embarrassed, she swept her hair over her shoulders so that she might have some sort of covering.

"Push your hair back over your shoulders."

She looked up at him, fighting against the temptation to beg. She would never do that.

"Come here."

Swallowing hard, she walked over to stand in front of him. She knew he was looking at her silk-clad body, and she resisted the urge to look up into his face until the desire to do so was too compelling.

The look in his eyes destroyed her.

If eyes could worship, his were doing so. Feeling strangely empowered, she whispered, "Is it—am I like you imagined?"

"Better."

His arms came around her, warm and hard, and he pulled her up against him. His body was incredibly warm through the silk, and she moved closer to that warmth and sighed, tension leaving her body.

They stood that way for a long time, Sean simply holding her, until he kissed her.

She felt like tinder catching fire as the kiss deepened. His lips were warm and firm, leading, coaxing, caressing. Then demanding. And she wanted him in a way she had wanted no other man in her life.

Then he held her away from him, the movement so smooth and steady it took her a moment to realize the kiss had been broken.

He held her for several minutes, and she could feel his heart racing. Alex gently placed her palm against his chest, and he caught her fingers, then kissed her palm.

"Let's get in bed."

Her body tensed, and he was quick to reassure her. "Nothing's going to happen, Alex. I give you my word. I just want to keep you close for a while."

She could have pointed out to him that Steve had probably left Bernard's by now, that she was too emotionally exhausted even to contemplate seeing another man, let alone carry on a coherent conversation. But the truth was, she wanted to be close to this man for a time, away from prying eyes and the need to conceal what she truly felt for him.

She could admit it to herself, but not to him. Not yet. If she did, she felt as if she would be totally vulnerable. She'd keep this new knowledge of the way she felt about Sean to herself just a little longer.

He lifted her so easily, with a masculine grace that made it seem he had held her in his arms this way many times before. She was frightened for an instant, and her fingers curled around the strength in his shoulders, needing his support. As Sean walked toward the bed, Alex softly rested her cheek against his.

There was such tenderness in this man, as well as stubbornness and pride.

He sat her down on the big bed, then pulled back the covers and helped her in. When he tucked the sheet and quilted bedspread around her carefully, Alex felt as if she was infinitely precious to him.

"Are you hungry? Did you eat dinner?"

She shook her head.

"Do you want something from room service?"

She shook her head again. Everything that had transpired tonight had exhausted her.

Linking her fingers around his neck, she gently pulled his head down to hers.

"Can we sleep? Just a little bit?"

"Anything you want."

She closed her eyes as she heard him slipping off his clothes, and a flare of painful excitement slipped through her. Then she heard the bedside lamp click off, and he was beside her, so close...

It took her a few seconds to realize he wasn't going to touch her, and she was thankful.

Alex reached out in the darkness until she found his hand. She grasped it firmly, linked fingers with him, then with a sigh, she turned her flushed face against the cool cotton of the pillowcase and slept.

When she woke, she saw him standing by the window, staring out at the dark skyline. He wore only pajama bottoms, his feet bare. She watched him, enjoying the sight of him during such a private moment.

"Sean?" Her voice was quiet in the silent room.

He straightened, and came to sit next to her on the bed.

"Do you feel better?"

"Much better."

"Alex, I'm not proud of what I did this evening, and I'm not going to try and make any excuses—"

She linked her hand with his, then placed a kiss on the back of his hand.

"Don't apologize. You didn't hurt me."

He looked at her for a long moment, then he said, "Hungry?"

"Yes."

"We'll order up."

They moved one of the tables right next to a large window, and called down to room service. Over dinner, they talked very carefully, skirting the more painful issues.

But later, back in bed with chocolate-covered strawberries and a bottle of champagne, Alex finally spoke from her heart.

"I can't go through with it, Sean. I can't watch you marry another woman. I'm not as sophisticated as you think."

He took another sip of champagne, watching her.

"If I asked you to trust me again, could you do it?"

"I want to. But I'm confused. Why are you taking part in this marriage if you don't love her?"

When he spoke, Alex knew he was weighing his words carefully.

"Alex, if I told you it had everything to do with loyalty and nothing to do with love, and that once the wedding is over, nothing will stand in our way, would you believe me?"

Slowly, so slowly, she nodded her head. "I would."

He looked up at the ceiling then, and she could see the small muscle working in his jaw. She touched his face, and his eyes were instantly riveted to hers.

"I don't deserve you," he said quietly. "I don't know what the hell I did to have you walk into my life, but I thank the gods every day that you did. And I'm not going to hurt you. I promise."

He turned off the light, and they lay in the big bed together, watching the first rays of dawn start to streak the night sky.

"Are you crying?" he asked suddenly. "Alex, darling, don't cry. We'll be fine." He kissed her then, his lips warm and reassuring against her cheek.

"I'm so happy." The words were muffled against his neck. "I'm just so happy."

MARCY FROZE, hearing the genuine malice in Louise's tone.

"Yeah, I've fixed her. Oh, no, nothing that simple. I'll tell you over dinner."

Both women were working late, but Marcy was sure Louise had no idea she could hear this conversation. She'd picked up the wrong extension, and now didn't dare set down the receiver for fear of discovery.

"Little Miss Rich Bitch thinks the rules just don't apply to her," Louise continued. "Well, I know exactly how to nail her. She picks on me, Randy, puts me down all the time. And in front of the others. I don't deserve treatment like this."

Marcy grimaced. Alex, pick on Louise? It was the exact opposite. Alex had bent over backward for her, and now Louise was going to stick it to her.

Not if I can help it.

"No, I don't want to talk about it over the phone. But let me tell you—" there was a hint of laughter in her voice "—Constance Bradford is going to crucify her when my little bomb drops."

Marcy froze, barely breathing. When Louise finally hung up, she set the receiver down.

The Bradford wedding. She's going to try to destroy Alex's career.

But how? And why? Grabbing her purse, Marcy slipped out the glass doors and ran silently down the hall.

"CATERING OFFICES, can I help you?" Marcy took the call the following day.

"Is Alex there?"

"She's sick, Sean. She went home at three."

"What's wrong? Is it serious?"

"Just a case of the current crud going around the office. She'll probably be back in a few days." Then Marcy said softly, "I bet you'd like her home address, right?"

"You got it."

"Your brother better be cute."

"I think you'll like him."

Sean jotted down the address as Marcy recited it to him, then hung up the phone and went directly to his car. He was at Alex's house in record time, with chicken soup from a deli, a fresh loaf of bread and everything helpful he could think of from the pharmacy.

But he hadn't counted on a blond bombshell opening the door.

"Does Alex live here?"

"The other side of the house. I'm Karin."

"Sean."

The brilliant blue eyes narrowed. "Aren't you the guy who's marrying Muffy Bradford?"

"One and the same."

"And you're bringing Alex chicken soup in bed— Forget it, it's none of my business. But mess around with my buddy's head, and I'll break both your legs."

He smiled. "I'll take that into consideration."

"Good. Just so you know." She closed the door.

There was no answer at the other door.

"I've got a spare key if you want it."

Sean glanced around at Karin. "Why would you help me out?"

"I guess," she said, grinning, "because I really do believe in blowing out your valves once in a while."

SEAN FOUND ALEX asleep when he let himself into her house with Karin's key. When she awoke a short time later he fed her chicken soup and toast, gave her an alcohol rub and sent her back to bed.

Sean had just sat down on the sofa to rest from the pampering he had lavished on Alex when the doorbell rang. A flustered-looking Marcy stepped through the door. "Louise is stirring up trouble," Marcy said, motioning wildly with her arms.

"Have a seat, Marcy." He directed her to a chair at the kitchen table. "Now start from the top."

"I don't know where she's messed things up, but she has. I've called almost halfway down this list, and everything is still on schedule. It gets me crazy."

"Why aren't you doing Louise's job? You're a lot more competent than she is."

Sean knew he'd hit a nerve when Marcy dropped her gaze to the table and whispered, "I don't know."

"Have you asked Alex?"

"Asked Alex what?"

Sean turned toward the sound of her voice. Alex was leaning in the doorway, wrapped in a turquoise-and-purple paisley silk robe with silk tassels. Her long hair was loose and she looked much better, her face less exhausted, her eyes clearer.

Sean helped her into one of the kitchen chairs, then touched her forehead gently.

"Not as hot as before. Do you want some juice? I brought orange and apple."

"Apple, please." But Alex was not to be deterred. "Asked me what?"

Marcy cleared her throat. "Alex, it's just that I've always wanted a chance to do some catering work. And I know I could! I've watched you and Phil and Lisa, even Louise. I couldn't be as bad as she is. So, do you think I might be able to—do something?"

Alex's expression was incredulous. "You never said a word about wanting to cater, Marcy."

"I just didn't think I could do it."

"Why not? Don't you think I know who was responsible for that Higgins wedding? It wasn't Louise."

"You knew? She used me until I got smart and stopped doing her work for her."

"Well," said Sean, setting down a glass of apple juice, "you can take over Louise's job once she's fired."

Alex sighed. "I can't fire her. There's too much work."

"Give Marcy the job. Louise isn't doing her work, anyway. And she's trying to destroy your own."

"What are you talking about?"

Sean glanced at Marcy. "She has to know. Alex may be able to figure out just what it is Louise is up to."

Marcy filled her in on the conversation she'd overheard. "She's thrown a wrench into the works somewhere, but I can't seem to find it."

"Give me the list," Alex said quietly.

They were all silent as she scanned it. On the third time through, she found what she was looking for.

"The flowers."

"How do you know?" Sean said.

"I'm sure it's the flowers. Constance Bradford could forgive everything else, but she wants flowers that will outshine the Jamison wedding. And you can't get flowers that special anywhere else but David's. All Louise had to do was call him up and cancel the order, implying that his flowers weren't good enough and we were going elsewhere. He's good—I think he's the best—but he's temperamental, and he doesn't always check things through. And he'd be too proud to call and scream at me. He'd just never do business with me again."

"So what are we going to do?" Marcy asked.

"Tomorrow morning, the three of us will go to his store."

"And if the flowers have been canceled?" Sean asked.

"Louise is history."

ALEX PUSHED open her office door and spoke quietly to Marcy.

"Send Louise in."

Her stomach was in knots. This was possibly the worst part of her job, but it had to be done. And her lingering fury gave her strength.

David Russell had been furious with her. The one hundred and twenty-five thousand dollar flower order had been canceled, with the implication that his arrangements for the Jamison wedding had been "not quite good enough" for the Bradfords. When Alex had swept into his store that morning, he'd started screaming.

After his outburst, she hadn't minced words. She told him exactly what had happened, then soothed his artist's ego and made sure the flowers were reordered.

Now Louise was going to get exactly what she deserved.

"Hi, Alex, you wanted something?"

"Louise. Sit down." The woman was incredible. She didn't even flinch.

"Louise, I spoke with David Russell today, and it seems that the order for the Bradford flowers was canceled. Do you know anything about it?"

Blue eyes opened wide, but Alex didn't miss the slight trembling of her hands.

"No. Should I?"

With those three words, Louise sealed her fate.

"I know you do, Louise. Clear out your desk and be out of

here within the hour. Don't ever ask me for a reference. I don't think I could stomach it."

The blue eyes narrowed. "You think you're so—"

Marcy, with perfect timing, opened the door. "Alex, Sean is here to see you. Are you busy with anything?"

"Nothing important," she said, looking straight at Louise. "I don't want to see you again before you leave."

Louise opened her mouth, seemed to think better of it, then swiftly left the office. She barely spared Sean a glance.

"So, you told her?"

"She lied. I didn't expect her to admit to it. But I'm glad she's gone." She looked up into his face. "And I'm glad you're here."

"MUFFY'S NOT feeling well. Bridal nerves, I suspect."

"I'd be nervous, too, if I was marrying Sean Lawton!"

There were polite female titters around the table. Constance had invited over thirty people for a quiet little sit-down dinner, but she was displeased by her daughter's behavior. Muffy had come down with the flu and was upstairs in her bedroom. Constance, who would have preferred to have shown her daughter off, was highly displeased.

John Bradford, down at the other end of the long dining room table, was studying his wife. Something wasn't right about this engagement and wedding. Sean and Muffy. The first time he'd seen them together, he'd thought they looked like a protective older brother with his delicate little sister. Perhaps that was what Muffy wanted—and he had felt old and tired that day, as well, realizing he'd abdicated the role of father in so many ways.

Maybe it was just too late.

He glanced up, watching Constance at the other end of the table. The chandelier gleamed softly above, the wallpaper was rich and opulent, a soft peach color. Silver clinked against china, and the crystal sparkled.

"Constance? I'm going to check on Muffy."

"I'm sure she's all right, dear. She's probably sleeping."

He felt a flash of rage. "I'll go up just the same."

John walked slowly up the huge staircase, then down the long hall to his daughter's bedroom door.

As he was about to knock, he heard the first sob. It was a small, stifled sound, and it tore at his heart.

He stood in the hallway, staring at the door.

Muffy had been an extremely private child, and she hadn't changed. If he walked in on her now, it would be embarrassing for her. Almost painful.

Confused, he stepped silently away from the door.

MUFFY TRIED to stop the next sob by holding her hand over her mouth, but it exploded out on her. She turned her head into the pillow and began to cry.

Where was Phillip when she needed him? She had to talk to him now.

Her hand strayed downward, until it rested protectively over her stomach. She'd first suspected when she'd been so tired in the mornings. Then the nausea. Thank God her mother rarely came into her room, for there was no way of explaining this to her without Constance becoming enraged. All of her plans would be spoiled, all her desires thwarted, if she knew her perfect daughter was almost three months pregnant with Phillip's baby.

Muffy's eyes filled with tears again. So frightened, so terribly scared, and there was absolutely no one she could confide in. No one she wanted to tell.

Except Phillip.

"WHAT DO YOU mean I can't leave tomorrow! I have to be in Los Angeles the evening of the seventeenth!" Phillip faced three of the security guards in their gray suit pants, white shirts and navy blazers.

"It's orders. Colonel Brimley has to open the bidding, and he's snowed in up in New Hampshire."

"Look," Phillip said quietly. "You cannot keep me here against my will. I'm leaving."

"Phil, be reasonable. We're miles from the nearest pay phone. This location was chosen because of its isolation. You couldn't make it to the airport in time if you started walking right now."

"All right. All right." All he could think about was Muffy. "There has to be a suitable compromise."

"There isn't one. There's only this. You can't leave this farm-house until the bidding commences, and it won't start unless Brimley gets to Washington."

There was no way out. The sky had been slate gray and ominous earlier this evening, and now a heavy rain was falling. You could barely see outside the windows. The news had predicted sleet later on, and possibly snow.

He was trapped.

"When do they think Brimley will make it down?" he asked. If Muffy cracks, if Constance finds out...

"Things are looking good for the next day or so. You won't be that late.

MUFFY'S HANDS were like ice. The wedding was tomorrow and still there was no sign of Phillip.

"Where is he?" she whispered as Sean led her to a corner of the spacious Gold Room.

"I don't know. Something must have come up at Stealthco. But I'm sure he'll be here in time for the wedding."

"Sean, what do we do if he's not here?"

She was looking at him as if he had the answers to the world's problems tattooed on his forehead. He loved Phillip like a brother, but Sean couldn't help contrasting Muffy with Alex.

He saw her the moment she walked into the ballroom. Just like that first night in her office, she took his breath away.

Her black dress was fitted, skimming her curves. He liked the style. A woman had to be truly striking to wear a dress like that. She'd coiled her hair on top of her head. It was a striking foil to her bone structure, the high cheekbones and square, strong jaw.

He looked to his heart's content. But he couldn't bring himself to meet her gaze. She trusted him. And he'd betrayed that trust.

"Sean. Sean!" The whisper had a tinge of desperation. "My mother's coming this way!"

As much as he longed to go to Alex and tell her the truth, he couldn't. Not until Phillip arrived. If he was totally honest with himself, he'd admit he was just as nervous as Muffy was. The wedding was tomorrow at three in the afternoon. There were eight hundred people invited, the cream of both New York and Los Angeles society. The rich and famous and powerful.

But just what was he going to do, if Phillip didn't show up before the minister asked him if he was going to have and to hold, love and cherish, till death do us part?

Nothing like making a total ass out of yourself in front of a cast of thousands.

"Hello, Sean."

Constance. Muffy was clinging to his arm as if it were a life-line.

"Hello, Constance."

"Ready for tomorrow?"

She looked so pleased with herself. He wanted to throttle her. But he smiled instead.

"As ready as I'll ever be."

"You won't change your mind about the morning suit?" Typical Constance, still trying to get her way.

"No." Even if he felt like a clown, he didn't have to look like one.

"Well, I'll leave the two of you to mingle, and I'll see you tomorrow, Sean."

Yes, indeedy.

He glanced up and caught Alex looking at him. Their eyes locked and held until a blush rose in her face and she looked away, her eyes dark and glistening.

And Sean wondered, for the first time in his life, if he'd found the deal he just couldn't make.

ALEX GLANCED away, furious with herself that he'd caught her looking at him.

And, ignoring all protocol when it came to overseeing a party of this importance, she walked over to the bar where Tony was mixing drinks.

"Perrier with a twist, Alex?"

"Something stronger."

The drink he handed her was long, cool and tropical—with a lethal kick to it and a tiny paper umbrella. Trust Tony to have a sense of humor.

"This'll do it." She took a long swig out of the tall, frosted glass as she started across the room.

What a world.

Now, in one of those romance novels where this would have been a marriage of convenience, she would know exactly what to do. Cool and regal, lightning-fast with the witty comeback, she would be parrying conversational sparklers with her hero, making him realize there was only one woman in the world he could ever love.

But the way these things really happened found Sean and

Muffy in the center of the room, surrounded by throngs of well-wishers, while she was on the sidelines, drinking a tropical bomb.

That about sums things up.

She glanced at her watch. Only an hour to go, and then she could legitimately leave. And leave she would. She was spending the night in her room at the hotel. The suit she was wearing to the wedding was already hanging in the closet.

Then from the group surrounding the engaged couple a small commotion arose. Alex almost choked on her paper umbrella when she saw Sean sweep Muffy up into his arms. The girl's head was hanging limp, her color was bad, and her mother was furious.

And he cut a wide swathe through the crowd, straight toward her.

"Where can she lie down?"

"Take her to my room."

And with Constance following them like a shark who smelled blood, Alex led the way to the elevator.

Once Muffy was on Alex's bed, Sean sitting beside her, Constance exploded.

"Look what she's doing to me! What is wrong with her. This is the wedding every girl dreams of having, and she faints at her own party!"

Alex realized that if Constance Bradford's facade was starting to crumble, they were all in big trouble.

"Mrs. Bradford, why don't you go downstairs and see to your guests? Sean, why don't you go with her?"

As she turned to him, she murmured, "Get her out of here."

Sean looked worried. "One of the guests is a doctor. I'll send him up."

The girl was sitting up in bed sipping 7-Up when the doctor arrived.

Alex moved away from the bed to give them privacy, but she could hear bits of the conversation.

"Anything you could have been allergic to?"

"No."

"Have you fainted before?"

"No."

Muffy looked so pathetic in her crumpled pink party dress that Alex's heart went out to her. She wasn't even given the satisfaction of hating the other woman.

And then, the million dollar question.

"Could you be pregnant?" the doctor asked gently.

Muffy paused, then covered her face and whispered, "Please don't tell my mother."

And Alex felt the blood leave her face in a rush as it began to roar in her ears. She lowered her shaking body into a chair.

Pregnant?

"How far along are you?"

"Almost four months."

Three months. You met Sean three months ago. They must have announced their engagement the second she missed her period.

"Have you been eating well, getting enough rest?"

Muffy started to cry. "I'm just so scared."

"And the father? Is he—" And here the doctor hesitated. "Is he the sort of man who's going to be there for you?"

"Oh, yes." Muffy hiccuped. "He's so wonderful, so loyal—" And dissolved into another bout of sobbing.

Alex felt her eyes filling. She remembered Sean's words. *And if I told you it had everything to do with loyalty and nothing to do with love—*

"Can you stay with her?"

Alex blinked. The doctor was speaking to her.

"Of course." No matter what she was feeling, she could not possibly take it out on Muffy.

"I want her to rest until the wedding." He lowered his voice. "She's a high-strung little thing, and there's a very real possibility she could lose the baby. Am I making myself clear?"

Alex nodded.

"Here's my number. I'm going downstairs to tell Constance her daughter is all right. I'll be at the wedding tomorrow. Don't hesitate to call me if you need help. I don't care what time it is."

"Thank you."

He left, then Alex went and sat in the overstuffed chair next to the bed and watched Muffy sleep.

Now, this is more like one of those novels. Jilted heroine with the other woman who's pregnant and could lose the baby if she doesn't stay quiet. If I was a heroine worth my salt, she'd be up doing the mambo—

But she couldn't. Even the joke fell flat in her mind.

Muffy was just too helpless.

But there's another person involved in this.

Before the night was over, she was going to pay Sean Lawton a little visit.

And tell him exactly what she thought of him.

"SEAN? ALEX. Could I come up and see you for just a second."

"Of course."

Muffy had slept for almost an hour. When she woke, she had sworn Alex to secrecy.

With Marcy watching Muffy, Alex took the elevator up to the Presidential Suite.

Sean was waiting for her.

"How's Muffy?"

At least he was concerned about her.

"Fine. I just—" She took a deep breath. "I just want you to know that she told me everything. I know what's going on now."

"You do?" He seemed incredulous.

"Yes. Why you're going ahead with the wedding. You're nothing if not loyal, Sean."

"Alex." His eyes darkened, then before she knew what was happening, he'd pulled her into his arms.

"I thought I'd lost you. I couldn't tell you what was going on. You understand that now, don't you? But now we can be together."

Her brain was shutting down, but she had just enough sanity left to dig the stiletto heel of her black pump into his foot.

"Ahhh!"

That got his attention.

He released her, then grabbed his foot and began hopping around the room, his face a grimace of pain.

"Pig with a capital P!" she shouted. Then, because this man had succeeded in driving her completely out of her mind, she pushed him over onto the big bed, watching him land with a resounding thwack.

"Just what in God's name did you think I was going to do when I found out?"

"Alex, I realize it was a bit of deception, but—"

"Oh, no, just schmooze me along, Alex the idiot. You let me think we had some kind of future together, when all the time you knew—"

"Of course, I knew. I wouldn't have done it if I hadn't known—"

"Answer me this, then, smart guy. Where are we all going to live? In your house in Malibu?"

"Alex, what are you—"

"I may be naive, but I'm not stupid! What were you doing, lining me up so you could be assured of having a continual good time in bed?"

"Alex, you don't understand—"

"No, you don't understand." Now, hating herself for showing any vulnerability, she started to cry. "I trusted you. I believed in you, and I thought we had something special. And I loved you, you big liar."

"Alex—"

"Don't touch me. I'm leaving now. I'm walking out that door and after this wedding is over, I never, ever want to see you again!"

She'd done it, pushed him past the brink. His eyes had darkened, his jaw was tightening.

"So you don't want to hear my side of it?"

"I wasn't aware that pigs could talk."

"Get out."

"With pleasure!"

But Alex was only halfway down to her floor in the elevator when she burst into tears.

"YOU CAN GO now, Phil. Colonel Brimley flew into Washington this morning and opened the bidding."

"It's too late." Phillip was sitting at the table, nursing the last of a bottle of good Scotch. He'd blown it. He wasn't sure what Sean and Muffy were going to do, but he knew he'd failed her.

He glanced at his watch. Almost noon. The wedding began at three. He'd never make it in three hours.

"Well, if you get off your butt and stop feeling sorry for yourself, you can just make it. The time change gives you six hours to get there. Add to that the company jet and a helicopter ride in from LAX."

Slowly, ever so carefully, he lifted his head.

"You're kidding."

"Nope. I explained that you were late to your own wedding. The company wants to bend over backward for you."

"Oh my God! I've got to pack. Where's my suit?"

"No time. Here's your jacket. Bill, Stan, get him to the jet. And sober him up on the way!"

A few hours later Phillip was over Texas when it occurred to him to call Sean.

"Is there a phone on this thing?"

"Sure." Stan and Bill exchanged looks. They hadn't exactly sobered Phillip up.

"Would one of you dial L.A. information for me? The—the Biltmore, that's it."

There was no answer in Sean's suite.

"Hey, Phil, buddy, are you sure there's a wedding going on at all, or was it just some ruse to ditch that lousy weather and head for the coast?" asked Stan.

"No. I'm not making this up. I've got to get hold of Sean."

Stan looked at Bill. Bill scratched his head.

"Maybe the hotel director."

They dialed again and reached the front desk. Bill put his hand over the receiver.

"How about the catering office, Phil? Maybe someone there can reach him."

"Catering offices, the Biltmore. Can I help you?" Marcy didn't mind slipping into her old role on a Saturday.

"Who is this? What? Wait, talk slower, this is kind of— What! Phil, slow down, I can't understand you."

Within minutes, Marcy knew the entire story.

"Yes. Yes, I'll get the message to Sean. That's right, you can land on the hotel helipad. I'll be up there waiting for you...."

"SHE'S HYSTERICAL, Ms. Michaels, you've got to help her."

"Don't tell her mother. I'll take care of it."

The bridesmaid looked really concerned, and Alex swiftly followed her to Muffy's room.

She was sitting on a small stool, sobbing.

"Muffy," Alex said softly, glancing around to be sure no one was within earshot. "Think of the baby."

Muffy grabbed both her hands. Her eyes were rimmed in pink. "I can't do this. I can't go out there in front of all those people. I don't know what I'm going to do."

"Muffy, you've got to get a hold of yourself—"

"No, you don't understand. I can't marry Sean. There's someone else."

And Alex, holding Muffy's hands and looking at this gentle little creature, suddenly knew exactly how Scarlett had felt at Melanie's deathbed.

"Muffy, no. Believe me, there isn't."

"There is! Oh, I know Sean has been strong for me and tried to make everything all right, but I don't know what he's going to do now! He didn't count on anything happening this way."

Muffy started to sob again as two of her bridesmaids crowded closer, murmuring words of comfort.

"I can't marry Sean. I don't love him, I—"

A total, absolute silence descended in the dressing room, and Alex knew, without looking up, that Constance Bradford had come in the door.

"Get out. Everyone get out." Her tone was clipped, and the bridesmaids scattered, their slippered feet pattering over the carpet as in a hasty rendition of Swan Lake.

"That means you, too, Alex."

Alex stood, Muffy still clinging to her hand.

"No."

"Get out right this minute or I'll have you fired. And you, get up." Constance grabbed Muffy's elbow and yanked her to her feet, causing her to let go of Alex's hand. "If you think you're going to ruin everything, young lady, just be sure you're willing to pay the price. I will make your life a living hell if you don't marry Sean Lawton!"

"I can't, I don't love him, I love—"

The hand came up before Alex could do anything about it, and Constance's palm cracked across Muffy's fragile cheekbone. She fell awkwardly, and Alex was down beside her in an instant.

"Get her dressed. Right now. I'm standing here until she walks out that door."

And Alex, knowing she was trapped with one sick cookie, reached for the lace confection that was Muffy's bridal gown. The three seamstresses had been called in, and those final stitches had ensured a perfect fit. Luckily, the veil covered Muffy's face so no one could see the redness of her eyes.

"Well, Alex, we have a wedding to run, don't we?" Constance's blue eyes were cold. It was no-holds-barred now that Alex had seen her slap Muffy.

"I'm not leaving her alone with you." Alex could feel Muffy trembling behind her.

"That's fine with me. Muffy's not going to do anything foolish now, are you, dear?"

"No." The one word was barely a whisper.

And at that moment, Alex knew Muffy had given up.

IT HAD BEGUN. The wedding of the year.

The trumpets had sounded, the procession was underway. Everything was going perfectly, and two people who didn't love each other were going to be joined together forever in holy matrimony.

Don't think about it, she instructed herself.

She refused to look up at the altar.

It was then, in the midst of the group leading the Renaissance procession, that she saw Marcy in full costume.

Sean saw Marcy at almost the same time, and his first reaction was surprise. Was Marcy supposed to be in the parade? She was trying to catch his attention.

Their eyes met. She glanced down.

He saw a small scrap of paper in her hand. The relief he felt was overwhelming.

And as Marcy passed Sean, she slipped him the note, smiled to a shocked Constance in the front row and skipped merrily on her way.

Sean knew Constance hadn't seen the exchange. He glanced down at the note in his palm, read it.

Hang in there, Father Lawton. The cavalry is coming!

And he smiled.

HE'S SMILING. How dare he? thought Alex.

She was as close to berserk as she'd ever been in her life, with the exception of last night in Sean's suite. What was Marcy doing in the Renaissance parade? Why was Sean grinning like a real groom? And Muffy...

As if on cue, the harpist began to play the familiar strains of the "Wedding March."

I can't bear it.

But she couldn't tear herself away. Muffy looked ethereal, a vision in lace, so delicate and fragile.

Sean, the rat, didn't look half bad in his tuxedo.

The crowd was silent. This was what they had come for. This

was the event of the Christmas season, and they were going to relish every second of it.

This is the worst day of the rest of my life.

"Dearly beloved, we are gathered here today..."

Alex rarely cried at weddings, but she could already feel tears gathering in her eyes.

What a mess. She doesn't love Sean; he doesn't love her, I still love him, and who knows if he still loves me or who in God's name loves Muffy....

Definitely the wedding of the year.

"Do you, Elizabeth Anne Bradford, take this man to be your lawfully wedded husband, for better or worse, in sickness and in health..."

Muffy's quiet "I do" was barely audible.

"Do you, Sean Lawton—"

Alex bit her lip, hard, but the tears started to roll down her cheeks.

"—to be your lawfully wedded wife—"

Alex swiped unobtrusively at her eyes.

"—as long as you both shall live?"

"I—"

Alex glanced up, her eyes wide, as she realized Sean was hesitating.

"I—" he suddenly turned to face the crowd, Muffy leaning heavily against him.

"I—want you all to know there's been a slight change of plans. I'm not the groom—he'll be arriving shortly. But in the meantime, I'd like to tell you about a boy and a girl who grew up together and faced the most unbelievable odds to be together."

Now, utter pandemonium broke out, excited murmurs were racing across the crowd. Alex, in total shock, still craned her neck to see the one face she couldn't wait to get a look at.

Constance Bradford was turning a lovely shade of purple.

Sean continued, his voice low and soothing.

"She was all of twelve years old when she told me she wanted to spend the rest of her life with this man. He fell in love with her at the same time, with her gentleness, her beauty..."

Sean went on to tell the rapt crowd the details of Muffy and Phillip's love story.

"...And so I agreed to the deception, knowing that these two wanted to build a life together, that they shared the kind of love that comes along only once in a lifetime...what I didn't count on was falling in love, myself.''

Alex couldn't meet his eyes. Her vision was blurring, her eyes were full of tears. How could she have ever doubted this man? Here he was, telling hundreds of people that he loved her.

"It was the most painful thing I have ever experienced, having to hurt the woman I love....''

The woman I love.

Alex knew she was a goner.

"So, to wind this all up, Phillip should be here any minute, and when he does arrive—''

"No!''

Constance Bradford finally broke, and it was a glorious sight. She rushed to the altar and grabbed Sean's other arm.

"Stop it! Stop it! You're going to marry my daughter! She doesn't love that spineless—''

"Yes, I do.''

Alex could have wept at the rapturous look on Muffy's face.

"You can't do this to me!'' Constance screamed. At that exact moment, a member of the press who had sneaked in dressed as a minstrel snapped several shots.

And Alex didn't even try to confiscate the camera.

When the crowd roared, Alex brought her attention back to the front of the ballroom, where Sean was stuffing a handkerchief tightly in Constance's mouth. Then he marched her back to her husband's side.

"John,'' he said, "please restrain her.''

"I've been trying to for years.''

That got the biggest laugh of all.

IT WAS THE strangest wedding Alex had ever attended. While she stood in the back of the ballroom watching total pandemonium reign, the servers, at Sean's request, began bringing the guests small plates of canapés and glasses of punch. The crowd was almost back under control until Muffy screamed, "Phillip!''

As she picked up the long bridal skirt and train with one hand and began to run toward her handsome groom, her face lit up with the purest of emotions, a love so overwhelming it almost hurt to look at her face.

Muffy was beautiful.

The crowd broke into spontaneous applause as she fell into his arms and burst into tears.

Just when the real wedding was about to get underway, someone yelled, "Hey, Sean, is she here?"

Alex, knowing exactly who this bozo was talking about, glanced at the nearest door. Even though two tall Renaissance men stood guard, she was sure they'd let her out.

Her feet started to move before she gave the matter coherent thought, but Sean was faster.

When he swept her up into his arms, she seriously thought about killing him.

"Put me down," she whispered furiously.

"I'm not letting you go again."

"Down. Now. I mean it, Sean. I'll punch you."

"I love you."

Sean set Alex down in front of eight hundred people, and she had no choice but to behave herself.

"Are you going to make it a double wedding?" the same bozo called out of the crowd.

"I haven't even asked her," Sean called back. Alex could see that Sean was feeling cocky.

"Why don't you ask her?" the man called out.

Then all she could see were Sean's blue-gray eyes, and suddenly the cockiness was replaced by the slightest vulnerability.

She stood perfectly still, knowing this was another moment she would remember for the rest of her life.

He fumbled—Sean fumbled!—in his pocket and brought out a small velvet box.

"Whatever it takes, Alex. Down on my knees, whatever you want. Forgive me for what I did, but I couldn't bear the thought of you with another man. I love you, and I want you in my life. Will you marry me, Alexandra?"

And she knew then that she would, if only to hear her name every day, just the way he said it.

When it was this right, it was so easy.

But she couldn't resist.

"Well..."

"Alex."

How she loved to torment this man.

"Yes."

There was another burst of applause when he slipped the diamond ring on her finger. And they both turned around just in time to see Phillip's incredulous face, hear "A baby?" come out of his mouth in a strangled voice and watch as he crumpled to the floor of the Crystal Ballroom in a dead faint.

"A FABULOUS WEDDING, dear. My Christie is getting married next June, and I'm going to make an appointment with you on Monday!"

"I don't know when I've had a better time at a wedding, Alex. You really outdid yourself."

Alex smiled as she felt a familiar arm curl around her waist.

"You've been praised enough. Dance with me."

"Whatever you say, Sean."

"Marcy and Brian certainly seem to have hit it off," she said, looking up at him.

"He likes her, Renaissance dress and all." Sean tightened his grip on her ever so slightly, then said softly, "I thought we could catch an evening flight to Vegas, get married and join Phil and Muffy on the yacht. How does the Caribbean sound to you?"

"What? No formal wedding?"

He rolled his eyes in disgust, and she burst out laughing.

"Alex, we could be married by midnight."

"Boy, you sure are in a hurry. What about my courtship? My engagement party?"

"Alex." The look in his eyes was deadly serious. "I don't want to wait any longer."

"I'm not asking you to wait." She held him closer. "What do you say we finish this dance then go get married?"

They made it to Las Vegas that very night, married joyfully, then flew to join Phillip and Muffy on the yacht, which Sean promptly rechristened Alexandra the Great.

SEIZE THE FIRE

Elda Minger

What am I doing here?

Morgan had asked himself the question countless times during the last two hours.

It's too good a part to pass up.

No, he corrected. *You wanted to see her again.*

Everything always came back to Delia. As he sipped his drink and eyed the crowded room, he studied her. Reality was so much better than all the nights he'd dreamed of her.

THE SURROUNDING peace and serenity couldn't have been more at odds with the way Delia felt.

She stood on the balcony of her father's Malibu beach house watching the gentle ebb and flow of the Pacific under a full moon.

Whatever had possessed her to think of Morgan Buckmaster for the part?

She tightened her fingers on the railing as she heard the glass door behind her slide open.

"I thought I'd find you out here."

Delia kept her back to him. Morgan Buckmaster was an expert at searching people's faces to discover the emotions that played across their features. The gift of an actor.

"You've become a beautiful woman, Delia."

"Thank you." She swallowed against the tightness in her throat. "I'm going to get something to drink. Would you like anything?" She was halfway across the large balcony when he spoke.

"You aren't afraid of me, are you?" There was a strange quality to his voice.

Delia turned mid-step, trying to control escalating emotions. "No," she stated flatly.

"Good." Morgan patted the rail. "Come back for a minute. Then, I promise you, we'll go inside."

Delia tensed as she felt his hand close over hers. Her stomach knotted in anticipation of promised pleasures. Morgan slowly raised her hand to his lips. They felt warm against the inside of her wrist. She glanced up. Once his gaze caught hers, she couldn't look away. The sensuous dark eyes she'd seen so many times in her dreams were studying her. Delia wanted to break free, but she couldn't.

"You have the softest skin," he murmured. "Eyes as blue as periwinkles," he breathed. "And lips as red—" his mouth was a heartbeat away from hers "—as a rose."

His lips touched hers gently, sensually. They were warm and firm. Experienced. Delia's legs started to shake as Morgan moved his hands over her bare back, and a heated weakness suffused her body. Delia longed to give in to pure sensation, letting Morgan take her higher and higher.

His hands touched her silk-covered hips and pulled her against him tightly, making her aware of his hard masculine strength, the clean scent of his cologne, the warmth of his body.

His lips teased hers apart, deepening the kiss, making her aware of his desire. She felt his tongue move inside her mouth, urging her response, making her want him. But she couldn't. Not this time. Not again.

Delia tried to wrench herself away from his grasp, but his fingers laced through her hair, coerced her to turn her face to his and bend her head back so his lips could kiss her neck and move lower still, to the slight shadow between her breasts.

Somewhere, as if in a very distant dream, she heard a deep voice boom out, "Come on. We're ready to cut the cake!"

Morgan finally released her. He was breathing deeply, his dark eyes burning as if lit by an inner fire, watching her.

She turned away from him, furious that he still affected her as no other man could. She ran to the sliding door, shutting it sharply behind her.

Her father's guests were by the large oak buffet table where a tiered cake glittered with sparklers. Though the dinner party had been small, the living room seemed quite crowded. All the guests were gathered around James Wilde, standing over his seventieth birthday cake.

"There you are!" He was clearly glad to see his daughter.

Delia smiled, her expression softening as she looked up at her father. James Wilde was a big bear of a man with a heart as light as a child's. When Delia had been small, she had worshiped him

Now, many years later, she still loved him with all the intensity she'd felt as a little girl.

Now she stood at his side. "Do you want me to help you?" she asked softly.

He shook his head, frowning. "Mary's getting out the champagne. Why don't you help her?"

Though Delia had resented Mary as a child, as a woman of twenty-eight she could understand that her stepmother suited her father. Their love was rare and wonderful to watch.

Delia walked into the kitchen.

"Has James talked to Morgan about the film?" Mary asked.

Delia shook her head.

Mary smiled. "James likes him. I can tell. I—"

"Mary, we're waiting!" There was a hint of humor in her husband's voice.

"I'm coming," she called, then said to Delia, "You'll have to talk to Morgan soon."

"I know. I will." As soon as Mary left, Delia leaned back against the kitchen counter.

Was it only three months ago that she'd thought everything in her world secure? Now the only thing that mattered was her father. And getting the film done.

She picked up two more bottles of champagne and walked into the crowded living room.

James had made it the favorite area of the beach house. It was expensively informal, with plush sand-colored carpeting and a west wall composed entirely of windows. The view of the ever-changing Pacific was magnificent. On the mantel rested three Oscars, silent testimony to James's acting career. Warm cream walls were almost entirely covered with photos. Delia as a child, James and Mary on the ranch, James with actors and directors from all over the world. An entire life was captured on those walls.

The cake had been cut. James was seated on a large leather sofa with Mary, opening presents. His delighted laughter filled the room and tore at Delia's heart. She stared at her father, her vision blurring.

"Do you need any help?"

Her eyes slowly focused on Morgan's dark face. He used to know her emotions so well. How much had he seen revealed in her face?

"Here." She thrust the two bottles she was holding toward
him. "Let's get the champagne out before it gets warm."

A short while later Delia found herself on the other end of the
sofa with Morgan. "What is it you do, Delia, besides lie out on
that balcony and sunbathe?" The remark could have been cruel,
but his tone wasn't.

Delia yearned to share her emotions with him—her excitement
and fear over her part in the film, her feelings about her father.
But her cautious side remembered emotional pain at his hands. *I
live from day to day and try to believe life will get better.*

"I'm a director," she said.

His dark eyes widened a fraction. "Everyone in Hollywood
wants to direct. What is it you really do?"

His refusal to take her seriously made her see red. Without a
word, she stood up and walked away.

She spent the rest of the evening by her father's side, surrounded by his old friends. But later on he approached her again.

"Did I offend you?" he asked.

"No," she answered coldly.

"How many films have you directed?" He seemed interested.

"Three."

"Big budget, were they?"

"Listen, you—"

But she was interrupted as Bob Rosenthal swept her into a hug.
"Lovely. The image of your mother," he said.

Delia was uncomfortably aware of Morgan watching the entire
exchange, as Bob gave her a quick kiss on the forehead, then
turned his attention to Morgan.

"Good evening, Mr. Buckmaster. Have you decided whether
or not you're signing on?" The producer's tone was friendly, yet
firm.

Morgan's dark glance was impassive. "I think so. I've always
wanted to work with James Wilde, and the script is brilliant."

Bob was pleased. "Then you'll be down at my office on Monday?"

Morgan nodded. "Who's directing?"

Bob seemed surprised. "Didn't James tell you? Delia is directing."

With confirmation of his suspicions, the skin around Morgan's
mouth whitened, and a muscle tightened in his jaw.

Yet he had too much business sense to lose his temper in front of Bob. He shook the man's outstretched hand. "I'll see you on Monday. And thank you."

He caught her eye. "Delia, could I talk to you for a moment?"

She was about to refuse when his fingers closed over her wrist. She nodded and allowed him to pull her gently away from Bob.

Once they were out on the balcony, Morgan got straight to the point.

"Why the hell are you directing this picture?"

"It's a major step in my career," she replied flippantly. "Surely you can understand that?"

"Isn't it really just a matter of letting Daddy buy you a film?" His tone was meant to wound.

Delia couldn't see for a moment, could hardly breathe, her anger at Morgan was so intense.

She clenched her hands into fists. And yet, she could see his point. The three films she'd directed so far had been low budget—and not very well distributed. She doubted Morgan would have seen them in England. And clearly she wouldn't have been given this opportunity if she wasn't James Wilde's daughter.

But wasn't that why she was doing this film?

"I guess it's just a matter of take it or leave it, isn't it?" Though she hated to do this to James, she wanted Morgan's final decision before the night was over.

"I'll see you tomorrow at noon," he said abruptly. "At my house for lunch. We'll discuss this...fiasco when you get there." And without a backward glance he slammed the glass door shut behind him.

DELIA WAS almost asleep on the chaise longue when Mary stepped out on the balcony.

"James is fine," she said. "I've got him settled for the evening." She sat down. "Thank you, Delia."

"For what?" She sat up.

"For the party. For finding the script, and all your endless talks with Bob. For making sure the entire film will come together." She paused. "For facing Morgan again."

Delia sighed. "I was surprised he accepted your invitation." She avoided Mary's eyes. "I'm going to have nothing but trouble with him." Delia suddenly realized one of the reasons she loved

Mary so much was because you could tell her anything and she would never judge you.

"I thought as much," the older woman replied. "He was watching you throughout the party."

Delia nodded. "Oh, he's quite hot on getting me back in bed again. He just doesn't think I can direct worth a damn."

"He'd be a fool to refuse the part. It's better than anything he's done in several years. Working with an actor like James will give him a chance to stretch himself."

Delia nodded. She just wasn't sure whether she wanted Morgan in the film for her father or for herself.

Mary stood, then leaned over to give Delia a quick kiss. "Get to bed soon, all right?"

"I will." There was something in her stepmother's expression that made Delia want to comfort her. She stood up quickly, put her arms around Mary and hugged her tightly.

As Mary slid the glass door open, Delia walked over to the rail.

Three months ago Dr. Taylor had found the tumors. James had gone into surgery immediately. They had thought the worst was over, but the malignancy had spread. Now it was only a matter of time.

So Delia had moved out of her town house and come back to her father's home, and all the while she'd thought about what would make the rest of her father's life as full as possible. And her idea for his final film was born.

She was no stranger to the intricate world of filmmaking. It was part of the legacy James had given her, and that was why she had planned the film as carefully as if she had been executing a battle. From the first call to her godfather, Bob Rosenthal, to finding the perfect script, to the party tonight. She had overseen it all.

DELIA believed nothing Morgan could do would unnerve her as much as their encounter on the balcony. But she was wrong.

He answered the door in his swimming trunks, his muscular body bronzed and dripping with water. "Shall we go into the living room?" he asked smoothly, taking her arm before she could say a word.

His living room turned out to be a small redwood deck with

separate levels. Bright tubs of herbs and flowering plants spilled their color and pungent fragrances into the spicy salt air. The steps led straight down to white sand and roaring waves.

Delia forgot her previous unease. "How lovely." She walked to the edge of the deck.

"I like it," Morgan replied, watching her.

"You spend a lot of time out here," she said, her eyes moving over his deeply tanned body.

He nodded. "When I first moved out here, it seemed like endless summer."

"I remember the weather in London." She immediately regretted the words.

His expression changed. "This is nothing like London."

She knew he wasn't just talking about the weather.

"Do you own this house?" she asked.

"I always lease...with an option to buy."

How like him, Delia thought. The perpetual gypsy.

"Can I help you with lunch?"

He shook his head. "Just sit right here." He led her to a small wooden picnic table with benches, then disappeared inside.

What kind of man had Morgan become? Before she could explore this thought further, Morgan reappeared.

"Lunch is served," he announced. He set a large blue-and-white ceramic bowl on the table, then returned to the interior of the house.

Delia recognized the earthy smell of pesto. It carried her back to other times, to their small kitchen in London. She had loved making this dish for Morgan.

Her thoughts were broken as he returned with a bottle of white wine and a bowl of grated Parmesan cheese.

He sat opposite her and proceeded to dish the pasta out into their bowls. Then he uncorked the wine.

There was something unbearably intimate about eating with Morgan again, even if they did eat in silence.

Then Morgan fetched another large bowl and proceeded to dish salad onto their plates.

It was delicious. He certainly hadn't been starving without her.

She watched as Morgan cleared away the dishes, then set out a small coffeepot. Pouring a tiny amount of coffee into a bowl, he mixed sugar with it until it created a thick, light brown paste. He spooned a little into one cup, then looked at her.

"Do you still take lots of sugar?" he asked.

He remembered. She was ridiculously, childishly pleased.

"Yes. It smells wonderful." She indicated the coffeepot in front of him.

"It's my one indulgence. There's a shop on Rodeo Drive where I buy Italian coffee." He poured the dark, fragrant liquid into both their cups. "It's expensive, but I have to have it."

The scent of espresso filled the air as Delia lifted the cup to her lips. If she closed her eyes, she could easily imagine herself back in Italy with Morgan.

Resolutely, she kept her eyes open. They had finished their meal, and Delia remembered the original purpose of her visit. *He's testing you.* She had to be on her guard.

"Let's sit down by the steps," he said.

As she followed him, the question that had nagged at her all afternoon surfaced with sudden clarity. Could she ever trust him, or was he acting with her again? How could she be sure? Could she work with a man she had once loved so intensely?

As if reading her mind, he said, "It won't be easy. You know it's very unusual for a director your age to be in charge of a film like this."

Delia stiffened. She knew Morgan too well.

"Yes, it is. I would never have gotten it if it wasn't for my father," she admitted quietly.

"At least you're honest. Are you scared?" Morgan had a talent for getting straight to the heart of the matter.

Delia thought quickly of her father, of the unguarded moments when she had glimpsed the pain in his face, the acceptance in his eyes. That was courage.

"No. Not of the movie."

"What are you scared of?"

She studied his face—the black eyes, chiseled facial structure, the strong jaw.

"Sometimes I think—" She stopped and set her coffee cup down. "I'm afraid of you."

His expression remained impassive.

"Is there another man in your life?"

"No. Only my father."

His arm slipped around her shoulders, his bare chest warm against her side. Delia knew he was going to kiss her. And she wanted him to.

"I've never stopped wanting you." His breath tickled her ear.

She felt sudden tears burn her eyes. *Wanting isn't the same as loving.*

"Why did you leave?"

Of all the questions Morgan could have asked her, this was not one of them.

Tears filled her eyes. She bowed her head and pulled her knees up against her face. Morgan let her sit like that for a long time. He stroked her hair, the back of her neck, her narrow shoulders.

Finally, she lifted her head. "Morgan, if we work together, I don't want to start up our old relationship. I want you to be in the film, and so does James. But that's it. Do you understand?"

"No." His answer was barely a whisper as he cupped her chin, turning her head toward his.

She pulled away as his lips met hers, then felt his fingers tighten; then his other hand touched her cheek, cupped her face and made her meet his kiss. It was a deep kiss, long and warm, without reserve. Delia struggled slightly, but Morgan took the lead with all the intimate skill she remembered. Soon she felt herself respond.

His lips left hers for an instant, then moved to her ear, her temple, then the tip of her nose and back to her mouth. She was holding on to him as if by letting go she might spin off the deck with the force of emotion exploding inside her.

His lips moved down her neck, then to her shoulder. "So sweet," he whispered.

The respite gave her a chance to breathe again. To think. He kissed her shoulder. In another instant she knew he would claim her lips again.

"No." With sudden clarity she knew she couldn't continue to let this happen. She pushed at his chest. "Morgan, *no.*" Her voice was low and firm.

He stood up and moved away from her, but his eyes never left her face.

"What is it you want, Delia?"

You. "I want you to work on this film." She swallowed nervously. "I want our relationship to be as professional as possible. On and off the set."

He sat down a few feet away from her, then leaned back on his elbows.

"Delia," he began, his voice low and intimate, "we're good together. We respect each other. And it isn't as if we're both virgins." When she didn't answer, he continued, "I don't understand you. I know you wanted to make love a few minutes ago."

She clenched her hands into fists. He knew her so well.

"I'm leaving, Morgan."

He was standing now.

"Will you be doing the picture or not?"

He approached her, and it took every inch of her willpower not to move away.

"Why do you act this way?" His dark eyes assessed her. "You're twenty-eight years old, Delia. Surely you can't be as innocent to the ways of the world as you act." His tone was slightly mocking.

I want you to love me the way I loved you. "I want to direct this film with a minimum of complications. If you want an affair—" she prayed her voice wouldn't tremble "—then we'll wait until after filming is completed."

His dark eyes narrowed. "I see. If I run after you like a child, I get the candy stick in the end. Is that it?"

Frustrated, she walked down the deck stairs and began moving around the side of the house. Her temper had reached its boiling point. "Damn you! The script's the best you've had in ages. You'd work beautifully with my father." She took a deep breath. "What the hell do you want?"

"You."

She was almost to her car when his hand closed over her upper arm. "Delia, wait."

She stopped. She wouldn't make a scene.

"I've never felt about any woman the way I feel about you."

She looked up at his face, seeking visual confirmation that he wasn't joking. But he was serious. She barely heard his next words.

"I've never stopped wanting you, Delia." He seemed confused.

"Let me go."

"What the hell is the matter with you!"

She moved toward her car.

"You were the one who walked out on me!" His voice was angry, harsh.

She stopped, confused. He sounded like a man who had been deeply hurt. Could she believe him? "One of the Finest Actors in the Western World," *Time* had christened him. How could she be sure?

"And no one walks out on Morgan Buckmaster. Is that it?" She opened the door and slid inside. Seconds later she drove out into the stream of traffic without looking back at him.

Delia drove as far as the next curve on Pacific Coast Highway, then had to pull over. Her hands were shaking so badly she could barely grasp the wheel.

She closed her eyes. Her body was so tense it hurt. After so many years, she was still angry with Morgan. How could she possibly work with him?

But the decision had already been made. Morgan wouldn't agree to do the film after the way she had treated him. She'd have to start considering other actors. James would be disappointed. How could she have done this to her father?

When she got home, Mary and James were out on the balcony. Delia avoided both of them and went straight to her room. Once inside, she threw herself on her bed and stared at the ceiling.

How could she ever tell James? *Maybe someone else should direct the picture.* The idea came to her swiftly, but she rejected it immediately. She rolled over and shut her eyes.

It seemed like only minutes later that Mary was shaking her gently awake. "Delia, Morgan's on the phone."

She felt dull and tired as she walked into the hall and picked up the phone.

"Hello, Delia. I called to tell you that while I still don't approve of the idea of your directing, I'll take the part." He paused. "I'm only doing this because I want to work with James Wilde."

She sat down suddenly, so lost in happiness that she had to concentrate to hear the rest of what he was saying.

"One slip and I'll insist on hiring a real director, so you'd better damn well know what you're doing. Am I making myself perfectly clear?"

"Thank you, Morgan. All clear. I understand, and I'll see you on the set."

She hung up before he could say another word.

*

THE STABLE smelled of straw and liniment as Delia walked past the row of box stalls. An early morning ride was just the thing to calm her before Morgan arrived later today.

They'd spent six weeks in Los Angeles, shooting interiors. And Morgan still hadn't come close to respecting her. He did his job, but he'd made it painfully clear that he was working with James, not with her.

She'd managed to shoot extra footage of her father, especially close-ups. So far the picture seemed to have invigorated James.

All exteriors would be shot at the ranch. Delia was thankful the May weather was mild with bright, clear sunshine. So far, everything was running exactly on schedule—and to budget.

Delia paused by one stall and peeked inside. Falstaff, her father's champion quarter horse, stood solidly inside, his chestnut coat gleaming faintly in the early morning light.

"What a good boy you are," she said. "I'm taking Cinderina for a ride today, or I'd take you. But you don't really like anyone but James on your back, do you?" She produced a lump of sugar from her pocket. Falstaff had a notorious sweet tooth. She held it out to him, her palm flat, and almost laughed as his soft lips tickled over her hand. She patted him.

Within fifteen minutes she had bridled and saddled Cinderina and was swinging up into the saddle when she heard a familiar voice.

"Cordelia Wilde, what's bothering you this early in the morning?" Tom Donahue, stable manager, short and wiry as a bantam rooster, came sauntering out into the cool morning air.

She smiled. "I just thought I'd take a ride, that's all," she replied, imitating his Irish brogue. She loved Tom dearly.

"Don't lie to this one." He jabbed at his chest. "It's worried you are about something, and I mean to find out!"

She sat back in the saddle and laughed. Some of the tension

left her chest, and she swung down and led Cinderina over to where Tom stood.

"It's James. It's the film. Morgan Buckmaster arrives today. Oh, Tom, I'm just so scared. It never stops."

"How's the old man?" Tom asked gruffly. He was the only one, other than herself, Mary and Dr. Johnson, the local physician, who knew of James's condition.

"The same. He's perked up because of the film. I hope he'll make it through all the exteriors—they're the first we shoot."

Tom nodded.

"I want this film to be good, Tom. I don't give a damn about my own career at this point. I just want it to be good for him—" As tears clogged her throat, she stopped talking. Then she went on, "I just can't believe he's going to die. He seems so cheerful some mornings."

"What does it take to direct one of these films?" Tom asked bluntly.

Delia sighed. "You have to be on top of everything. The actors' performances are brought out by whatever I can give them to work with. I pick the order—" She started to laugh. "Oh, what the hell, I'm in charge of the whole damn thing!"

Tom smiled. "You can be pretty bossy when you mean to be, miss. I don't understand what your problem is. Surely all these people have to know it's your first time for such a big show."

"Morgan," she murmured softly—not even aware she'd spoken aloud.

"Morgan, is it? You're worried about the famous Mr. Buckmaster?"

Delia felt her face grow warm. "He took the news about my directing badly," she admitted.

"Delia, girl, the man probably doesn't even know how to sit a horse. He has his fears like anyone else. Don't you understand that?"

She shook her head. Not Morgan. She thought of him as the devil himself, scared of nothing.

"Don't shake your head at me. I know people. I'll take care of this man if he troubles you."

The image of Tom up against Morgan was so amusing, Delia bit her lip to keep from smiling. Dear Tom.

THE BREAKFAST nook was a favorite spot inside the ranch house. But Delia barely took in the cheerful blue-and-white decor as her eyes settled on Morgan and the young woman next to him.

Belinda Peters was to play James's daughter. Her romance with Morgan was one of the chief conflicts in the script. Delia had to admit she was perfect for the part. Her blond hair was shot through with streaks of pure gold. Her blue eyes were set in a face composed of startling classic features. She looked like a young Grace Kelly—the perfect foil for Morgan.

They sat close together, both dressed for traveling. Delia was suddenly aware of her own jeans and sweatshirt, and that she smelled of horse.

She bent and kissed her father. "Hello, Dad." He looked tired. "Tom and I went riding this morning." She turned to address Morgan and Belinda. "I hope you both had a good flight."

Belinda nodded, then spoke, "One of your men met us at the airport. I don't think we could have found the place otherwise." She smiled at Delia, her features perfect and glowing.

At that moment, Mary came in with a tray of waffles and a pitcher of heated syrup. A silence descended as everyone began to help themselves to food.

"I'm going to take off my boots," Delia announced, then exited gracefully.

She reached her room, surprised to find her hands trembling. *From seeing Morgan?* No. *From seeing him with Belinda?* Ah, now we're getting close. Even after weeks of filming in Los Angeles, she still wasn't sure how close they were.

So what's it to you? You don't care anymore. She ran a comb through her wind-tangled hair and pulled it back off her face with a band.

They were all still at the table when she returned.

Tom finished his waffles and pushed back his chair. "James, I'd like you to see the Arabian stallion I talked with you about. He's a mean one—but once I gentle him he'll be good to the mares, I can assure you."

Delia concentrated on cutting her waffle. Frank talk at the table about the horses was nothing new, but with Morgan here, it made her uneasy. She looked at her father.

His deep blue eyes were sparked with interest. "Mary, we'll be out by the barn." The two older men got up as Mary began to clear the table. Belinda offered to help. Delia realized she and Morgan would be the only two people left, so she started to get up.

"Delia, stay." The softness in his voice surprised her. "You've barely started to eat. Don't make me feel responsible for your skipping breakfast."

She couldn't let him know how he affected her. "It isn't you," she said hastily. "I want to go out to the barn and see the new stallion."

"Then you won't mind if I come along?"

He had trapped her. Her eyes met his for just an instant. *Touché,* she thought.

TOM JOINED them at the rail. He patted Delia on her shoulder. "Come on, miss. You're the one who always names them. Give this wild one a title worthy of all that fire!" He grinned. "Your father is absolutely delighted. I haven't seen him look so good since—" He stopped, aware of Morgan behind him.

Delia frowned. "Black as sin, wild as the wind—" She played with the words. Suddenly, she laughed. "Hades!" she shouted, turning to Tom. "Hades, king of the underworld!"

"Hades it is," Morgan repeated. He leaned on the fence. "You know, now that I'm finally here, I can understand why you missed it so much. As we were driven in, all I could see were mountains and sky. London must have been awfully confining."

"At times. At times it was..." She stopped herself. At times it had been the most exciting place on earth, but only because of Morgan. "At times it was very pleasant." Such a tame word to describe what she and Morgan had shared.

He was watching her now, like a hawk eyeing a mouse. "Your stepmother prepared the guest house for Belinda and me."

Delia felt as if all the air were being squeezed out of her lungs.

"I'll be sleeping in the main bedroom," he continued, "but Belinda said she'd take the smaller bedroom off the kitchen." When she didn't reply, he said, "We're not sleeping together, despite what you may think." And with that he turned and walked away.

Delia didn't look back. She kept her eyes on the animal in the corral. The long black mane and tail fluttered in the spring breeze;

the obsidian eyes flashed.

"I should have named you Morgan," she said.

"CUT!"

Delia bit her lip and tried to control her temper. Morgan was already creating problems. She motioned him over to her with an impatient flick of her hand.

His walk was smooth and assured. Any other actor might have looked anxious. Not Morgan. Was it her imagination or was he enjoying this?

She clenched her hands. "Dan—" she turned to her cameraman "—tell everyone to take a break. We'll be back in fifteen minutes."

They were twenty feet away from the set before she directed her first question to Morgan.

"Would you mind explaining to me just what you were doing out there?"

He seemed amused. "Just playing my part, ma'am," he drawled in his best western accent.

"Come off it, Morgan. The way you were delivering your dialogue—it wasn't the way we discussed it the other day."

The change in him was startling. "Are you saying that I don't know how to do my job?" he asked softly. But there was steel in his voice.

"No, that's not what I'm saying at all," she snapped. They were wasting valuable time. "I want you to run through the scene the way I explained it to you. You're meeting Mary Anne—Belinda—for the first time. She's the daughter of the rancher you'll eventually have to fight. But there's a tremendous sexual attraction between the two of you, and I don't think you'd be so hostile immediately. Do you understand?"

He smiled, but it didn't reach his eyes. "I've been told that I'm *very* hostile, when all I'm trying to do is convince a particular woman of how sexually attracted I am to her." The look in his eyes left no question about the identity of this particular woman.

Delia averted her gaze, hating herself for the telltale blush she could feel on her cheeks.

"Morgan, I don't care how attracted you are to *anyone*." *Especially me.* She glared up at him. "We're going back, and you're going to run through that scene the way I want you to. Is that absolutely clear?"

"And if I want to try it another way?"

"I'll listen to you, and if I think it might work, you can try. But I want the scene on film my way first! Is that clear?"

"Perfectly." His response was clipped, frigid.

"Thank you." She spun away from him and began to walk rapidly back to the set.

The rest of the day was one long disaster. Morgan did everything she requested. But it seemed as if some inner light had been extinguished. He just didn't project. Belinda was patient through take after take, but Delia could see the actress was tiring.

The sky was darkening when Dan tapped her shoulder. "I think we'd better wrap it up for the day. We won't get anything else done."

Delia nodded, then bent her head so the older man couldn't see the tears starting. *Toughen up. Fast.*

Blinking the dampness away, she faced him. "Thanks, Dan. You did a good job today."

She touched Belinda's arm gently. "Don't be late for supper. Mary's making fried chicken." She grinned. "You were terrific. It's difficult doing the same lines over and over."

Belinda looked amazed. "I....it's...thank you."

"You take direction well."

"Thanks for being so understanding. It's curious about Morgan, isn't it?"

Delia made no comment, and the young woman continued, unaware of any tension.

"I mean, his work today. Usually he's the one who pulls the rest of us up."

"You've worked with him before?" Delia said.

Belinda nodded. "It was a play in London—his first leading role. I was in the crowd scene, but all of us that could stayed for Morgan's rehearsals." Her blue eyes sparkled with the memory.

But Delia had stopped listening as her own memories rushed back. She could see Morgan's face, more boyish, more *vulnerable*, as he bounded up the stairs to their flat and caught her in a bear hug. He had told her about the play, about the part. She had gone to see every single performance—except the first. Bad luck for the actor, Morgan had reminded her. She had been so proud of him, and they had been so happy together.

"Will we start with the same scenes tomorrow?" Belinda's voice startled her back to the present.

"Yes. Yes, I think so." They were close to the ranch house now, and Delia noticed Tom by the paddock railing and turned toward Belinda.

"I'm going to talk to Tom just a minute before dinner, but you go on in."

"Thanks, Delia." Belinda started for the house.

Tom's eyes were on Hades, and Delia knew he was trying to figure out the best way to gentle the animal.

"What do you think?" she asked softly.

He grinned slowly. "I'm thinking that devil is going to be quite a handful—but I like them that way!"

"What's the best way of taming an animal like that?" Delia asked nonchalantly. "Suppose you know him pretty well, or think you do, but you still get unexpected trouble?"

Tom narrowed his eyes. "Then I'd make sure he was feeling all right, that he was healthy and rested. But if it's not health, then you have to get to work and make the animal come to you."

"But what do you do?"

"With this one? I'll start tomorrow by going to his stall and offering him a bit of sugar. If he takes it, then we can go on."

Delia felt Tom place his palm on her head and gently ruffle her hair. "Mind you, I'm not suggesting you give Morgan sugar lumps. But then, a man is a different animal altogether."

"You always know, don't you?"

He smiled. "Dan told me you and Morgan had a little talk and the rest of the afternoon was wasted. It's not that hard to figure out."

"If Morgan were a horse... What I mean is—"

"What you mean is, how the devil are you going to get the man to respect your direction."

"That's it exactly."

Tom continued to watch the stallion. "Darling, I'd have a talk with him after dinner. With a full stomach and some good company, he might see reason. Does he know about James?"

"No," Delia admitted. "I don't want anyone to know. I don't want anyone to pity him. I want him to have this last picture just the way it's always been."

"I know." Tom reached into his pocket for a lump of sugar. He took her hand and placed it in her palm.

Slowly, ever so slowly, she reached out her hand as far as she could over the fence, the sugar held flat.

The stallion began to approach, and as he did, she watched his eyes. Big and black, they registered a certain amount of fear, then curiosity.

Delia barely breathed as he came nearer; then, suddenly, she felt velvet lips move over her palm for the sugar.

Daring further, she reached up and patted the silken neck. The stallion wheeled and trotted to the center of the paddock.

Tom's expression was proud. "You're the first! You see! You help them sense you're not going to hurt them, and they respond." He gave her a brief, hard hug. "Your da will be proud." Without another word, he headed for the barn.

Delia began to walk toward the brightly lit kitchen. Approaching the back door, she almost tripped over the figure sitting on the steps.

"Oh!" Strong male hands caught her by the waist. She found herself looking down at Morgan.

He squinted up at Delia's figure in her tight jeans. She was thinner than when he'd lived with her. He didn't like the slightly worried expression behind her deep blue eyes.

He had thought it was he who was making her so tense. Tonight he knew for sure.

He had caught enough of her conversation with Tom to know she was talking about him. But he had no intention of jeopardizing the picture. They were still right on schedule.

What scared him most was that as a man who placed great value on being in control, he had never felt more out of control in his life. And vulnerable. To her. And to his own feelings.

"What are you doing here?" Delia demanded.

He reached up and took her chin in his hands. "I could ask the same of you. Why don't you watch where you're going?"

She backed away, and he dropped his hand. "Forget it, Morgan. I don't have time to play games with you." She started to brush past him.

"Delia, wait." When she didn't listen, he grabbed her and started to drag her away from the kitchen door.

She didn't make a sound, though she twisted and struggled.

Morgan didn't enjoy this. He had simply wanted to talk with her, to try to make her understand what he was feeling. He was having a hard time dealing with his part, with his work obligations. It was time they settled their relationship once and for all.

He eased her up against the barn wall. The bright light from inside spilled across her face. She looked defiant, yet vulnerable.

Morgan studied her face—remembering other places, other times—and without really knowing why, he lowered his head and touched his lips to hers.

She resisted at first. He smiled against her mouth as he felt her begin to respond. Maybe this was a good way to settle their differences. Fires as hot as those that had blazed between them couldn't be dampened. He heard himself groan with pleasure as her mouth began to open underneath his.

Her hands slowly slid up his chest and around his neck as she clasped him against her. The feel of her firm breasts against his chest was a sweet aphrodisiac. He reveled in her closeness, her scent, the feel of her slender body, her trembling warmth. When he heard a small groan escape her lips, the sound excited him further.

"Morgan, no—" Before she could say anything else, he claimed her lips again.

This time he deepened the kiss, slipped his tongue inside her mouth and explored her melting sweetness. She responded in kind.

Morgan felt his hand move, as if with a will of its own. His fingers moved down her shoulder, tenderly caressing, until they cupped her breast. He held her gently, and when she didn't resist, he began to lightly stroke the tip. It was already hard with desire.

She broke the kiss, put her hand over his. "Morgan, no!"

This time he stopped.

He looked down at her face in the dim light. "Delia, we have to talk."

She shrugged her shoulders, tried to extricate herself gingerly. He wouldn't let her go.

"What happened in London?"

Her bright blue eyes were huge pools of disbelief. "Morgan, why are you bringing this up?"

"Because I want to know." He cleared his throat. "Because I loved you, and—" *Because I still love you.*

She was staring at him now as if she thought he was crazy. Her body trembled.

"You're cold." Morgan wrapped her more tightly in his arms. "Let's go inside."

They walked into the warmth and light of the barn. Tom was locking the tack room and heading toward the kitchen. He didn't look up.

Good man, Tom, Morgan thought. He walked quickly, his arm around Delia, until they were inside a vacant stall. Closing the door, he let her go.

"Why did you leave me in London?" he asked.

She looked cornered. "Morgan, you're out of your mind! That was six years ago! Why do we have to discuss the past right now?"

"Because I want to. *Why did you leave me?*" The words came out harsher than he'd intended. She just gazed at him mutely, and for a moment he thought she was going to run into his arms and surrender. He watched as she came nearer.

"You bastard!" She swung her fist hard enough to connect with his stomach. He doubled over, grunting with surprise. Morgan tried to reach her, but Delia was a fury to be reckoned with.

"Why the hell did I leave *you?* You have nerve, Morgan! You were gone long before I *ever* left! And if you were so much 'in love' with me, why didn't you come after me?" She picked up a handful of straw and threw it at him, then flung herself against his chest.

Morgan stumbled and felt his back hit the hardwood box stall. Suddenly it seemed that everything he'd ever really wanted in life was slipping rapidly away. How could he ever make Delia understand that the intense feelings he had for her had always frightened him? He had to try. Even if, deep inside, he thought he'd fail. Because he'd never deserved the gift that was Delia.

He didn't know what to say, what to do, to re-create what they'd once had. He wanted to ask her to come back to his room and spend the rest of the evening. The rest of her life.

When he raised his gaze to hers, she was staring at him. Her voice was low, almost inaudible. Ashamed.

"I'm sorry, Morgan. I—I went crazy." She looked as if she were about to cry. "It won't happen again."

Before he could reply, she walked quickly out of the stall and down the corridor.

*

DELIA COULD feel her entire body trembling by the time she returned to her room. Locking the door, she dropped down on the bed and buried her face in the pillow.

How could you have responded to his kiss? Now he knew how she felt. Her body, her deepest feelings—she hadn't been able to lie.

It was several minutes before she heard soft knocking. Morgan?

"Who's there?"

"Mary."

She got up and unlocked the door. "I brought you some dinner. I thought you might be tired and would want to eat in your room." Mary's eyes were serene.

"Thanks. How's Dad?"

"Fine. He's sitting by the fire. You might want to come out later. He wants to talk to you."

"Give me an hour." She still had to see the dailies from yesterday's shooting, but they could wait until tomorrow night if James needed her.

JAMES WILDE was lying in a reclining chair, a crocheted afghan around his thin legs. The fire snapped merrily, giving the dimly lit room a golden glow. King, his German shepherd, lay quietly by the chair.

"Hi, Dad." Delia gave her father a quick kiss on his forehead and sat down next to him. "How're you feeling?"

"Not too bad." But his voice sounded rough and tired. James seemed to burn from within. The doctor had told her the cancer was eating him alive. Delia glanced away.

"Tom tells me you're having trouble with Morgan."

Delia's head snapped back up quickly, all her senses alert. "A little bit. But nothing to get worried about."

James laughed softly. "He's a good man, Delia. You need someone strong. Someone who can give you a real run for your money."

"Oh, come on, Daddy!" She could tell the familiar endearment pleased him. He patted her hand.

"I don't want to think about leaving you alone."

The tears were just behind her eyes now.

"Take a good look at Morgan, Delia. He's attracted to you. I could see it if my eyes were closed."

I know. But for all the wrong reasons. "Attracted or not, I wish he'd listen to me on the set."

"He'll respect you in time." James closed his eyes. "He's just having difficulty because you're a beautiful woman."

Delia didn't answer. For a time they sat in front of the fire, bathed in the warmth.

"You remind me of your mother. I called her the other night."

"You did?" She tried to keep the amazement out of her voice. Delia couldn't remember the last time her parents had spoken.

"We talked about you." He reached for her hand this time, as if to prevent her from pulling away. "She told me about Morgan. Don't look so astonished. I'd suspected for a while. Delia, darling, whatever is the matter with you?"

"I'm so sorry, Daddy. It's just—" With an angry gesture she wiped away the tears sliding down her cheeks.

The gentle slapping of house slippers against the hardwood jolted Delia out of her thoughts. Mary came into the room bearing a tray of freshly baked brownies.

James broke the spell. "Mary, my dear. We were just talking by the fire." He sat up. "How lovely of you to bring tea." It was then that Delia realized the three of them weren't alone. James went on, "Morgan, how nice of you to stop by."

She didn't want to look at him. Not after what had happened in the stable.

James continued, "I was going to call you and ask if you'd mind running lines with me tonight."

She couldn't avoid him any longer without being rude. The words faded as Delia glanced up and saw Morgan's face. His eyes surprised her. Warm, filled with an almost tender light. It was a look she'd never seen before.

When he moved to sit beside her, Delia didn't even flinch; she simply handed him a cup of tea, thinking of the countless times they had performed this intimate ritual in London. Another quick look at his face let her know Morgan remembered, too.

240

ELDA MINGER

ELDA

An hour later, Delia leaned back into the couch comfortably. The fire had a somnolent effect, and she felt her eyelids growing heavy. James's and Morgan's voices were somewhere in the background.

"WAKE UP, sleepyhead." Delia heard a soft voice that seemed far away.

"What?" She opened her eyes to find Morgan's face very close to her own. "Where's Dad?"

"He went to bed."

"Oh." Delia stood up and stretched lazily. "I'd better be heading to bed myself. We've got a long day ahead."

Morgan patted the cushions beside him. "Give me a few minutes, Delia. We have to talk."

She eased herself back down on the couch. "Okay." She folded her arms in front of her, as if for protection.

"Delia, I'm having a very hard time working with you on this film."

She felt herself begin to bristle. "It hasn't been easy for me, either, Morgan. But this picture is very important to me." *Could she tell him why?*

"I know you may not believe this, but I never stopped loving you." His dark eyes were intense. "I don't believe you stopped loving me, either." Morgan simply stated it as a fact.

Delia couldn't deny the truth. "Yes." She nodded, her eyes on his face. A soft warmth began blooming deep within her body.

"Come here." He patted the space next to him.

She remained where she was until his hand caught hers, and he pulled gently until she came to rest in his arms. She didn't resist as his fingers tightened in her hair, tilting her head back as his lips moved over hers.

It was a soft kiss, a slow kiss. He was giving her plenty of time to respond. She moved closer and parted her lips to deepen the intimacy between them.

She felt him ease her down on the couch, then slide one leg over both of hers. His lips left hers; his head came up slowly.

"Delia." His voice was tight. "I don't think I can work with you on a professional level with this between us."

Slowly, feeling as if she might break apart at any moment, she got up off the couch and walked over to sit on James's chair by the fire.

"Now tell me, why is it you can't work with me?" She was amazed at how steady her voice sounded when she felt as if her heart were breaking.

"I've never been in love with my director before."

She shook her head. "I'm not buying that, Morgan."

"Why does directing this film mean so much to you?" he asked harshly. "And why are you so unconcerned about how I feel?"

"I'm not unconcerned. It's just impossible for me to get a replacement."

"I could ask Joseph Bates to fly up."

You bastard. Delia stiffened with rage at the mention of their mutual friend. With Joe directing, the film would be nothing but a shoot-'em-up Western. She couldn't do that to James. She wanted to give him one last great character before he died.

"No." She stood up. "I'm sorry. You have to understand, Morgan, that I take my work as seriously as you do."

"Then you may have to find yourself another actor."

"Fine." Delia's voice shook as she walked quickly out of the room. She heard Morgan leave, then went back into the living room to check the fire.

But once in bed, she couldn't sleep. His face, his voice haunted her through the night. He said he loved her. But he couldn't work with her.

There was no answer.

AFTER AN EARLY morning ride, the corral seemed to rush up to meet her—and Morgan stood right beside it. Dismounting, Delia handed the reins to Tom, sure he sensed her need to be alone to talk with Morgan. As man and quarter horse headed for the barn, she faced Morgan.

His expression was that bland, smooth mask she hated. "Did you decide?" he asked.

"There's a flight back to Los Angeles at ten this morning," she replied. "If you can pack by eight, one of the men can run you to the airport."

There might have been a slight stiffening of his body, but his face didn't change at all.

"So you're staying on," he said.

"Yes."

"Why, Delia?"

The hint of pain that had broken through his mask tore at her heart. Delia wanted to tell him. She needed someone to share the painful secret of James's dying.

But she didn't. Instead, she touched him lightly on the arm. "I have to. If I don't do this film, Morgan, I'll never be able to live with myself. Please try to understand."

Before he could reply, the kitchen screen door slammed. James was walking slowly toward them. He had been so delighted when Morgan had agreed to do the film. Now he would have to be told he was leaving.

She didn't say anything as James came up to the rail and leaned companionably next to them. Then she decided to get it over with. "Morgan has something to tell you, Dad."

James turned toward the younger man. "I could certainly use some good news."

For once, Delia noted with satisfaction, *he's shaken.* She'd seen Morgan's eyes widen just a fraction, seen his lips tighten when she'd spoken. The silence seemed to stretch forever. Then finally he spoke. "Delia said we could begin shooting our first scene today."

When his words finally sank in, she put her hand on his arm and gave it the gentlest squeeze.

Thank you, Morgan. For giving us another chance.

"THAT'S A WRAP!" Delia called out, delighted with the results. She looped her arm through her father's and smiled up at him. "You're really cooking."

James was in his element. "It had a lot to do with this man." He gestured to Morgan.

"Thank you, Morgan. That last take was excellent, and I'm sure we're going to use it." Facing everyone, she shouted, "That's it for today! I'll see you all at eight tomorrow morning!"

She turned away from Morgan, concentrating on her father. James looked good today. His deep blue eyes, so like her own, were sparkling. But Delia also knew he had an almost superhuman ability to concentrate on a scene. She didn't know how much longer his strength would last.

She was grateful when Tom clapped James on the shoulder and the two older men headed for the pickup truck Tom had driven out to location.

Delia jumped when she felt a pair of strong warm hands settle on her shoulders.

"I have to admit, you're really pulling it out of him. That was the best I've ever seen James."

"Thank you. You're pretty hot stuff yourself."

He laughed then, throwing back his head and looking more boyish than he had in a long time. "You've got guts, Delia. You may just make it, after all."

She decided to play along, liking this new side of him. Sticking her hands in her back pockets, she grinned. "We'd better hurry if we're going to catch dinner."

He surprised her then. "I thought we might go out to dinner tonight."

She couldn't resist. "Won't Belinda be lonely?"

He mock scowled. "She won't even notice I'm gone."

"Do I get a chance to clean up, or do you want me smelling like a horse?"

His dark eyes were suddenly serious. "I'll take you any way I can get you."

She looked away. "Meet me in the living room in an hour, okay?"

It was the longest hour she'd ever lived through. Delia finally settled on a cranberry hand-knit sweater, a mid-calf length black skirt and boots. Tired of her constant wardrobe of jeans and sweats, she also wanted Morgan to appreciate her as a woman and forget she was his director.

The expression in his eyes was reward enough. He devoured her.

"Don't wait up," she called to Mary. Miraculously, her voice didn't tremble.

They drove into Jackson and chose a steak house where the food was good, solid and unpretentious. After a simple meal of steak and salad, they faced each other over coffee.

"You've changed," he said softly.

"Good or bad?"

"Both. You're more confident. Much more in control than you used to be. I like that."

"Go on."

"But...you seem harder. As if nothing can get to you. And the picture...it's almost an obsession."

"It is," she admitted. "I'll be relieved when it's over."

"Why did you recommend me for the part?" he asked suddenly.

Delia was about to reply that it had been for James. But she wanted to be honest with Morgan.

"I wanted to see you again."

"Did you miss me as much as I missed you?"

She nodded. "I missed you terribly. Why didn't you ever call me?" she asked.

His mouth tightened. "This may still be very hard for you to understand, but I resented who you were terribly. James Wilde's daughter. You had everything in the world. How could I possibly have provided for you? But the one thing I wanted to do more than anything was to ask you to marry me."

She couldn't say anything—she was stunned by his admission. Wanting to hold the moment, she laced her fingers through his and held on tightly as he continued.

"And what could I have offered you? A little flat in London that barely had hot water half the time? I wouldn't have taken any of his money if I'd married you, Delia. I wanted to provide for you. I needed that."

He talked rapidly, quietly, as if he'd missed his chance before and it had stayed all bottled up inside for the past six years. If there was any chance for their future, it had to be said now.

"You had a family, and it was obvious that you were an adored child. I had no family to offer you, not even a bad one. I thought I pulled you down. And I couldn't do that, Delia. Not the way I felt about you."

"Why couldn't you tell me any of this before?"

"I didn't even know most of it consciously. All I knew was that I thought you deserved better, so I did everything in my power to push you out of my life. At the same time, I kept trying to prove myself to you, that I was good enough for you. It was all that ever mattered to me."

"I know that feeling," she said. "I feel that way about my father. And deep inside I feel like I don't always measure up."

Then Delia said softly, "I think we'd better get back. We have a lot to do tomorrow."

THEY PARKED the car outside the garage, then walked slowly toward the house. The stars were bright overhead, and a gentle breeze blew the scent of crisp mountain air around them.

When they reached the kitchen door, Delia stood on the cement step so that she was almost level with his eyes. "I had a wonderful time, Morgan. It meant so much to me that...we could talk like that."

He didn't reply, but the pressure of his hand on her arm increased slightly.

"Good night," she whispered. Then she leaned forward and kissed him gently on his cheek.

She heard his quickly indrawn breath; then his arms encircled her and he just held her. She could feel his heart pounding, the warmth of his breath on her neck. Delia wanted to stay with him forever.

"Come back with me."

"Morgan—"

"Not to make love. Just to sleep with me. I want to hold you next to me all night."

She hesitated for a second, but Delia knew it was what she wanted, too. She also knew she was playing with fire.

"I promise," he breathed, "just to hold you."

She slid her arms around his neck, then laid her cheek against his shoulder. "Yes."

He picked her up easily and carried her toward the guest house. Mary had moved Belinda to one of the guest bedrooms in the main house, so Morgan had the little house all to himself.

He maneuvered the door open gently, then carried her over the threshold and into the darkened bedroom.

Delia tensed for just an instant as he laid her down on the bed. Then he sat next to her and began to take off his shirt.

She stood up and began to unzip her skirt, stepped out of it, then drew her sweater over her head and stepped out of her boots. Clad only in her silk slip, bra, bikini and stockings, she turned her back on Morgan and reached behind her for the hook on her bra. As the straps slid down over her upper arms, she saw him lying on the bed, bare chested, watching her.

"You're just as beautiful as I remembered," he said.

She removed her stockings, slip and finally her tiny lace bikini. Feeling strangely shy—hadn't she slept in the same bed with Morgan many times?—she sat down on the edge of the bed. A heartbeat later, she felt his hand on her waist, his fingers warm.

"Climb in. You must be freezing."

She moved underneath the covers, and then he was beside her, his body warm and hard, comforting in the darkness.

"Come here," he whispered.

She turned toward him, burying her face against his chest, loving the feel of his rough hair on her cheek. She sighed softly.

"This is what I missed the most." Morgan's breath tickled her ear.

"Me, too."

He moved his hand slowly down her back until he cupped her buttocks gently. It was as if he were discovering her body all over again. Though they weren't going to make love, they had time to be truly intimate.

"Thank you for coming back with me."

She kissed the tender skin just underneath his ear. "My pleasure, Morgan."

When she awoke, she was aware of him instantly. He was beside her, his muscled, rough leg entwined intimately with hers. One large hand was splayed over her breast, holding it gently, the other was between her thighs, warm against the smooth skin.

With a soft exhalation, Delia glanced at the bedside clock. Five twenty-three. It was still dark. She tried to move, but their bodies were entwined in such a way that she couldn't.

She moved back against him, trying to ease his hand out from between her thighs, when she felt his strong arousal.

He shifted in his sleep, and his fingers pressed her more intimately. Delia started, then shifted. She'd have to wake him.

"Morgan?" she whispered.

"Hmm?" His voice was still sleepy.

"Could you move your hand for just a second?"

He did, his fingers settling on her waist.

"Your other hand?"

He complied, moving it to her shoulder.

Both touches had been soft, nonsexual. Yet as his hand

squeezed her shoulder, Delia knew she wanted him to make love to her.

She raised her thigh gently and reached between her legs to touch him intimately. She trailed her fingertips over the taut flesh, then grasped him more firmly. Shifting in front of him, she brought the tip of his masculinity to her most intimate place.

She felt his hand tighten at her waist; then it slid slowly, luxuriously, to the back of her thigh. He pushed lightly, and she raised her leg a bit more as he shifted his hips behind her and entered her just the tiniest bit.

She groaned at the exquisite sensation. His hand moved again, and she felt his palm pressed firmly against her abdomen, fingers apart. He moved his hand down until one of his fingers was tangled in the soft curls of hair between her thighs. As he found the spot he wanted, he began to move his fingertip over it, slowly. So slowly.

She arched her hips, bringing him more firmly inside her. He groaned, and she felt his hand tighten slightly on her stomach. His other hand eased her head back so his lips could claim hers.

It was the most tender of kisses, his lips soft and warm. She opened her mouth at the same moment he thrust again, gently. She moaned against his mouth, then turned her head away and buried it in the pillow. It felt so good, so right. She had wanted this from the first moment she'd seen him on her father's balcony. This slow sensuality. She wanted Morgan to make her body sing with life.

And she wanted him. More than any man she'd ever known. She wanted him because she loved him. She'd never stopped loving him.

The feeling was the same, but different. She'd made love to him before, but in six years they'd become different people. So it was a combination of old and new. And achingly tender.

She moved her hips back, suddenly hungry for all of him, but his fingers tightened on her stomach, then moved lower. She stopped. His mouth moved to her shoulder, and he bit it gently, sending shivers through her body. Though she had started their intimacy, he was going to finish it. She felt him move, his motions smooth and graceful as he positioned himself behind her. Then he thrust strongly, once, twice, as he filled her completely, the sensation extremely satisfying. She felt his hand move back down, unerring as he found her again and began to slowly build her excitement. At the same time, his other hand moved underneath her body. She shifted slightly, then sighed as his fingers closed over one of her breasts, the soft, kneading caresses making her nipple pucker and harden.

He took his time, building passion until she thought she would float right out of her body and shatter. As a feeling of inevitability began to overtake her, she heard him whisper against her ear.

"Yes." His voice was still husky with sleep. "So good."

The sound of his voice touched off her response, and she strained against him as she reached her peak. It was a violent culmination for both of them, and she gasped as her body shuddered and finally was still. She could feel his body trembling with the aftermath of their passion.

He kissed her shoulder, then moved back, still inside her but not touching her other than where their bodies were intimately joined. When Delia stopped trembling, she slowly looked over her shoulder at him and smiled.

He moved closer until their bodies touched completely, his front to her back. She heard his labored breathing close to her ear. After several minutes she eased apart from his strong arms, then cradled his head against her breasts.

When he caught his breath, he smiled down at her, then kissed the tip of her nose softly.

"So much for my good intentions," he murmured, nuzzling her. "God, you smell good."

She moved her body against his, delighting in the way they fit so closely together.

He cupped her buttocks and pulled her tightly against him. "It was wonderful." He kissed her cheek. "You don't know how many evenings I've lain awake, wishing you were here with me, making love."

"I've had the same dreams."

"It was better than I remembered," he said, grinning wickedly. "Didn't you say something about an eight o'clock shoot?"

She sat up in bed. "Oh, my God. It's ten after seven!"

"Better get a move on." He got out of bed and stretched. "You have your choice, Delia. A quick shower with me or breakfast."

"So who needs to eat?" she replied quickly.

THE NEXT WEEK passed quickly for Delia. Filming was coming along brilliantly; the chemistry between James and Morgan was perfect. Delia let them have their heads, and she knew that she was seeing film history in the making. Neither actor had ever been this outstanding in a role before.

If her days were filled with filmmaking, her nights were filled with lovemaking. It was an unspoken agreement between Morgan and herself. No commitment had been made, but she moved in a few of her clothes. They spent evenings together at the house with James. Delia watched the way her father would laugh as Morgan made his early days in the London theater come alive.

For a brief time, James was filling the role of the father Morgan had never known; Morgan the son James had never had. There was laughter and warmth in their evenings together, and Delia was content to sit back and watch the two men dearest in the world to her enjoy each other's company.

Many evenings, Morgan would ask James to get out the video-cassettes he had of his older films. They would watch James's performances, and Morgan would ask countless questions. Delia watched as James patiently explained what he thought had made a scene work, and why. And she sensed her father's contentment. He was passing something on to Morgan, and perhaps in that sense, he wouldn't die.

*

"QUIET!" Delia's voice was low, but it carried perfectly. The set was closed today; only the minimum number of crew were present. Today was the scene the entire film rested upon—James's confrontation with Morgan.

She had tried to film the scene on Monday and Tuesday, but Mary had forewarned her that James wasn't feeling well. So Delia had juggled her scenes and ended up directing Morgan and Belinda. But today James felt better, and Delia knew it was time.

James and Morgan looked at each other for a second; then Morgan nodded his head slightly. Delia picked up the signal, and the cameras began to roll.

Delia willed herself to remain calm, but her nails were biting into her palms. *Please, let him be able to do the scene.* She had already looked through the lens. The weather was perfect, early summer in all its glory.

She could hear Morgan delivering his lines angrily, letting James know he was going to take Belinda whether he wanted him to or not. Morgan caught fire every time he shared a scene with James, and he was doing brilliantly today. When you watched Morgan act, you forgot he was playing a part.

"Cut. That's it." When the cameras stopped rolling, Delia ran to her father.

"Dad, that was—"

"I'm tired, Delia. Could you walk me to the trailer?"

She held his hand tightly and put her arm around his shoulders as she led him toward one of the trailers they'd set up on the edge of the clearing.

Once inside, James lay down, and Delia poured him a glass of water.

"Drink this." For the first time in his long illness, she was scared. He held her arm as he drank.

The soft knock on the door stopped her thoughts, and she eased James back on the bed.

Morgan stood at the door, a look of concern on his face. "Is James all right? He seemed—"

"He's tired." Delia stepped outside and closed the trailer door softly behind her. She didn't want any rumors, anything to harm the film. She was almost finished, and then she could devote full time to James.

"Please, Delia, don't shut me out."

Did he know? Delia decided to share as much as she could. "He's getting old, and...Morgan, he can't give over all that energy and not feel the strain. Not at his age."

"Tell me how I can help you."

"Find Tom. Bring him here. Ask him to drive the truck as close as he can."

Without another word he vanished around the side of the trailer.

Delia went back to her father and laid her fingers against his cheek. The skin was thin, his color bad. An understanding of what was going to happen to him ripped through her body, searing her with a pain so intense she couldn't move.

"MORGAN, wake up!"

He shot up in bed, his body covered with sweat. He reached

for Delia and drew her against him. *She's still here.*

"You're shaking!" She drew him down against her, cradling him in her arms as if he were a small child. He buried his face against her shoulder, ashamed she should see him this way.

"What's wrong?" She touched his shoulder.

"A dream...it's stupid. Nothing."

"It had to be something for you to be crying out like that. Tell me, Morgan."

When he didn't say anything, she whispered, "Let me be strong for you."

"I feel like such a...fool."

"No. You can tell me anything, Morgan."

"Tell me what's going to happen after filming is finished."

"You mean us?" she whispered.

"Yes."

She put her arms around his neck and moved her body against his. "I don't know. I just know I want us to be together," she said softly.

"Are you sure?"

"Yes."

"I can't take it a second time."

"Was that what you were dreaming about?"

He nodded.

She kissed his cheek, then his lips. "I'll never leave you. I couldn't if I wanted to. I love you so much, Morgan, it's like you're a part of me."

He sighed, then hugged her tightly. "You're the only good thing that's ever happened to me. I want you to know that."

She answered him with a kiss, and he responded, wanting to be as close to her as possible. Wanting to know that when he woke in the morning she would still be beside him.

BUT HE couldn't sleep that night, so he left the warmth of their bed and silently walked toward the barn. When would Delia trust him enough to tell him what was on her mind? They were so close in so many ways—their talks, their lovemaking—yet there was still one more bridge to be crossed. There was an important part of her she kept separate from him. And he wanted to share her problems as well as her happiness.

Over and over he thought of what it might be. Directing the film was a big step in her career. Did she think she wasn't up to it? She brought something special to the film that all the actors had responded to. A caring, a perspective that was totally devoid of personal ego. If he was honest with himself, Morgan had to admit she was one of the best directors he'd ever worked with.

Her father? But he'd asked her, and Delia had said he was simply not as strong as he'd once been. And Delia wasn't the sort of person to worry about something without reason.

Their relationship? He frowned. Perhaps she was worried about what was really going to happen.

That had to be it. It had been difficult at first for both of them. But she had made the first step, had sent the script over, invited him to her father's party. She had been the first to put her heart on the line.

You still don't think you're good enough for her. Admit it. Though he had amassed a fortune, built a career that was astounding in its breadth and scope, he still felt he never quite measured up. Delia was an unattainable goal.

He remembered the feelings of inadequacy that had flooded him when they'd talked about their childhoods. Delia had told him stories of French finishing schools, skiing trips to Gstaad, vacations on the Riviera. She'd been in the news from the time she was born, on a movie set before she knew how to walk.

He'd been fighting to stay alive.

He walked around the corral slowly, trying to decide what he was going to do. By the fifth time around, he'd decided.

Let her make the decision. Ask her to get married. You make the commitment, and have the guts to see if she'll have you.

Being here in Wyoming with Delia and her family had brought him to this decision. They were good people, and he could only hope some of that goodness had rubbed off on him. It made him understand how Delia had turned out the way she had. Including her mother, Danielle, whom he had met once in Paris, Delia had been shaped by a remarkable array of people.

When he walked silently back into his bedroom, Delia was still asleep. He undressed and got into bed beside her. But he didn't touch her. He simply looked at her for a long time before he finally fell asleep.

DELIA RINSED the soapsuds from the large pot Mary had made chili in, then set it to dry. She welcomed the mindless routine of the chore, wanted to blank out the future.

James had finished the picture. But giving out all that energy had cost him. Mary was by his side constantly, except when Tom took over briefly. Delia rushed to him at the end of each shooting day and spent weekends with him.

I should have never attempted it. Yet the second the thought came to her, she dismissed it.

The kitchen door opened, and she turned to see Morgan come in. He unbuttoned his jacket but kept it on.

"Working hard?" His voice was gentle.

"I just finished. Why weren't you at dinner?"

"I had an errand to do in town."

"Would you like some coffee and apple pie?"

"Only if you sit with me."

She cut him a piece of Mary's pie and poured him a cup of coffee.

"Did you eat anything tonight?"

"I grabbed a hamburger in town."

He set down his fork and put a hand over hers.

"I'm going in to see James. Would you like to come with me?" Delia asked.

"Take a walk with me first." His eyes were burning with a peculiar intensity as they stepped outside.

They walked until they were on the far side of the fence; then Morgan stopped. He cupped her face in his hands and spoke softly. "I want you to think about this before you answer."

She looked up at him, puzzled. For just an instant his face looked more vulnerable than she'd ever seen it.

"I love you very much, Delia. Will you marry me?"

Of all the things she'd thought he was going to ask her, this was the very last. She stared at him for a long moment, then started to smile.

"Yes." The last of their problems could be worked out with love.

He stepped closer so that their bodies were touching and lowered his head to kiss her. It was the sweetest of kisses, almost shy. He surprised her once again.

"I'm glad you said yes." He laughed shakily. "I didn't have anything planned if you'd said no."

"How could you even think I'd refuse you!"

When she was able to think coherently again, she grasped his sleeve. "Let's tell James and Mary."

They headed back toward the ranch house.

James was sitting by the fire, Mary at his side knitting a sweater.

"Dad?" Delia called softly.

He opened his eyes and smiled at her as she sat down next to him. "Morgan and I are going to get married."

He looked as if he hadn't heard her for a moment; then his face creased into a smile, and he closed his eyes. When he opened them again, they were suspiciously bright.

"I give you both my blessing." He included Morgan in the loving look he gave Delia. "I was hoping this would happen." He sat up in his chair, and energy seemed to fill his body. "Mary, we need champagne, and where's Tom? This calls for a toast." Extending his hand, he clasped Morgan's firmly. "Welcome to the family, son."

Morgan sat next to Delia, and it seemed as if tension were leaving his body. She took his hand and gave it a squeeze. Living totally for the moment, Delia basked in the warmth of the room.

Once the champagne had been poured, James raised his fluted glass. "To Morgan and Delia. May your marriage be filled with warmth and laughter, love and happiness. May you be a constant source of joy and strength to each other. May you always take care of each other. Delia, I love you very much. Morgan, there isn't another man in the country I would rather my daughter marry. Thank you for the good news." Soon the room was bubbling with conversation.

Morgan touched her arm. "I didn't give you your ring yet," he said softly.

"You bought a ring?" she asked. "When?"

"This afternoon." He handed her a small velvet box.

Delia opened it slowly, then caught her breath. An exquisitely cut, sparkling diamond.

"Oh" was all she could say.

He slid the ring on her finger. A perfect fit.

"How did you know my size?"

"Mary. I asked her this morning."

When Delia looked up at her stepmother, she saw her tears. "Thank you, Delia. This means so much to both of us. Morgan, you have no idea how happy I am."

Delia watched as Morgan kissed Mary softly on her cheek, then shook hands with Tom. Her father, sitting back in his chair, fairly glowed with contentment.

They stayed for an hour; then Mary signaled Delia with her eyes that James was tiring.

"We're going to leave you to your fire," Delia announced. "I'll see you all in the morning."

She kissed Mary and Tom good-night, then knelt by her father. "I'll see you tomorrow," she said softly, then kissed his cheek.

"Good night, my princess." Delia felt her throat tighten. He hadn't used her pet name in years. "I love you."

She squeezed his hand. "Always, Daddy."

"Morgan," her father said softly. "Take good care of her. I'm entrusting her to you."

"I will."

"Make her happy. Don't let her brood too much. And never let a day go by without telling her how much she means to you."

"Dad!" Delia was embarrassed.

"I will."

DELIA DIDN'T sleep well that night, and was awake by five. Knowing she wouldn't be able to fall back asleep, she got up and began to dress.

"Where are you going?" Morgan asked sleepily.

"Out to see the sunrise."

"Want some company?"

"I'd like that a lot."

Once outside, they walked over to the corral and faced the mountains. The sky was dark lavender, the palest tinge of sunlight visible at the edge of the horizon.

"Beautiful," Morgan murmured.

Delia tucked her hand in his arm and leaned against him. She heard some noise from the barn; then Falstaff came galloping into the corral, his large hooves thundering. He neighed, and the noise came out an angry squeal.

Tom joined them at the rail. "I don't know what's gotten into him. He was restless all night."

Falstaff came up to the rail and snorted. Delia began to pat the silken head. "It's okay, boy. It's okay." She pitched her voice low, and it seemed to quiet the animal.

The sun was rising now, washing the pale morning light with tinted hues of pink and gold.

"There's nothing like this anywhere in the world," Delia said softly to Morgan.

They watched the sunrise silently. Falstaff trotted back to the far end of the corral and began to buck, hooves kicking against the fence. The harsh sound carried in the still morning air.

"Hey, now!" Tom leaped into the corral and began to run toward the horse.

"I don't know what's wrong with him," she said to Morgan. "He's usually—"

"Delia!" Mary stood on the kitchen steps. Even from a distance Delia could see that her face was contorted with pain.

No.

Her heart began to pound, and she started to walk, then run, toward her stepmother.

MORGAN STOOD frozen at the fence as realization came crashing down around him.

He was dying. My God. She made the film because he was dying.

Tom was at the fence moments after Delia left. Tears were running down his face, and he made no attempt to disguise his grief.

"God be with you, James Wilde," he said.

"I'm entrusting her to you." James's words came back to Morgan with new meaning. They were not simply the words of a pleased father-in-law; he had asked Morgan to take care of his daughter for all time.

*   *

THE REST OF the day had an air of unreality. Once the ambulance came and took James away, Delia wandered around the ranch house, wondering how everything could still look the same. The sun was high in the sky, the weather serene. Several quarter horses still grazed out in the paddock, and Hades pranced restlessly in the corral.

Morgan stayed by her side constantly. While Tom comforted Mary, Delia was conscious of Morgan watching over her. He looked awful; his face was pale, his eyes dark with pain. Yet he answered phone calls, talked to neighbors as they dropped by with casseroles, salads, loaves of homemade bread—all sorts of foodstuffs. Delia felt detached from it all, yet the people in the valley were a great comfort to Mary. As they kept coming in the door, offering help in any way they could, Delia realized how many friends James and Mary had, how much they were loved.

Early that evening, as the sun began to set, Delia walked out to the corral. She had to get away from the endless condolences. Somehow she felt closer to her father when she walked the land.

Falstaff was out behind the barn in one of the paddocks. When he saw her, he began to walk slowly toward the rail.

Delia scratched behind his ears absently. The thought of her father never riding his favorite horse again brought quick, stinging tears to her eyes, but she pushed them back. She couldn't cry for James. Not yet.

She heard quiet footsteps behind her.

"Are you coming in for dinner?" Morgan asked.

She concentrated on patting Falstaff. "No. I'll eat something later."

"Delia, tell me how to help you."

Her restless hand stilled, but only for a moment. "I've been thinking, Morgan." She cleared her throat. "There is something. I want to finish the film."

"Do you have enough footage of your father?"

She nodded. "I knew we wouldn't have much time once we got here. I wanted to film the exteriors, and we just made it."

"So the principal work left is with Belinda and me."

"Yes."

He squeezed her arm gently. "Then we'll do it. Whatever it takes, we'll finish the film."

She put her hand over his. "Thank you, Morgan."

THE NEXT two weeks seemed to fly by, and Morgan remembered them as a time of hard work and feverish intensity. He watched

Delia, and it seemed to him the film consumed her. She barely took time to eat or sleep.

His and Belinda's final scenes caught fire, the emotions blazing between their characters. There was no safety net for the risks they took as actors. It was James's death, Morgan was certain, that gave their performances such a fine edge. He had given them all a chance to see their own mortality.

The morning they left for Los Angeles, Morgan got up early and showered, then headed out toward the barn. He stopped at the corral, watching as Hades circled the enclosure restlessly.

Tom had worked miracles in the time he'd trained the Arabian. The animal was beginning to trust again. Quite an achievement.

Mary came out and joined him at the rail. She was silent for a moment.

"I want to wait a while before the funeral," she said quietly. "James asked me to scatter his ashes at the foot of the mountains." She gazed at the horizon. "I won't have it turned into one of those celebrity circuses, but I would like it very much if you would come back with Delia."

He was touched.

"What will happen when you and Delia go back to Los Angeles?" she asked.

Morgan sighed. "We're into the home stretch. She has to edit the film, then show the final cut to the studio."

"When will it be over for her?"

"A director's involved with every stage of production. The film will have to be edited, then dubbed. Delia said it could take up to eight weeks—if she's lucky. It's supposed to be a Christmas release, and it must be, to qualify for next year's Academy Awards. She'll just get it in under the wire."

Mary's eyes were worried as she watched Hades. "I don't like the way she looks."

"I don't, either. I wish she'd eat more. She sleeps, but she still seems tired."

"You're going to have to take care of her these next few months. Maybe even until the picture opens."

"I know." He hesitated for a moment, then decided to confide in Mary. "She doesn't seem to be...it's as if she's keeping all her feelings locked away. You seem to have mourned James, let him go. I keep sensing Delia hasn't let any of her feelings out."

Mary smiled, but her eyes remained sad. "They had a difficult relationship, James and Delia. He wanted to be a good father so desperately, but in the earlier years he barely knew how. And then, as his fame grew, it became harder and harder for Delia to be his daughter.''

He gripped the rail tightly. ''Did Delia ever tell you that we knew each other before?''

''I knew. She came back to the ranch when she left you. James was on location, so it was just the two of us.''

''I never meant to hurt her. I wanted to marry her, take care of her.''

''I know you did. I know you loved each other very much.''

''Just as she had trouble being James's daughter, I had trouble accepting who she was. I had this crazy idea she might think I wanted to use her. When we started seeing each other, I had no idea who she was. Only that I cared for her.''

Mary put her hand over his and squeezed.

''I...pushed her away from me before she had a chance to...but I wanted to build a life with her, but first—''

''First you had to be a success.''

He wasn't surprised she understood.

''Sometimes I wonder if we'll ever find a time to simply be together, if we'll even marry. Both times I've been with Delia we've been caught up in the middle of something crucial.''

She patted his arm. ''You'll have that time. You must have faith, Morgan. Faith that things will work out.'' She smiled up at him, her eyes serene. ''You love her very much, and once the film is over, you'll both find a way.''

''I promise you I'll take care of her, Mary.''

''I know you will. Now let's get both of you on that plane.''

MORGAN LISTENED to the shower running as he toweled his hair dry in the bedroom.

Only one more night of this lunacy and it will be over.

He'd grown to hate the film because of what it had done to Delia. The last week had been the worst. The film was right on schedule; it had been finished exactly eight weeks after they flew back from Wyoming.

She seemed to come to life only at the studio, and then it was by sheer effort of will. He'd come to expect her mood swings, from her jittery, wired high to the lethargic, empty low. He'd continued to bring her food but hadn't had the heart to stay around and make sure she ate it.

She's a big girl, he thought, his mood foul. *She can take care of herself.*

The minute he saw her step into their bedroom, he admitted the lie.

As she slowly unwound the thick blue towel, he studied her surreptitiously.

Too thin. Too pale. One more night. He could put up with anything, knowing he would soon have Delia back the way she'd been before.

He dressed quickly, slipping on his jeans, shirt and sweater. Industry people usually went to screenings after work, so the dress code was casual. All anyone cared about was whether the film worked.

Delia was wearing what he teasingly referred to as her Japanese coolie outfit. Full pants, cropped short. Soft cotton in a brilliant shade of royal blue, with a matching tank top. Now she was studying her reflection in the mirror, and he could tell she wasn't pleased.

Her arms are too thin.

She reached for her jacket and slipped it on, concealing them.

Her hair was drying naturally, wavy and full. She rushed through the minimum amount of makeup, then reached for her bag.

"Ready?" she asked.

He nodded. She walked toward him, her flat sandals noiseless against the deep carpeting. There was nothing to trip her, but she stumbled against him, and he caught her by her upper arms.

Even through the jacket he could feel her. Burning up.

Delia didn't resist as he pulled her slowly toward him, turning her so they were face-to-face. Her color was high, her eyes dilated. Why hadn't he seen it before? Because they hadn't been sleeping in the same bed.

"How long have you been sick?" he asked.

"I can make it through—"

"How long!"

She lowered her eyes, and he loosened his hold. "Just the last few days. But I slept in the limo on the way home, and I feel better—"

He felt her forehead. Burning. "Like hell you do. I'm taking your temperature. Damn it, Delia, don't you care what you do to yourself?"

"We don't have time! We have to be at the studio—"

"No, we don't."

"I told Bob we'd—"

"I don't give a damn what you told Bob."

"I have to be there!" She crossed the room to the door, but he grabbed her and half dragged, half carried her to the bed.

She began to cry. "Don't do this, Morgan."

He put his cheek against her hot skin. "Delia, you're in no condition to go tonight. Call it off."

Her body tensed. "I can't." There was a note of desperation in her voice. "The vice-president of advertising is going to be there, all the publicity people...Morgan, I can't just cancel the screening! It has to be a Christmas release to qualify for—"

"I don't give a damn. They can all wait one week."

"Spoken like a spoiled, egotistical star! You're so used to getting everything your way you can't take anyone else into account. Damn you, Morgan, I'm going to this screening if I have to crawl there on my hands and knees."

The film had become her life.

He decided to try one last time.

"Let him go, Delia," he said softly. "Let James go. The film isn't going to bring him back." He hated saying the words and for a moment she almost crumpled.

But she stiffened when she heard the knock on the door.

"Bob." She looked up at him, an imploring expression on her face. "Please, Morgan. Just give me tonight? I won't ask for anything else. Ever."

She was going to go.

Delia stepped back, away from him, opened the door and walked out.

MORGAN SLIPPED into the back row just as the lights went down in the small studio screening room. Delia was in the third row, seated next to Bob. He'd caught a glimpse of her blue jacket before the lights dimmed.

The air conditioning was too high. Delia was freezing and Bob had taken off his jacket and draped it around her shoulders.

But Delia still couldn't get warm.

She concentrated on the screen in front of her as her vision of the film began to unroll, frame by frame.

There was total silence when James first appeared on screen, and Delia studied him. *Perfect.* The first shot, his first words. She knew instinctively that the only way she'd ever get through this evening was by looking at the film dispassionately. He wasn't James Wilde, her father, but a character in a film.

She shivered and pulled Bob's jacket closer around her. Though she was cold, she was sweating. Bob put his arm around her and gave her shoulder a gentle squeeze.

"James is wonderful. Delia, thank you for giving him this."

His words were her total undoing. She tried to study the screen again, but the images blurred.

The first sob tore out of her body, loud in the quiet theater. She covered her mouth with her hands as her shoulders began to shake. Bob tightened his hold, the gentle pressure a lifeline.

Delia made it through the first hour without breaking down again. And she knew she'd been privileged to work on a masterpiece. Morgan and James set fire to each other, each actor making the other reach higher, dare more. As Delia watched both men she loved, her hand over her mouth, her eyes filled with tears.

By the time James's climactic scene was reached, she was a quaking bundle of nerves. It seemed like only a few days ago that she'd helped her father walk to his trailer. But even then she'd known. It was the scene of a lifetime.

As James talked on about Mary Anne, his cinematic daughter, Delia felt her tenuous control snapping.

I can't take any more of this.

She put her hands over her face and began to sob. This time she couldn't stop. The audience was perfectly quiet, utterly engrossed in the film, but also respecting Delia's grief. Everyone knew what she'd gone through after her father's death to get this film ready in time for a Christmas release.

THE LIGHTS came up, and Delia wiped her hands over her wet face. The tears were streaming down her face; she couldn't make them stop.

People were coming by.

"Beautiful film, Delia."

"Bob, it's going to be a hit. I can feel it."

"James was wonderful."

Voices swirled around her, but all she could think of was what an utter mess her life was.

Watching Morgan's last scene with Belinda, she'd remembered that day's filming. He'd kissed her, given the scene to her, come back with her to Los Angeles and put up with eight weeks of insanity so that she could finish her dream.

What had she given him back? She'd snapped at him, stopped listening—she'd done everything wrong it was possible to do in a relationship.

Her body felt unbearably tired, but she pushed herself out of her seat. Call him. *Tell him how much you love him.*

Delia felt as if she were swimming through a sea of thick, humid air. She was no longer sweating; she felt as if she were being burned alive. There were too many bodies, too close. And her legs weren't working. She looked out into the sea of faces, and for an instant she thought she saw Morgan rushing down the aisle toward her, pushing people out of the way.

Then her legs gave way, and she fell.

SHE WOKE UP in an ambulance, Morgan's tense face close above hers.

When she opened her eyes again, she was in a hospital bed, the smell of antiseptic and alcohol strong in her nostrils.

"Morgan?" The word was barely a whisper. "Don't leave me. Please." The words were harsh and raw against her throat.

"I'm not going to leave," he said quickly.

There was someone else in the room. Turning her head, she saw a doctor standing on the other side of her bed.

She looked away from him, toward Morgan. She had to tell him now, all the reasons she loved him, before she fell asleep.

"I was wrong, Morgan. What I did." She tried to sit up but was astonished to find an IV running out of her arm. She searched for his face.

"I was wrong to go tonight—"

"Delia, stop—"

"It was stupid. You were right. I never meant to hurt you, but I've been awful—"

"Delia, the doctor's going to give you a shot to make you sleep. I don't want you to worry about anything."

"Don't leave me." She clung to his hand, her eyes smarting. "Please, Morgan, stay with me."

Scared of needles, she looked at Morgan as she felt it prick her skin.

"I love you." It was the last thing she said before she fell asleep.

*

EARLY MORNING sunshine spilled over the redwood deck of Morgan's beach house. Delia gazed out over the ocean, totally content.

Her picture had swept the Academy Awards. Best actor, Morgan Buckmaster. A special award for lifetime achievement given to James Wilde.

Best director, Delia Wilde.

It had been a night of wild celebrating, and she and Morgan had gone to every party in town. They'd danced the night away, driving home just before dawn.

But she couldn't sleep. She'd slipped out of her backless cowl dress and put on her pink robe. Morgan had gone into the kitchen to make a pot of coffee.

So much had happened since the screening. She'd only been hospitalized for a week; then Morgan had driven her back to his beach house.

They were married exactly one week later at the ranch. It had been a quiet ceremony, with only Tom, Mary, Bob and a few other very close friends present.

He'd taken her away to Tahiti for a month. And it was while nestled in a private bungalow that they really began to talk to each other.

Her thoughts were interrupted as she heard the glass door behind her slide open.

"I thought I'd find you out here," he said, handing her a cup of coffee. He looked as wired as she felt and had changed out of his tuxedo into a pair of faded jeans.

They drank their coffee in silence, grateful for the respite from their partying. When Delia set her cup down, she looked up at him.

"So what do you want to do, Best Actor?" she teased.

He took the last sip of his coffee before answering, "I just want to be with you."

She smiled as he traced her cheekbone with his finger. "So what do you want to do, Best Director?"

"Funny. I just want to be with you, too."

His mouth quirked upward. "At last, we agree on something."
He was silent for a minute, just holding her as they stood by the
redwood railing.

"Are you tired?" she asked.

"Not particularly."

She leaned back in the circle of his arms. "What do you want
to do? I mean, right now."

He kissed her cheek. "You're the director."

She ran her hands up over his bare shoulders, up into the softness of his hair. "Give me a minute. I'm sure I'll think of something."

She teased him, touching him as long as possible, then finally
exerted the gentlest of pressures and brought his lips close to hers.

"I think you should kiss me," she said softly.

It was a light, playful kiss, perfectly in tune to the moment.

When he lifted his head, she glanced up at him. "Do you make
a habit of sleeping with all your directors?"

He swatted her bottom. "Just this one." He kissed her again.

She couldn't think when he broke the second kiss; could only
rub her cheek against his chest.

Morgan's voice held a hint of laughter in it. "Where do you
think this next scene should take place?"

"Oh, the bedroom. Unless you want to shock the neighbors."

"And what's my motivation?"

As he swept her up into his arms, she kissed the tip of his nose.
"You have to answer that one." She looped her arms around his
neck as he stepped inside and began to walk toward their bedroom.

"My motivation? I love you, Delia Wilde. I love you very
much."

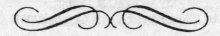

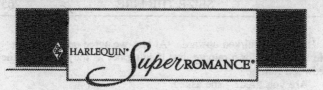

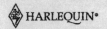

AMERICAN *Romance*®

Heart, Home & Happiness

Save $1.00 off the purchase of any 2

AMERICAN *Romance*®

series titles.

$1.00 OFF!

any two American Romance series titles.

RETAILER: Harlequin Enterprises Ltd. will pay the face value of this coupon plus 8¢ if submitted by customer for this product only. Any other use constitutes fraud. Coupon is nonassignable. Void if taxed, prohibited or restricted by law. Consumer must pay any government taxes. For reimbursement submit coupons and proof of sales to: Harlequin Enterprises Ltd., P.O. Box 880478, El Paso, TX 88588-0478, U.S.A. Cash value 1/100¢. Valid in the U.S. only.

Coupon valid until December 31, 2001.
Valid at retail outlets in the U.S. only.
Limit one coupon per purchase.

107427

5 65373 00033 5   (8100) 0 10742

HARLEQUIN®
Makes any time special ®

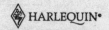

AMERICAN *Romance*®

Heart, Home & Happiness

Save $1.00 off the purchase of any 2

AMERICAN *Romance*®
series titles.

$1.00 OFF!
any two American Romance series titles.

RETAILER: Harlequin Enterprises Ltd. will pay the face value of this coupon plus 10.25¢ if submitted by customer for this product only. Any other use constitutes fraud. Coupon is nonassignable. Void if taxed, prohibited or restricted by law. Consumer must pay any government taxes. Nielson Clearing House customers submit coupons and proof of sales to: Harlequin Enterprises Ltd., 661 Millidge Avenue, P.O. Box 639, Saint John, N.B. E2L 4A5. Non NCH retailer—for reimbursement submit coupons and proof of sales directly to: Harlequin Enterprises Ltd., Retail Marketing Department, 225 Duncan Mill Rd., Don Mills, Ontario M3B 3K9, Canada. Valid in Canada only.

Coupon valid until December 31, 2001.
Valid at retail outlets in Canada only.
Limit one coupon per purchase.

52602968

Visit us at www.eHarlequin.com
T5V3CHARCAN
© 2001 Harlequin Enterprises Ltd.

HARLEQUIN®
Makes any time special ®

Emotion, excitement and the unexpected
That's

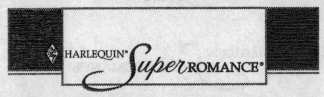

Save $2.00 off the purchase of any 2

series titles.

$2.00 OFF!

any two Superromance series titles.

5 65373 00051 9   (8100)0 10744

Visit us at www.eHarlequin.com
T5V3CHSUS
© 2001 Harlequin Enterprises Ltd.

Emotion, excitement and the unexpected
That's

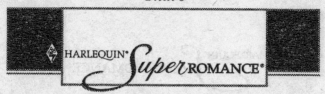

Save $2.00 off the purchase of any 2

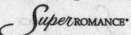

series titles.

Visit us at www.eHarlequin.com
T5V3CHSCAN
© 2001 Harlequin Enterprises Ltd.

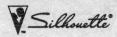

SPECIAL EDITION™

Life, Love and Family

Save $2.00 off the purchase of any 2
SPECIAL EDITION™

series titles.

$2.00 OFF!

any two Special Edition series titles.

5 65373 00051 9   (8100) 0 10743

Visit Silhouette at www.eHarlequin.com
T5V3CSSEUSR
© 2001 Harlequin Enterprises Ltd.

Silhouette®
Where love comes alive™

SPECIAL EDITION™

Life, Love and Family

Save $2.00 off the purchase of any 2

SPECIAL EDITION™

series titles.

$2.00 OFF!

any two Special Edition series titles.

```
52603482
```

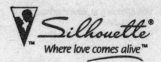

Where love comes alive™